# THE END OF BLISS

This is a work of fiction. Names, characters, businesses, organizations, places, events and incidents either are the product of the author's imagination or are used fictitiously. Any resemblance to actual persons, living or dead, events, or locales is entirely coincidental.

Published By Fairlight Press



ISBN: 061569764X

ISBN 13: 9780615697642

# THE END OF BLISS

Rhonda Ringler Cutler

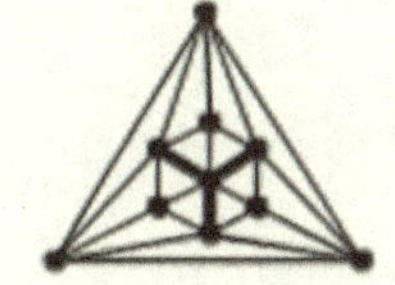

Fairlight Press

**For Anthony**

# Chapter One

## *August through December 1929*

---

"Eau de Nil," the draper said. He removed the bolt of satin from the shelf and placed it on the cutting table.

"Eau de Nil," Edith murmured. She loved the way the words felt on her tongue, against the roof of her mouth. "Eight yards, please."

Eyebrows raised, the draper began unfurling the bolt. "Sure you need eight? Most dresses take four, five at most." Caught in a shaft of late afternoon sunlight, the rippling fabric did indeed glimmer like a river. The draper glanced up, his glasses sliding down his nose, the cutting wheel poised against the selvedge. "Because once I cut..."

Edith nodded. Now that she had seen this fabric, nothing else would do.

Since spotting the pattern in *Vogue*, Edith had thought of little else. With its low-cut draped back, bias cut skirt, and floor-skimming mermaid pleats, she was sure it signaled a fashion revolution, that the decade soon to begin would be a stylish era in which women, at long last, would once again be expected to dress like adults instead of prepubescent girls. In bed the night before, as Reuben lifted up her nightgown and hoisted himself on top of her, as he eased her legs apart and himself in, Edith scarcely noticed what was happening. She was too busy imagining the dress she already knew she had to have made. The fabric would be satin, the color a powdery pastel, perhaps mauve, maybe a green. She pictured herself crossing a ballroom, the other guests moving to the sides to clear a path for her, a vision so intoxicating that, for once, when she felt Reuben's back arch and his legs jerk, she didn't immediately wriggle out from beneath him, content to lie there quietly with her thoughts.

But before Edith had even left the store, her elation gave way to a giddy sort of remorse. It hardly seemed possible that the single parcel of fabric dangling from her arm had cost $50 when, for the same money, she could have bought three or four perfectly decent off-the-rack dresses. On top of that, she would still have to pay to have the dress made. She stood outside the draper's door, wondering if, despite his warning, she might be able to persuade him to take the fabric back. She knew she was being ridiculous. Reuben was always bragging about how rich they were. And unlike most of her friends' husbands, he was generous. Whenever she asked him for money, his wallet would come flying out, no questions asked. It was just that... she didn't know exactly what it was except that she found spending money on extravagances—and the fabric *was* an extravagance—as terrifying as it was thrilling. The draper spotted her, laid down the bolts he was carrying, and headed toward the door. Embarrassed, for she was certain he could read her thoughts, Edith hurried away.

The day was sweltering, the air thick, the sky bleached white by the sun. Edith had taken a taxi to the draper but now, as penance, she decided to take the Main Street bus home. The bus was a rattling old thing, the springs and stuffing pushing through the torn cloth seats. Most of the windows were sealed shut, and the smell of exhaust filled the stifling air. Edith pulled the pattern from her purse and patted it open on her lap. As her eyes traveled between the pattern and the bag of fabric wedged between her calves, she began to relax. So what if, for the cost to have this dress made, she could buy ten off-the-rack dresses? They'd all be commonplace dresses that, by this time next year, she wouldn't be caught dead wearing. A dress like this would never go out of style. A dress like this, whether it was the first or fiftieth time she wore it, would always make her feel beautiful—and there was no way to put a price on that.

A woman got on at the next stop. Though the bus was nearly empty, she sat down directly across from Edith. She had lank blond hair and a flushed face and was wearing a faded shirtwaist with a frilled collar and a floppy beige hat. After positioning her own parcel—a string bag filled with groceries—the woman began to stare at Edith. This continued for several stops, unnerving Edith, until finally the woman pointed her finger. "Edith Rosenthal! This is the last place I'd expect to bump into you."

Edith smiled warily. Now that she studied her face, the woman did seem familiar. She was younger, too, than Edith first assumed.

The woman extended a rough, red hand. "Audrey Lloyd. Except it's Carney, now."

Audrey Lloyd. Of course. They had gone to high school together. For a while, they had even called themselves friends. The only thing they'd really had in common, though, was the fact that they were both poor, with mothers who were forced to take jobs. In Audrey's case, this was because her father had died, whereas Edith's father had simply tired of being married.

"Mine's Merkal now. What a surprise," Edith said, her tone cool. She shook Audrey's hand, withdrawing her own quickly. Terrified lest Audrey start reminiscing about those miserable years, she yanked the cord, though there was a good half-mile until her stop. Without waiting for the bus to come to a halt, Edith hurried toward the door, nearly tripping over the splayed legs of a napping boy.

By early September, the dress was ready. It was even more spectacular than Edith had expected it to be. So beautiful that each time she thought about wearing it, the occasion never seemed special enough. Then, in October, the world changed.

Black Thursday was followed by an even blacker Tuesday. There were reports from New York City of crowds mobbing banks, of men jumping from the windows of Wall Street skyscrapers. But in Sea Forth, it was as if the world had been stunned into a sort of paralysis. The streets and stores became eerily quiet.

Edith had recently hired a tradesman to repaper the dining room. He was supposed to start by the end of the month. One night at dinner, she reluctantly asked Reuben if they should postpone the project.

"Absolutely not," he said, bringing his palm down on the dining table for emphasis. "If everybody begins thinking like that, my God, this country really will be in a pickle."

"But this thing with the stock market, how long do you think it's going to last?" Edith asked.

"It'll be over before you know it. What's happening is healthy. The market's attracted way too many bozos, buying and selling stocks they don't know the first thing about. This sure as heck will drive them out. Once it does, things will be better than ever."

Edith cut Reuben a slice of the poppy seed cake that Magda, the cook who came to them twice a week, had baked that afternoon, and then cut a smaller slice for herself. "So you're not scared?"

"Scared? No!" Reuben reached across the table for the cream, ladled an enormous dollop, and then, holding the spoon above his cake, watched it slowly make its way down. "I'm actually thinking of sticking my toe in the market. God only knows when we're going to see stocks this cheap again."

This alarmed Edith. Reuben rarely discussed their finances with her and never sought her approval when it came to such matters, which was fine with her as she generally found the subject boring. But what if Reuben were wrong? It seemed crazy to start gambling with their money now. "I wish you wouldn't."

"I said 'sticking my toe.' You think I'd put all this at risk?" Reuben took in the dining room and the foyer beyond with a sweep of the arm. "Have some faith, Edith, not just in me. Your country. The greatest country the world has ever known."

As October rolled into November, the rhythms of life resumed in Sea Forth. On the streets, people began to smile at one another again. One of Edith's friends organized a bridge game and another a casual supper, during which the chatter was only rarely punctured by the most fleeting of references to events in the wider world. Edith found that hours could pass without her thinking about the stock market, which she still didn't understand despite Reuben's patient attempts to explain it. Then in mid-November, an ivory-colored envelope came sailing through Edith's front door mail chute. The envelope was addressed in large, loopy handwriting to "Mr. and Mrs. Reuben Merkal," below which, instead of a street address, was written "Bliss." But then, no street address was necessary. Everybody in Sea Forth knew their house by name, just as they knew the story behind it. How Reuben had built this house as a present for Edith, surprising her with it on their wedding day, though until then he had never built anything grander than summer bungalows for city folk. How he had "Bliss" chiseled into the stone lintel above the front door. At the time, she hadn't the heart to tell him that as touching as she found the sentiment, she was mortified by his need to make a public display of it.

On the envelope's back flap, in smaller script, were the names Gladys and Paul Herbert. The Herberts were one of the most prominent couples in Sea Forth. Edith and Reuben were invited to many of the same parties they were and twice had invited the Herberts to their house. Both times the Herberts had declined, claiming prior obligations. Edith had been baffled and hurt by their failure to reciprocate. The Herberts were known to be great entertainers. Her friends had all been to their house, many more than once.

Too excited to fetch the letter opener, Edith ripped open the envelope. Inside was a dinner invitation. Pacing the foyer, Edith read it out loud, returned it to the envelope, pulled it out, and read it again. What was wrong with her? Why did she always assume the worst? Of course, the Herberts' failure to reciprocate had not been intentional. With people as busy as the two of them, such oversights were bound to occur. As for the timing of the invitation, could it be any more fortuitous? If Paul, a Wall Street lawyer and one of the wealthiest men in Sea Forth, still saw fit to entertain—well, maybe things were not as bleak as they seemed.

On the morning of the party, Edith took the dress from her closet and held it up against herself in front of the mirror. In those terrifying first weeks following the crash, often when she opened the closet door, she would stroke the dress wistfully, sorry she'd held off wearing it, wondering when she would have the chance again. As she backed away from the mirror, Edith tried to picture herself the way the other guests would. She found it hard to accept what her eyes told her—that she was an attractive, stylish woman. As a girl, she had been chubby with unruly hair and bad posture. Midway through adolescence she realized these problems could be corrected and, in the summer between tenth and eleventh grade, she devoted herself to doing just that. By the time she started school in September, she was hardly recognizable. Teachers, even classmates, commented on how she had "blossomed." Still, she remained on the periphery. She was never invited to parties, never asked on dates. It was not enough to change how she looked, she realized, without changing who she was. She dreaded becoming like her mother who, while technically still married to her long-absent father, had the penny-pinching traits and sour outlook Edith had come to associate with spinsterhood. By studying other women, Edith formed a composite of the woman she hoped to make herself into, consisting of this one's bell-like laugh, that one's way of fluttering her hands while she spoke, another's graceful gait. She went about this transformation stealthily, adopting one trait at a time, so that no one, not even her mother, suspected what she was up to.

It was after eleven. Edith had seen no one—not Reuben who, as usual, had crept out before dawn, nor Jeffrey, whose nanny, Mrs. Goldsmith generally waited for Edith to summon her before bringing the child in. After laying her dress across the bed, Edith sat down at her dressing table and pulled out her jewelry box. Cracked pink leather, embossed in gold, it had been an eleventh birthday present from her father, the last he was to give her, though he took two more years to disappear from her life entirely. The box opened to reveal a ballerina who at one time twirled to Beethoven's "Moonlight Sonata" but who now stood still. For years, except for some dime-store trinkets, the box had remained empty. Now it was filled with bracelets, earrings, rings, and brooches. All were presents from Reuben, who bought her jewelry for her birthday, their anniversary, for Mother's Day, and for Christmas. He gave her jewelry even on his own birthday, a tradition he began the year they were married.

Weeks ago, Edith had decided upon her pearl drop earrings. Now, as she held them up against her face, she wondered if the dress called for something more dramatic, such as her gold-and-pave diamond set, although having worn them to the Flemings' party in September, they were sure to be remembered. Or perhaps her sapphire and platinum earrings, except that would mean rethinking her bracelets and rings, which were gold. These were not decisions to be made lightly; the wrong jewelry was like an off-note played upon a piano. Just as Edith had decided to stick with the pearl drops after all, she heard a knock on the door.

"Sorry to disturb you, ma'am…" The top of a curly brown head peeked out from behind the nanny. "The boy wants to kiss his mummy good morning before we go out." Mrs. Goldsmith gave Jeffrey a nudge. He stood beside her, giggling, his face buried in her skirt.

"Come." Edith waggled her fingers.

Mrs. Goldsmith prodded Jeffrey, but he refused to budge. She shook her head and exhaled heavily. Not that Edith was fooled. She knew it delighted Mrs. Goldsmith that Jeffrey preferred her to his own mother.

To hide her embarrassment, Edith began fiddling with her jewelry. Why did she find being Jeffrey's mother so hard? Motherhood was meant to be the most natural of states, as instinctive as eating or sleeping. It had never been that way for her. At least while Jeffrey was still a baby, she was able to hope that as he grew older they would have more in common. But Jeffrey was four now, and their relationship was more strained than ever. Hardly a day went by when he didn't tell her he hated her. She often wondered if getting rid of Mrs. Goldsmith might make a difference. But Jeffrey adored Mrs. Goldsmith, and she depended on her too much.

"Is that what you're wearing tonight?" Mrs. Goldsmith made a beeline for the bed. "Satin, right?" she asked, rubbing the hem between her fingers. She motioned Jeffrey over. "Feel it, darling. Isn't it slippery?"

Edith fixed her eyes on their hands, hoping they would get the message to leave the dress alone.

"The color, what would you call it—aquamarine?" the nanny asked.

"Eau de Nil." The words were barely out of her mouth before Edith regretted them. Mrs. Goldsmith was sure to think she was putting on airs. "Water of the Nile," she explained.

"Water of the Nile! That's a good one. Back in Liverpool, my neighbor, Guy, he'd been in the army. Come to think of it, it might have been the navy. Anyway, according to Guy, the Nile had to be the dirtiest river in the world."

Jeffrey had thrown himself across the dress, a blissful expression on his face.

"Or maybe it was the Ganges he was talking about."

"Please get him off my dress," Edith said. The last thing she needed was a palm print or a bit of Jeffrey's morning soft-boiled egg on her dress.

"That was it. The Ganges."

"He might soil it."

"No, I'm wrong. It was the Nile."

"For God's sake!" Edith grabbed Jeffrey's arm and yanked him up. With a remarkable show of strength, Jeffrey freed himself from Edith's grasp. He glared at her before disappearing behind the nanny.

Edith fixed her eyes on the sculpted carpet swirls. She did not want the nanny to see how they had filled with tears. No doubt, her son thought she was an ogre. And while Mrs. Goldsmith might be better at masking her feelings, she probably did, too.

"It's just that tonight's so important," Edith said. She took a few tentative steps toward Jeffrey and crouched so that her face was level with his. "Darling, Momma still hasn't gotten her morning kiss."

Jeffrey mumbled what sounded like his first "I hate you" of the day and then began giggling.

"If you don't mind, I've got a million things to do," Edith said, rising. She headed to the closet for her bathrobe, suddenly self-conscious that she was still in her nightgown, the outline of her breasts, the darkness of her nipples visible beneath.

Edith waited for the sound of the front door slamming, the sign that Mrs. Goldsmith had taken Jeffrey out for his walk, before going downstairs for something to eat. She took two slices of the baked ham and dished out a few spoonfuls of the beet and onion salad left over from the previous evening. As she sat eating at the table, she stared at the still unopened newspaper. She was afraid to look at it, but she was overcome by the sort of morbid curiosity that compels people to stare at car crashes. There was no need to read the articles; the advertisements said it all. Though Christmas was still three weeks away, the Manhattan stores had already marked down their merchandise drastically. At Bonwit Teller's, Russian mink coats had been reduced from $350 to $230. At Arnold Constable, evening wraps once priced at $275 were selling for $160. At Macy's, the price of evening mules had been slashed from $16.89 to $7.94.

Edith pushed the paper away. To her, the most terrifying thing about the past month was how powerless it made her feel, as if she, along with everyone else, was stranded in a leaking boat in the middle of a roiling sea. Had it not been for Reuben, she would have fallen apart weeks ago. A few nights before, she had bolted awake, breathing hard. Reuben touched her shoulder. "Are you okay?"

"I had a bad dream," she said. He asked what about and she admitted the stock market.

He laughed. "Whoever thought the day would come when my wife would start dreaming about the stock market. How many times do I have to tell you that there's nothing to worry about. I'll bet you a diamond brooch that, by this time next year, this mess will be long forgotten."

Edith found Reuben's words so reassuring that she had quickly fallen back asleep. Though now she wondered, how could he be so sure? She opened the newspaper again and began thumbing through it. With big, bold headlines throughout, the articles were all peppered with words like "panic," "crash," "crisis," and "catastrophe." Reuben was awfully smart, especially when it came to business. But did he really know what he was talking about, or was this just his inherently optimistic nature speaking, bolstered by a large dose of wishful thinking?

By the time Edith left for her beauty parlor appointment, she knew Mrs. Goldsmith and Jeffrey would be heading home from the playground, stopping along Main Street to do the errands at the butcher shop, the produce store, and the grocer, where Mrs. Goldsmith would stand proudly to the side while Jeffrey reeled off the shopping list. It was easy for Edith to imagine the sort of greeting she would get were she to bump into them. Mrs. Goldsmith, who savored her slights—real and imagined—would greet her coldly as she drew Jeffrey to her side. And Jeffrey, who took his cues from his nanny, would scowl at her, perhaps tell her again that he hated her.

Because of this, Edith decided to take the laneway that ran behind the shops, on the other side of which were the sheds that once housed carriages but were now used mainly for cars. The unpaved path was rutted and muddy, and the stench of garbage filled the air. Edith prayed she wouldn't run into anyone. If she did, what could she say? That she was trying to avoid her nanny and son? Later, after she crossed back to Main Street, Edith paused to look around. These days, she was always on alert for clues as to how bad things really were. Outside of Baldwin's Men's Furnishings, a liveried driver held open the door of a glossy black Cadillac for a smartly dressed woman, while a salesclerk loaded her parcels into the trunk. On the opposite sidewalk, she spotted two red-faced and huffing teenage boys lugging an enormous fir—a Christmas tree, of course. The street had been done up for the holidays, with red tinsel wrapped around the light posts and berry-studded holly wreaths nailed to the merchants' doors. The perennial crèche had been hauled onto the small lawn in front of the Long Island Bank & Trust. These were all reassuring signs, yet Edith couldn't shake the feeling that the holiday atmosphere was all surface, propelled by a collective determination to carry on as if nothing had changed.

Edith's own transformation—which involved having her hair colored, cut, and coiffed and her nails painted a scarlet red complete with pale quarter moons—took several hours so that by the time she arrived home, dusk had fallen.

Reuben was already home from work. Through the French doors that led from the living room to his office, she could see him at his desk, busy with the paperwork that consumed nearly as much of his time as the building of the bungalows themselves. When he heard her, Reuben smiled and motioned her inside.

"Where's Jeffrey?" she asked as she bent over to kiss the top of his head.

"Still napping. Mrs. Goldsmith's resting, too." Reuben closed his ledger, catching a stack of bills between its pages, and stood. "Did you get your hair done?"

Edith patted her hair, so heavily lacquered that it was unyielding to the touch. "You like it?"

"Very smart," Reuben said, as if he knew the first thing about women's hairstyles. He wrapped his arms around Edith's waist and drew her close.

Reuben was still in his flannel shirt, jeans, and construction boots, and Edith could smell the faint, but not unpleasant, stew of sweat and earth she had come to associate with him. As she rested her head on his shoulder, she glanced toward the stairs. For a few hours, she had managed to put Jeffrey and Mrs. Goldsmith out of her mind. Now, the memory of her humiliating morning came flooding back. She dreaded seeing them, especially her son, and longed to escape to her bedroom before he awoke.

Edith freed herself from Reuben's embrace. "I have to get ready."

"You've got two hours! First, don't I at least get a real kiss?"

"You're still dirty. Besides, I just got my hair done."

As Edith headed toward the stairs, she glanced over her shoulder in time to catch the hurt on Reuben's face as he sat back down and returned to his bills.

Upstairs in her bedroom, Edith changed into her dressing gown and then sat in front of her vanity. After laying out her makeup and assortment of brushes, puffs, and wands across the mirrored surface, she studied her face. With her snub nose, round eyes, and small, pink mouth, Edith considered herself pretty enough—in a Kewpie doll sort of way. The main problem with her features was in their placement, crowded toward the middle of a face that was too broad and square. Still, a woman had to work with what God gave her, and through years of experimentation, Edith had learned to make the most of her looks.

This evening, Edith decided to go for a Hollywood effect. She covered her face with an ivory pancake foundation and then penciled in sharp, inverted Vs for eyebrows, years of too-vigorous plucking having reduced her own to a few wispy strands. She followed this with rouge, garnet lipstick, fashioning her upper lip into a cupid's bow, several applications of black cake mascara, and, finally, a liberal dusting of pressed powder. Edith was still "putting on her face" when Reuben appeared. She did her best to ignore the reflection of his emerging nakedness as he stripped off his clothes. But he soon appeared close behind her, his loosely belted robe revealing a hairy expanse of chest and stomach. As he pressed himself against her back, she felt his penis grow hard.

"I still haven't gotten my kiss," he murmured.

Edith pressed her fingertips to her forehead. "Can't you see I'm doing my makeup? Later, when you're clean and I'm finished, I promise you'll get your kiss." She gave him a playful push but noticed from her vanity mirror the same hurt appear on his face as before. She swiveled around on the stool, intending to apologize, but he waved his hand.

"You're right. You need to get ready, and I stink." He padded out of the room. A moment later, Edith heard the whoosh of the bathtub taps.

As usual, Reuben was dressed before Edith. While he missed a few spots shaving and would have left the house without his cuff links had Edith not noticed, overall, she judged him as presentable. Other women were always telling her what a handsome husband she had. Reuben did have lovely doe-shaped eyes and a warm, full-lipped smile, soft features rescued from the feminine by his strong chin and aquiline nose. Yes, Edith supposed, he was handsome. It was just that swarthy and standing at 5′8″—only a couple inches taller than she was—he was so different from the husband of her girlish dreams, who'd been tall, blond, and fair like Leslie Howard.

"This is nice. Is it new?" Reuben asked as he zipped up Edith's dress.

Edith was about to remind him how she had modeled the dress for him on the day she brought it home. How, when she posed on the stairs, her hand poised on the newel post, he'd told her she looked like she had stepped out of one of her fashion magazines. Instead, she just said yes, for even then she had realized that she could have been wearing a potato sack, and he still would have thought she looked beautiful. Her infatuation with fashion was as baffling to him as his infatuation with her body was to her, the way the merest glimpse of her flesh was enough to send him into a sexual swoon.

Downstairs, as Edith stood by the foyer mirror, fiddling with her silver fox boa so that the snout bit the tail and the paws hung just so, she could hear Jeffrey and Mrs. Goldsmith talking in the kitchen amid the clattering of pots and pans. "We should say goodbye to him," she told Reuben, though this was the last thing she wanted to do.

"You'll just get him upset." Reuben was panting, having just sprinted outside to start the car so that it would be warm for her.

"We can't leave without telling Mrs. Goldsmith." Edith could just imagine the nanny's reaction when she discovered they'd left without saying goodbye, a combination of outrage and smug satisfaction, for she would surely take this as vindication for all the bad things she had ever thought about Edith.

"We're already late." Reuben pressed his hand into the small of Edith's back to urge her on. "When she sees we're not here, she'll figure it out."

As Edith and Reuben stepped onto the flagstone path, Edith heard Mrs. Goldsmith call out to them. She looked over her shoulder. Her eyes locked with the nanny's, visible through the front door's glass insets and full of rebuke, before she continued on.

"How lovely to see you," Gladys said as she opened the door. Her voice had a questioning inflection as if she had forgotten having invited Edith and Reuben. She pressed her cheek against Edith's and made a kissing sound and then surprised Edith by doing the same to her other cheek, repeating the routine with Reuben. Then Gladys craned her head and, spotting one of the maids, directed her to show them into the living room.

Paul was at the bar, tongs in hand, dropping sugar cubes into several rows of champagne glasses. Edith already knew from her friends of the Herberts' tradition of kicking off their parties with champagne cocktails, made with real French champagne, too, a tradition they refused to allow a nuisance like Prohibition to interfere with.

While Gladys—bucktoothed, with watery, blinking eyes and nearly six feet tall but as stooped as an old lady—had grown even homelier over the years, Paul's looks had improved. Indeed, Edith found it nearly impossible to connect the impeccably groomed man at the bar, with his custom-made suit, brilliantine slicked hair, and Clark Gable mustache, with the boy she'd grown up with, who'd been plump and sloppy, his shirttails always hanging out, and shoes in need of a polish. But that was before Gladys' father had taken an interest in him and agreed to finance his college and law school educations, both at Columbia, on the proviso that Paul join his law firm upon graduation. Around town, it was generally assumed that Gladys, too, had been part of this deal.

The guests gathered around the Herberts' red brick fireplace were all members of Sea Forth's business community. Edith had been hoping for at least a few new faces. There was Marianne

Rule and her husband George, both of whom worked in her family's jewelry store, and Harry Groschal, a lawyer who sat on the town planning board, and his wife Rosemary. Bunny Fleming and her husband Arthur, the owner of a Franklin car dealership, and Stu Joseph, Reuben's accountant, and his wife Lydia were also there. Finally, there was Marcus Fellowes, senior vice president at the Long Island Bank &Trust and Reuben's lender, and his wife Adele. It occurred to Edith that every man there was also involved in the local real estate market, be it as an investor, an accountant, a banker or, in Reuben's case, a builder. She couldn't help wondering if the reason the Herberts had finally invited her and Reuben was not because they wanted to get to know them better but because Paul, who had begun to dabble in real estate, reckoned Reuben was someone he should get to know better.

The living room was smaller than Edith would have expected—no more than half the size of her own—and a bit tired looking, with a worn maroon velour divan, matching armchairs, and a moth-eaten Oriental rug. Still, evidence of the rumored Herbert wealth was everywhere—in the crystal vases, all filled with long-stemmed roses, the enormous oil family portrait that loomed above the fireplace, and the hand-painted porcelain figurines in the back-lit display case. It was especially evident in the number of staff on hand to assist Gladys with this dinner party of fourteen: the white-coated kitchen staff of three, complete with chef in toque, and the two maids—one tall and dark and the other short and fair—dressed in black uniforms topped with white aprons, who were now circulating among the guests with gleaming trays of canapés, of which there seemed to be an endless variety—smoked salmon and chopped egg and swirling mounds of cheese, all atop coin-sized bread rounds and crowned with paper-thin cucumber slices, shawls of dill, or jaunty olive and pimento caps.

Reuben and Edith had just crossed the living room threshold when Edith spotted Marcus Fellowes approaching. "Oh God," she sighed. Her visceral dislike of Marcus baffled her nearly as much as it did Reuben, for Marcus had never said or done anything that could be interpreted as being the least bit offensive.

Quite the contrary. He was unfailingly polite to her. Moreover, as Reuben often reminded her, were it not for Marcus' willingness to lend him whatever sums he needed, on a moment's notice and on the most favorable terms, Reuben's business wouldn't be nearly as successful as it was.

Reuben gave Edith a sharp look and whispered, "Be nice."

Striving for what she hoped was a convincingly warm smile, Edith asked after Marcus' children.

"All well, thanks for asking," Marcus said. She expected him to ask about Jeffrey. Marcus never just asked how Jeffrey was, rather would pepper her with questions, such as what sports Jeffrey enjoyed, did he like playing board games and, if so, what games. They were questions she often had to fudge the answer to and which would leave her feeling embarrassed about her inability to feign the slightest interest in his five children, whose names and ages she could never get straight. Instead, Marcus turned to Reuben, asking, "Are you free?" Before Reuben could answer, Marcus had grasped his elbow and was leading him off to a quiet corner.

By then, Marianne, Rosemary, and Lydia, who had formed a group, had spotted Edith. Marianne, her many bracelets jangling, was waving her over. Edith had known these women her entire life, but it was only during the past few years that she had begun to think of them as friends—though the choice had really been theirs, not hers. Reuben's financial success had finally canceled out factors, such as her religion and her poor, fatherless upbringing, which once made this an impossibility. As Edith headed toward them, she glanced over at Marcus and Reuben. She was unnerved by the grimness of their expressions, the way Reuben kept nodding while Marcus spoke, the strangled way Marcus sucked on his cigarette.

All three women had their eyes fixed on Edith, their heads inclined toward one another, their smiles artificially bright. Edith could tell they'd been talking about her dress and that they didn't approve. Not that she approved of the way *they* were dressed, like fraternal triplets, all in the dropped-waist shifts with scooped necklines and knee-length skirts that were all the rage, but which

Edith was convinced would soon seem like relics from another era. She had the dress made simply because she knew it would be beautiful, but now realized that the dress made her stick out in a way she hadn't anticipated. She longed to change course and join the frumpy Adele and simpleminded Bunny by the windows instead. But it was too late for that.

"I was about to tell the girls a story," Rosemary said. Marianne and Lydia shifted to allow Edith into their circle. Rosemary looked around to make sure she could not be overheard. "You know Hattie, my cleaning girl, the one who got herself knocked up?"

"They're no better than animals," Lydia murmured, shaking her head.

"Well, she finally had her baby, a girl. And in a hospital! I thought they all just went out to the fields. Last week, she brought the ugly thing around, though God knows why she thought I'd want to see it. Told me she was all set to call it Nellie when she heard this new name and changed her mind. Guess what it is?"

The women shrugged.

"I'm not telling unless you guess."

A volley of names sallied forth, mainly those of movie stars: Theda, Greta, Myrna…

"You're not even warm," Rosemary roared.

More names followed – exotic ones like Annabelle and Isolde and old-fashioned ones like Patience and Prudence.

"Give up?" Rosemary paused to prolong the suspense. "Placenta."

There was a moment of stunned silence before Lydia spoke. "Placenta?"

"You heard me."

"Oh dear," Marianne tittered. "That's awful!"

Edith smiled uncertainly. The story was funny and at the same time not. The only Negro she had ever really known was a cook Reuben and she once had, a woman so dim-witted and ugly that Edith could barely stand having her around. Even so, it was horrible to think of any child, even a Negro child, having to go through life with a name like that. "I hope you told her what it means."

Rosemary laughed. "What, and spoil the fun? Besides, it's none of my business!"

"Great story!"

The women turned around, startled to see Paul standing outside their circle, brandishing a drink.

"Though I must say," he continued, "I'm with Edith on this one. Not very nice, Rosemary."

Paul turned his attention to Edith. "You strike me as a woman who could use a champagne cocktail." As he handed her the drink, he looked her up and down. "Nice dress. Different. I like that."

The other women were silent, their expressions disapproving, as if Edith had deliberately invited this attention. Edith wondered if Paul was trying to embarrass her or if he simply enjoyed playing the wolf. There had long been rumors of his dalliances, but then Paul was the sort of man people loved to gossip about. Successful, handsome, and rich, he was the closest thing Sea Forth had to a home-grown celebrity.

To Edith's relief, Reuben, all traces of grimness gone from his face, now joined them. "She's something, isn't she?" Reuben placed a proprietary arm around her shoulders.

"That she is," Paul answered. Then Paul launched into a series of questions about the financing for Reuben's latest project, questions Edith found so inscrutable, as were Reuben's answers, that they might as well have been talking Greek. She became bored and had begun to think about wandering off when Gladys appeared in the archway. Caught in a shadowy swath that accentuated the hollows beneath her eyes and the ridges of her clavicles just visible above her schoolmarm's gray wool dress, she looked cadaverous. "Dinner is served," she called out, her soft voice somehow managing to trump all conversation.

The place cards were resting against the water goblets, each name a miniature work of art in gold calligraphic script. Edith was disappointed to see whom her dinner companions would be: to her left, Marcus Fellowes, and to her right, the rotund Arthur Fleming, who, with his off-color jokes that no one ever found half as funny as he did, would be hardly better company. At least the table was beautiful, set with gold-rimmed ivory bone china and an Irish linen tablecloth with matching napkins, the edges tatted in lace as intricate as a spider's web. At the table center stood a six-branched candelabrum, the multifaceted wineglasses reflecting its candlelight like a thousand tiny flames.

By the time the first course was served—a beef consommé flecked with squares of carrots—talk had begun to fly in all directions, even through the tall candelabrum, the guests weaving in and out of conversations like dancers in a minuet.

"Seen the new Franklin?" Arthur asked, tugging at Edith's sleeve.

"I'm not sure," Edith answered.

"You're not sure?"

"All cars look pretty much the same to me."

"You're telling me you can't tell a Franklin from a Ford?"

"Maybe from a Ford," Edith said, though she wasn't even sure about that.

Marianne piped up from the other end of the table. "I've seen it. It's a real beaut, though frankly, if you'll pardon the pun, when it comes to style, the Packard's got them all beat. That's what I want for Christmas—a bright yellow Packard."

"Hey, George, at least she's not asking for a Cadillac," said Stu.

"First you've gotta learn how to drive, hon," George said, "and it ain't gonna be from me."

"You know that the Franklin's engine's air cooled, same as an aeroplane's?" Arthur asked.

Marianne shrugged. "Big deal."

"That's the problem with you ladies," Arthur said. "Too concerned with the way something looks instead of what's inside."

"Seems to me the same thing could be said about you men," Rosemary said.

Paul pointed his index finger at Rosemary. "Touché." He winked in what Edith thought was her direction. Then Paul's face turned serious as he dropped his spoon to his saucer, patted his lips, and placed his napkin beside his plate. "I hate to interrupt the fun, but there is something I've been dying to ask Marcus, and given how my wife saw fit to sit him down there in

Siberia…" He glanced around the table with an apologetic smile. "Well, I'm sure I'm not the only one who'll be interested in what he has to say. Tell us, Marcus, what's the feeling around the bank these days?"

All eyes turned toward Marcus as he cleared his throat.

"Surely, you don't believe the pap Washington's been selling us," Paul said, "that we've already seen the worst?"

"I'm not sure I'm qualified to speak on behalf of the bank," Marcus said.

Paul looked toward Adele, Marcus' wife, his eyebrows raised. "Is he always so modest? If the head of the credit committee and the best darn one the bank's ever had isn't qualified to speak for the bank, you've got to wonder who is."

"Well, yes, of course. It's been a pretty wild ride these past few weeks, I don't mind telling you," Marcus said. "But the feeling at the bank, if I may be so presumptuous as to speak on behalf of the entire bank, the feeling at the bank is that—well, we have faith in our president, in our secretary of the treasury, in the board of governors, and in the heads of the big banks, Mitchell and so forth. We believe, and I'm sure you'll agree, they're very capable men. I'm sure—we're sure—they'll put into place whatever measures are necessary to get us out of this thing."

The lighthearted atmosphere of minutes before had evaporated, and the guests waited in suspense while Paul tore a hunk from his roll, placed it in his mouth, and chewed.

"But how can you, and by 'you' I mean the bank of course, be confident they, and by 'they' I mean those jokers in Washington, know what those measures should be when this country has never experienced anything like these conditions before?" Paul asked.

Gladys gave Paul a reproachful look. "Let poor Marcus finish his soup. I, for one, am dying to hear about Bunny and Arthur's trip to Florida. Was it simply divine? I hear some of the hotels in Miami are not to be believed. What about the weather? They get some nasty hurricanes down there, don't they?"

"Oh yes! They had a doozy just a few weeks before we arrived," Bunny said. "Palm trees ripped out by their roots. Houses tossed around like toys. At least, that's what the bellboy told us.

Our weather was perfect, though. Nothing but blue skies. It actually got kind of boring." She smiled in a way meant to convey she was kidding. "Although," she continued, "people did keep to themselves. It was right after the crash, you see." Bunny clapped her hand to her mouth. "Oh dear, we're not supposed to talk about that, are we, Gladys? Our hotel! Whoever built it thought of everything. And the service! Beach chairs, towels, drinks. Just a snap of the finger and there they were."

"Arthur, did you get a sense what property values were like?" Paul asked.

Arthur played with his fork. "Things looked okay to me. The place wasn't as crowded as I'd expect. Maybe that was why we got the service we did."

Paul laughed. "I'm of the opinion that the '26 bust in Florida was a bellwether, so to speak. Marcus, would you agree?"

"Paul," Gladys said.

"You'd rather talk about palm trees? So would I. Except this seems a little more important."

The tall maid peeked her head through the door.

"Come in," Gladys snapped.

The maid charged in, the short one trailing behind. "Are you finished, sir?" "Are you finished, ma'am?" they asked as they moved around the table, their lowered heads and flushed cheeks making it clear that they'd been eavesdropping from behind the door.

Paul waited for them to leave. "Marcus, like I was asking—"

"I'll tell you the real problem," Stu interrupted. "It's the way we let every Vito, Paddy, and Moshe into this country. The dregs of Europe—no other country would put up with it, that's for damn sure. You wonder why we've got an unemployment problem?"

The group went silent, struck by the collective realization that there was one couple at the table who was not of Protestant stock. Edith stared down at her plate, wishing she could escape to the powder room. She had known Stu forever. In high school, he had even asked her out. After taking her to a cheap café, barely speaking two words to her as she forced down her burger, he said, "Let's go." *Go where?* She was too unsure of herself to ask. He drove to the beach. She naively assumed he'd suggest a walk. Instead, he jumped on top of her, practically suffocating her with his mouth. Somehow, she managed to free herself and escape from the car. She began to walk home when he pulled up alongside her, rolled down the window, and said, "All right, I made a mistake. I just figured..." As he drove her home, she wondered, *figured what?* She realized that his behavior had something to do with her being poor or Jewish, perhaps both. He was a bigot then and was still one now.

She was surprised when Reuben spoke first, even more so by how unperturbed he sounded.

"I was reading in the paper the other day that things don't look all that bad. Retail sales may be off a bit, but factory production is still pretty strong."

"And if retailers can't move their merchandise, how long do you think manufacturers will be able to keep that up?" Paul asked.

"Not long, I'll admit. But Paul, maybe they're seeing things you're not," Reuben said. "With all due respect, sometimes you wheeler-dealer types forget that Wall Street and Main Street are two different animals. This thing going on with the stock market may hurt your pocketbook, but it barely touches the lives of most folks."

Paul formed a bridge with the tips of his fingers. "You believe that?"

"I do."

"You believe that even if corporations can't raise capital, and banks run out of money to lend, or worse, can't pay their depositors back, the little guy on Main Street won't feel a thing?"

"I'm not saying there'd be no impact—"

"You do realize that your theory flies in the face of basic economics?"

Harry Groschal raised a finger. "Paul, I don't hobnob with industry chieftains like you do, and I'm certainly no expert on economics. But I know one thing. If people start believing the worst is going to happen, the worst will happen. What we need most now from Washington and you Wall Street types is reassurance that you're on top of things. And as the leaders in our community, we can do our part by putting on a good show, which means not running around acting like the sky is falling."

Arthur raised his wineglass. "Amen." Reuben leaned across the table to clink glasses with Arthur and then behind Bunny to do the same with Harry.

Marianne Rule clapped her tiny hands together. "Bravo, Harry, I'm all for happy talk. The store's been like a morgue. Even though we're getting close to Christmas, nobody wants to buy jewelry."

Paul leaned back and crossed his arms. "So that's the answer? Happy talk. You don't think the problem might be that we've been talking too happy, pretending that the patient's just got the sniffles, when the reality is he's come down with double pneumonia?"

The maids burst through the swinging doors. As they stood on either side of Paul, they removed the silver domes from their platters, revealing a standing rib roast, new potatoes, and baby peas with pearl onions. The smaller maid set the roast in front of Paul.

Paul sniffed at the roast with closed eyes. "I'm sure these people are starving. I know I am. Nothing sharpens the appetite more than a good argument." He picked up the carving knife, ran it back and forth across a whetstone, and began to carve.

For the rest of the meal, there was no more talk about the economy. Indeed, there was so little talk that, by the time dessert arrived, the guests were all sneaking glimpses at their watches.

"Coffee and tea will be served in the living room," Gladys announced.

The guests shuffled in behind her like schoolchildren being sent off to the principal. Except for the clatter of cups against saucers, the clink of spoons against cups, there was more silence as the maids came around with silver urns, cream pitchers, and sugar bowls.

"Coffee, please," Edith said. She normally took tea after dinner but felt the need for something stronger.

Reuben was stretched out in an armchair, his head resting against the lace antimacassar, his face relaxed and genial as he puffed away at one of Paul's Cuban cigars. Paul had taken the armchair opposite his. He, too, was smoking but with a distracted expression that said he couldn't wait for his guests to leave.

As Edith sipped her coffee, she looked around at the other guests. Only Reuben seemed relaxed. The others seemed as anxious to escape as Paul was to see them go. She had found it hard to follow the discussion at the table, let alone decide whether Paul or Reuben was right. Not that it mattered. No one, not even men as smart as those two, could predict the future, and, to her, that was the most terrifying thing of all.

Edith and Reuben arrived home to find Mrs. Goldsmith in the living room, her bare feet resting on the coffee table, which was littered with magazines and half-drunk cups of milky tea. A mountain of cigarette butts rose from the scooped back of the swan-shaped Lalique ashtray on the side table. Mrs. Goldsmith was not supposed to relax in the living room. Edith had placed an easy chair in Jeffrey's playroom for that purpose, but the nanny always seemed to "forget."

"I wasn't expecting you for hours! Mustn't have been much of a party," Mrs. Goldsmith said. She swung her feet off the coffee table and pushed them into her slippers.

"We were tired." Edith undid the clasp of her fox as she walked over to draw the curtains, an apple-green silk moiré with a rippled surface. They smelled of cigarettes, so she opened the windows to air them overnight.

The nanny groaned as she bent to gather up Edith's fashion magazines. "Mind if I borrow these? They're saying hemlines are going to drop this spring. I say hallelujah."

"How's Jeffrey?" Edith asked.

"Why didn't you say goodbye? When he realized you'd left, did he ever bawl! Poor thing, it took forever to calm him down."

The nanny forgot to clear one of the cups. When Edith brought it to the kitchen, Reuben was by the stove. He often made himself a mug of hot milk before bed. She watched as he stirred a large wooden spoon around the small enamel pot. He was particular about the oddest things, and one was that a metal spoon should never be used to stir milk. He turned and smiled. "Arthur's looking fatter than ever, don't you think? And that Rosemary! She's a lefty, and all evening long I kept getting that bony elbow of hers in my ribs." He brought a spoon of milk to his lips. "Perfect."

Edith placed her palm on the counter to steady herself as she unfastened her shoes. Her feet had swelled during the evening and she wiggled her toes against the linoleum floor. She was ashamed of her feet and hid them from everyone except Reuben. When she was growing up, her mother got her shoes for free from her Uncle Morris' store. Most of her friends also got their shoes there, for Uncle Morris had a reputation for careful fittings and quality shoes. But Edith got only cast-offs that never fit, and her feet bore the scars. Bunions protruded from the sides, and her toes turned under like animal claws.

Edith studied Reuben's face above his mug. His eyes looked tired but untroubled. She longed to ask what he really thought about the discussion at dinner but was afraid. He rinsed his mug and placed it in the drying rack.

"As usual, you were the most beautiful woman there," he said, drawing her close.

Edith placed her hands on Reuben's chest. "I'm tired."

His lips pressed against hers, he said, "Surely, not that tired."

When she freed her mouth and pushed him away, Reuben's face turned angry. She followed him out of the kitchen and up the stairs. "I was just upset about what Paul said," she said and grabbed his jacket fabric. "I do want to make love."

"The last thing I want is to force you."

"Really I do."

Reuben didn't look convinced, but Edith knew how impossible he found it to turn down any opportunity for lovemaking, no matter how insincerely proffered. As they passed Jeffrey's door, they heard him sigh. Reuben asked if they should look in on him.

"We might wake him," she whispered and tugged him away.

Later, Edith would be convinced that was the evening they made their second child, a daughter they named Harriet.

# Chapter Two

## April 1930

---

Pink glimmers of daybreak were visible from between the branches. Reuben slipped out of bed, careful not to disturb Edith, burrowed so deep beneath the covers that only the top of her head was visible. The house was chilly. Before putting on the coffee, he decided to start the furnace.

The basement was damp and musty. Reuben's sole miscalculation in building the house was his failure to realize how high the water table was, even this far from the bay. Whenever it rained heavily, water would puddle in the corners of the basement, the dampness traveling up its walls and infecting the rest of the house.

After four days of rain, the forecast was for clear skies and mild temperatures. As Reuben shoveled the cold ashes from the bottom of the furnace into the ashcan and added fresh coal from the bin, he wondered whether the good weather would entice people out from the city. There was no question that "things" were slower this year although it was too early to become alarmed, especially given how lousy the weather had been. Even in good years, his first sale often did not occur until after Memorial Day.

Reuben waited to make sure the fire caught. He stared through the door grates, mesmerized by the coals as they turned from black to orange. As the furnace began to pump out a beautiful, dry heat, he held up his hands, which had become stiff from the cold, and wiggled his fingers. No, he wasn't really worried. It probably wouldn't be a great year, but he couldn't imagine that it would be a disaster. His bungalows were more than fairly priced. And while plenty of people might have lost their jobs or savings, plenty more hadn't. The world might be revolving less quickly, but it hadn't ground to a halt.

Reuben was the first to arrive at the construction site. He waited in the truck for his workers, reading the newspaper and sipping at his thermos of coffee. A mist clung to the earth, but the sky was clear. The forecast had been right. The day was going to be fine.

He read nearly every article to the end, even those in which he had little interest. He believed a businessman needed to stay well-informed. The news was a mixed bag. On one hand, steel production remained depressed, and unemployment was at historically high levels. On the other, the stock market had been steadily, if modestly, improving for nearly a month. Reuben derived comfort from this, his theory being that in the same way the stock market had led the country into this mess, it was sure to lead it out.

Reuben glanced up from his newspaper just as the owners of the two wood-frame houses across the road emerged from their front doors. Their houses were eyesores, with flaking paint and broken windows covered over with tar paper. Their sagging, wraparound porches and scrubby front yards were crammed with bed frames, worn automobile tires, and empty kerosene cans. The men looked like twins. Both had thatched blond hair, lanky, loose-limbed frames, turkey necks, and pointy noses.

The men went to work on the vegetable garden between their houses. One shoveled topsoil out of a wheelbarrow and carted away rocks, while the other tilled the soil. Reuben knew their last names—Gruber—but little else about them.

From the start, Reuben worried that their houses would make his bungalows harder to sell. He might not even have purchased the land had he not gotten it for such a good price. Immediately after the closing, he introduced himself to these men, with the intention of asking if they'd be interested in selling. Before he'd gotten five words out, they began spewing forth such a string of invectives, some directed at the man who had sold Reuben the land, some at Reuben himself, that he had given up the cause as hopeless.

Reuben wondered if it might be a different story now. The men used to drive off together each morning, presumably to jobs, in the truck they shared. Now, just one did, and only three days a week. Between them, the men had close to a dozen mouths to feed and, from the looks of one of their wives, there was about to be another.

He'd probably be able to get their land for a good deal less than it would have cost him a year ago. With nine of his bungalows nearing completion and only enough land to build three more, if he didn't come up with another project soon, he'd be forced to let most of his men go. But go where? In this economy, the only thing they'd be going to would be certain poverty. There was more than an acre of land between those houses—enough for four, possibly five more bungalows.

Reuben stepped down from his truck. "Got a moment?" he called. The brother wielding the shovel rested it against the house while the other continued to till. "Reuben Merkal," he said, extending his hand.

"I know who ya are." The brother pulled a tobacco pouch and rolling paper from his breast pocket. As he rolled two cigarettes, he motioned for his brother to join him. With cocked heads and crossed arms, their cigarettes dangling from their mouths, they waited for Reuben to continue.

"I'm thinking of putting up more bungalows..." Reuben stopped himself. Why should the brothers care what he did with the land after they sold it? "I'm wondering if you fellows might be interested in selling." When the brothers' expressions didn't change, Reuben found himself babbling on. "I don't have to tell you how tough times are. Still, I'm prepared to pay a good price. Might you be interested?"

The first brother shrugged. "It depends."

"Of course," Reuben said. "As the saying goes, everything's for sale, provided the price is right."

"What sort of number did ya have in mind?" The man picked a piece of tobacco off his tongue and flicked it to the ground.

Reuben's eyes were drawn to a woman's shadowy figure behind a second-story window. If these men were as desperate as he suspected they were, he could probably get the properties for a song. But he wouldn't try. A man had to be able to live with himself. "Given that it's just the land I'm interested in, I was thinking, say, $750 per property."

The first brother's eyes shot to his brother's. "We'll have to think about it." The other brother grunted in agreement. Though they kept their faces impassive, their eyes betrayed their excitement.

Reuben had been prepared to go up another $100. He knew now he wouldn't have to.

"I understand. It's an important decision." Reuben held out his hand to shake theirs. Again, the brothers ignored it.

The second brother tossed his cigarette to the ground and ground it out. "Yeah." Then, they turned around and headed back to their garden.

That afternoon, Reuben left work early. He wanted to get to the bank before it closed in order to line up his financing, so if the brothers did decide to sell, he could move quickly. Experience had taught him that even desperate men could become foolishly sentimental when it came to their family homes.

The bank, across the street from the cathedral, Sea Forth's grandest structure, was its second most imposing. Set back behind a small lawn enclosed by a wrought-iron fence, it was built in the classical tradition, complete with Doric-style pillars. The bank's interior was just as impressive. The vaulted ceiling in the banking chamber was painted midnight blue and affixed with gold stars arranged to form the constellations. The floor and internal pillars were marble, the walls paneled in mahogany. On one side of the chamber were the wired tellers' cages. The clerks sat across from them on a raised platform, behind desks lit by curved-neck brass lamps with green glass shades.

Reuben regarded it as auspicious when he found Marcus not locked away in his office as usual, but bent over one of the clerk's desks, running his finger down a column of figures while the clerk followed along.

"Hello, friend," Reuben called out. The round-faced, boyish-looking clerk raised his eyebrows at this impertinence, clearly mistaking Reuben, dressed in a flannel shirt and blue jeans, for a laborer.

Marcus appeared taken aback. The clerk jumped to his feet, his insolent expression gone. "Mr. Oldham and I were just going over the accounts," Marcus explained, shaking his head. "Well, I hardly need to tell you." His arm slung around Reuben's shoulder, Marcus led him not to his office, which was where they usually met, but to the conference room. "My office looks like it's been hit by a tornado," he said. "Credit files everywhere. You wouldn't believe the trouble some folks around here are in."

"I hope I'm not interrupting anything," Reuben said.

Marcus shrugged. He removed a gold cigarette case from his shirt pocket. "You're a cigar man, right?" he asked as he tamped his cigarette against the conference table. As he sucked on his cigarette, his eyes traveled to a spot above Reuben's head, where they remained until his secretary arrived with coffee.

"A real sweetheart," Marcus said after she left. "Efficient, too. And I'm going to have to let her go. Also, the clerk who sits behind Oldham, and one of the tellers."

"It's always hard to let people go, especially in times like these," Reuben said, reminded of his own crew, all of whom lived from one payday to the next.

"Times like these?" Marcus stubbed his cigarette out on the rim of his ashtray. "When have we known times like these?"

"What about 1918?"

"Oh, it was bad," Marcus said. "But this is of a different magnitude altogether. Hardly a day goes by when I'm not presented with yet another catastrophe."

Reuben smiled sympathetically, though he suspected that Marcus might see things as being worse than they really were. As the bank's chief credit officer, Marcus was probably consumed by the bank's problem loans. As sorry as Reuben felt for those borrowers who were about to lose their businesses, or worse, their homes, he also couldn't help feeling that many of them would have brought these problems on themselves. Also that Marcus and his people were, if anything, even more to blame, for as bankers they surely should have known better than to lend them such outrageous sums in the first place.

"Surely a downturn this sharp can't go on for very long," Reuben said. "People still need to eat and clothe themselves. They still need to put roofs over their heads."

"You would think so. But what if people get to a point where they can't even afford the necessities? That's something I'm beginning to see—and not just among those who were already struggling. Middle class folks, too." Marcus laced his hands. "How's your business looking?"

"Too early to say. Not that I'm worried. In a business like mine, all you need is a few good weeks to make your year. And using your own bank as an example, while one teller might be losing his job, two are keeping theirs. Given that I'm only looking to sell twelve bungalows, all I need to find are twelve buyers who still have jobs."

"Or at least haven't lost them yet." Marcus pulled out another cigarette and rolled it around in his fingers as he spoke. "Remember what Paul said last December? That we were in for something uglier than we'd ever seen? The crash scared me plenty. Even so, I meant it when I said I was sure that our government and the heads of the big banks would figure out a way to get us out of this. Know what I believe now? That not even Paul foresaw just how ugly things would get. That this country—forget 'this country'—that the *world's* on a downward spiral the likes of which we've never seen."

Though the conference room was warm, Reuben suddenly felt cold. He took a sip of coffee to warm up and, as he placed the cup back on the saucer, ended up spilling some. While it was true that Marcus might be too tied up with the bank's bad loans to be completely objective, it was also possible that what Marcus was dealing with was indicative of what was happening everywhere. Maybe he'd been kidding himself to think his business would be spared when businesses everywhere were failing. After all, no one needed to buy a summer bungalow. "How bad do you think things are going to get?"

"You tell me."

Reuben's thoughts returned to the morning. He pictured himself standing before the brothers, outlining his proposition. To succeed, a businessman had to be an optimist. But there was a thin line between being an optimist and a fool.

The men sat in silence for a moment before Marcus spoke. "I didn't mean to scare you. What did you want to talk with me about, anyway?"

"Since when does a friend need a reason to stop by?" Reuben asked.

Marcus raised his eyebrows and then stood. "It's always great to see you. It's just that if there's nothing we need to discuss, I've got several rather urgent matters to attend to." He opened the door for Reuben. "Let's have a real meeting in June. By then, you should have a good idea about the sort of season you're going to have. Don't forget you have that big payment due in September. There's nothing a banker hates more than unpleasant surprises."

Reuben was hanging up his jacket when Mrs. Goldsmith appeared in the dining room archway. She had a floral print apron tied over her uniform. "The boy and I are making a cake."

Jeffrey was standing on a chair that had been pushed against the counter. He, too, was wearing an apron and was clumsily working a wooden spoon around a red-rimmed mixing bowl. The kitchen was hot from the oven. Jeffrey's face was flushed and his curls lay plastered against his forehead.

"Daddy!" Jeffrey clambered down. Still brandishing the spoon, he flung his arms around Reuben's hips.

Reuben pushed him away, discomforted by the press of Jeffrey's face against his groin. "What kind of cake are you making?"

"A delicious cake," Jeffrey said. "I'm going to be a baker when I grow up."

Mrs. Goldsmith ran the corner of a tea towel around Jeffrey's mouth, which was smeared with chocolate batter. "I thought you wanted to be a milkman," she said, feigning surprise. She gave his mixing bowl a few turns with the spoon and then tipped the batter into a pan. She smiled at Reuben. "He's certainly an odd one. I thought all little boys wanted to be baseball players or firemen."

Reuben knew Mrs. Goldsmith didn't mean to be hurtful. Just the same, her words stung, tapping into his fear that there was something wrong with a boy who preferred baking cakes to playing baseball.

Mrs. Goldsmith looked over her shoulder at Jeffrey as she filled the mixing bowls with soap flakes and warm water. "I'm warning you now so there will be no tears later—there'll be no cake until after dinner." She handed Jeffrey a tea towel and a washed bowl. "Careful! Wet things can be slippery." To Reuben, she added, "He's a wonderful helper! The best this nanny's ever had."

"Where's Mrs. Merkal?" Reuben asked.

Mrs. Goldsmith pushed a strand of hair from her forehead with the back of a soapy wrist. "The boy keeps asking the same thing." She lowered her voice. "I hope you don't mind my saying that it's wrong for a woman in her state to do the running around she does. You should talk to her."

On several occasions, Reuben had voiced the same concern to Edith. She always laughed him off, telling him that she never felt better. In truth, she did look robustly healthy. Recently Edith had shocked him by saying, "I enjoy being pregnant; it's motherhood I can't stand." While she'd meant this as a joke, Reuben suspected there was a grain of truth to it.

"I'm sure Mrs. Merkal knows what's good for her," Reuben said.

"I hope so." The nanny drew Jeffrey close and kissed the top of his head.

Seeing Jeffrey and Mrs. Goldsmith had taken Reuben's mind off his meeting with Marcus, but as he headed upstairs, Marcus' words came flooding back. Reuben had only dabbled in the stock market, so while he'd suffered losses, they had not been large enough to make an appreciable dent in his family's lifestyle. All winter, he'd continued to pour money into his business, convinced that because his bungalows were inexpensively priced and because he was only trying to sell twelve, he wouldn't be hard hit. What if he was wrong? Not only were most of his savings tied up in the business, he had borrowed heavily against it, with, as Marcus reminded him, a large principal repayment due in the fall.

Exhausted, Reuben didn't bother to remove his work clothes or shoes before stretching out on top of the bedspread. He quickly fell asleep.

When Edith woke Reuben, it was already dark. The bedroom door was ajar, and through it he spotted several shopping bags resting against the banister.

"What's this?" Edith asked, pointing to Reuben's shoes. The bedspread and curtains were recent acquisitions. She claimed the old ones had begun to look tired, though they had looked fine to him.

Reuben eased himself up against the headboard and pushed the bedspread out from underneath. "Why didn't you tell Mrs. Goldsmith where you were going?"

"I did tell her," Edith answered. She took off her jacket, placing a piece of tissue paper between the back and sleeves before folding it away. As much as Reuben wanted to believe her, he suspected it was Mrs. Goldsmith who was telling the truth.

"You're not ill?" Edith pressed the back of her hand to his forehead.

Reuben couldn't resist running his hand up her arm. She had lovely cool skin, softer even than Jeffrey's. "I'm fine. I see you've done some shopping."

"Maternity clothes," Edith said as she stepped out of her skirt. For the first few months of her pregnancy, she'd only grown fuller. Now, he could see the beginning of a bulge. Edith, of course, was hoping for a girl. He pretended to be as well. Secretly, he longed for another boy, a real one this time.

"What about the stuff you wore with Jeffrey?"

Edith pushed aside the clothes in her closet to make room for her new outfits. "I gave those away years ago."

Reuben remembered now, how when Jeffrey was an infant, he arrived home one evening to find cartons of clothing by the door. "What's this?" he called out, drawing Edith to the foyer. She was still breastfeeding, and there were milk stains on her blouse. Her hair was disheveled, her eyes red. "My maternity clothes," she said, "because one thing's for sure, I'm never doing this again."

At the time, Reuben chalked up her behavior to a case of the baby blues. But as the years passed, Edith never changed her mind, refusing to allow him near her unless he put on a condom—except for that one time after the Herberts' party. Yet, if she did not seem elated by her pregnancy, nor did she seem distraught.

Reuben fixed his gaze on the shopping bags, now strewn empty across the carpet. He was afraid if he looked directly at Edith, he would lose the resolve to say what was needed. With Edith, there was never a good time to raise the subject of money. On the few occasions he'd suggested they cut back, she reacted as if he were attacking her. Invariably, he would find himself reassuring her that they had nothing to fear, which, until this afternoon, he believed. "I stopped by to see Marcus."

"Oh." Edith's tone was wary. She went behind her closet door to undress. She was modest about her body, rarely allowing him to see her naked, even when they made love.

"I'm glad I did."

Edith emerged with her satin bathrobe belted high above her stomach. "So what did the great pontificator have to say?"

"I'm trying to be serious."

Edith slid down into the armchair. "Okay, be serious."

"Apparently, he's up to his eyeballs in problems. Businesses failing left, right, and center."

Edith smiled impatiently.

"Because my business is seasonal, so far, this stock market thing hasn't had much of an impact on it. I fooled myself into thinking that I wasn't going to be hurt. After talking with Marcus, I'm not so sure."

"The man's a ghoul. All you have to do is look at him to see he enjoys scaring people."

"Edith, please," Reuben said. "I'm trying to tell you what an idiot I've been. Of course we'll be hurt. It's not as if I'm selling milk or eggs. No one needs a summer home."

"Remember that story about Chicken Little? The way he ran around telling everyone how the sky was falling? Marcus is like Chicken Little. You told me yourself that there's no way to tell ahead of time what type of season you'll have."

"This year is different."

Edith walked over to the window. "Do you mind telling me how different?"

She's no better than a child, Reuben thought. How she acts as if all I'm trying to do is scare her. "Different enough that if we're smart, we'll start thinking about ways to cut back."

Edith spun around. "This is about the dresses, isn't it? If you're that unhappy, I'll return them. Though what do you expect me to wear? Flour sacks?" She scooped up the shopping bags and stormed over to the closet.

Reuben sighed. "It's not the dresses. Of course you need things to wear." *But why seven, wouldn't three or four have done?* he wished he had the courage to add. "All I'm saying is that we need to protect ourselves in case the worst does come to pass."

"How bad do you think things are going to get?" Edith asked softly.

"It's too early to tell. But let's say the worst does happen, and none of the bungalows sell. Things could get tough."

"Then why the hell are you always bragging about how much money we have?"

Reuben reminded himself to stay calm. "We have money. Enough to keep us going for several years—but only if we're careful."

"Several years? I thought you said this thing would be over in a year or two?"

"I've changed my mind."

Edith clutched her stomach. "I think I'm going to throw up."

"You haven't been nauseous in months!"

"I need the toilet," Edith said as she ran from the room, her hand pressed to her mouth. Behind the bathroom door, Reuben could hear her gagging. He wondered if it had been a mistake to speak so bluntly. Getting her this upset couldn't be good for her or the baby.

When Reuben arrived at the construction site the following day, he was startled to find the brothers seated on the stoop of one of his bungalows, their expressions as genial as they'd been distrustful the day before. Somehow, the sight of them enraged him. "The deal is off," he said, waving his arm to shoo them off his property.

The brothers clambered down the steps. "We're ready to take your offer."

"You heard me." Reuben couldn't bear the thought of seeing their faces crumple, so he stomped off. It had rained all night, and mud spattered over his boots and up his trouser legs. He kept walking, past the last of the bungalows, deep into the woods behind them, though it was hard going between the mud, tangled vines and thorny bushes. Finally, he rested his back against a tree trunk and closed his eyes.

Reuben heard the men calling, "Mr. Merkal?" "Reuben?" They followed him into the woods. Reuben stood still, terrified lest the snap of a branch or the rustling of leaves betray his whereabouts. He felt wretched, knowing how disappointed they would be, knowing how hard they would find breaking the news to their wives. Long after the men had given up their search, Reuben remained where he was. Had it not been for his workers, whom he knew would start to worry, he might have stayed there all day.

# Chapter Three

## *September 1932*

---

It was not yet eleven, but the sky was already white, the air devoid of the breezes off the Great South Bay that usually provided Sea Forth with some respite from the humid Long Island summers. Reuben moved his folding chair to the lawn outside of bungalow number six. A week of high temperatures and no rain had turned the grass to straw. There were no trees in front of the bungalows. Reuben had his men bulldoze them, as it was cheaper to build without having to navigate around trees. The last Sunday before Labor Day, it was also the end of the summer season. With it would go Reuben's last hope of selling his bungalows that year.

Reuben had spent every Saturday and Sunday since Memorial Day outside of bungalow six, the same place he'd spent his weekends for the past two summers. More than two years had passed since he'd made a sale. Besides advertising in *The New York Times, The Daily News* and *The Daily Mirror,* which he continued to do at painful expense, he didn't know what else he could do to turn the situation around.

He had placed some furniture inside of bungalow six to give prospective buyers an idea of how it would look furnished. He rarely used the bungalow himself, even though logic told him there could be no harm in taking an occasional break. But if he were being logical, he would have concluded long ago that there was little point in sitting outside the bungalows at all. The cars that passed rarely slowed down. The ones that slowed down rarely stopped. The people who did get out to look did so mainly out of boredom or curiosity. The only serious lookers were those trying to figure out what to ask for their own bungalows—not an easy question in a market where, with each passing day, real estate was worth less. Reuben's original asking price for the bungalows had been $5,000. At the beginning of this summer, he'd reduced his asking price to $3,000, a price that would generate barely enough cash to pay off his construction loans.

As he sat there, Reuben wondered what else he could do to make Edith comprehend how precarious their finances had become. She claimed to be doing all she could to economize. And she had cut back; there was no denying that. She no longer served meat every night and, when she did, it was often a cheap cut, braised or potted as a way of making it tender. A couple nights a week, they now ate leftovers, quite a change from the old days when the leftovers usually went home with Geraldine, the maid who now came to them only twice a week. Reuben had also noticed how rarely she treated herself to a new hat or dress these days, which, given how she loved looking stylish, had to feel like an awful sacrifice. But she refused to fire Mrs. Goldsmith, despite the fact that Harriet was nearly two and Jeffrey was in school all day. And she still visited the beauty parlor each week, a minor indulgence to be sure, but one that rankled him, given how few his own pleasures were.

The press of the sweat-drenched hatband against his forehead soon became more than Reuben could bear, and he tossed the hat to the side. He'd brought the Sunday papers but found it impossible to concentrate. Every crunch of automobile tires down the dusty road would bring him to his feet. After these cars passed, it would take him several minutes to get over his disappointment.

As the day wore on, Reuben could feel his scalp burning. His pants and shirt became so sweat-drenched that they clung to him like a second skin. The chirp of the cicadas had turned to shrieks, drowning out his thoughts. He was wildly thirsty, too, having finished the last of his thermos of lemonade within an hour of arriving. So far, not a single person had stopped by, and Reuben harbored few illusions that anyone would. Still, he was determined to remain seated outside of bungalow six until the sun set, if for no other reason than so later, when he lost his business, as he surely would, he would be able to console himself with the thought that he had done everything he could to prevent this from happening.

By late afternoon, Reuben had lapsed into such a stupor that when a Cadillac the color of cherry licorice pulled up, he barely took in the glare of its whitewall tires and the gleam of its wire-spoke wheels, or the silver seraph poised for flight on the front of its hood. Even the sight of the tall, broad-shouldered figure dressed in a navy blazer, nautical cap, and white duck pants striding toward him failed to rouse him from his lethargy. It was not until Paul Herbert was standing over him that Reuben realized who he was.

"Hello, Sport," Paul shouted over the cicadas. "I was hoping to find you." Paul was one of the few men Reuben knew who wore rings, and the large square ruby on his right pinky caught the sunlight as he thrust out his hand. Reuben wiped his sweaty palm on his pants leg and rose. The blood rushed from his head, causing him to collapse back down into the chair.

Paul crouched. He chewed on a blade of grass as he studied Reuben's face. "Let's get you inside," he said, hoisting Reuben up. As Paul guided Reuben toward the bungalow, he fanned his face with the newspaper. They smelled the dead rat before they saw it, trapped between the kitchen cupboards and the wall. "I'll get a stick," Paul said.

The stench combined with the bungalow's musty heat sapped Reuben's last bit of strength. He opened his mouth in a futile grab for oxygen before slumping to the floor.

When Reuben came to, Paul was slapping his cheek. "Good God, it's heatstroke," he heard Paul say. Paul smelled of cigar and of something fruity and alcoholic, smells Reuben would have normally found pleasant but which made his stomach heave. He watched in horror as his vomit splattered onto Paul's two-tone oxford shoes.

Paul rubbed at his shoes with the wadded newspaper. "Is the water on?"

"No water." Reuben had never bothered to turn it back on after the winter. It was too much, Paul finding him like this—Paul, who was thriving in spite of the dismal conditions that were destroying him. It hardly seemed possible that a few years ago, he'd been sitting in Paul's living room, puffing away on one of Paul's cigar, confident that his place in Paul's world was secure.

Paul placed two fingers to Reuben's wrist and checked his pulse against his wristwatch.

"Sport, I'm taking you to the hospital!"

Reuben wiped roughly at the tears dribbling from his eyes. He had cried when Edith got a fever after giving birth to Jeffrey, when it seemed for one agonizing day that she might not make it. He had surprised himself by crying at his father's funeral, for if he had loved his father at all, it had been a tepid sort of love. But those were the only times he could recall crying as an adult. Why was it happening now, in front of Paul of all people? Had he shown Paul his savings passbook, he could not have made the precariousness of his financial situation any more obvious.

Paul's car rode so smoothly that Reuben was quickly lulled off to sleep. He awoke to find Paul's car parked outside the hospital emergency room entrance, with the driver's side door open and Paul gone. Through the hedges beyond the hospital's driveway, Reuben could see his mother Jenny's white-frame house. She and his father had moved out to Sea Forth shortly after Edith and he were married, except back then, the hospital had been a genteel nursing home. While his mother complained constantly about the ambulances whose drivers, she was convinced, kept their sirens going just to torment her, Reuben suspected that she secretly enjoyed living next to the hospital. When he visited, he would often find her seated by her bedroom window, watching its comings and goings. He glanced up, hoping she was watching now. For some reason, he liked the idea of causing her to worry. But it was too light to see inside the windows.

Paul returned with an orderly who helped Reuben into a wheelchair. Reuben thanked Paul, assuming he would leave, but Paul brushed away his extended hand.

"I'm not going anywhere until I'm sure you're okay," Paul said.

"You've already done enough," Reuben said. Now that he was able to think clearly, he began to wonder why Paul had stopped by the bungalows. It just didn't make sense that he might be interested in buying one.

"Don't be ridiculous. Besides, I've got nothing better to do."

Reuben doubted this. These days, he and Edith were invited to few parties, in part because they lacked the funds—and also the heart to reciprocate. Still, Edith continued to read the society page of the *Sea Forth Beacon* religiously, something that struck Reuben as a form of self-torture, a torture she inflicted upon him as well by her insistence on reading to him from the gossip columns. If these columns were to be believed, the Herberts hardly ever spent an evening at home.

"Stay where you are," Paul said, as if Reuben, whose wheelchair Paul had positioned in the one corner of the emergency room where the sun wouldn't reach him, had the strength to leave. When Paul returned, there was a pretty red-haired nurse by his side. "Meet Miss Latham," he said, giving her a nudge forward.

Miss Latham pushed Reuben past the half dozen or so people who had been waiting there longer than he had. "Undress completely," she said in the examining room, handing Reuben a hospital gown. Though she didn't appear to be a day over twenty, her starched white cap and uniform invested her with authority. "The job makes the man" had been one of Reuben's father's favorite expressions, which had always struck Reuben as ironic given that his father had never risen beyond assistant comptroller with the New York City Board of Education. His own job, building bungalows, had certainly made him and, as Reuben was beginning to realize, could unmake him as well.

Paul returned with *The Sunday News*. He settled down on a wobbly wooden chair and rested his right ankle upon his left knee to form a ledge. *The Sunday News*, he informed Reuben, was not the sort of paper he normally read, but it was the only New York City paper the gift shop carried. Reuben went behind the screen to undress. He knew that Paul would regard such modesty as odd in a man, but he could not bear the thought of removing his clothing in front of him.

"Goddamned communist," Reuben heard from the other side of the screen. "Spoiled momma's boy. Not fit to be dog catcher, let alone president of the United States." Because his mind still wasn't working quickly, it took Reuben a moment to realize that it was Governor Roosevelt—presidential candidate Roosevelt, whom Paul was maligning. Reuben would have almost preferred that Paul had been talking about him. Of course, Paul was a Republican. Paul's parents, being truck farmers, would have been Democrats if they were anything at all, and as a young man, Paul would have been one as well. But that part of Paul had long been obliterated, along with his flat Long Island accent and unkempt appearance. As soon as he emerged from behind the screen, Paul would want to talk with him about Roosevelt. The idea sickened Reuben. Patrician though he was, Roosevelt understood suffering in a way the cold-hearted Hoover never could. The way it transcended the physical hardships to include the anguish it caused a man to see what it had taken him a lifetime to achieve, destroyed in a few years. But to defend Roosevelt to Paul, one of the most powerful men in Sea Forth—let alone someone who might well have saved his life—struck Reuben as disrespectful, not to mention imprudent.

"Mr. Merkal, are you decent?" trilled a feminine voice. A true angel of mercy, Miss Latham had rescued him, at least for the moment.

Reuben, feeling ridiculous in the skimpy hospital gown, shuffled over to the examining table with his back toward the wall so as not to expose his buttocks.

"Paul was right to bring you here," Miss Latham said as she prepared to take Reuben's pulse. Her fingertips were delightfully cool. As she counted his heartbeats, Reuben caught a whiff of her violet scent.

"Paul," not "Mr. Herbert." Miss Latham seemed unaware of having made this slip. Nor did Paul's expression change. Reuben had never taken much notice of the gossip about Paul's philandering. But had he caught the two of them in bed, Reuben couldn't have been surer now that the rumors about Paul were true.

Miss Latham prepared a salt and sugar water solution and then watched with a stern expression as Reuben drank it.

"I'm fine. Please go home," Reuben told Paul, though he suspected it wasn't just concern for him that was keeping Paul there. He really was feeling better, which, in an odd way, was disappointing. Had he been seriously ill, he might have felt less embarrassed about putting Paul through so much trouble.

"Sorry, Sport. When you go, I'll go, and not a minute before." Paul winked at Miss Latham, who gave him a sly smile in return.

"Where've you been?" Edith called out from the living room. With its northward facing aspect, it was the coolest room in the house. She was playing solitaire on a portable card table. Jeffrey was sprawled out on the carpet beside her. Reuben was pleased to see him finally playing with the toy soldiers Mrs. Goldsmith had given him the Christmas before.

"The hospital," Reuben said.

Edith gathered up the cards and returned them to their brown suede box. "Is your mother sick?"

"It was me. I got heatstroke." Miss Latham had actually called it *heat exhaustion*, but *heatstroke* sounded more dramatic.

Jeffrey looked up with a concerned expression. "Daddy, are you all right?"

"Don't I look all right?" Reuben held his arms out wide.

Jeffrey looked over toward Edith. "Mommy?"

"You heard Daddy!" Then Edith dropped her voice. "How on earth did you get that?"

Reuben found this an extraordinary question. Edith knew the way he spent his Saturdays and Sundays. "It's brutal out there."

Jeffrey tugged at Reuben's trouser leg. "Look what I've done." He'd arranged the soldiers in concentric circles – gray, blue, gray, their horses gathered in the middle, their noses touching.

Reuben knelt down and gave Jeffrey's shoulders a squeeze. "That's really clever, kiddo, but don't you think they should be fighting? They are Civil War soldiers."

"I don't want them to fight. They're friends."

Reuben shook his head, not sure how to respond. It seemed wrong to insist that Jeffrey make his soldiers fight. On the other hand, he surely had a duty to encourage Jeffrey to behave – well, more like a normal boy.

"I'll tell you what, buddy," Reuben said. "After your old pops has a bit of a rest, the two of us will play soldiers. You can be the north and I'll be the south, or the other way around, and we'll have ourselves a grand old war."

"Jeffrey can wait," Edith said. "You still haven't told me what happened."

"The nurse told me I should drink plenty of fluids," Reuben said. He headed toward the kitchen, Edith following behind, and opened the Frigidaire. Its cold air felt so good on his face that he moved his head from side to side. The Frigidaire was less than a year old. Edith had ordered it without asking his permission and had made such a tearful fuss when he insisted she send it back that, in the end, he gave in. It was, he had to admit, a marvelous invention.

"Know what I'd love? Some of that lemonade," Reuben said, rooting around the shelves.

"I'm afraid it's gone," Edith said. "How about some ice water?"

With six lemons sitting on the windowsill, Reuben thought the least Edith could do was offer to make more. But when she didn't, he decided not to ask.

As Reuben downed the water, Edith asked, "How did you get to the hospital?"

"Paul. He stopped by to see me." Reuben held out his glass for Edith to refill.

"Paul Herbert!"

"What other Pauls do we know? He waited there while they re-hydrated me. Insisted on driving me home, too."

"Why didn't you invite him in?"

Reuben went to the sink, splashed some water on his face, and poured himself another glass. "I knew he'd be anxious to get home."

"You should have at least offered him a cool drink."

"I'm sure he can get water at home. Maybe I should put some sugar in it. The nurse told me to take in lots of sugar and salt."

Edith opened the white metal sugar canister. They both kept their eyes fixed on the glass as she spooned in three teaspoons. "Oh dear, I guess that means the car's still at the bungalows. I told Mrs. Goldsmith we'd pick her up at the station."

"When she doesn't see us, I'm sure she'll know to take a cab."

Jeffrey appeared at the doorway. "Harriet's crying."

Edith cocked her ear. "God, she is." She ran to the base of the stairs. "Darling, Mommy will be right up," she called. She then returned to the kitchen. "How will she know?"

"Who know?" Reuben asked.

"Mrs. Goldsmith. It will probably take her an hour to realize we're not coming." Edith opened the refrigerator, took out the milk, and poured it into a pan. "Go tell Sister that Mommy's heating up her milk," Edith told Jeffrey. "What if there are no cabs?"

"She'll walk. It's only a mile, for God's sake!"

Edith poured the milk into a bottle and screwed on a teat. "What did Paul want?"

"How should I know? As soon as I stood up to greet him, I passed out."

"You should call and thank him. That way you can find out what he wanted."

"I already thanked him. Besides, if Paul wants to talk, he knows where to find me."

"Why don't I call?" Edith asked.

"You'll do nothing of the sort. Whatever Paul wanted to talk about is my business. That child upstairs? She's your business. Go take care of her."

Edith glared at him. "I'm sorry you got sick. It makes me sick thinking of you sitting out there week after week. But you're wrong. It is my business. Do you want to know what I really think? That for some crazy reason, you're afraid to hear what Paul has to say."

# Chapter Four

## October 1933

It was only when Reuben caught someone staring at it—his right little finger gone to the second knuckle—that he remembered it was no longer there. It happened so long ago, when he was a builder's apprentice. He turned his head from the lathe for an instant and off it came. His body understood what had happened before his mind did. His finger lay among the wood shavings that carpeted the floor. His blood, bright and garish, was splattered everywhere. At first, he felt nothing except bewilderment. Even after the pain coursed through him, it was as if what happened had happened to a stranger, with the real Reuben watching from a safe distance.

That afternoon, Marcus Fellowes was doing the staring, and it was only when Marcus looked away, embarrassed, that Reuben understood. Had Marcus never noticed his finger before, or had he simply forgotten? Marcus had asked Reuben to his office, and the two men were sitting catty-corner, Reuben sunk low in the worn, plaid couch and Marcus in the stiff-backed, black leather chair. These were the same positions they'd occupied many times before, although on those occasions, there had always been a tray with coffee, cream, and shortbread cookies on the table. Today, the table was bare, save for a single thick manila folder. "Reuben Merkal," its tab read, printed in large block letters. A stack of folders, similar to Reuben's and neatly tiered so that the names on their tabs were visible, sat on Marcus' pine veneer desk. One of the tabs read "Arthur Fleming." Reuben hadn't realized that Arthur was also in trouble.

Marcus smiled expectantly. Reuben opened his mouth and then shut it; he was not going to initiate a discussion he knew would end badly.

Marcus leafed through Reuben's folder. "Perhaps you can fill me in on how things are going," he said, tapping the folder's spine against the tabletop before setting it back down. A horsefly landed on the folder and walked its length before taking off again.

Reuben had anticipated the question and rehearsed his response. "Traffic through the bungalows has really picked up," he'd spoken to the medicine cabinet mirror that morning as he shaved. "Two couples seemed especially keen. One even asked for the plans." He'd practiced not just what he would say but how he would say it, so that he would appear optimistic, but not foolishly so, and he had left the house confident in his ability to pull off this lie.

Now that he was looking into Marcus' eyes instead of his own, Reuben's courage deserted him. "I don't have to tell you how tough things are. I spent every weekend at those bungalows. I was sure that if I couldn't sell them, I'd at least be able to rent them."

Marcus pulled a rumpled handkerchief from his suit and wiped his forehead. Edith once said that Marcus reminded her of a basset hound, a description Reuben found more apt now than ever. There were bruised hollows where Marcus' cheeks should have been, and the skin beneath his eyes sagged like turned-out pockets. "I'm sure you recall our correspondence from last fall," he said as he pulled a letter from the folder. He patted it open on the table so that Reuben could follow along.

Reuben winced as Marcus recited the terms he had agreed to last autumn, a 2 percent increase in the borrowing rate in exchange for a twelve-month moratorium on principal repayments. He recalled how effusively he'd thanked Marcus when he proposed these terms, how he pumped his hand again and again until Marcus grasped his forearm to make him stop. Back then, a year's reprieve had seemed like an eternity. He'd been convinced that as soon as Roosevelt was sworn in, conditions would start to improve.

Marcus returned the letter to the folder. "Just this morning, I read in the paper that three thousand banks failed last year. That's ten a day. I'm sure I'm not telling you something you haven't figured when I say it's day to day here. I don't want to call in these loans, but I have to do something."

"What good would calling them do?" Reuben asked. "I have no cash. And my inventory—right now, you'd be lucky to get five cents on the dollar." He shifted uncomfortably. Since work at his sites had stopped, he had gained a good deal of weight. The waistband of his pants was slicing into his waist, his jacket pulling across his back.

"I have to go back to my board with something. They don't give two hoots what the stuff was worth two years ago or might be worth two years from now. They only care about bringing in enough cash to keep this place going." Marcus pulled a pack of cigarettes from his breast pocket, offering one to Reuben before lighting one for himself. He seemed to have forgotten that Reuben only smoked cigars.

Reuben stood and began to pace. He was afraid that if he didn't keep moving, he would lose control. "Until these past couple years, was I ever so much as a day late on my payments? Weren't you always saying that you wished all your customers were like me? Marcus, as your friend, I'm appealing to you. Give me more time. Say three or four months. If I haven't worked things out by then, do what you have to and I'll understand."

Marcus inhaled deeply on his cigarette. "Have you thought of doing something with your house? Even in this market, that house has to be worth something."

"You're not asking me to sell my house?" In the days leading up to this meeting, Reuben had racked his brain, trying to come up with every condition that Marcus might propose in exchange for not calling the loans. This one never occurred to him.

"If you deed the house to us, we could sell it and pay down a portion of your loans. I'm sure the board would look favorably upon such a demonstration of good faith."

Reuben could hardly believe his ears. He rested his hand on Marcus' desk to steady himself. "You want me to give my house to the bank?"

"Not give, exchange. Instead of paying your loan down with cash—"

"I built that house. It was a wedding present for my wife." Reuben looked over toward the window. Its beige drapes didn't quite meet, and the slice of pure blue sky visible between them seemed like a tease from another world.

"There's no way I can approach the board about a rescheduling without offering something." Marcus' voice was apologetic. "Come up with something else. It doesn't have to be the house."

Reuben glanced down at the manila folder, which contained copies of his loan agreements and his correspondence with the bank. Did Marcus say what he did just to scare him, so that when he placed his real offer on the table, Reuben would jump at it? Reuben had never known Marcus to be a conniver, but if he'd learned anything over the past few years, it was that when people's backs were up against a wall, they became capable of all sorts of things.

Reuben could feel Marcus' eyes upon him as he did a mental inventory of his assets. His stock portfolio, once a small fortune in its own right, was nearly worthless now. He had a few thousand in a savings account, not at Marcus' bank, thank God. Three thousand in government bonds that he'd vowed, for his children's sake, never to touch. A couple thousand in cash in the safe in the basement. Edith's jewelry. But his wealth was largely tied up in the business and the house. The business into which he had poured his heart, his soul, and every ounce of his energy. The house he'd built not just as testimony to his love for Edith but as the embodiment of the life he envisioned them leading together. Now Marcus was asking him to choose between them.

"Why can't I sell the house and turn the proceeds over to you?" Reuben asked.

"Because it will take time to sell the house. If I don't give the board something tangible right away, they're going to make me call in those loans."

"So, if I deed the house to you, you'll leave my business alone?"

Now Marcus looked over at that snatch of blue sky. "Of course, we'd still expect you to service the remaining debt. But speaking as a friend, if you turn the house over, I should be able to persuade the board to agree to almost anything."

Reuben told Edith that Marcus had asked him to come in. She had some idea, too, of the trouble he was having servicing his loans. But how close they were to losing everything—that she didn't know. Indeed, to keep her from worrying too much, he'd made a habit of reassuring her that things were not all that bad. Now, Reuben wondered if he'd made a mistake. Perhaps if he had been more open, she'd be better prepared for what was to come.

On the way home, Reuben detoured down to the bay. He walked to the end of the pier where he watched the seagulls skim the silvery water. He was angry with himself for not foreseeing the possibility that Marcus might ask for the house—and angrier still for caving in so quickly and asking only in return that Marcus release the lien on one of the bungalows so, if God forbid it ever came to that, his family would have a place to live.

Earlier, the sky had been clear, but meringue-like clouds had drifted in from the west, a pink and orange sun playing hide and seek behind them. A barefoot boy with a fishing pole came scampering down the pier, a bucket of worms slapping against his thigh. The boy, who looked to be about Jeffrey's age, rolled up his pants and dangled his feet in the water. Reuben had looked forward to the time when Jeffrey would be old enough to take fishing, hiking, and camping, activities that, growing up in the city, he used to dream about. But Jeffrey showed a perplexing lack of interest in the sorts of things most boys enjoyed. Reuben squatted and watched the boy impale a squirming worm on a fishhook and cast his line. He remained until his knees began to ache. "I hope your luck is better than mine," he said, getting up. By then, he had been away from home for several hours and was concerned Edith would start worrying.

On Main Street, the awnings above many of the shops were tattered and faded, their windows streaked with dirt. The patches of earth between the sidewalk and the road were littered with bottle caps, scraps of paper, and dog droppings. It seemed as if every third storefront was vacant, and "For Let" signs hung in the windows of many apartments. In front of the hardware store, furniture and clothing were heaped on the sidewalk, something that was becoming a common sight around Sea Forth. Thank God, his situation would never come to that. Between the bungalow and his mother's house, at least his family would always be assured of having a roof overhead.

By the time Reuben saw Adolph Friestadt emerge from his apothecary with a broom, it was too late. A German Jew who had settled in Sea Forth around the time he and Edith were married, Friestadt considered him a friend although why he should was a mystery to Reuben, who gave him little encouragement. Another mystery was Friestadt's decision to sweep the pavement during the middle of the afternoon when the sidewalks were their most crowded. It dawned on Reuben that Friestadt must have seen him coming, and the broom was his excuse.

Reuben quickened his pace as he tipped his hat, but Friestadt scurried in front of him, blocking his way. "You in a hurry?" Friestadt asked. Then he answered his own question. "Of course not, what's to be in a hurry for these days?"

Before Reuben could answer, Friestadt had taken hold of his arm and was steering him toward the alley. "We've got to talk."

The alleyway smelled of urine and rotting food. At the other end, there was a sleeping bag and a clutter of household goods. "Who's minding the store?" Reuben asked, hoping this would jar Friestadt into remembering it was unattended.

"Does it matter? Who comes in don't have money anyway." Friestadt poked his head out of the alley. "Just making sure we've got privacy. You know Carl Waldmann?"

"The guy with the furniture repair shop?"

"That's the one. Edna Silverman says, and she's not one to make up stories, that Waldmann is trying to start up one of those Nazi parties here in Sea Forth." Friestadt backed away, waiting for Reuben's reaction.

Reuben was only vaguely aware of the Nazis and the political situation in Germany. He had enough on his mind without worrying about the goings-on thousands of miles away. He mumbled, "That's awful."

"That's all you have to say? You think it can't happen here? Let me tell you. When people are scared, they look for a scapegoat. And right now, people are very scared."

"With all due respect, Adolph," Reuben said, "I think you're making the same mistake many foreigners make, which is assuming this country is more like your own than it is. Edith and I have many Gentile friends. We have them to our home. They invite us to theirs. There are no distinctions." Reuben recalled the Herberts' dinner party, how Stu Joseph had complained the government was letting in too many Jews and other foreigners. Because Stu was always spouting off about one thing or another, at the time, he had shrugged the comment off as just more of Stu's vitriol. Now, Reuben wondered how many of the other guests had secretly agreed with him.

Reuben motioned to his watch. "I should have been home an hour ago."

"Who's stopping you? First, let me tell you something. Sometimes you have to be an outsider to see these things." Friestadt began to sweep so furiously that Reuben could taste the swirling dirt and feel it beneath his lids. "The German Jews, they thought they were accepted there, too."

It was nearly four o'clock when Edith heard the front door open. Mrs. Goldsmith had taken the children out, but Edith could tell by the soft, slow way it closed that it was Reuben and that the meeting had not gone well. By the time she got to the foyer, he had hung up his suit jacket and was loosening his tie.

"Let me get cleaned up first." Reuben avoided her eyes as he headed for the stairs.

"No," Edith cried. She followed up the stairs behind him.

Reuben went straight to the bathroom, shutting the door behind him. Edith banged at the door, pleading for Reuben to let her in. She heard the whoosh of the taps. She pressed her head against the wall and hugged herself, too frightened to be angry with him.

"Can I come in now?" Edith asked after several minutes had elapsed. There was no answer. Now that the taps had been turned off, there were no sounds at all coming from the bathroom. She remembered reading of how the wife of a local stockbroker had found her husband dead in the bathtub, his wrists slit. "Reuben!" she screamed, for the first time actually trying the knob. It was unlocked.

Reuben was sitting on the toilet bowl in his undershorts. The tub was filled, but Edith could tell by the bath towels folded along the edge that he had not been inside.

He nodded toward the wall tiling. "You once pointed to a flower and told me that you couldn't imagine a more beautiful shade. I wanted this house to be perfect for you." He was bent over, his hands resting on his knees. Beneath his undershirt, Edith could see his pale skin and dense, matted hair. Everything about him seemed sad, the pallid sheen of his calves, the way his muscled arms pressed against his soft middle, the sides of his temples where his hair had become sparse.

"I never could figure out where you got the idea that lavender was my favorite color." Edith moved closer so that their knees were touching. "Tell me, before I go crazy." She laced her fingers through his, so that there was one of hers, then one of his, except where his missing little finger would have been.

"We're going to have to give it up," Reuben said.

"Give what up?"

All Reuben could do was shake his head.

"Tell me, damn you," Edith cried, unlacing their hands, balling hers into fists.

"The house. We're going to have to give up the house."

# Chapter Five

## November 1933

"Bliss." The corny name had always embarrassed Edith. Whenever someone asked if they were the family who lived in Bliss, she would cringe. Now, more than an embarrassment, the name seemed a mockery. Bliss. Where Reuben had intended for them to remain until they went to their final homes beneath the earth. Where their daughter was meant to be married. Where their son was supposed to move his family after they were gone.

Not that Edith had ever been as fond of the house as Reuben was. She never told him that as touched as she had been by his decision to surprise her with the house, she would have greatly preferred to have been involved in its design. If only he had shown her the plans, she could have pointed out how a kitchen should never face west, that the dining room was too small to seat more than ten comfortably, and that a master bathroom should be located off the bedroom instead of across the hall.

What Edith now realized was that Reuben's decision to build the house without consulting her was the first sign of a pattern that was to define their married lives. As much as Reuben loved her, he didn't regard her as his equal. He saw her as unworldly and simple and believed he had an obligation to protect her from unpleasant truths the same way one protects a child.

But if Reuben had treated her like a fool, she had behaved like one. Who else but a fool would have believed him when he insisted he had everything under control? The bungalows were still unsold, weren't they? How many nights had she woken to find his side of the bed empty? Had Reuben regarded her as a true partner, he would never have considered deeding the house to the bank without first consulting her. Not his house or their house, but *her* house. After all, the house had been his wedding present to her. Except, of course, it wasn't really hers and never had been.

At the same time, Edith also believed that while Reuben should have consulted her, in the end, there was room for only one decision maker in a marriage, and that should always be the husband. As angry as she was, she felt it was her duty to support him, and for days she managed to keep her feeling hidden behind a sympathetic mask—until one night at dinner, when she shocked herself as much as Reuben and the children by screaming, "I forbid you to give this house away," words she underscored by ramming the ladle into the bowl of mashed potatoes, scooping up a mountainful and dumping them onto a plate.

"Pass these to your father," Edith told Jeffrey, shoving the plate into his hands.

After doing as he was told, Jeffrey slumped down so that his face was inches from his plate. Harriet, still in a high chair and too young to understand, jammed her fingers in her mouth and began sucking furiously. Edith had intended to break the news of the move to the children gently but, once released, she found her fury impossible to reign in.

"First thing tomorrow, you call that bastard and tell him the deal is off!" she yelled.

Reuben's voice was calm. "I'll do nothing of the sort." He stuffed a piece of meat in his mouth and chewed.

"Tell him you should have spoken with your wife first."

"Jeffrey, finish your dinner." Reuben's eyes had turned into such angry slits that Edith was momentarily silenced.

"Have you given a moment's thought about how this will affect the children?" Edith asked more calmly.

"What do you think?"

The pained expression on Reuben's face told Edith that he had given it a lot of thought. She ignored it, because she wanted to hurt him. "I'll tell you what I think. That your business means more to you than your own family does."

Reuben threw down his napkin and gave the table such a violent shove that the dishes clattered. "That's rich, coming from you. When was the last time you earned a nickel or, for that matter, lifted a finger to do anything?" He stormed from the room. A moment later, she heard the front door slam. Edith listened for the sound of the car engine, but there was none. Later, she would find Reuben's car keys, along with his wallet, on the foyer table. With false composure, she began eating her dinner and insisted the children finish theirs. She asked Jeffrey about school, as if there was nothing the least bit upsetting about what had just happened.

It was after midnight when Reuben returned. By then, Edith was frantic with worry and sick with shame for having lashed out at him in front of the children. Upon seeing her this way, Reuben's face flooded with relief. He looked stiff with cold, his face and ears painfully red, his nose and eyes running.

Edith threw herself against him. "I can't tell you how sorry I am."

Reuben patted her back in that gentle way of his that she always found so comforting. "I'm the one who should be sorry. Not just for this, for everything."

Arm in arm, they headed upstairs, where they left their clothes in a pile beside the bed. Edith wrapped her leg over his side, pressing herself close to warm him up. Within minutes, they were making love.

So, when Edith awoke the following morning, she was surprised to find that her anger had returned, as fierce and uncontainable as it had been the evening before. "I thought this was the kind of decision husbands and wives made together," she shouted at the still-sleeping Reuben.

Reuben's eyes flew open. He swung his legs over the side of the bed, taking the covers with him. "Damn you! I'm only trying to make sure we'll be able to keep putting food on the table."

Edith railed at him for more than a week. No matter how she screamed and threatened, how many doors she slammed or tears she spilled, it was as if she had an endless store of rage. Reuben stopped shouting back. Indeed, he said little. He left the house early in the morning and didn't return until sunset. She had no idea where he went, except that it wasn't to his construction site where she learned work had stopped months ago. Eventually, Edith wore herself out. Now, instead of being engulfed in tears and screams, Bliss was immersed in silence.

When weeks passed and Reuben heard nothing from Marcus, his memory of their meeting began to fade until it seemed no more real than a barely remembered dream. He began to hope Marcus had become too preoccupied with his other problems to give more than a passing thought to his.

It was late November when Marcus called.

"I was about to call you," Reuben blurted. He instantly regretted having uttered such an obvious lie. Though he was the only one at home, he turned so that he was facing the wall and cupped his hand over the mouthpiece. "Edith wanted me to ask if we could stay through December. She feels not having Christmas here would upset the children."

Marcus paused. "I didn't think you Hebrews celebrated Christmas." He sighed. "I suppose I can get the board to agree to that."

Reuben sensed there was something insulting in what Marcus said but couldn't decide if it was his use of the word "Hebrews" or his presumption that his family didn't celebrate Christmas. Even so, Reuben didn't feel insulted so much as irrationally grateful and found himself thanking Marcus effusively and reminding him to give his best to Adele and his daughters—until Marcus interrupted him, claiming an urgent call.

From the foyer, Reuben could see past the living room into the sunroom, which he used as his office. It hardly seemed possible that in six weeks, he would be living someplace other than this house, which had become as much a part of him as his arms and legs. He didn't have a clue where that someplace might be, except that it wouldn't be a bungalow. That would be asking too much of Edith. He should have already been making inquiries about what apartments were available to let. Only, no inquiries seemed discreet enough, even if the day was not long in coming when the whole town was bound to find out anyway how desperate his situation had become.

Reuben supposed they could move in with his mother. As unpleasant as that prospect was, it was not nearly as unpleasant as the thought of living above the Main Street shops or in a tiny bungalow. And there would be the added advantage of not having to pay rent, which, of course, he would offer to pay and, of course, his mother would refuse. Edith wouldn't be happy, but, these days, she was rarely happy anyway. And given that the only person she saw most days was her feeble-minded housekeeper, Antoinette, his mother might even welcome the companionship.

Reuben arranged to have lunch with his mother the following day. On the walk over, he struggled to come up with a way to explain his predicament. It pained him that his relationship with his mother was such that he had to take such care with his words. He imagined her listening politely, her head tilted, an unreadable smile on her tiny, pinched face. She would not be fully sympathetic. Over the past few years, she'd warned him repeatedly what a mistake it was to keep pouring money into the business.

Jenny was dressed in her customary uniform of a high-necked, old-fashioned blouse fastened with her cameo brooch and an ankle-length, pleated skirt. She was seated on her horsehair couch, the Philco on the side table tuned to the "Westinghouse Theatre Story Hour." As he bent to kiss her, she leaned away to turn off the radio.

"You're late," she said. "Everything will be ice cold."

"Only a few minutes."

"Twelve minutes." While Jenny's eyes were no longer good enough to make out the hands of her wristwatch, she had an uncanny sense of time.

"I prefer my food cold," Reuben said.

"Well, I don't." Jenny pressed one knotted hand into the sofa arm, anchored the other against the cushion and attempted to stand. She managed to put no more than a finger's width of space between herself and the sofa before collapsing back down.

Reuben stood there, afraid that whether he offered to help or didn't, she was sure to get angry. Finally, he held out his arm, so it would be her decision whether to take it.

Jenny swiped it away with impressive force for a woman whom old age had reduced to less than five feet and one hundred pounds. "If I want your help, I'll ask."

"Suit yourself." Reuben headed off to the dining room, pleased with himself for having mustered the courage to answer her this way.

The food was already on the table. Their plates each contained two shriveled potatoes, a few brown-edged slices of lettuce, and a chicken leg and thigh covered with beige gooseflesh. Reuben often wondered if Jenny regarded the unappetizing meals she served him as a test of his love, for the mother he recalled from his childhood had been a wonderful cook with an almost magical ability to transform a cheap cut of meat and some root vegetables into a fragrant stew. Even her meatless dinners—and from necessity, there were many—had been delicious.

When Jenny made it to the dining room, her face was flushed and she was breathing hard.

"At least let me help you into your chair," Reuben said. This time, Jenny didn't refuse.

Reuben's plan had been to warm up his mother with stories about the children, but now that he was seated across from her, he didn't see the point. His mother was too shrewd to be won over by a few anecdotes about grandchildren she had never been all that interested in.

"The bank will only grant an extension on my loans if I agree to deed Bliss to them," Reuben began. He cut into his chicken thigh, and a puddle of pink liquid squirted onto the plate.

"Oh." Jenny's tone was wary. Her arthritic fingers bent inward like claws and, after several tries with her cutlery, she gave up and clasped the chicken leg between her palms. "Whose idea was that, that Fellowes character?"

Reuben nodded.

"You told him nothing doing, of course?" Jenny's eyes had turned fierce behind the thick lenses of her steel-framed glasses. "Didn't I warn you not to go ahead with that last group of bungalows?"

Reuben resisted the impulse to argue the point, to remind his mother that he'd already owned the lots, and with building materials and labor so cheap, he made a calculated gamble. "I should have listened," he murmured as he excised a purple vein from his chicken and placed it on the rim of the plate.

Jenny smiled, pleased by this admission. Her expression quickly soured as she looked around the table. "Antoinette!" she called.

Antoinette burst through the swinging door. "Merkal?"

Reuben's heart sank. It was hard enough to get down this meal without having to look at Antoinette. Her face reminded him of a beaver's, with the decayed teeth that protruded over her bottom lip, her broad, red-tipped nose and small lash-less eyes.

"You forgot the bread." Jenny shooed her with the back of her hand.

Antoinette looked puzzled. Then her eyes widened with comprehension. "Merkal wants bread," she said to Reuben. "Merkal wants bread," she repeated as she shuffled toward the kitchen.

Reuben added, "I agreed."

"Agreed to what?"

"You asked if I accepted Marcus' offer. It was the house or my business."

"The house is worth something."

"It's already done."

"So why are we discussing it?"

"We're not discussing it. I'm telling you."

Jenny leaned across the table. "Is there something wrong with the chicken?"

"The chicken's fine." Reuben popped a piece in his mouth to prove it.

"I suppose you're planning on moving your crew in here."

As always, Jenny was one step ahead of him, voicing his thoughts before Reuben had the chance. It became a matter of pride to convince her that this was not what he had in mind. "We're moving into one of the bungalows. Marcus agreed to release the lien on one if I deeded Bliss to the bank."

"The four of you in one of those dollhouses! You wouldn't have room to turn around."

"We'll just have to sell some things. I'm still working out the details." Reuben wrinkled his forehead to give the impression he was thinking. "Maybe we should move into an apartment. I hear there are plenty of vacancies on Main Street."

"I can just picture Edith living above a store."

"She did once."

Jenny snorted.

"I can't lose the business—not now, when things are about to pick up."

"The eternal optimist. You'll move in here, of course." Jenny leaned out of her chair and called, "Antoinette, dessert." She turned back to Reuben. "Baked apples. There's nothing your father enjoyed more than a baked apple."

The apples were in rose-patterned china bowls, now chipped and faded, that Reuben remembered from his childhood. He stared down at the puckered apple sitting in a puddle of brown liquid. It was odd, but he had no recollection of his father ever even having eaten a baked apple.

"She forgot to core them. You'll have to eat around it." Jenny pushed her apple aside. "I'm thinking the one on the corner of Manor and Cornwall."

"What?"

"The yellow one with the large maple. I think it's a maple, anyway."

Reuben stared at her.

"The bungalow! I can just imagine Edith and me under the same roof! No, a bungalow is perfect for me. I'm finding the stairs difficult these days, anyway."

As obvious a solution as this seemed, the possibility hadn't occurred to Reuben. He tried to control his excitement. "Mom, I could never ask you to do that." He dug his spoon into the apple. It was nearly raw, but he ate it all, including the core.

Reuben arrived home to find Edith sprawled, stomach down, on top of their bed. "It's very kind of her, don't you think?" he asked. "You should call and thank her."

Edith buried her face deeper into the pillow.

"She'll be taking Antoinette, though her chickens will have to stay. She even offered to have Antoinette help around the house when she comes by to feed them."

Edith lifted her face. "Antoinette. The chickens. Oh yes, it's very kind of her."

"It is. Especially since we should be thinking about letting Geraldine and Mrs. Goldsmith go."

Edith laughed. "Aren't you always saying what an imbecile Antoinette is? Besides, I've already cut Geraldine back to twice a week. As for Mrs. Goldsmith, how do you expect me to look after the children?"

*The same way your mother looked after you and my mother looked after me,* Reuben wanted to say. "You'll just have to manage." He stroked her hair, which was free of the lacquer she normally used and as soft as Harriet's. "It's your place to tell them."

Edith rolled onto her side. "You're the want who wants to fire them."

"They deserve to hear it from you."

Edith gave him a knowing smile. "'Deserve' is an odd way to put it. As if they've earned the right to be fired. I won't do it."

Reuben wasn't surprised by how Edith answered, just disappointed, for there was nothing he hated more than firing people. It was the real reason he'd kept his workers on long after it had become obvious that this was no ordinary downturn. He looked around the bedroom. Edith's dressing table, which she usually kept in such deliberate order—with her ivory-handled brush and comb to the left of the mirror and her crystal perfume flasks to its right—was in disarray. Lipsticks, their swivel tops off, powder puffs, eye pencils, and mascara brushes were scattered everywhere, as were her necklaces, rings, bracelets, and brooches, making it look as if a thief had rifled through the partly-opened drawers. Her clothing was flung about, including her undergarments, which she was normally so modest about.

"If you insist on acting like a child, I'll do it," Reuben said.

"You treat me like a child. Why shouldn't I behave like one?" Edith answered.

While Reuben fired Geraldine right away, it took him a week to work up the courage to fire Mrs. Goldsmith. He was afraid she might start crying as Mrs. Goldsmith was almost unnaturally attached to the children. But Mrs. Goldsmith betrayed no emotion, save a flicker of sympathy when Reuben told her that they were forced to give up Bliss. She even beat him to the punch line.

"It would be madness to keep me on," Mrs. Goldsmith said. Only her hands betrayed her anxiety. She had twisted the tassels of her shawl so tightly around her fingers that their tips had turned white.

By evening, Reuben sensed that Mrs. Goldsmith's attitude had changed. He could hear it in the slap of her large feet in their stretched-out oxfords against the kitchen linoleum and in how fiercely she whacked the wooden mallet into the lamb cutlets for the children's dinner.

The following morning, Mrs. Goldsmith cornered Reuben in the kitchen. "They're going to suffer," she whispered, motioning toward Harriet, who was seated in her high chair across the table from Edith in the breakfast nook.

"Of course, they'll miss you terribly. You'll have to visit." Reuben spoke loudly so that Mrs. Goldsmith would get the message that he wasn't prepared to hide anything from Edith.

Mrs. Goldsmith leaned closer. "That's not what I meant. She doesn't know the first thing about looking after them."

Harriet began banging her Peter Rabbit cup against her tray, sending juice spilling onto the floor. Edith was hunched over the table, her hands wrapped around a coffee cup, which she had yet to touch, and so lost in thought that she didn't even flinch.

Mrs. Goldsmith strode over to the table and yanked the cup out of Harriet's hands. Harriet began to scream.

"You had your chance," Mrs. Goldsmith said, wagging her finger. "You're not getting Peter Rabbit back until lunchtime."

The old toaster had to be watched, but Harriet's tantrum had distracted Reuben, and his toast burned. He brought the blackened slices over to the sink and scraped at their charred surfaces. Mrs. Goldsmith pressed in beside him and rinsed Harriet's cup. She pulled a dishtowel from the swivel arm and ran it roughly around the cup's insides.

"I've held my tongue for years. If I didn't speak up now, I couldn't live with myself," Mrs. Goldsmith whispered.

Edith looked over at them. Reuben could tell she knew they were talking about her—also that she didn't care. Her face was swollen, and even from this distance he could see how red her eyes were. "I think she wants something," Edith said, flicking her hand in Harriet's direction.

Harriet was standing on her seat and reaching over the tray.

"See what I mean!" Mrs. Goldsmith cried as she hurried over to Harriet, catching her just as she was about to topple over.

# Chapter Six

## December 1933 and June 1934

Once Reuben had dispensed with the nasty business of letting Mrs. Goldsmith go, he became unnaturally cheerful, as if he were actually looking forward to moving into the Main Street house.

"Let's make our last month here a happy month," he told Edith. "Living on Main Street will be a great adventure," he told Jeffrey. "From your bedroom window, you'll be able to see all sorts of goings-on. You'll be able to hear the ambulances and train whistles and go to the corner store all by yourself. And Antoinette's chickens, you'll surely enjoy taking care of them."

Edith went through their last month at Bliss like a sleep-walker. "We're going to have to make some tough decisions," Reuben told her. They had accumulated so many things, and the Main Street house wasn't half the size of Bliss. But what to keep? What to give away? Edith found herself incapable of making the simplest decisions. And because Reuben was unwilling to make them for her, she knew they would end up bringing everything with them, cramming the items that didn't fit in the house into the derelict barn toward the rear of the property.

Reuben hired two of his laborers, burly Italian brothers, to help with the moving. "These boys couldn't tell china from Bakelite," he told Edith. "Pack the breakable stuff yourself." He was about to leave to go help his mother move when he waved her over. The brothers had started in the living room. One was removing the hooks from the drapes while the other wrapped a painting in butcher paper. "Keep an eye on them," he whispered. "They're good kids, but they know they're about to lose their jobs."

Edith dragged cartons and a pile of newspaper into the dining room. She opened the china closet and stared at her china set and the remnants of what had been her mother's set. Why bother packing any of it? She wouldn't be entertaining at Main Street. The dining room was one of the nicer rooms, reasonably sized with an attractive crown molding. It was the rest of the house—the claustrophobic front hallway, the living room with its water-stained ceiling and buckling walls, the noises in all the walls that Edith recognized from her childhood to be the scrabbling of mice.

Without saying anything to the brothers, Edith put on her coat and left the house. It was a gray day with a biting wind. The evening before, it had snowed heavily, and deep drifts covered the shrubs that hugged the house. The sidewalks hadn't been shoveled yet, so Edith had to walk in the road, where the slush seeped through her boots, numbing her toes. She walked for nearly an hour until finally the cold became unbearable and she ducked into a cinema. Later, she would be unable to recall the name of the movie she'd seen, let alone what it was about.

It was late afternoon when Edith returned to Bliss. By then, the contents of the house were in cardboard cartons, the drapes down and folded, the carpets rolled up, and the paintings wrapped. The dull light from outside, spilling across the bare rooms, cast angry shadows, making the house look cold and haughty, like a scorned lover.

At Main Street, Reuben had left the front door open to air out the place. But even the cold air couldn't mask the stew of old woman, camphor, damp, and rodents that Edith had come to associate with the house. Now, that odor would be the first thing she would smell upon waking up, the last thing before going to bed. With time, it would seep through her pores so that no matter how hard she scrubbed, she would be able to smell it and would forever be worrying that others could as well.

Jenny had left behind much of her furniture, including her harp, which Edith had never heard her play but which Reuben claimed she once played beautifully. It was an enormous thing with a gold-painted, scrolled frame. "She wants Harriet to learn how to play," Reuben explained when he returned from Jenny's bungalow. "She says a well-bred girl should know at least one musical instrument."

Quaint as this notion was, it was one Edith also believed. But the idea of Harriet playing the harp revolted her. In the one photo she had seen of Jenny as a young woman, Jenny had been seated behind this harp, her hands poised above the strings, her pale hair spilling over her shoulders. This photo was proof positive of how much Harriet resembled her, something Jenny claimed from the moment Harriet was born but was only now becoming apparent to Edith. Because Jenny had once been a beauty, this would have pleased Edith if only she didn't dislike her mother-in-law so.

Before entering the kitchen, Edith steeled herself. It had been years since she last agreed to eat in Jenny's house. After Isadore died, Jenny's already casual housekeeping standards became nonexistent. As for Antoinette, it was a mystery to Edith what it was she did around the house.

The kitchen was even worse than Edith had imagined. A patina of grease covered the stovetop and walls. Charred spills like miniature volcanoes rose from the floor of the oven, and a foul puddle of water marked where Jenny's icebox had stood. There were mouse droppings inside the drawers, sticky with jam, honey, and God knows what else.

Over the past month, Jenny had reminded Edith and Reuben repeatedly about how the house was a loan, not a gift, and because of that, they were not to do anything to it without her permission. As Edith mounted the stairs, she wondered if this meant they were supposed to ask Jenny before they repaired the dripping faucets or nailed down the creaking floorboards—or replaced the window sashes, so rotten, Edith could peel the wood off with her fingernails. This was the first house that Jenny and Isadore had owned, and neither ever fully grasped how they were solely responsible for its upkeep. They became masters of accommodation. If an electrical outlet stopped working, they would use another. If a pipe leaked, they would place a bucket beneath it. Reuben did whatever repairs they asked him to do but no more. He never really forgave them for not seeking his advice before buying this house and, because of that, he was determined to let them live with the consequences.

Inside the bedroom that had once been Jenny and Isadore's, then Jenny's, and would now be Reuben and hers, the wisteria vine wallpaper had faded to near nothingness, and water stains reached out from the corners like giant hands. On the floor, Edith found Jenny's hairbrush. It hadn't been cleaned for years, and the bristles were thick with fuzz and Jenny's long gray strands. The handle was strangely pitted. Only later did it occur to Edith what had caused that pitting—mice.

For the first few months after they moved, Reuben would park his car across the street from Bliss almost daily, turn off his engine, and stare at the house. It soon became obvious that the bank wasn't looking after the house properly. An enormous branch that came down during a snowstorm lay across the driveway for weeks before it was cleared away. When a window was smashed, it was patched over with a piece of cardboard, which, after that fell off, was never replaced. Beyond these obvious signs, the house exuded such a distressing aura of neglect that by spring, Reuben had stopped coming by.

Yet, when June came, Reuben was overcome by a compulsion to see the house again. On the drive over, he steeled himself for what he was about to see—the grass grown high, the shrubs he had so lovingly tended, withered and brown due to the unusually dry spring, more windows smashed, perhaps more serious vandalism.

Instead, he found the lawn mown, the evergreens trimmed into precise conical shapes, and white and pink impatiens planted along the borders of the neatly tended flowerbeds. A bat and ball rested against a tree stump, all that remained of the enormous maple that once graced the front lawn.

Reuben had wanted the house to be sold, if only to insure that it would be looked after again. Now that it had been sold, he felt sick. He pressed his forehead to the steering wheel to calm himself, then succumbed to the temptation to give the house one last look. His eyes locked with Gladys Herbert's just as she was coming down the steps.

Gladys spun around, her first instinct apparently to hurry back into the house. Then, she turned back and with a broad, if not entirely convincing, smile, continued down the front path. Reuben sat frozen, his hand on the starter key, foot pressed to the clutch. Gladys was just feet away when he finally managed to start the car. Through his rearview mirror, he saw her standing in the road, watching open-mouthed as he sped away.

That it was Paul Herbert who was now hanging his clothes in his closets and crapping in his toilets made Reuben feel as if he'd been raped. He could just picture Paul rubbing his hands together when hc heard Bliss was available and exclaiming, "What an opportunity." He wondered why none of his old friends had told him, assuming they knew—which, of course, they would. The Herberts had probably already invited all of them there to dinner.

Reuben arrived home to find Edith stretched out on Jenny's stiff-backed, riveted couch, their plush divan having been too large for Main Street's small living room. She had a paperback spread open on her lap and was filing her nails, the shavings drifting like light snow onto the pages.

"You won't believe this," Reuben said.

Edith turned to him warily.

"The Herberts bought Bliss. They're already living there."

Edith went back to her nails. "So?"

"Well, what do you think?"

"It was for sale, wasn't it?"

"It doesn't bother you that it's people we know? Friends?"

Edith dusted the shavings off the book and then held out her hands, testing the edge of each nail with her finger pad for smoothness. "Friends? They were never our friends." She picked up a bottle of red lacquer and banged it against her palm to mix the contents.

Reuben watched as she applied the lacquer, recalling how she used to have a standing Friday appointment at the beauty parlor, during which the manicurist would attend to her nails while the beautician did her hair. Now, she went to the beauty parlor only once a month to have her hair colored and cut. She never complained about this, had pretty much stopped complaining about everything. Yet, he could sense her resentment, rushing like a poisonous stream beneath the surface.

He walked over to the windows, opening them wide. The overgrown lilac bushes pushing against the side of the house were in bloom, and their scent flooded in. He sniffed in deeply as he rested his palms on the windowsill and looked out at the darkening sky. It, too, was lilac, like a spreading bruise.

"Before you know it, things should be on the upswing," Reuben said. "Mark my word, by the time summer's over, two, maybe three of those bungalows will have sold."

"Shut the window, please," Edith said. She raised her book so that her nose was practically touching the page. Reuben kept staring at her until, with an exasperated sigh, she tossed her book to the side. "What!"

"I'm just curious what you think," Reuben said.

"About what?"

"The bungalows, whether you think they'll sell this summer."

"Do I look like a fortune teller? If they sell, they sell, if they don't, they don't."

"I think it's a little more important than that."

"I can't predict the future, and neither can you."

Reuben ran his fingers through his hair. "Damn it, Edith, I'm just looking for a little reassurance."

Edith returned to her book. Reuben began to pace. He knew his pacing would annoy her but didn't care. As he crossed the room, he kept glancing at her, trying to read her feelings from the small part of her face not hidden behind her book. She remained determinedly focused on the page, though Reuben couldn't imagine she could be absorbing much of what was there. Did Edith really not care that the Herberts had bought Bliss? Or was she just pretending because she wanted to hurt him? Reuben suspected it was the latter, but then, why did she want to hurt him? Was it possible she was still angry with him for agreeing to deed Bliss to the bank? Surely by now, she must have come to her senses enough to realize that he had no other choice.

# Chapter Seven

## October 1934

---

"A person shouldn't hear news like this over the phone," Marcus said. He was seated at the edge of Reuben's recliner and had on his coat, brown tweed, its frayed leather buttons still fastened. He was holding an envelope in his large, liver-spotted hands. "As it is, I'm not sure we did you any favors by keeping you going so long." Marcus placed the envelope on the side table. "Besides, I have to put the bank's interests first."

Reuben struggled to keep his voice calm. "You promised that if I deeded the house to the bank, you'd leave the business alone."

"I said I'd do my best and I did. I got you close to another year."

"Nine months."

"I didn't come here to argue." Marcus pulled a cigarette from beneath his coat. His hands trembled as he lit the match. He had always been jowly, but his face was so slack now that it reminded Reuben of melting wax. "I was hoping some of the bungalows might go this summer."

"So was I."

"The board wanted to pull the plug in June. I held them off."

Reuben thought back to all those Saturdays and Sundays he'd spent at the bungalows, waiting for the buyers who never came. "What makes you think the bank will have better luck?"

"That remains to be seen. But the bungalows are beginning to look shabby, and the feeling at the bank—"

"Don't give me that bullshit. You're the bank!" It infuriated Reuben that Marcus could be so cowardly as to pretend to be merely one voice among many, when every businessman in town knew that at the bank, his was the only voice that mattered.

"All major decisions are made by committee."

"But surely, the committee has to rely on the advice of someone."

"Of course." Marcus tapped his ashes into a Lalique ashtray. The living room was crammed with such pieces, brought over from Bliss—Edith's hand-painted porcelain china figurines and sterling silver candy dishes, now hopelessly tarnished, Reuben's lead crystal decanters for port and whiskey, now empty.

The question that had been nagging at Reuben since June and had driven him to the telephone many times, though he'd never mustered the courage to dial, demanded to be answered: "How much did they pay?"

"How much did who pay?"

"The Herberts."

Marcus paused. "That sort of information is confidential."

The information was not confidential but rather a matter of public record, obtainable through town hall. Still Reuben had to hear it from Marcus. "More bullshit. I need to know!"

"If you must, it was around $14,000."

Reuben shut his eyes to steady himself. "You let them steal it."

"The house is only worth what the market will bear."

"How nice it must be to still have friends at the bank."

Marcus rose. "I don't want to hold your dinner up."

As Reuben stood to leave, he felt the blood drain from his head. He collapsed back down, clasped his hands between his thighs and lowered his head.

Marcus touched his shoulder. "Are you okay?"

Reuben waved him away.

"I want you to know how sorry I am. I didn't sleep a wink last night."

Reuben lifted his head. There were dark smudges beneath Marcus' eyes, and his complexion was gray. "Marcus, like you said, business is business. Why should I care what you sold the house for?"

"Paul struck the deal with one of our board members. I didn't even know about it until after the papers had been signed."

Reuben still felt light-headed but got up anyway. "I'll see you out."

It was raining heavily, the drops pushed along by a slashing wind. Reuben turned on the porch light. He was about to warn Marcus about the wobbly porch step but changed his mind.

It wasn't until later that Reuben remembered the envelope Marcus placed on the side table. The envelope had not been sealed, and Reuben wondered if Marcus intended to read the letter to him but lost his nerve. It was short, two paragraphs, a formal notification demanding the outstanding loans and exercising the bank's right to the supporting collateral, effective immediately.

Edith was waiting for Reuben at the kitchen table, nibbling on a cracker as she paged through a magazine. When Reuben told her that the bank was taking possession of his business, she seemed relieved. "At least now that it's behind you, you'll be able to make a fresh start," she said.

Reuben had to fight the urge to grab her shoulders and shake her until she understood that, in the same way that one never gets over the death of a child, he would never be able to put the loss of his business behind him. Instead, he said, "Right," adding that he was exhausted and was heading upstairs.

As tired as Reuben was, he was unable to sleep. All night, he lay awake, watching the rain stream down the window while Edith slept peacefully beside him, oblivious to his fury, which by dawn had extended beyond Marcus and his bank to include her.

By then, the rains had lightened, and the streetlights were wreathed in halos, the moon covered in a mist as delicate as a bridal veil. Reuben dressed in his old work clothes—a flannel shirt and dungarees—and carried his boots downstairs so as to not wake Edith. He made the same breakfast he used to make when he needed to get to his sites early—coffee and buttered raisin toast. Within fifteen minutes, he was in his truck.

The storm had wrested the last leaves from the trees, forming a slippery carpet. The tires on Reuben's truck were nearly bald, and the truck skidded several times on the way to the bungalows, once missing a utility pole by inches.

By the time Reuben arrived at the bungalows, the rains had drifted off to the sea. The sky was a washed violet, the sun's blood-orange corona visible over the horizon. Two flatbeds were parked by the curb, beside which a quartet of men dressed much like Reuben were standing in a huddle. One read from a clipboard while the others stamped their feet and rubbed their hands together. When they noticed Reuben, the man with the clipboard shooed the others to work. The men began gathering the spare building supplies—the timber and plywood, the rolls of insulation and asphalt roofing, the bags of concrete and plaster mix—and loaded them onto the trucks while the man with the clipboard ticked them off. They worked silently and efficiently as if performing a dance they'd rehearsed many times.

It infuriated Reuben that Marcus hadn't even waited for the bank to open before ordering his men to the site. Was he afraid that if his men didn't get there first, Reuben would cart off everything that wasn't nailed down? It was fine for Marcus to insist he was only doing his job, but had it been Paul Herbert instead of him, would Marcus have dared to ask for his house or reneged on a promise to leave his business alone?

Reuben clenched the steering wheel, imagining that it was Marcus' neck beneath his grip. He recalled how, once, when the two of them were negotiating a loan, Marcus had said, "Don't jew me down." When Reuben flinched, Marcus had been quick to add, "I meant it as a compliment. Everyone knows what shrewd businessmen you people are." *You people.* The tribal instinct was easy to disregard, so long as there was enough to go around. But as soon as things turned tough, it became a different story. Adolph was right.

When he could no longer bear to watch, Reuben shifted the truck into gear and headed downtown. By then, the sun was over the horizon, the moon faded to a ghostlike disk. Main Street was beginning to come alive. Reuben parked outside the bank, which would not open for another hour. He was sorry that he hadn't thought to take a beam from the site so that he could ram it through the bank's plate glass window. So what if the police threw him in jail? His life was over anyway.

At half past eight, a light flicked on inside the bank. Reuben got out of his truck. The front door was still locked. He began pounding on it until he drew a middle-aged woman, as full-breasted as a pigeon, to the window. She pointed to her watch, shook her head, and then disappeared back into the shadows.

"Goddammit, open up," Reuben screamed. He was aware that a small crowd had gathered behind him, but he didn't care. He banged on the door until his fists became sore. After giving it a last kick with the side of his boot, he pushed his way through those friends and neighbors whose opinion of him once mattered so much. Instead of returning home, he drove to Mowbray. There were trucks parked outside of Bliss as well. The house had been in near-perfect condition, and Reuben couldn't imagine what the Herberts thought needed to be done. He got down from his truck and, crouching over so as not to be seen, went over to the dumpster. Among the plasterboard, copper wire, and pieces of pipe, he found the lavender bathroom tiles as well as fragments of the glazed white ones with which they must have been replaced.

# Chapter Eight

## January 1935

It was the sort of drowsy Sunday afternoon Edith once loved, when she and Reuben would lounge about the living room, he with his newspapers, she with a romance novel. But that was back in the days when, by the time Sunday rolled around, they both longed for a break from their social merry-go-round, when their surroundings were both beautiful and comfortable.

As soon as the family finished lunch, tinned cream of mushroom soup followed by macaroni and cheese, Harriet fell asleep on the couch, her index finger in her mouth, a habit left over from babyhood. Jeffrey escaped to his bedroom.

"What do you think he does up there?" Edith asked. She and Reuben were still at the dining room table, finishing their tea.

"I wish I knew. He's a strange kid." Reuben picked at his teeth with the silver toothpick he always used after meals, a disgusting habit in Edith's opinion.

"What an awful thing to say." Edith wished she were able to sound more like she meant it. While "strange" might be a bit harsh, Jeffrey certainly was different. He'd always been a boy who cried too easily, a loner who preferred his own company to that of other children. She had no doubt that he was teased in school. Boys who preferred drawing to playing ball and who sat huddled in a corner during recess always were.

"You don't think I worry about him? I just don't know what else to do," Reuben said.

Edith began stacking the plates. She was sorry that she had raised the subject of Jeffrey when the mere act of talking about him was enough to upset her. Reuben did try with Jeffrey, even if his efforts usually came to nothing. The week before, when it snowed, he'd washed off the trash can lid and then pleaded with Jeffrey to go sledding. But Jeffrey would not be budged. Not only did he hate the cold and hate getting wet, he said, he was terrified of going fast.

Reuben gathered the Sunday papers. "I think I'll head upstairs for a rest."

A rest from what? Edith wondered. After Reuben lost the bungalows, she'd resisted the temptation to insist he look for work right away. Given his mental state, no one would have hired him anyway. But now four months had passed, and he still hadn't shown the least inclination to start looking.

"Can I have a word with you?" Edith asked, catching his arm.

Reuben raised his eyebrows.

Edith wished she'd had the chance to clear away the luncheon dishes first. But moments like this, when the children weren't about and neither of them was angry, were rare. She pushed the plates toward the center of the table and sat back down in what had become her customary seat, the one closest to the kitchen. Reuben took his customary seat, too, at the head of the table, which secretly rankled her, for she couldn't help feeling he had forfeited the right to sit there.

"It's time you looked for work," Edith said.

Reuben picked up a crust of bread from Harriet's plate, mopped up some cheese sauce, and ate it. "Do you have any idea how bad things are?"

Edith resented his implication—that she was too unworldly to know about such things. But she was determined not to lose her temper, knowing that if she did, Reuben would go storming from the room. Speaking slowly so as to keep her voice steady, Edith said, "There have to be some jobs out there."

"Maybe I should take one digging ditches."

"If that's all there is."

"A bit of a comedown, wouldn't you say?"

"In times like these, there's no room for pride." Edith had read these words in *Good Housekeeping*. As soon as she parroted them, she recognized them for what they were: words that seemed sensible enough on the page but were impossible to live by. "You're right. I'm hardly in a position to tell you how to look for work. I do know one thing, though, and that's how much people like and respect you. Why don't you call some of your old friends and see if you can stop by?"

Reuben headed upstairs, this time without the newspapers. He sat down at the desk he'd had custom made for his study at Bliss—walnut, straight-legged, and unadorned, except for its gold-embossed leather top. Too large for any room in this house, it sat in the landing outside of the master bedroom. He actually preferred the view of Main Street to the one he had at Bliss of shrubs and grass. But the hallway was so narrow that even with his chair pushed against the opposite wall, his stomach pressed into the desk's edge. Outside it was damp and gray, the street deserted except for a mother who stood hugging herself for warmth as her son circled around the sidewalk on his tricycle. By now, Reuben recognized many of the tenants who lived above the shops across the street, though he and Edith had yet to introduce themselves to a single one.

He felt ashamed for having put Edith in the position of having to beg him to look for work when any man with an ounce of pride would have started looking months ago. He resolved to make Edith proud of him again, even if it did mean digging ditches.

He decided to make a list of people to contact, so that first thing Monday morning, he'd be able to start his calls. He pulled out a writing tablet, replenished the inkwell built into the desk, and then deliberated over which fountain pen to use. It seemed important to choose carefully, as if the right pen might bring him good luck. He selected the Waterman gold nib pen his parents had given him for his twenty-first birthday.

Reuben opened his address book. Starting with the A's, he copied down names and telephone numbers. Nearly all belonged to men he once regarded as friends, except so much time had elapsed since he'd spoken to most of them that he couldn't help worrying how they would react to this call out of the blue.

By the time Reuben got to J, he had filled an entire page. But this exercise, instead of giving him hope, made him feel more ashamed. He couldn't be blamed for everything that had befallen him. Still, not everyone had failed as abysmally as he had. All of these men had managed to hold on, some more firmly than others, but they had all held on.

Reuben buried his face in his hands. Though he had cut back on nearly every expense, he continued to make the premiums on his life insurance policy, even though the company that held this policy, the Mutual of Toledo, was in danger of going under. Maybe the thing to do, while the Toledo was still breathing, would be to kill himself, not by slitting his wrists or putting a gun to his head—for he was sure suicide would void the policy but in a more ambiguous way. He could take the car out on a snowy evening and run it into a tree.

Reuben imagined the "accident"—not the moment of impact but the seconds leading up to it. Then, he pictured the funeral service and burial and wondered which of his former friends would show up, whether the chapel would be empty or full. He wondered whether Edith and his children would grieve deeply or hardly at all. By then, he already knew that he was too much of a coward to kill himself. A man who could barely muster the courage to look for work could never deliberately drive his car into a tree.

In all, Reuben made appointments with ten men. On Wednesday, he set off for the first of these meetings. The temperature was in the teens, and the winds pressed against him like a relentless hand as he struggled down Main Street. Nose dripping, eyes tearing, fingers and toes numb, as he trudged up narrow, worn staircases to small, rundown offices, he tried not to dwell on the folly of his mission. While the hard times might not have destroyed these men's livelihoods, they'd certainly had an impact. Men who once occupied several rooms now shared single rooms with their sole remaining employees, their secretaries. As a young man, Reuben had been determined never to work in an office, chained to a desk as his father had been. Now he found himself envying these men, envying the fact that they still had a place to go and were performing services people were willing to pay for.

These visits were even more of an ordeal than he had anticipated. The forced cheeriness, the obligatory questions about the men's families and feigned interest in their responses, the falsely upbeat answers to questions about how he was doing—it all depleted him. As the day wore on, his ability to put on a good front flagged.

"My days are pretty dull," he admitted during his last meeting with Stu Joseph, the accountant who used to keep the books for his construction company.

"I'd go bonkers if I didn't have a place to escape to during the day," Stu said. He swiveled his chair around and punched some numbers into an adding machine already trailing several yards of tape. "Usual end-of-the-month crush," he explained as he transcribed these numbers onto a sheet of green ledger paper. The clanging steam radiators were pumping out so much heat that Stu had opened both windows. A lash of frigid air whipped around the room, ruffling papers and rattling the closet door against its hinges.

"It's tough on Edith, though she's been a real trooper," Reuben said.

Stu held up his hand. "Miss Lehmann, that letter's got to make the evening post. How's Edith, anyway? Still such a looker?"

Miss Lehmann looked up. "Just finishing." She gave the carriage return a shove, its ping underscoring her words.

As Stu proofread the letter, Miss Lehmann read along, too, looking over his shoulder. "I couldn't have said it better myself." He signed his name with a flourish. "She's a real gem, aren't you, doll? Better bundle up. Poor Reuben here still looks frozen."

"Maybe this isn't a good time." Reuben had to shout to be heard over the truck rumbling down Main Street.

"No time's ever good. I'll close the windows." When he was seated, Stu began punching more numbers into the adding machine. "Don't mind me, I'm listening."

"I figure I owe it to Edith to at least get out and talk to people," Reuben said. "Not that I have any real expectations."

Stu whipped the tape from the adding machine and unrolled it on his desk. "It's pretty miserable out there, and I'm not talking about the weather. For all his WPAs and NRAs and TVAs, I can't see where Roosevelt's made a damn bit of difference." He pulled his pencil out from behind his ear and pointed it at Reuben. "Except to bring us that much closer to communism."

Reuben smiled weakly. Roosevelt's name had come up in nearly every one of his meetings. He found the vitriol with which several of these men regarded Roosevelt astonishing. As far as he was concerned, the only thing that Roosevelt was guilty of was a willingness to try anything that might lift the country out of the mess it was in.

"You don't agree?" Stu asked.

"At least the man's got ideas."

Stu clasped his hands and leaned forward. "Want my opinion? What this country needs is someone like Hitler. Someone ruthless enough to run this country like an army."

Reuben's mouth dropped open. Was this Stu's idea of a joke? He regretted having let Stu's "Moshe" comment pass at the Herberts' dinner party and decided not to make the same mistake twice. Smiling, so as to dilute the sting of his words, Reuben said, "Perhaps you've forgotten who you're talking to."

Stu waved his hand. "That's the problem with you people—you're too damn sensitive. All I meant was that the man has balls."

Reuben decided it was best to drop the subject. "Getting back to my own situation..."

"Say what you like about Hitler. At least he knows how to get things done." Stu looked out the window. "What a day! I promised to take Lydia to Miami Beach this winter. Except, thanks to Paul, I've never been busier. You heard that I'm doing his books, now? It'll be months before I can even think of taking a vacation. The guy's a genius."

Several other men had brought up Paul's name. "Have you called Paul?" "If anyone can help, Paul can." Always spoken with such bland earnestness, it was as if these men had already forgotten in whose house Paul was living.

"I figured it was time to let people know that I was ready to start looking for work." Reuben held up his hand. "Not that I came here to ask for a job."

"I hope not!" Stu looked up at the clock. "Five already! Where did the day go?"

"I wanted to make sure people knew that I was willing to look at other things besides construction."

"Like what?"

"I don't know what. That's why I'm out talking to people."

"Of course, you'll want to get back into the building business. Even in good times, when you get to our age, it's just about impossible to change fields."

"It's just that construction is deader than dead."

"Everything's dead. My clients are dropping like flies—manufacturers, retailers, everyone except Paul. What about those public works projects? You know, building roads or bridges."

"Unless you're a civil engineer, I think what they're looking for is brawn, not brains. Someone who can operate a bulldozer."

Stu raised his eyebrows. "So?"

"You're not serious."

"You think you're the first one who's come by looking for work?" Stu walked around to Reuben's side of the desk and squeezed his shoulder. "Buddy, if you're serious about getting a job, you better be prepared to take anything. Can I ask a blunt question? You didn't blow through all that dough already?"

Reuben brushed Stu's hand from his shoulder and stood. "I've already taken up too much of your time. If you do hear of anything…"

"Don't hold your breath." As Stu opened the door, his eyes dropped to Reuben's stomach. "Put on a few pounds, huh? You should get out more, do a little walking. It's not as if you don't have the time."

A few days later, Reuben summoned Edith to the kitchen table. He always paid the bills himself but decided it would be a good idea if she knew how much it cost to run the house. "No matter how you cut back," he began, "you still have to pay for electricity, for water, for coal. A telephone, though plenty of people manage without one. You still have to buy bread and milk."

Her elbows on the table and chin resting on the back of her hands, Edith waited for him to continue.

Reuben was about to explain that he wasn't trying to talk down to her, when the kettle whistled. He jumped up, but Edith waved him back down. "My job," she said chirpily. She brought the white enamel kettle over to the table, filled his cup, and then handed him a White Rose teabag, saying, "You first."

"That's ridiculous."

"Aren't you the one who's always saying watch the pennies and the dollars will take care of themselves? Besides, I'm getting used to weak tea."

"Suit yourself," Reuben said. It seemed to him that Edith's periodic economizing crusades were less about saving money than inflicting pain—by serving powdered milk instead of fresh and Postum instead of coffee, by insisting he listen to the radio in the dark. He let the teabag seep a nice long time before passing it to her.

"Like I was saying," Reuben continued. He patted the bills open and turned them around so they were facing her.

Edith took a long sip of her tea. "Explain to me again why we're doing this?"

"Because I think you should know," he answered, the conviction already drained from his voice. He spooned three teaspoons of sugar into his tea to offset the bitterness of having let the bag seep so long. "Because I thought you'd want to know."

"Not particularly." Edith gave the bills a shove, sending them to the floor. "What good is knowing what it costs to run this house when you refuse to tell me how much money we still have?"

Reuben gathered up the bills. He knew Edith had a point. On the other hand, when it came to women and money, a little knowledge could be a dangerous thing. "I hope you're planning on coming with me to my mother's."

Edith rubbed at her right temple. "I've got a headache." She shuffled over to the sink where she kept a bottle of aspirin. Reuben couldn't tell how many aspirin she took, except that it was more than two.

"Maybe you've forgotten everything she's done for us."

"Us! She did it for you."

Harriet burst through the back door. "Daddy, Tony let us feed the chickens!" She was red cheeked and breathless, her blue cap askew, her long hair spilling down across her unbuttoned coat. She threw her arms around Reuben's neck, kissing him on both cheeks.

Reuben laughed and pushed her gently away. "Get that," he said, addressing Edith. "She's Tony now."

Antoinette returned, Jeffrey holding her hand tightly. It amazed Reuben how attached the children had grown to this simpleminded woman, especially Harriet, who followed her from room to room while she cleaned, a rag tied around her head and a dust cloth tucked into her waistband just like Antoinette.

Jeffrey pulled two feather-coated eggs from his jacket pocket and placed them on the table. "For dinner," he said.

There were more chickens now than ever. Reuben had no idea where they all came from, but he had to admit the stupid animals turned out to be a godsend. Not only did they provide breakfast most days and dinner occasionally, there were usually enough eggs left to sell. Antoinette would pile them in Harriet's baby pram and go from house to house. On a good day, she might make two or three dollars. She would sort the change into piles and leave it on the kitchen table.

"I'd like the kids to come," Reuben said to Edith, who was pressing a folded, wet tea towel against her forehead.

"You know they unsettle her. Anyway, I need to lie down."

"Would you like to come to Nana's?" Reuben was not sure why he asking, rather than telling, the children that they were going. According to Jenny, he was too soft on everyone—his children, Edith, his workers. She insisted this was the real reason his business had failed.

Jeffrey ran to the broom closet. "I'm bringing this for Nana!" He held up the whisk broom and then stuck it between his legs and careened around the room.

Reuben knew immediately where Jeffrey got this from. Edith, whom he'd overheard more than once refer to Jenny as "the old witch."

"Put that back," Reuben yelled.

Jeffrey slung the broom over his shoulder and pointed the end toward Reuben. "Bang, bang. I'm going to kill you."

"Drop that!"

"Stand back or I'll shoot!" Jeffrey began swinging the broom wildly. The end caught the back of Harriet's head, sending her sprawling to the ground. For a moment, she lay stunned and silent. Then, she let out a wail that brought Edith back to the kitchen.

"What happened?" Edith cried. She fell to her knees beside Harriet.

Reuben glanced over at Antoinette, who shook her head as she placed a protective arm around Jeffrey. Edith caught this look and, misinterpreting it, said, "She did this?"

Jeffrey, who'd begun to cry, said, "I didn't mean to hurt her!"

Edith looked between him and Antoinette and then down at the broom. "What would he be doing with a broom?" she asked.

"Jeffrey's telling the truth," Reuben said. "He was planning on giving it to my mother. I hardly need to tell you where he got that idea from." Reuben picked up the broom and began rolling the handle around. "That was before he got the even brighter idea of pretending it was a rifle."

By now, Harriet had stopped crying and was sitting up.

Edith parted the back of Harriet's hair. "She's already got a lump."

"He gave her quite a whack." Reuben kneeled down on the other side of Harriet. "Just like he's going to get from me." He tried to glare at Jeffrey but was unable to pretend that he was really angry. Now that he knew Harriet was going to be fine, he was happy about what Jeffrey had done. It was so boyish, so normal.

# Chapter Nine

## *April 1936*

It was after ten, and Reuben still hadn't changed out of his pajamas. Some days he never did. He was always so tired, he wondered if something might be wrong with him. Like cancer. His father had died of it, and he had heard that it often runs in families.

"If you did more, you'd feel better," Edith told him the other day. Before he had a chance to explain that it was because he was so tired that he couldn't do more, she cut him off. She no longer seemed interested in anything he had to say.

He was in his recliner, reading the newspaper, when Edith came down the stairs. She was wearing the black Persian lamb coat he'd surprised her with for their seventh anniversary. He hadn't seen her wear it in years, hadn't seen her wear any coat besides her green cloth one, though even he could tell how worn its fabric was and how outdated its boxy shape. He wondered if she was meeting a man and then told himself not to be ridiculous.

As Edith gathered her gloves and purse from the foyer table, Reuben was struck by the whiteness of her skin, the gleam of the coil of hair pressed against the nape of her neck. He called out, wanting to tell her how nice she looked. When she turned around, her expression was so impatient, the words caught in his throat. "I was wondering where you're off to," he said.

"Out." She slammed the door behind her.

Reuben picked up *Newsday*. Over the past couple years, his eyes had weakened, and he had to hold it straight out in front of him in order to read. He scoured the paper for signs that things had started to turn around, more out of habit than anything else. It was too late for him. He felt no more connection with the successful builder he'd once been than he would have with the fading photograph of a distant relative.

Reuben wished he hadn't spotted the article about Paul Herbert. But given that he did, he had to read it. The article, which was written with the sort of breathlessness normally reserved for debutantes, related how Paul had waited on the sidelines until 1932, when he reckoned things had become about as cheap as they were going to get. It was then that he began to buy not just stocks and bonds but the houses, land, silver, and artwork of his neighbors. By the reporter's calculations, this scheme had already turned Paul into a millionaire. The article closed by revealing that Paul had recently surrendered his partnership in his father-in-law's law firm. It quoted him as saying, "I had no choice. The management of such a large portfolio is a full-time job."

Reuben wasn't sure why he found Paul's success so upsetting. Paul hadn't bought his house to hurt him. Indeed, he should be flattered that Paul admired Bliss so much that he was willing to sell his own house and move his family to the opposite side of town. But every time he read about Paul or heard his name, he felt like a spear had been thrust through his heart.

The phone rang, startling Reuben—it rang so rarely these days.

"Have you seen my window?" It was Adolph. Reuben had to resist the temptation to place the phone back in the cradle.

"What about your window?"

"Come."

"I'm busy," Reuben said. "Tell me what happened."

"Just come," Adolph said. "It's urgent."

It took Reuben's mind a moment to register what he was seeing—"JEWISH SWINE, GO HOME" scrawled across Adolph's display window in red paint. Reuben was still staring at the graffiti when Adolph emerged from his store, lugging a bucket of sudsy water and a pile of rags.

"Goodman and Kimmel. Haft, the tobacconist, too," Adolph said. "I didn't realize he was Jewish, but Goodman assures me he is."

Reuben placed his hand on Adolph's shoulder. "It's vile," he said. He tried to think of something comforting to say but was too shaken.

Adolph dunked the rags into the bucket and squeezed out the excess water. "Funny thing is, they left Pullen alone, even though he's the most Jewish looking of all of us."

"I'm sure this was just some kids' idea of a joke," Reuben said lamely.

"A joke? I think it's a little more than that. Hating Jews is like a virus. Once it gets started, you'd be amazed how quickly it spreads." Adolph began covering the window in large soapy swirls.

"Razor blades are probably a better idea," Reuben said.

"Razor blades?"

Reuben followed Adolph into the store. He had never before noticed the store's reassuring clove smell or the logic with which the items were shelved. He remembered vaguely what a dimly lit and dusty place the apothecary had been before Adolph took it over. Yet people still spoke nostalgically about old Mr. McIver who, unlike Adolph, always greeted his customers with a broad smile and a compliment. That Adolph was the more knowledgeable pharmacist did not seem to matter.

"Give me some blades," Reuben said when they were back outside.

"I didn't ask you here for that, but thanks," Adolph said. "This morning, I came in through the back door, so I hadn't seen the window. Would you believe, several customers stopped by and didn't say a word? If it hadn't been for Adele Fellowes, I might have gone the whole day without knowing."

"They were probably too embarrassed," Reuben said. Both men began to scrape. Red flecks of paint showered from the window, landing on the pavement like specks of blood.

"Embarrassed? They probably thought it was a big joke. Tell me, am I really so loathsome?"

Reuben looked at Adolph in astonishment. "You must know this is nothing personal."

"Nothing personal?"

"The pranks of a few hooligans don't mean the world is against you."

Adolph shook his head. "For an intelligent man, you really are naive. The world is against me and you."

"There, good as new," Reuben said once they'd finished. "Except that now, the window needs that wash. Can you handle that by yourself?"

"I could have handled this myself. What I can't do alone is fight this thing. If we don't, we could end up in the same pickle they've got themselves into back home."

"Adolph, do yourself a favor and forget about it. In a week's time, no one else is going to remember it." Reuben didn't really believe this. In fact, he believed the opposite—that this was the sort of incident that would remain imprinted in people's minds for years. At the same time, the last thing Sea Forth's Jews needed was to draw more attention to themselves.

"Can I count you in?" Adolph asked.

At that moment, Reuben saw Edith turn the corner onto the opposite sidewalk, a single parcel in her arms. He could tell she was upset by the rapidity of her gait, by how she was holding her chin a fraction higher than was usual.

"My wife, look," Reuben shouted, grateful for the opportunity to escape Adolph. He waved his arm to attract Edith's attention.

Edith clutched the parcel tighter to her chest.

"I'll be in touch," Reuben said.

Adolph continued to scrub at the window. Without looking around, he said, "Tell your lovely wife I said hello." While Adolph always used words like "lovely" and "charming" when referring to Edith, Reuben sensed that he didn't really like her.

Edith had lowered her hat veil over her face. Beneath it, Reuben could see that her cheeks were blotchy, her eyes red. He offered his arm, expecting her to refuse it, but she laced her own through his.

"Just a bunch of hooligans." Reuben patted her hand for reassurance. "Adolph, of course, is up in arms."

"Adolph." She laughed harshly.

"They got Goodman, too. And that funny little stationer, Kimmel. Also Haft, the tobacconist. Did you know he was Jewish?"

"Are you sure it's such a good idea to be seen in public with him?"

The same thought had crossed Reuben's mind, but hearing Edith say it made him wince at its ugliness. "You're not frightened?"

Edith paused. "Not so much frightened as embarrassed. Like I've been caught doing something I shouldn't have been."

"I understand," Reuben said. Edith had put into words precisely what he had been feeling, although why he—or she—should feel this way, he had no idea.

As they walked, Reuben listened to the clack of Edith's heels and the slap of his own shoes against the pavement. He buried his fingers beneath the nap of Edith's coat sleeve. As she leaned against him for support, her breast brushed against his arm. He found himself getting aroused and prayed that this closeness between them would last long enough for him to take her up to their bedroom. It had been months since they had made love.

The day was chilly but clear, the sky blue except for a few threadlike clouds. The branches of the elms planted along the grassy strips between the sidewalk and street were swollen with tight green buds. Mere saplings when he moved out to Sea Forth, they now stood several stories high.

Reuben lifted his face toward the pale, early spring sun. "What a perfect day."

Edith looked at him in amazement.

"I was talking about the weather, of course," Reuben said.

"I hope Antoinette remembered to hang out the laundry. It's been sitting in a moldering heap for days." Edith did not remove her arm, but Reuben could tell she had withdrawn. The closeness between them had been as ephemeral as the clouds above.

When Adolph opened the door to his apartment, he was stooped over, his palm pressed against the small of his back. "I'm not used to such exertion," he told Reuben as he led him into the living room.

Until the hour before, Reuben had been unsure whether he would come to this meeting. When Adolph called on the morning after the graffiti incident, he told Reuben that all the other "interested parties" agreed that something had to be done. But Reuben could tell by the empty bridge chairs scattered about Adolph's living room that several of those parties must have had second thoughts.

Adolph's living room was small and like Reuben's own living room, crammed with mismatched furniture of a scale intended for a much larger space. There was a glass-fronted china cabinet cluttered with knickknacks that Reuben reckoned must have belonged to Adolph's wife, dead now for six or seven years. Jammed into the corner was a grand piano with magazines and books piled atop its closed lid. There was also a stiff-backed Victorian couch, much like the one Jenny had left behind at Main Street and above which hung a portrait of a stern-faced man with muttonchops, its gilt frame providing one of the few spots of brightness in a room where the upholstery fabric, carpet, and lamp shades were all in shades of brown.

Reuben recognized all the men except one. There was Goodman from the bakery, Kimmel the stationer, Haft the tobacconist, and Pullen, the tailor whose window had been spared. The man he didn't recognize, named Marder, was the only man dressed in a suit. Adolph's son, Ernest, was stretched out beneath a blanket on the couch. Reuben recalled Adolph telling him that the boy was unwell and hadn't attended school in years.

"I've prepared an overview," Adolph said when Reuben was seated. He waved a sheet of paper and pushed his wire-rimmed spectacles up the bridge of his nose. "Fellow Jews," he read, "we must take a stand against the oppressors who would drive us out of Sea Forth in the same way our brethren are being driven from their homes in Germany. Our tragic history shows what a mistake it would be to wait for things to blow over. Our means will be peaceful. We will seek to educate our Gentile neighbors about Judaism and the disproportionate contribution our people have made to the arts and commerce. At the same time, we must be prepared to do whatever is necessary to defend our right to live where we choose in peace."

As soon as Adolph finished, Haft stuffed his copy in his breast pocket. "I think you're asking for trouble," he said. He retrieved his pipe, tamping down the tobacco with his forefinger.

"The boy," Adolph said, motioning toward his son.

"Calling one incident 'a campaign' is downright..."—Haft glanced down at the box of matches he was still clutching—"incendiary."

"And that statement about our disproportionate contributions," Marder chimed in, "is the kind of thing that will make them hate us even more."

"Particularly that bit about commerce," Kimmel boomed. "They already think a cabal of Jewish bankers runs the world."

Reuben was always surprised by what a manly voice Kimmel had, for while his torso and head were normal sized, his arms and legs were child-sized. In his store, he had to stand on a crate to see over the counter.

"I never intended to distribute this outside the group," Adolph said.

Goodman stretched his muscular baker's arms overhead and cracked his knuckles. "Adolph, for a man with such strong opinions, this is awfully namby-pamby. Education! We all know there's only one solution to what our Gentile friends call the 'Jewish problem,' which is to get out of their hair and get them out of ours. We need a Jewish homeland. Truth is if they ever did accept us, it would mean the end of the Jewish race."

"Problem is, aren't we supposed to wait for the Messiah?" Kimmel asked.

"The Messiah!" Goodman laughed. "It's time we ditched that religious crap. For two thousand years, while we've been waiting for the Messiah, they've been trying to get rid of us. One of these days, they'll succeed. Look at Germany, man."

The men fell silent. From the outside hallway, Reuben heard the wail of a baby, a mother's soothing words, and then a door shut. Ernest had shifted onto his side and was looking from one man to the next. Beneath the woolen blanket, just the sight of which made Reuben feel hot, his body looked skeletal. But he had an animated face, and his dark eyes were lively and intelligent.

Kimmel turned to Reuben. "Reuben, what do you think?"

Reuben stared at the carpet as he tried to gather his thoughts. He thought back to the day when Adolph forced him into the alleyway. Since then, he'd seen articles in the newspaper about the German-American Bund and how they'd set up a youth camp not ten miles away. Perhaps Adolph wasn't so crazy after all.

"I agree with Adolph," Reuben said, though he was not entirely sure what he was agreeing with.

"Thank you." Adolph sounded surprised.

"Why don't we write letters to the editor?" Pullen suggested. "Of the *Sea Forth Beacon*, I mean."

With a chop of his hand, Goodman dismissed the idea. "Never. You gotta sign those letters with your full name, address too, or else they won't publish them. It's bad enough what those pigs did to our windows. That would be suicide. Nobody would ever shop at my store again."

Reuben thought this was a wild exaggeration and was amazed when the other shopkeepers nodded.

"God forbid we end up making things worse for ourselves than they already are," Adolph said. "But we've got to do something."

Haft stood. With a finality that made clear that the other men could count him out, he said, "I wish you all the best of luck." A few minutes later, Marder, who'd sat there the entire time with his arms crossed and a sour expression, also left.

Pullen's stomach gave an audible growl, and Goodman said, "Maybe that's a signal that we all should start thinking about heading home." With a slap to the thighs, he stood and walked over to Ernest, ruffling his hair. "Not a peep out of you all evening. If only my own kids could keep their mouths shut, they might learn something, too. You like jam rolls? Get Poppa to stop by the store tomorrow, and I'll send some home."

"Wait," Kimmel cried. "We still haven't decided what to call ourselves or whether we should invite women to our next meeting, let alone what to do about the graffiti."

It hadn't occurred to Reuben that this meeting wasn't intended to be a onetime thing. He glanced over at Adolph, who, fingers pressed to his lips, was looking thoughtful. With a sigh, Goodman dropped his coat over the sofa arm.

"No women," Adolph said, an opinion that Goodman and Pullen vigorously seconded. "As for your other questions...," he shrugged.

"I'm not saying we forget about what happened, but maybe the wisest thing would be to take a wait-and-see approach," Pullen said. "If we get together, say once a month, before long, we should know whether this was just a stupid prank or a signal that something more dangerous is going on."

"Like the Bund," Reuben said.

"Like the Bund," Adolph seconded.

"Nonsense," Goodman boomed, again reaching for his coat. He looked over at Ernest. "The Bund is just a bunch of losers who get their kicks out of dressing up like storm troopers and drinking too much beer. I'm willing to keep on meeting, but the minute the rest of you try and blow this up into more than it is, I'm out."

As Reuben headed home that evening, the air was sweet with the promise of spring. The street was filled with strollers and a line had formed outside the cinema where *A Night at the Opera* was playing. Recently, Reuben had been surprised to read that the Marx Brothers were Jewish. When he mentioned this to Edith, she'd shocked him by saying, "With those schnozzles, that horrid wiry hair, what else could they be?" It was the sort of comment his father might have made. He lacked Edith's knack, or the knack his father had had, for sniffing out Jews. As far as he could tell, Jews were no uglier than any other race. At the same time, he couldn't help feeling unreasonably proud of Harriet's pale skin, blond hair, and fine features – and of Edith and himself for producing a child who could pass for a Gentile.

It was not until he and Edith were about to apply for their wedding license and he needed his birth certificate that Reuben learned that the family name had once been Moskowitz. His father made him guess where he'd gotten Merkal from and, when Reuben couldn't, pulled a tin of baked ham from the cupboard. "Smoked and packaged by J. R. Merkal & Sons," his father read off the label. "All these years, it was right there under your nose." Was it any wonder that, as a boy, he never thought to question his father's contention that to be born Jewish was to be born blighted? Indeed, when Reuben first met Edith, he'd been disappointed to learn she was a Jewess. Even the word was ugly, hinting of something dark and disreputable. Yet, Edith, with her ivory skin, cushiony mouth, and thick-fringed eyes, was anything but. Not only was her speech free of the nasal twang and grammatical mistakes so common in the girls, Jewish and Gentile, he'd grown up with, she had beautiful table manners. And though Reuben knew nothing about women's fashions, he could tell that Edith dressed with an elegant flair. In short, she was the sort of woman any man would be proud to call his wife. He soon began to see Edith's Jewishness as a good thing. For no matter how they each changed over the years, that was one thing they would always have in common.

# Chapter Ten

## *July 1936*

It was after ten at night when Jenny telephoned. "Where were you?" she asked.

"Asleep, of course," Reuben answered.

"I forget the last time I had a good night's sleep," Jenny sighed. "How are the children?"

A steamy night, Reuben had stripped off his pajamas. Afraid one of the children might come stumbling down the stairs, he wrapped Edith's afghan around his middle. "Something the matter?"

"I had a fall, but don't worry I'm fine." She told him the last thing she remembered from before she passed out was eating her dinner, a bowl of Campbell's tomato soup and saltines.

"I'm coming over."

"I told you I'm fine. Besides, Antoinette will be back in the morning."

Reuben told Jenny that he would be there in ten minutes. He knew it was what she expected, despite her words.

The right side of Jenny's face was bruised from her eyebrow to the base of her nose, and her eye was swollen and red. She limped as she led Reuben into the living room. Her ankle, she told him, was just a little bit tender.

"You're coming with me," Reuben said.

"I am not," Jenny said.

"Then why did you call?"

"I thought you'd want to know. I am your mother. Though, God knows, you stop by so rarely, it's a miracle I don't forget. As long as you're here, you might as well help me into bed."

As Reuben led Jenny to the bedroom, he noticed a smile play across her face. She felt as fragile as a bird as he eased her into the rocking chair where she claimed to have nursed him as an infant. Given the way she was now, it was hard for Reuben to imagine anything but vinegar flowing from her breasts. Yet the mother he recalled from his childhood had been joyful and affectionate.

After folding down her counterpane, plumping the pillows, and straightening the blankets, Reuben got a nightdress from the dresser drawer, cotton muslin now yellowed. Years ago, she had embroidered pink and purple roses across the bodice, but so many threads had unraveled that they were no longer recognizable as flowers.

"I'm fine, go." Jenny grabbed for the nightgown.

"Not until you're in bed." Reuben waited in the living room for her to undress. When fifteen minutes had gone by, he called through the door, "You all right?"

"I told you to go home."

"Not until I know you're okay." Reuben waited a little longer, and then after a quick knock, he opened the door slowly to warn her. Jenny was sitting on the side of the bed, the nightgown by her side.

"Let me help."

"Leave me alone." Jenny raised her arm to push him away.

Reuben leaned against the dresser. For the first time he could recall, he felt like it was he, not she, who was in charge. Emboldened, he asked the question he had long wondered about. "Why do you always seem so angry with me?"

Jenny placed the nightgown across her lap and began smoothing out the wrinkles. "I'm not angry. Just upset. In case you haven't noticed, I've had an awful fall."

"I don't mean just now."

Jenny looked up at him. "I don't know why."

Reuben was surprised to realize he understood. These days, he often felt murderously angry with Edith for reasons that had little to do with her. "Are you sure I can't help?"

This time, Jenny didn't push him away. He knelt in front of her and unbuttoned her blouse. Then, she held out her arms so he could slip it off. It made him think back to how, as a boy, he would become wilder and wilder as the day wore on, running around their small apartment until he collapsed. Jenny, too, would kneel as she undressed him for bed, pausing every now and again to kiss him on the forehead.

"This is ridiculous," Jenny murmured as Reuben helped her beneath the covers. He spread her sparse gray hair out on the pillow and placed her arms on top of the blankets.

"I'm leaving now," he told her.

"Haven't you forgotten something?" Jenny pointed to a glass on her night table. "My teeth, could you fill it with water?" By the time he returned, she had removed her dentures, now resting on her night table. Reuben realized that he had never before seen his mother without her teeth.

"She has to move in with us," Reuben told Edith the following morning.

Edith didn't answer. She was at the sink, hulling strawberries from the patch Antoinette had planted the year before.

Reuben reached around her and grabbed several.

"They're for dessert," Edith said and gave his arm a shove.

He dropped them back into the colander.

Her voice softened. "I didn't mean you couldn't have any. Just don't make a pig of yourself."

"I'm not crazy about strawberries anyway." Reuben sat down at the table and watched as Edith gave the strawberries a final rinse and tipped them out into a cut-glass bowl. He waited for her to turn around before speaking. "I want you there when I tell her. She'll never agree if she thinks you don't go along."

"Does it have to be today?"

Reuben knew Edith was hoping that if she could put off this visit long enough for Jenny to heal, he might no longer see the necessity of her moving in with them. "She thinks you don't like her. She's never come right out and said so, but I can tell." Reuben folded his arms and tipped his head. "Well, you don't, do you?"

"I have things to do." Edith wiped her hands on her apron and then hung it on a hook by the pantry door. While her motions were matter of fact, her face had turned pale. Reuben realized he had stumbled on the truth and Edith knew it. When he told her again that he wanted her to come with him, she didn't argue.

As Reuben backed out of the driveway, his arm slung over the seat, his head twisted back, Edith was reminded of how handsome she once found him. His face had not so much aged as gone slack. His eyelids drooped, and there was a wilting quality to his mouth that made Edith think of her father whose face, for the first time in years, she was able to recall.

On the way to Jenny's, Reuben detoured, taking the coastal road that ran beside the Great South Bay. The sky had turned leaden, and the waves were choppy.

"I think we're finally going to get some rain," Reuben said and stuck his hand out of the window. It had been a dry spring, and for weeks he'd been going on about how worried he was for the farmers until Edith thought she would go mad. She shifted so that her back was to him. Her temple had that tight feeling that signaled the start of a headache, and she pressed her forehead against the cool window glass.

A few months before, Edith heard that the bank had sold the bungalows, and all to the same person, though who this person was remained a mystery. Rumor had it that an agent had represented him and that even the bank didn't know his true identity. Edith was surprised to see that most of the bungalows were already occupied. She glanced over at Reuben, but he was staring straight ahead, his expression unreadable.

For several minutes, Reuben rang Jenny's doorbell and banged on the window. "I should have brought the key," he said. "Do you think she's okay?"

"I'm sure she's in the bathroom or sleeping," Edith said. She found herself hoping that Jenny had died. She wasn't proud of herself, but there was no denying this would make her life easier. At least she would no longer have to worry about Jenny's moving in with them.

Reuben was about to go around to the back door when they heard the *slip-slap* of bedroom slippers. The door opened slowly, and Jenny's small, bruised face peeked out.

"Was I expecting you?" Jenny asked, though they had called to say they were coming just hours earlier. She looked peeved as if they had interrupted something important. "As long as you're here, come in." She offered Edith her cheek and then withdrew it before Edith had a chance to bestow the obligatory kiss. Jenny was dressed in her usual outfit—a high-collared white blouse and long pleated skirt but had buttoned the blouse wrong so that it gapped comically. Her bruise was a rainbow of purples, greens, and yellows, and while the swelling in her eye had gone down, the sclera was streaked with red.

"I'll see about coffee," Jenny said and then waited for Edith's customary offer to help so that she could refuse it.

For once, Edith decided not to play along. She took a seat on a stiff-backed chair, which, except for color, was a miniature replica of one Jenny left behind at Main Street. The cottage depressed her. The ceilings were so low that she could practically touch them, the rooms small and square, and the windows narrow and widely spaced. "The cottages were never meant to be lived in year-round," Reuben used to say, but the reality was that virtually all of them were. All were identically ugly with red asphalt roofs, clapboard siding, and porches barely wide enough to accommodate chairs.

"I managed to turn up some chocolates. Your favorite—bonbons," Jenny said as she struggled back with the coffee tray and a gold foil-wrapped box.

Jenny's hands were so arthritic that her fingers bent over practically to her palms, crossing one another on the way. As Jenny slid the chocolates across the coffee table, Edith thought of how she might have found it within herself to admire the way Jenny coped, if only Jenny were less judgmental. The chocolate had a musty undertaste. Edith brought her napkin to her mouth and discreetly spit it out. She was folding her napkin around it when she caught sight of a tubular creature and opened the napkin. There were dozens swarming about in the chocolate and cherry cream glop.

Edith began to gag. Reuben rushed to her side and began thumping her back. He picked up the discarded chocolate. "My God, weevils."

Jenny brought the candy box close to her eyes. "There's nothing wrong with them." She popped a chocolate in her mouth to prove it.

Reuben snatched the box away and smashed his thumb into one of the bonbons. "Nothing?" he asked, holding out an infested caramel mess.

Jenny turned away, refusing to look.

"Mother, two days ago you fell, now this." Reuben's voice had an authority Edith had forgotten it could have.

"Now what?" Jenny countered.

"It's just a matter of time before you forget to ignite the pilot light and asphyxiate yourself or—well, something serious. You're moving in with us. You'll take the bedroom next to the bathroom. Antoinette can move back into the attic."

"Isn't that Harriet's bedroom?" Jenny asked.

"Harriet can move in with Jeffrey."

*I will not cry,* Edith told herself. Jenny, Antoinette, all of them under the same roof. It was too horrible to contemplate. If only she could move into the bungalow and leave Main Street to the lot of them.

"I'm not going anywhere. Besides, you can't sleep a boy and girl together."

"When the time comes that it's no longer appropriate, I'll turn the side porch into a bedroom," Reuben said.

Jenny began gathering the coffee things.

"Let me do that," Reuben said. He tried to wrest away the tray, but Jenny refused to let go and, for a moment, it looked as if the cups and saucers were about to go crashing to the floor.

"You always did blow things out of proportion," Jenny said.

Edith watched them disappear into the kitchen. It occurred to her that neither had asked what she would like, which, of course, was that things remain as they were, as awful as they were. That way, maybe one day, Jenny *would* forget to ignite the pilot light.

Edith decided to leave. If Reuben couldn't figure out why she'd left, well, that was his problem. The rain they'd been promising had finally arrived, the droplets as fine as sea spray. As Edith walked up the hill to Main Street, she recalled how disappointed her mother had seemed when she confided her hunch that Reuben was about to propose, and also her intention to accept. Her mother had wanted Edith to marry a college man, someone who would make his living, if indeed it were necessary for him to make a living, by his brains. This had been Edith's dream, too, but by age twenty-one, she was beginning to get scared. And while Reuben was not yet wealthy, she could tell by the way his eyes would shine when he talked about his dream of turning the South Shore of Long Island into the sort of summer paradise he fantasized about growing up in Flushing, that one day, he was going to be.

By the time Edith reached Main Street, the rain and winds had picked up, causing the branches of the elms alongside the sidewalk, heavy with bright green leaves, to sway as if in time to music. Still, Edith walked slowly. She dreaded the thought of returning home but no longer had a single friend on whose doorstep she could just show up.

Edith stopped outside what had once been a grocery store. Hand-lettered signs advertising weekly specials for June 1933 were still plastered to its window. She pressed her face against the dirty glass, cupping her hands around her eyes. The store's shelves were still crowded with goods as if the store had merely closed for the night. Nearly half the storefronts on Main Street were empty. Edith doubted that the merchants who once ran these stores would have had much in the way of savings. How were they managing to feed their families, assuming they were managing? For years, she had been surrounded by evidence of other people's suffering. Yet, this had affected her very little other than to remind her of all she had lost. After the bank took Bliss, she and Reuben had retreated from the world, ashamed, as if what happened to them had come about through some moral failing of their part, when the truth was, they could no more have prevented it than a piece of seaweed caught on a wave can prevent being flung against a shore.

Reuben was in his pajamas, settled in his recliner, when Edith arrived home. He was holding a cigar—Edith hadn't seen him smoke one in years—and cutting off the end with his old sterling silver clipper. He raised his eyebrows but said nothing about her unannounced departure from his mother's house.

"The more I talked with Mother, the more I became convinced that this fall was a one-off thing. Providing Antoinette sticks around, things should be fine the way they are. For now, anyway." Reuben lit the cigar and inhaled as he waited for her reaction.

Edith was relieved. At the same time, she couldn't help seeing Reuben's capitulation as evidence of a lifelong inability to stand up to his mother. Does he realize, she wondered as she settled down on the couch, how his stomach now pushes against his pajama buttons or how the skin beneath his chin has grown as loose as a turkey's wattle? She pulled off her shoes. The leather, stiffened from the rain, had rubbed her heels raw. As she buried her chilled legs beneath the mohair afghan, now pilled with age, Edith recalled how she used to rest her back against the sofa arm and place her feet in Reuben's lap. How he used to give them marvelous massages.

As Edith sat there, she studied Reuben. Had he really been such a good businessman? Or had he simply been lucky? She thought about the bungalows and how there was one person out there who still had enough money to buy them. Then she recalled that day at the end of the summer of 1932, when Paul Herbert had stopped by, clearly intending to talk business but ended up driving Reuben to the hospital instead. "I bet it was Paul Herbert who bought your bungalows," she said.

Reuben placed his cigar in the ashtray. "That's ridiculous. Who told you that?"

"Just a hunch." But Edith knew.

Later that afternoon, Reuben said, "What you said about Paul—if it was him, don't you think word would have gotten out by now? Besides, what possible use would he have for bungalows?"

# Chapter Eleven

## *August 1936*

Edith hoisted her slip up to her hips, sat down on the edge of the bathtub, and pressed her legs against the porcelain, the coolest thing in the house besides the refrigerator. Downstairs, Reuben was sprawled out on his recliner sleeping, his mouth hanging open like a fish's, the newspapers spread across his lap. Soon enough, he'd be up, demanding his lunch.

For a house so shrouded with overgrown bushes that it was impossible to see outside, it stayed confoundingly hot. Reuben said this was due to the lack of insulation, the same reason why in the winter, even with the furnace pumping and a fire roaring, the house remained damp and chilly. He kept talking about laying more insulation in the attic one day, but if Edith had learned anything, it was that when Reuben said "one day," what he really meant was "never."

Edith had to get away. Day after day, the two of them padding about the house, trying to avoid each other—it was too much. She assembled her makeup tools beside the sink. She always applied her makeup there rather than at her dressing table because the light in the bathroom was harsher and therefore merciless in revealing her imperfections: the starburst of veins that had formed on her cheeks, the lines that now fanned out from her eyes, the vertical worry crease that had settled in between her eyebrows. She would never consider going outside without makeup. "Putting on her face" was one of the first things she did every morning. She'd been doing this for so long that her made-up face had become her real face, more familiar to her than the one she saw when she got up each morning or before she went to bed.

After penciling in eyebrows, applying mascara—Rubinstein's Noir, lacquering her lips with Curtis' Vamp Red, and rouging her cheeks, Edith returned to her bedroom. She sat down at her dressing table and again studied her reflection. She closed her eyes and then opened them quickly, pretending that the face staring back belonged to a stranger. She parted her lips and threw her head back, Hollywood style. What she saw pleased her. While her face had finally shed its youthful pudginess, except for that crease between her eyebrows, it did not yet betray the disappointments of the past several years.

The fact that she was looking so attractive made it all the more horrid to have nothing to wear but frocks and hats so outdated, Edith could barely stand to look at them. In a few years, her looks would be gone. So, even if the time came when she would be able to keep up with the fashions again, what good would it do? A spent rose in a crystal vase was still a spent rose.

Edith settled on a white and red checked linen dress and white straw hat adorned with plastic cherries. She selected a yellow parasol. It did not go with her outfit, but her red one had become so tattered she'd thrown it away. Few women still carried parasols, but Edith was too careful about her skin to go without one on a day like this—or without gloves, for she believed nothing betrayed a woman's age more mercilessly than liver spots.

The thermometer beneath the large pedestal clock in front of the Long Island National Bank & Trust read 94°. Most of the merchants had let out their awnings. But with so many vacant storefronts, much of the sidewalk was unsheltered, and people moved slowly, as if trapped in amber.

Because Edith had been holding her parasol low and to the front, she didn't see Adele Fellowes until she'd practically bumped into her.

"What a surprise!" Adele sounded genuinely glad to see her. She took Edith's hand and looked her up and down with such gravity that Edith was afraid she was passing judgment on her outfit.

"How do you manage to look so crisp?" Adele asked. "You always were a marvel!"

These days, Edith so rarely received compliments that she found herself gushing, "I was thinking the same about you. That dress is awfully smart. The color, would you call it peacock blue? It matches your eyes perfectly."

With her pear-shaped body and stumpy legs, Adele was the furthest thing from a fashion plate. And her dress, while bright, was matronly and unflattering.

She released Edith's hand and glanced down at it with a puzzled expression. "Really? I've never much liked it, but it's the coolest thing I have." Adele looked up smiling, and Edith could tell she wanted to believe Edith was being sincere. "How are those darling children? Jeffrey and Harriet, right? Is her hair still such a gorgeous blond?"

"They've gotten so big you wouldn't recognize them. And yes, her hair is as light as ever." Edith steeled herself for the question she knew was coming.

"And Reuben, what's he up to?"

"Oh, this and that," Edith said, thinking of how, these days, Reuben spent most of his time either in bed or collapsed in his recliner. "And Marcus?"

"Working as hard as ever. It's a mystery to me how he keeps it up." Adele touched Edith's arm. "Just the other day, Bunny and I were talking about how much we miss the old times. Didn't we used to have fun! Remember to tell Reuben I asked after him. And don't be a stranger. Promise you'll call."

Only after she and Adele had said their good-byes did Edith realize how much this chance meeting had unnerved her. For a while, she had felt as if she hated all her old friends, the Herberts, the Groschals, the Rules, and especially the Fellowes. While this was no longer the case, time had done little to dull her grief over what she and Reuben had lost. Reuben insisted that what happened to them had been strictly business, that there was nothing personal about it. Edith was not sure. While in most ways, she and Reuben had been like their friends, in one important way, they hadn't been. And she, having grown up around Gentiles, should have known better. By the time she started high school, girls in whose homes she once spent nearly as much time as in her own had stopped inviting her over or accepting invitations to hers. She had not been asked to pledge a sorority. Nor had she been asked to her senior prom.

As word of Reuben's success got around, invitations began to arrive at Bliss, to dinner parties on the bay side of Main Street, to cocktail parties on the yachts moored in the harbor. She and Reuben were even invited to black-tie soirees at the Bayview Country Club, where they might come as guests but would never be welcomed as members. While many of these invitations were from the same women who had kept her out of their sororities, Edith accepted them eagerly, convinced that the rejection she experienced as a teenager had been nothing more than the by-product of a less enlightened era.

As Edith walked on, the shops became fewer and less respectable. Interspersed among them were several bungalows that Reuben had built. These bungalows were set close to the street on narrow lots, set off by chain-link fences. To catch what little breeze there was, their doors and windows had been left open, and the sounds of crying children and blaring radios spilled onto the street. Though these bungalows were less than a dozen years old, they already looked dilapidated, their siding buckling and the asphalt peeling off their roofs. Once, it hadn't mattered to Edith how cheaply Reuben built his houses. Now, it mattered a great deal. She felt sorry for the people who bought them, people who, back then, would have thought they were getting a bargain.

Edith leaned against a fence and removed a pebble from her shoe. Her feet had swollen from the heat, causing blisters to form on her heels, and her dress was sticking to her back. She was about to head home when she noticed the cross street, Corona Avenue, and recalled that a specialty store had opened there a few months earlier. She was curious to see how the store was doing, which she had heard was not very well.

Edith had never been down Corona. Nor, she supposed, had most of Sea Forth. The street was mainly industrial, filled with drab red buildings that hummed with the sound of sewing machines. The store, plain brick unadorned by fretwork, looked as if it, too, had once been a factory, and she might have passed right by it were it not for the poster-board sign that hung above the windowless double doors. *Emporium* it said in gilt lettering against a glossy maroon background.

Edith paused outside the doors, fearful of running into yet another woman from her old set. Then the door opened, and a tiny woman with alarmingly rouged cheeks stumbled out, revealing an interior of such luxuriousness that Edith couldn't help but be drawn inside. There were crystal chandeliers as multitiered as wedding cakes and carved alabaster planters as tall as men. The floor was made of purple-veined marble, and brass sconces illuminated the polished mahogany walls. At the center of the space was a rotunda containing the stairway to the second and third floors, which formed galleries around it. A skylight, through which sunlight poured, bathing the store in an ethereal glow, topped this rotunda.

Edith was standing there transfixed, when she smelled something. Not the perfume-like scent one would expect to find in a place like this. Something sulfurous. She looked around, sniffing, until she located the source—the planters, where the chrysanthemum arrangements were so spent they appeared mummified.

As Edith wandered the floor, she noticed other signs of neglect. How many bulbs on those gorgeous chandeliers were out, how badly the brass sconces needed polishing. Most of the merchandise was crammed onto the shelves, that is, if it weren't still lying where the last customer left it. It was not as if the salesgirls were too busy to put their departments in order. The store was nearly deserted.

And yet, there were also signs of an acutely original fashion eye—silver fox-trimmed jackets and cashmere wraps embroidered with seed pearls. Also, white cotton blouses with delicate lace inserts. Nearly all were displayed with such indifference that the store might as well have been selling rags. How was it possible, Edith wondered, for someone who put so much money and imagination into refurbishing this space and selecting the merchandise, to fail so miserably at the simple tasks that would make the store an appealing place to shop?

Edith was almost back to Main Street when she heard her name. She turned around to see a small man hurrying toward her, one arm arced in a wave, the other holding his Panama in place.

"Mrs. Merkal, what a surprise!" The man was panting, and his round face was flushed. "Didn't ya hear me screaming?" He was still several feet away when he extended his hand. Then, noticing her bewilderment, he withdrew it. "Heavens, I've given you a fright. Fred Adler. From the store. It's been donkey's years since we met, but I never forget a face, 'specially one as lovely as yours."

Edith had not the slightest recollection of having met him. "Mr. Adler, a pleasure." As she extended her hand, she was glad she had worn her finest pair of summer gloves, with their neat stitching and mother-of-pearl buttons. His hand was so small it barely fit around hers. Everything about Fred Adler was child-sized. The top of his head barely reached Edith's chin.

He stepped back and held out his arms. "As beautiful as ever. Unbelievable. But I've always said some women are like fine wines. They just improve with age. Others, of course, turn to vinegar."

Edith lowered her eyes. "Well, I wouldn't know about that, although they do say beauty is in the eye of the beholder."

"Speaking of beautiful things, have you been to my store?—what a stupid question! Why else would you be on this godforsaken street? Some folks say I was crazy to locate so far off the beaten track, but I say if Mohammed won't come to the mountain, let the mountain come to Mohammed. Or maybe it's the other way around." Mr. Adler stopped, noticing that Edith seemed confused. "What I'm trying to say is that, if you figure out what people want, they'll flock to you. Here I am rambling on when what I'm really interested in is what you think."

"Well," Edith said as she tried to figure out what to say. "You've certainly done marvelous things to the interior. Those chandeliers, those marble floors. That rotunda!"

Mr. Adler's smile faded. "Ya know, I got those chandeliers from a hotel they were knocking down in Montauk. The sconces, too. And that marble, it comes straight from Italy. Carrerra, the place is called, or is it Carrerro? What about the merchandise?" He circled his hand upward. "The ambiance?"

"The ambiance. It's rather large, isn't it? Room for all sorts of departments, but I guess that's what this sort of store is all about."

His expression turned impatient. "That's not what I meant. The ambiance, the atmosphere. These days, shopping is supposed to be more than just shopping. The customer is supposed to have a retailing experience."

Edith didn't have the foggiest idea what he meant by ambiance, much less by retailing experience. Irritated by this ridiculous man, she looked at her watch. "One o'clock, oh dear, I was expected somewhere fifteen minutes ago."

"I didn't mean to hold you up. Just one more question—is the Emporium the sort of store you'd visit again?"

"Absolutely," Edith said, too enthusiastically. "No question about it."

As Edith continued home, she went over the conversation. She recalled hearing that Mr. Adler came from a family of retailers. What kind of retailers? She couldn't decide whether it was a stroke of genius or a sign of madness to open a women's specialty store in times like these. And she suspected that Mr. Adler's understanding of the term "retailing experience" was little better than her own. Off the top of her head, she could come up with a half dozen necessary improvements. She would place a sign on Main Street to direct customers. Then she would paint the exterior a pastel shade to distinguish it from the neighboring factories and warehouses. She would replace the tacky poster-board sign with one in brass, the wooden doors with glass, and while she was at it, install a canopy over the entrance, replace the concrete steps with limestone, and junk the utilitarian handrail in favor of something sweeping and ornate. What a shame, she thought, that the store wasn't hers to run.

# Chapter Twelve

## *October and November 1936*

"I've decided to look for work." Edith practiced saying these words as she lay across the rumpled bed sheets. She had come up to the bedroom for her purse but instead flopped on the bed. It was her marketing day, a day she always dreaded, convinced that each nickel she parted with was bringing the family that much closer to the poorhouse. How much closer, Edith didn't know. Reuben was no more forthcoming about their finances than he had ever been. Whenever she thought they had to be scraping the bottom of their savings, he would manage to come up with a few dollars. With the solemnity of a sacred ceremony, he'd pull the bills from his money clip and press them into her hand. Then, he'd wait for her to thank him, as if he'd given her a gift instead of money to run the house.

From the hallway came the sounds of Antoinette's Hoovering the carpet. Edith got up and locked the door, certain that Antoinette lacked the common sense to knock before entering. It was hard to believe that not so long ago, she'd had a full-time housekeeper and an English nanny. She'd had an allowance, too—money that, after paying for the food and other incidentals, she was free to spend however she pleased.

The ceiling was full of cracks. Edith recalled how, when she was small, she would pretend that the ceiling of the tiny bedroom she shared with her mother was heaven and make angels out of the cracks, who would look after them while they slept. How nice it would be to still believe in angels, Edith thought, beings who would make sure they didn't starve. Edith wondered what her mother would say if she could see her now. Perhaps she could. If there was a heaven, her mother was surely there. Only now could Edith fully appreciate the sacrifices her mother made on her behalf. How demeaning it must have been for a woman of her breeding to take the jobs she had at the duck farm and then in the button factory where she spent six long years on the assembly line (studying shorthand, bookkeeping, and typing late into the nights) before she was finally promoted to the front office.

Edith's mother drummed into her the importance of marrying a man with prospects, drawing upon the sorry example of her father to reinforce the point. Edith's father had been so handsome and personable that her mother had been the envy of her girlfriends. These charms had blinded her to his selfish nature and aversion to hard work, traits her mother was forced to confront before Edith reached her first birthday, when she woke up one morning to find his side of the bed empty and the Maxwell House coffee tin, in which she had been saving up to buy a bedroom set, gone.

From time to time, Edith's father would show up unexpectedly. He would sweep Edith into his arms, covering her face with kisses. He took her to carnivals, circuses, and double matinees. All she had to do was admire a doll or a dress, and it was hers. As a child, Edith thought it a great injustice that she was forced to live with her stern, frugal mother when she had this wonderful father. As these visits drew to a close, she would beg her father to take her with him. "There's nothing I'd like more," he would say, "but you know your mother." When Edith was thirteen, her father stopped visiting altogether. When the weeks turned into months and the months into years, and there was not so much as a word from him, her love for him shrank and then hardened into a sharp pebble. By the time Edith was eighteen, she was determined to follow her mother's advice and marry someone who was steady, reliable, and ambitious. A few years later, Reuben came along. Although he wasn't the tall, blond college man Edith had dreamed about, he was kind and handsome, and it was clear he would be a good provider. So when he proposed, Edith accepted readily, certain that, with time, the affection she felt for him would deepen into love. Well, the joke was on her. Here she was, pinching pennies in a dilapidated house that stank of mouse and mold, no better off than if she had ignored her mother's advice and married a man who looked like Leslie Howard, married a man for love.

"I've decided to look for work," Edith said again. She tried to imagine how Reuben would react. He wouldn't be happy, but what choice had he left her? Reuben thought it was undignified for a woman to work, unless she was a spinster. Then it wasn't undignified, merely sad. Edith had never thought to question his attitude, despite the example of her own mother, who had worked at all sorts of jobs—most of them menial—but who had always conducted herself with, if anything, too much dignity.

Of course, deciding to look for work was one thing; finding a job was another thing altogether. Her mother had taught her table manners and scraped together the money for dance lessons. When Edith began to slump, her mother made her walk around with a schoolbook on her head and eat her meals with a broomstick wedged beneath her arms. She'd taught Edith the social graces necessary to snare a man from a higher social station—or failing that, one on the way up. It never occurred to either of them that Edith should also learn a trade. Recently, Edith had begun to see the irony in this. Her mother had been taught the same social graces by her mother and ended up working in a factory.

Edith decided to wait until evening to speak to Reuben. If the past several years had taught her anything, it was to control her tendency to speak her mind before she had thought through how and when to do it. As soon as dinner was finished, Edith sent the children to their bedrooms. Both went without protest, clearly relieved to escape the tense atmosphere that pervaded the rest of the house.

It was the first really cold night that autumn. Earlier, Edith had insisted that Reuben build a fire. He didn't approve of fireplaces, believing they drew more heat out of a room than they added. He had stomped out of the house, coatless, grabbing the first twigs he could find. Then he balled up the newspaper along with one of Edith's treasured fashion magazines. An hour later, the fire was still spitting and sputtering and not adding a bit of warmth to the rooms. But a perverse determination to keep it going had taken hold of him, and he kept fiddling with the damper.

"Are you finished?" Edith asked after this had gone on for at least ten minutes.

"No." Reuben gave the fire a strong poke, sending cinders flying about.

"It's hurting my eyes. Besides, I've got something to tell you."

"First, make some coffee," Reuben said. He never drank coffee after dinner, but Edith decided not to point this out. "Bring some biscuits, too."

By the time Edith returned, Reuben had gotten the fire going.

"There." Reuben wiped his hands on his trousers and sat down on his recliner, his expression blandly innocent. "Just half a cup. Any more will keep me up."

Edith poured the coffee, waiting for him to add cream and sugar before speaking. "I've decided to look for a job."

Reuben put his cup down with a clap. "Really." He grabbed a cookie topped with an insipid pink icing, Harriet's favorite. "What sort of work, may I ask?"

"I don't know. I'll have a better idea once I start looking."

Reuben adjusted his recliner so that it was upright, and then leaned forward. "That's novel. Most people, I dare say, would go about it in reverse."

Edith looked through the archway to the clutter of dirty dishes on the dining table that she still needed to clear, wash, and dry before she went to bed. Her confidence began to desert her. "It's not that I don't have ideas."

The fire was roaring now, sending ghost-like shadows up the walls and making the room too hot.

"What sort of ideas?" Reuben asked. There was malice in his voice.

"I thought I could work in an office or maybe in a store. A person can't be too choosy in times like these."

"You're half right. That's true enough for the person looking. For those hiring, it's a different story." Reuben picked up the *Saturday Evening Post* from the magazine pile beside his recliner and began flipping through the pages. "Not that I don't think it would do you good to see for yourself how tough things are."

"What, to teach me a lesson?" Edith asked.

Reuben held the magazine out in front so that Edith could no longer see his face.

As she headed through to the dining room, she called back, "What makes you such an expert?"

"Want my honest opinion?" Reuben asked. "Don't waste your time. No one's going to hire you."

As Edith cleared the table, she could see Reuben's feet, now shoeless, one crossed over the other, through the dining room archway. He rarely helped around the house and never in the kitchen, which he regarded as the woman's domain. Reuben's father once told her that, at heart, Reuben was lazy. It used to drive her crazy the way Reuben refused to defend himself against the cruel things his father would say. According to Reuben, his father was "just a pathetic old man, too bitter about his own failures to be proud of his son."

As Edith swished the Ivory Flakes around the dishpan, she wondered if there might be a grain of truth in what Reuben's father said. Perhaps his father detected something lurking beneath Reuben's youthful vigor—that there was a mechanical aspect to Reuben's ambitions, as if he'd been given a script, pointed in a certain direction, and told to go. Like a windup doll, Reuben might have continued on course forever had the bad times not arrived. Edith had grown to believe that had Reuben a shred of pride, he would have come to regard what happened to him not as a fatal blow but as a test of character. He would be determined to start over, if only to prove that he was still the man she once took him to be. Clearly, he had given up on himself, leaving her no choice but to give up on him as well.

Before heading out each morning, Edith gave herself a pep talk. Yes, times were hard and she had no office skills, but she was well-spoken, intelligent, and good-looking, many cuts above the typical office gal. People took to her, particularly men. Moreover, things seemed to be looking up. Just recently, several storefronts on Main Street had been let.

As she trudged up the stairways that led to the offices above the Main Street shops, Edith would visualize herself clacking away on a typewriter or unflappably attending to an enormous switchboard. She would knock on the office doors in a firm, self-confident way as if she would be doing these businesses a favor by accepting a job with them. Reality soon wore her down. More often than not, she'd be asked what she wanted from behind a closed door. When she replied that she was looking for work, she'd be told to go away. On those rare occasions when she was invited inside, it was invariably by some sympathetic secretary, who figured she could use a glass of water.

Edith had nearly made her way down the length of Main Street when a dumpling of a man with a pink, hairless face actually did invite her into his office.

"I was about to make myself a cup of coffee," he said. "Can I offer you one?" Though Edith refused, he returned carrying two mugs. "Figured you were just being polite," he said as he set the mugs down.

The coffee was fragrant and strong, brewed not instant, and Edith sipped it gratefully. It was a raw day, and she was feeling thoroughly chilled.

"Name's Fowler," the man said. "I'm an accountant. Been in practice thirty years. My wife used to take care of the correspondence and answer the phones, but lately, she hasn't been up to it. To be honest, business is awful, but it's gotten to the point where I figure I've got to bite the bullet and train up some other gal." He pulled out a legal pad and his fountain pen and said, "Okay, shoot."

"Shoot?" Edith asked.

"Your experience. You have worked in an office before?"

Edith wondered if she could get away with saying that she used to work in her husband's office. She knew that if Mr. Fowler asked too many questions, she risked tripping herself up. Still, she had nothing to lose by gambling that he wouldn't. "My husband is—was a builder. I pitched in when things got busy. Helped with the typing and filing, answered the phone, that sort of thing."

"Great, you type. You wouldn't believe the amount of typing here. What's your WPM?"

"WPM?"

He looked up. "Your words per minute?"

"My words per minute." Edith looked around at the putty-colored walls, bare except for a calendar with a photograph of Jones Beach, courtesy of the Long Island National Bank & Trust, and a framed Norman Rockwell illustration of a man wearing a green eye shade. "To tell the truth, I couldn't say."

"Forty words a minute? Fifty? Sixty?"

Edith had no idea whether these were considered slow, medium, or fast typing speeds. She said, "That sounds about right."

"Forty, fifty?"

"Fifty. Right, fifty."

"Do you take dictation?"

Edith wanted to bolt. But having gone this far, she answered, "Absolutely."

"What sort?"

"Dictation. I take dictation."

Mr. Fowler pushed his pad and fountain pen to the side, clasped his hands, and leaned forward. "Mrs. Merkal, you seem like a lovely woman. A smart one, too, and my guess is that you'd be a fast learner. Even so, surely you don't think you could waltz into a job like this and pick it up so quick that you'd be able to fool me?" He stood and extended his hand. "If you'll excuse me, I've got a busy afternoon."

Edith fumbled into her coat. "Thanks for your time," she mumbled, not daring to look at Mr. Fowler.

"Wait," he called from the doorway as Edith was about to head down the stairs. "I'm sorry I embarrassed you. I hope you won't mind my being honest. Without experience, no one's going to hire you for an office job. Why don't you stop by Kresge's? It seems every time I drop in for a cup of coffee, there's a new face behind the lunch counter. You know where else you might look? The grocery store."

Though Edith knew this was good advice, there was no way she could bring herself to take it. She, a waitress at Kresge's? A cashier? The women who worked at such jobs were a different breed, lower class. It was bad enough being forced to look for office work, but to ask the same merchants—who in a sense had always worked for her, repairing her shoes and delivering her groceries—whether she could now work for them was unthinkable. Not to mention, how humiliating it would be when her former friends stopped by.

Thanksgiving came late that year and, by the following week, the Christmas decorations were up. Green and red tinsel had been wound around the utility posts, and wreaths hung from the traffic lights. A skating scene was displayed in the window of Kresge's, complete with cotton snow, an aluminum foil lake, and sleds made from wooden matchboxes. Outside the Long Island National Bank & Trust was the same crèche they'd been hauling out for years, much the worse for the wear with Joseph now missing his nose and the baby Jesus' face reduced to a featureless blur.

It had rained for two days, and when the skies finally cleared, Edith decided to take a walk. Dusk had fallen, and the still slick sidewalks and roads gleamed beneath the streetlights. The clearing skies had brought out shoppers, who, full of early Christmas cheer, greeted friends and strangers alike with warm hellos and big smiles. Edith did the same, unwilling to betray how low she was feeling. She walked for a long time in a sort of daze, until she found herself standing in front of the Emporium. While she had thought about the store a great deal since her visit in August, she had not been back. Her reason for staying away was simple: she was afraid of bumping into Fred Adler.

The Emporium, too, had been done up for Christmas. The chrysanthemums had been replaced by poinsettias and the stanchions wrapped in red foil. A Christmas tree, decorated with strings of popcorn and blinking colored lights, had been positioned in front of the staircase that wound through the rotunda, and green and red felt stockings hung from the shelves. But the decorations, instead of making the store feel festive, had the perverse effect of calling attention to the tarnished brass, spent light bulbs, and haphazardly displayed clothing in the same way that makeup sometimes makes a homely woman look even less attractive. The store was nearly deserted. Behind the horseshoe-shaped makeup counter, a lank-haired salesgirl was scrabbling through the contents of her purse, which she had dumped onto the counter. Across the aisle in Leather Goods, a salesgirl perched upon a stool, her shoes dangling off her feet, was flipping through a magazine. In Millinery, two salesgirls, trying on hats, butted hips as they vied for space in front of the mirror.

As Edith wandered through the store, she kept an eye out for Mr. Adler. She was afraid of bumping into him. At the same time, in her mind, she talked with him: "Mr. Adler, I couldn't help noticing how carelessly your merchandise is displayed. It should be organized by style, color, and size. How else do you expect your customers to find anything? On a slow day like this, surely your salesgirls have the time to put things in order. And speaking of your salesgirls, it's shameful the way you let them take advantage of you. You need to walk the sales floor more, let them know they're being watched. Tell them what needs to be done. And remind them that there are plenty of gals out there who would kill for their jobs."

Edith was so engrossed in her thoughts that when she felt a tap on her shoulder and turned around to find the real Fred Adler standing behind her, she gasped. Had he been watching her? Could he tell what she'd been thinking? As she thrust out a hand to shake his, she gushed, "Mr. Adler, what a surprise!"

Fred Adler was grinning, his face so lit up that it reminded Edith of one of his Christmas ornaments. "Mrs. Merkal!" He took her hand, which, to her astonishment, he proceeded to kiss. "I'd just about given up hope of ever seeing you again, when whaddaya know, God answered my prayers!"

"I've just been so busy," Edith said.

"No need to make excuses." Mr. Adler leaned in close and asked, "Do you have a moment?" His breath smelled of peppermints and something nastier underneath. Rotting teeth, Edith decided, though the teeth in front looked fine. Too fine, in fact, to be real.

Could she say she had an appointment, Edith wondered, as Mr. Adler looped his arm through hers? No, she'd used that excuse last time. She could say she had to get home; after all, it was about the time when most housewives began dinner. But he looked so pleased to have this opportunity to show off his store that Edith didn't have the heart to disappoint him.

As Mr. Adler led Edith toward the opposite end of the floor, not a single salesgirl made the slightest pretense of acting busy. His reaction surprised Edith. She could have understood angry or embarrassed—even resigned. Instead, he had a far-off look and vague smile, as if he were escorting her not through the real Emporium but the Emporium of his dreams. He led her to Accessories, where they stopped in front of a wooden bin filled with impossibly tangled scarves.

"I want your opinion," Mr. Adler said as he craned his head around, looking for the salesgirl who was nowhere to be seen. His dreamy expression now gone, he muttered to himself as he dug through the bin. "Here!" He pulled out a pale silk turquoise scarf and draped it across his arms. It was one of the most beautiful scarves Edith had ever seen. Silver threads were sewn onto its surface in imperfect, concentric circles, like the ripples formed when a pebble is thrown into a stream. Inside the circles were clusters of pearls. "Look at this." He folded over the edge. The back was the reverse of the front, silver with turquoise threads, and equally beautiful. "Try it on."

"I'd prefer not to." Edith saw no point in trying on a scarf she knew she couldn't afford.

"You don't like it?"

"Not particularly. I find it rather...garish."

Mr. Adler raised his chin defiantly. "Garish? I think it's beautiful." He dropped the scarf back into the bin. "I'm beginning to think that maybe it's me who's crazy."

Sorry that she had hurt his feelings, Edith touched his forearm. "Garish was the wrong word. What I meant was striking, loud—but not in a bad way. Really, I think it's lovely. Just not right for me. For a redhead, perhaps. Yes, that color would look divine against red hair."

"It's not supposed to be worn like a kerchief." Mr. Adler pulled the scarf out again and looked at it quizzically. "It's from Japan. All the best silk is. You're sure ya won't try it on?"

Edith took the scarf and walked over to a swivel mirror. Of course she knew such a scarf, stiff with embroidery and pearls, was not meant to be worn on the head. As she draped the scarf around her neck, Mr. Adler watched from behind. Red hair! The scarf made her dark hair gleam and her skin glow. She had nearly forgotten the way a beautiful garment could transform a woman.

"You're right," Edith admitted. She longed to know how much the scarf cost but didn't have the nerve to peek at the price tag.

"There's one in red, too, with gold threads."

"It's very special." Edith handed it back.

"I'm glad someone appreciates it. It's been sitting there for months." Mr. Adler returned the scarf to the bin.

Edith looked around. "I imagine things should start picking up—with Christmas so near."

"You would think so."

"I suppose things are difficult everywhere."

Mr. Adler dismissed this with a wave. "Don't kid yourself. There's plenty of money out there. Plenty of old money and plenty of shysters who've cashed in on other people's misfortune."

Edith wondered if this was a sly reference to her own troubles. Everyone else in town knew about them, so why wouldn't he? "I have to leave." She began buttoning her coat.

"We're getting a shipment of chiffon dresses in after the New Year you won't want to miss." Mr. Adler held out his hand. Edith was about to extend her own but, remembering his earlier kiss, kept it by her side.

Outside, Edith paused in front of the display window. The mannequins—dressed in green and red plaid dresses with black patent belts and pleated skirts guaranteed to make the slenderest hips look enormous—had been artlessly posed around a table piled high with boxes covered with foil wrap. The end of a metallic banner emblazoned with "Happy Holidays" had come loose and fallen across one of the mannequin's shoulders.

She thought about how once she wouldn't have thought twice before buying that scarf, how it had been more than a year since she'd treated herself to a dress. And even that one had been nothing special, just something to wear that wasn't too narrow in the shoulders or long in the waist. She wondered how much Mr. Adler knew about her financial situation and if by "shyster" he'd been referring to Paul Herbert, for by now, it was an open secret that Paul Herbert had indeed been the purchaser of the bungalows. She tried to recall what she had heard about Mr. Adler. Very little, except that he was not native to Sea Forth and that it was his wife, not him, who came from money.

Edith strode back through the front doors. It was nearly closing time and, as she crossed the floor, she could feel the trail of resentment she stirred up in the salesgirls, desperate to bolt. She found Mr. Adler standing where she had left him, beside that bin.

His face filled with delight. "You've come back for the scarf!" He pulled it from the bin. "You won't regret it."

Edith took the scarf. "A scarf like this deserves a prominent place." She draped it across the shoulders of the nearest mannequin.

Mr. Adler scratched his chin. "It doesn't go with what she's wearing."

"At least here, it will be noticed." Edith moved close enough to smell his peppermint. Astonishing herself with her boldness, she whispered, "I have some ideas that might interest you." Mr. Adler raised his eyebrows rakishly. "About the store," she said primly. "Is there someplace we can talk?"

"Why not here?"

Edith said what she had to in one great rush. "I couldn't live with myself if I didn't tell you what I really thought. While you've got some lovely things, you're going about selling them the wrong way. You need to make this place more stylish. Poor people can't afford what you sell, but the rich ones want to buy from a place that looks posh. You treat your merchandise like it belongs in Kresge's. And your salesgirls. Let's just say you need to hire a better class, even if it means paying more. Women who dress and act like ladies."

Mr. Adler smirked. "Mrs. Merkal, with all due respect, do you have any idea how hard it is to hire quality help, even in this economy? Ladies don't want to work as shopgirls; they want to shop. Even if they did, do ya think their husbands would let 'em?"

Edith grabbed his arm. "Have you tried—to hire ladies, I mean?"

"Let me put it this way: Would *you* be interested in working here?"

Edith smiled. "As a matter of fact, I would."

"He's putting me in charge of accessories—scarves, shawls, belts, gloves, that sort of thing, because he can tell I've got impeccable taste." Edith crossed her arms as she waited for Reuben's reaction. The family was eating dinner, in what she still thought of as Jenny's dining room, the four of them stranded at a table that could comfortably seat twelve.

Edith winced as Reuben cut into his lamb chops. She liked to think that over the past few years she had turned into a passable cook, but tonight her mind had been on the store instead of the stove. The chops were so overcooked that they were nearly impenetrable and the carrots so undercooked, they crunched. And with the mashed potatoes, she had achieved the nearly impossible of making them watery and lumpy at the same time.

When it became obvious that Reuben wasn't going to answer, Edith turned to Jeffrey. "It looks like the cat's got Daddy's tongue. What do you think?"

Jeffrey gave his mother a sidelong glance. "I think it's great." He began to rap his knife against the rim of his plate.

"Stop that." Edith placed her hand on top of his.

"You heard your mother." Reuben grabbed Jeffrey's other arm. "If you can't behave like a normal person, you'll have to leave the table."

"Let go!" Jeffrey yanked his arm free. He rubbed at the spot Reuben had grabbed. "I hate him," he muttered, just loud enough for Edith to hear.

Don't cry, she silently begged him, afraid this might infuriate Reuben, who didn't think boys, even ten-year-old boys, should cry.

Reuben dropped his fork. "Did you see that?"

"What?" Edith asked.

"That," he said, pointing to Jeffrey. "You haven't noticed that he's developed a twitch?"

"What's a twitch?" Harriet asked, looking from her father, to Jeffrey, and then Edith, with a smug expression, as if what was going on at the table had nothing to do with her.

"It's when your eyelid opens and shuts..."

"For God's sake, Jeffrey doesn't have a twitch. Daddy doesn't know what he's talking about."

"Like when Jeffrey's face goes like this?" Harriet squeezed her cheek so that her eyelid closed.

Reuben gave Harriet an indulgent smile.

Harriet tossed her braids, which Antoinette had fastened with bright red ribbons, behind her shoulders. "A twitch," she repeated softly before placing some carrot slices in her mouth. She chewed daintily, patting her mouth with her napkin between bites.

"You just took me by surprise," Reuben said. "I didn't even know you were looking."

Edith closed her eyes and shook her head so that Reuben would know how extraordinary she found this. "Where did you think I was on all those days?"

"What about the children?"

"What about them? You're around." Edith knew that would shut him up. Reuben picked up his lamb chop in his hands and began gnawing at it. He eats like an animal, she thought.

# Chapter Thirteen

## *March 1937*

Edith had been working at the Emporium for several months when an attractive woman with auburn hair approached the accessories counter. The woman was wearing a tailored pink mohair suit, which she had paired with a white silk blouse with a broad jabot. Her makeup had been well applied, her bright pink lipstick and pale mauve eye shadow complementing her outfit. In all, she was the sort of refined but fashion-conscious customer the store was meant to attract but rarely did.

"Mrs. Merkal," the woman said, extending a perfectly manicured hand, each nail a glossy rose oval.

Edith racked her brain trying to recall who this woman was. She wondered if they had met socially.

The woman laughed. "Eliza Browning, Jeffrey's first grade teacher."

Edith could have stared at this woman all day and not realized who she was. Back when she was Jeffrey's teacher, Miss Browning had never worn makeup or styled her hair. Her dresses looked like they came from a thrift shop. She used to bite her nails and tear at her cuticles so viciously that it hurt Edith even to look at her hands.

"I guess I've changed," Miss Browning said as she smoothed down her already perfect hair with her left hand, a gesture clearly meant to draw attention to her ring finger. "Oh, my ring," Miss Browning said as if Edith had been staring at it, which Edith had been doing her best not to. "It's true. I'm getting married. An old maid like me." She held out her hand. "It's something, isn't it?"

So it was, with its large, pear-shaped diamond and glittering baguettes. The sort of ring Edith would have loved. Her own engagement ring with its small and cloudy diamond had been a disappointment. She had been expecting so much more. She hadn't yet known about Bliss, which had sucked up nearly all of Reuben's savings. After a few years, Edith put the ring away and never wore it again. Reuben promised her a new one for their tenth anniversary, but by then, the bad times had hit.

"Tell me about him," Edith forced herself to ask.

"He's a doctor—ear, nose, and throat." Miss Browning placed her hand down on the counter so she could admire the ring herself. "I saw him about a sinus infection, and before I knew it he'd asked me to marry him. The wedding's next month. I'm looking for a scarf to pair with the suit I'll be changing into after the reception." Miss Browning pulled a swatch of gray fabric from her purse.

One of the first things Edith had done after starting at the Emporium was to replace the bin with a glass-faced, shelved cupboard, where she organized the scarves by color, folded into triangles, and tiered so that their edges were visible. Edith pulled out a dozen or more scarves, all of which were either too dull or loud, or just not to the liking of Miss Browning.

"What about that one?" Miss Browning pointed to the turquoise and silver scarf.

While Edith had placed that scarf with others of similar hue, she'd hidden it toward the bottom of the pile, with only a sliver of fabric showing. Often when the store was quiet, she would lift up the scarves on top of this one, and just stare. She could not recall ever wanting anything as much as she wanted this scarf. But at fifteen dollars, the scarf cost more than she earned in a week.

"Really?" Edith asked.

Miss Browning nodded.

"If you wish," Edith said, careful to inflect her voice with the right note of disapproval.

"You don't think it would go?" Miss Browning draped it around her neck.

"It wouldn't be my choice, but I suppose you could get away with it."

Miss Browning looked puzzled. Not only did the scarf contrast beautifully with the fabric swatch, it was as if it had been made with her fair coloring in mind. "I think it's beautiful," she said quietly.

"I'd love to see it get a home. It's been sitting here for months." Edith pulled out a purple floral print. "Personally, I think this one's a lot smarter."

Miss Browning looked doubtful. "That reminds me of something my mother would wear."

"Oh dear, no." Edith held it up to Miss Browning's cheek. "Not only does this scarf bring out the color of your eyes, unlike the other, it's not something you'll grow sick of."

Although she didn't look convinced, Miss Browning followed Edith's advice. As she was leaving the store, Edith saw her remove the scarf from her shopping bag and study it with a worried expression.

A few days later, the turquoise scarf sold anyway to an old woman with a heavily powdered, leonine face. She pointed and said, "That one," ignoring Edith's suggestion that she look around before making up her mind. Sorry that she had talked Miss Browning out of buying the scarf, Edith felt such a stinging resentment as she rang up the sale that she was unable to look at the woman as she handed her the parcel.

Watching that old hag walk away with the scarf she had coveted for so long was a turning point for Edith. During her coffee breaks and her free minutes after lunch, she took to wandering through the other departments. For a while, Edith kept her resolve not to waste money. Then one morning in April, she noticed a brooch made of polished cut stone, meant to resemble a flower, with aquamarine petals and a pink center. The more she stared at it, the more it seemed as if the brooch's center were an eye trying to let her know that the brooch was meant for her. The brooch was just a foolish piece of costume jewelry, something she once wouldn't have been caught dead wearing. But it was such a cheerful thing. As its faceted petals refracted the artificial light, they seemed to emit happiness.

The pasty-faced salesgirl gave a huff of annoyance when Edith asked if she could get a closer look at the brooch. She shook her head as she rifled through her apron pockets and the pockets of her skirt before finally finding the key to the display cabinet beneath the sales receipt pad, still secured with a rubber band from the previous evening.

"Kinda hurts your eyes, don't it?" the salesgirl said as she rubbed the brooch against her sleeve. She placed it on the black velvet display cloth. "God knows what you'd wear it with. I suppose you could pin it on a coat or something."

Edith turned the brooch over. Two dollars—a lot for a piece of costume jewelry with rough metal prongs and a sloppily glued-on clasp. But as Edith held the brooch against her heart, she felt a kind of euphoria.

Edith never regretted buying the brooch, although she wore it rarely and self-consciously. Or the slouch hat made out of the softest purple felt she bought the following week. Or the belt made of burgundy pressed leather she bought a few weeks later. She smuggled these purchases into the house and buried them in her lingerie drawer so that Reuben wouldn't find them.

Edith soon began to buy herself a gift every payday. Sometimes it was as modest as a lipstick, other times as expensive as a dress. By July, she was no longer hiding her purchases, having come to regard them as deserved rewards for her hard work. "Is that new?" "That looks nice." These were the sorts of things Reuben would say when he noticed Edith's purchases. At least there was one thing about which the two of them agreed—that he had no right to tell her how to spend her money.

"You know what I heard?" Wally Kimmel asked. "That the Ku Klux Klan has started up a chapter in Queens." It was the first Monday of the month, which over the past year had become the regular date for the BJAAS' meetings.

"I haven't read nothing in the papers," Hal Pullen said.

"This kind of thing, you don't read about in the papers," Adolph said. "Who told you?"

Wally shrugged. "In my business, you hear things."

"It's only Negroes they hate, right?" Reuben asked. What he had read about the Klan's activities down south sickened him—the cross burnings, how they would tar and feather a Negro for using the wrong public toilet or cut off his testicles just for looking at a white woman.

"Niggers or Jews, it's all the same to the Klan," Wally said.

"They're the guys who dress up like ghosts, right?" Hal asked.

"Yeah," Morris Goodman said. "Though I find it hard to imagine those shmoos getting away with parading around Queens in bed sheets."

The men fell silent. From inside the bedroom came the static sounds of a radio. It had been months since Ernest attended a meeting. When the men asked Adolph how Ernest was doing, his answer was always the same, "Not so good."

"What else did you hear?" Morris asked.

"What else? How long does it take to buy a newspaper?" Lacing his fingers behind his head, Wally tilted his bridge chair back so that his small feet lifted off the floor. "My question, gentlemen, is what do we do about it?"

The men shifted in their seats, waiting for someone to come up with an answer to what Reuben was sure they all had to recognize as a rhetorical question. They couldn't come up with an answer because there wasn't one. Anti-Semitism was as old as Christianity. Older. For a long while, Reuben used to ask himself why he kept coming to these meetings when the only thing the men accomplished was to scare one another out of their wits, especially given that over the past year, there had been no incidents in Sea Forth that carried even a whiff of anti-Semitism. He came to realize that anti-Semitism was everywhere, that even if it wasn't grabbing you by the throat, that didn't mean it wasn't hiding behind a wall, biding its time until the moment was right to strike.

Morris broke the silence. "What do we do? We move to Palestine, that's what. The world is shit, and nothing we can say or do will change that." The men were still arguing when Hal got up. He stretched, his shirt pulling away from his pants and revealing a mound of doughy flesh. "I promised Trudy I'd be home in time to say goodnight to the boys."

Until recently, Reuben hadn't realized that the pretty blond woman who worked in Hal's shop was his wife. With her straight back and long neck, she looked as graceful as a swan, even bent over a sewing machine. Hal and his wife had two sons, both excellent students, both good-looking like their mother. Despite the economy, his shop was doing so well that he had recently expanded into the vacant space next door. How was it, Reuben wondered, that Hal, who was just a tailor and in every way unexceptional, had managed to make a success of his life when he had failed so miserably?

Reuben decided to use Hal's departure as an excuse to make his own getaway. "I promised Edith I'd be home early, too," he said. It pained him to have to pretend that he had a wife who still cared about him. At the previous meeting, he noticed a candle burning in a plain glass tumbler and had asked Adolph what it was. "It's a Yahrzeit candle," Adolph explained. "According to the Jewish calendar, today's the anniversary of my wife's death. The candle's supposed to burn for twenty-four hours." Adolph showed him a photograph of a fresh-faced woman with a halo of blond curls. "Wasn't she a beauty? Seven years she's gone, and still not a day goes by when I don't miss her."

"You can't leave yet," Wally protested. "We haven't settled anything." Wally referred to himself as a confirmed bachelor, though Reuben couldn't help wondering whether he'd ever had the opportunity to marry given that he was so starved for companionship that he would keep the men there all night if they let him. Reuben ignored this remark, retrieved his hat, and closed the door quickly behind him. He pretended not to hear Hal call to him as he hurried down the stairs.

The evening sky was a satiny purple and the air dry with a hint of late winter bite. Eager to evade Hal, Reuben walked quickly. His mind traveled back to photos he'd seen of Klansmen in *Life* magazine, stripped of their absurd peaked white hoods, men about to go on trial for a lynching. It was the very ordinariness of these men's faces that Reuben found most disturbing, the way they looked no different from men he passed on the street every day. Reuben thought of Patsy, the colored cook Edith hired shortly after they were married. While they would have preferred a white woman, a Negro cook was all they could afford.

Patsy had a broad, shiny face, the color of chocolate pudding. She had a flat nose and wore her hair in tiny pigtails fastened by strips of rag. Reuben found everything about her ugly, from her man-sized hands with their pink palms to her square, flat feet. In order to eat her food, he had to force himself not to think about who had prepared it.

Patsy was with them for a year, arriving early each morning by foot and staying until dinner was over and the kitchen was sparkling. He would never have known she had children, except that one died. When she returned to work, red eyed and silent a few days later, it never occurred to him to offer his condolences.

Then, Patsy was gone. Edith fired her, without notice, and hired a sullen Irish woman, someone who had no business calling herself a cook. Patsy, at least, could cook. Back then, he never gave a thought to what hardship it would have caused Pasty to be suddenly deprived of a wage. This was because he had never regarded her as being fully human, which was exactly the way the Nazis—and the Klan—felt about him.

That evening, Reuben saw a profile of Paul Herbert in the *Sea Forth Beacon*. He had recently been elected to the school board. The photo that accompanied the article had been taken on the steps of Bliss. Paul had an arm around Gladys, who was more stooped than ever. His other hand was on Lawrence's shoulder.

Except the house was no longer called Bliss. A large plaque above the handrail simply said "20 Mowbray."

The article described Paul as a private investor. "Real estate, art, antiques, wherever I spot opportunity," he was quoted as saying. "I look for discrepancies between how an asset is priced and what I believe to be its intrinsic value. The successful investor is always one step ahead of the crowd. The best opportunities are often right under a person's nose—all a person has to do is open his eyes to see them. The real estate here in Sea Forth is a perfect example. Right on the bay, with fertile soil, accessible to the city by rail and road. There's nowhere for prices to go but up."

A week later, while Edith was at work, Mr. Forrester, Jeffrey's principal, called the house. "I was hoping you and Mrs. Merkal could meet with me at one."

"What about?" Reuben asked, though he had his suspicions. The previous day, Jeffrey had returned from school with torn clothing, his face filthy, and his palms scraped raw. Jeffrey refused to tell him what happened, but it was clear he had been in a fight. Secretly, Reuben couldn't help being pleased. Boys were supposed to get into fights.

"We'll talk then," Mr. Forrester said.

Afraid if he left a message, Edith might not get it, Reuben drove to the store. He had been there only once before, months earlier, and was surprised to see how much busier the store seemed. Edith's counter had been relocated from the side to the center of the store, directly in front of the impractical winding staircase. She was waiting on two women, who appeared to be mother and daughter, both dressed in pale blue suits and navy blue hats. She had draped a lime green scarf around the younger woman's neck and was arranging the ends into a many-looped bow. To Reuben, the result looked ridiculous, like something that belonged wrapped around a present, but the women seemed delighted. As he approached, a flicker of annoyance crossed Edith's face, but she quickly composed herself and began playing with the scarf.

"Here's another way to wear it," Edith said, retying it so that it hung in a V across the woman's chest like a baby's bib.

Addressing the women, Reuben said, "Excuse me." He leaned over the counter and dropped his voice. "Jeffrey's principal called. He wants to see us at one."

"Can't you see I'm busy?" Edith said.

Reuben held up his hand. "That's all I came to tell you. I'll pick you up at ten to one."

"You'll have to go by yourself." Edith smiled toward the women. "Be with you in a second."

"We can come back," the younger woman said.

"No, we're finished. So nice of you to stop by." Edith extended her hand to Reuben. "Ladies, you mustn't leave without seeing the chiffons we just got in. Just the ticket for spring."

Reuben stood there, hands tucked into his dungaree pockets, except for the thumb looped into the brim of his cap. He shifted from side to side, and cleared his throat as Edith pulled out a pile of scarves in Easter egg colors and began demonstrating the many ways they could be tied. Reuben couldn't help marveling at how Edith had managed to learn them all, even if this did strike him as an enormous waste of time and energy. The women were certainly impressed. Even Edith seemed surprised when they decided to buy four scarves.

As soon as the women left, the smile vanished from Edith's face. "Were you trying to humiliate me?" she asked.

"This is your son we're talking about. Maybe Jeffrey wouldn't have so many problems if things were different."

"What are you implying?"

"Perhaps if you were around more..."

"Get out."

"I'm not leaving until you say you'll come."

"I'm calling the security guard." Edith raised her arm to show she was serious.

"Most mothers wouldn't dream of missing a meeting with their son's principal. It strikes me as rather..."

"Rather, what?"

"Unnatural, that's what." Before Edith could answer, Reuben stalked out of the store. He derived such immense satisfaction from having gotten the last word in, that he was almost glad that Edith had refused to come. He was nearly back home before it dawned on him that he hadn't won the argument, after all. He was going to the meeting alone, wasn't he?

Mr. Forrester was a prune of a man, with a mouth like a sewn purse and small, washed-out eyes that looked even smaller behind the thick lenses of his spectacles. He was dressed in a brown wool vest and worn tweed jacket that reeked of pipe tobacco.

If Mr. Forrester was surprised by Edith's absence, he hid it, murmuring "what a shame" when Reuben explained how she was unable to get away from work. He played with an octagonal glass paperweight as he spoke. "Has Jeffrey told you about yesterday?"

Reuben admitted that Jeffrey had refused to tell him anything.

Mr. Forrester nodded. "There have been several occasions when I considered inviting you in but decided not to trouble you. This time, Jeffrey gave me no choice."

Reuben's eyes traveled to the wall where the paperweight, having trapped a glint of sun, was projecting a rainbow. It was a mild day, and Reuben could hear the children on the playground then the sound of the whistle summoning them back to class. "What happened?" he asked.

Mr. Forrester cleared his throat. "I don't think Jeffrey is entirely to blame. The others don't make it easy for him. But that doesn't excuse what he did." He paused, picking up the paperweight again. Reuben was suddenly grateful that Edith wasn't there. He felt a chivalrous urge to protect her from whatever Mr. Forrester was about to say.

"We're inclined to believe the other boys as we questioned several individually and their stories were consistent. It was Charles Eldridge's birthday earlier this month, and he's been bringing his present, a catcher's mitt, to school every day, leaving it on his desk. Yesterday, when the children came back from assembly, the mitt was gone. The teacher found the mitt in Jeffrey's cubby, buried beneath some papers. She ordered Jeffrey to remain in during recess, but before she could stop him, he scooted out the door, apparently tackling Charles on the playground. Then he straddled Charles and threatened to pour gravel down Charles' throat. That's when the other boys came to Charles' rescue, perhaps too enthusiastically."

"Jeffrey doesn't even like baseball," Reuben said.

"Which makes his actions all the more puzzling." The principal shook his head.

Reuben ran through the other possibilities. Maybe one of the boys planted the mitt in Jeffrey's locker, and it was because Jeffrey was innocent that he refused to stay back. Perhaps the boys jumped Jeffrey and made up the story about him tackling Charles. Given how timid his son was, that made a good deal more sense to Reuben than the principal's version. He said nothing, however, afraid of sounding overprotective.

"We're at a loss as to what to do. I'm sure I'm not telling you something you don't know when I say he's different from other boys. How does he behave at home?"

He's as much of a mystery to me as he is to you, Reuben wanted to say. Instead, he said, "Like an eleven-year-old boy. A bit shy, but nothing out of the ordinary." He was tempted to ask whether Jeffrey had any friends but was sure he knew the answer.

"To be honest," Mr. Forrester said, "I'm more concerned about the boy than with how to punish him. That's not to say he isn't being punished. Not punishing him would send the wrong message to the other children. What I've decided to do is to keep him apart. Make him take lunch alone. Remain in the classroom during assembly. Sit by himself in class. I'm hoping this way he'll learn that to be a part of civilized society, one must play by its rules."

To Reuben, it seemed as if this punishment couldn't be more wrongheaded; isolating Jeffrey would just make him feel even more like a pariah. Again, he decided to say nothing. Mr. Forrester, after all, was the principal.

"Perhaps you can reinforce this at home. Send him straight to his room after school. That sort of thing. Just for a few weeks. No point being too punitive." Mr. Forrester stood, signaling that the meeting was over.

On the way out, Reuben peeked in the door window of Jeffrey's classroom. While the rest of the children were painting with watercolors, Jeffrey had been banished to the corner, where he had been made to sit cross-legged, facing the wall.

# Chapter Fourteen

## August and September 1938

"Your silver wedding anniversary? How old were you when you got married? Twelve?"

The petite redhead laughed. "Hardly." She leaned across the counter, cupped her hand, and whispered, "I'll be forty-eight next month."

"You're kidding!" Edith was astonished to learn this woman, Mrs. McKenna, was nearly a decade older than she was. Yet, as Edith looked more closely, her face did reveal clues to her real age—crows' feet, a slack jaw line, a sagging brow. What made the woman seem so young was the sparkle in her eyes and the genuineness of her laugh. Mrs. McKenna was shopping for an evening wrap to pair with the strapless ice-blue gown she had bought for her anniversary party.

"For such a delicate dress, you don't want anything that looks heavy. On the other hand, September is so unpredictable. Make sure whatever you buy has enough length, so that if it's a chilly evening, you won't freeze," Edith said. She pulled several wraps from the display case but unfolded only one, a silver chambray embroidered with sequins. "This one will turn heads," she said.

After she became a saleswoman, it hadn't taken Edith long to figure out that if you presented the customer with too many choices, you risked confusing her so that she would end up buying nothing. Edith stepped out from behind the counter.

"May I show you how it's supposed to be worn?" Another thing Edith discovered was that most women, including those who could whip up a pair of curtains in an afternoon or produce a perfectly flaky pie crust, were all thumbs when it came to tying a wrap or scarf. "How many people are coming?" Edith asked as she knotted the wrap.

"Close to a hundred. My husband's even asked our minister. He wants us to renew our vows!" Mrs. McKenna shook her head in mock exasperation.

"Nothing wrong with being a romantic." Edith recalled how romantic Reuben had once been. How he never forgot her birthday or their anniversary. How he used every occasion, including his own birthday, as an excuse to buy her presents.

Edith stepped back, chin in hand. "It's missing something." She returned behind the counter, where she rifled through a drawer until she found a brooch with cloisonné flowers in shades of blue. She fastened the brooch at the shoulder, and then adjusted the shawl downward so that the brooch would be visible from the front. While the brooch was the sort of touch that Edith believed made a wrap like this, it was also one that would never occur to most women.

"What about shoes and a bag?" Edith asked as she rang up the sale.

"I haven't even started to look."

"Can you spare a minute?" Until she began working at the store, Edith hadn't realized what an exceptional memory she had. Not only did she know just about every piece of merchandise the store carried, her mind had them cataloged. All she had to do was think, blue gown, silver wrap, and the shoes and handbag to pair with them would spring to mind.

Edith escorted Mrs. McKenna over to Shoes. She had no intention of handing her over to bucktoothed Darlene Fedder, the salesgirl there. It wasn't that Darlene had no taste; she had astonishingly bad taste.

"The customer insists I take care of her. Be an angel and look after my department until I'm finished," Edith told Darlene.

Darlene glared at her as she mumbled, "Sure." From the corner of her eye, Edith watched Darlene head not toward her department but to the Ladies' Room, the only place besides the cafeteria where the girls were allowed to smoke. Edith knew Darlene didn't believe her. She wished she could make Darlene understand that by looking after Mrs. McKenna herself, she was only doing what was best for the store.

"This is the shoe you want," Edith said, holding up a pair of silver sling backs that Mrs. McKenna recognized to be perfect. After ringing up the shoes, Edith steered Mrs. McKenna over to Handbags, where she also dispatched the girl in charge over to her own department, with instructions to relieve Darlene, assuming she was there. Mrs. McKenna had come in only for a wrap but, by the time Edith was finished, she had bought nearly three hundred dollars' worth of merchandise. As Edith escorted her to the front door, she looked shell-shocked, though because Edith had not tried to sell her anything that she didn't love herself, she was sure later on Mrs. McKenna would thank her.

One day in August, Gretel Hinderman steered Edith to an empty lunch table. "I've been dying to talk to you." She and Edith often ate together. Like Edith, she was middle-aged, and her husband was out of work, though, in his case, this was due to an industrial accident that had left him crippled.

Edith leaned across the table eagerly. The other salesgirl in Better Dresses, Gretel's department, had been growing steadily larger, and Edith was sure she was finally going to learn whether the girl had gotten herself pregnant.

As Gretel removed her sandwich—strong smelling liver paste on coarse brown bread—from its wax paper wrapping, it occurred to Edith that her expression lacked the malicious glee she'd expect in someone about to share a piece of gossip.

Gretel pulled a piece of paper from her smock pocket. It was Edith who had suggested to Mr. Adler that the salesgirls wear smocks to make them immediately identifiable to the customers, give them a neat appearance, and hide their largely unfashionable clothes. What she had nothing to do with, was Mr. Adler's unfortunate color selection. Pepto-Bismol pink, the other girls called it.

Gretel scanned the lunchroom, a depressing place with murky green walls, the only natural light coming from a series of tiny street-level windows that ran along the base of the ceiling.

"Did you see it?" Gretel whispered.

"See what?" Edith asked.

"The flyer! Didn't you check your mail slot this morning?"

"I forgot." The truth was that Edith had checked her mail slot, but nothing was there.

"Read it under the table."

The flyer was a typed mimeograph, full of misspellings, the d's, b's, and o's smudge-filled:

> The workers strength is in their numbers. Only by banding together can the humbel workers offset the Power of the Boss. The union movement has rescued our miners and factory workers from inhumen working conditions and starvation wages. It's our duty to our families to demand the same for ourselfs!!!! Sisters, lets celebrate Labor Day by meeting by the picnic tables at Hecksher State Park at 12 Noon. A representitive from the Retail Clerks Nationel Protection Association will be there to talk with us about forming a local chapter! Lets assert our collective power. Rain date, the following Sunday.

Edith refolded the note and slid it back to Gretel. "My God, it's scandalous," she said, though she was not exactly sure what unions did, except that they sent people out on strike and were somehow related to the Red Peril.

"Scandalous? We're talking about forming a union, not robbing a bank."

"If you ask me, getting involved with something like this is a good way to get yourself fired."

"Isn't that the point? He can fire one of us, but he can hardly fire the whole lot. Take my husband. If his plant had been unionized, he might still be collecting a wage."

Edith motioned for Gretel to keep her voice down. "This isn't a factory. There's nothing wrong with working conditions here."

"How different is it? We do all the work so that he can get rich."

"What makes you think Mr. Adler's getting rich?" Edith was astonished that Gretel could think this when the store was so often empty. Where did she think the money was coming from to buy the inventory or pay the rent, not to mention the weekly wages of Mr. Adler's forty or so employees? She might not know as much as Gretel did about unions, but at least she had the common sense to figure out that.

"Of course he's making money. He's a Jew, isn't he?" The words had barely left her mouth when Gretel realized what she'd said. "Oh dear! I didn't mean to insult you." Gretel shook her head as she placed her lunch remains in her brown paper bag and swept the crumbs onto the floor.

Edith was more shocked than insulted. How had Gretel figured out she was Jewish? With her small nose and fair complexion, she had never thought of herself as looking particularly Jewish. She longed to escape to the Ladies' Room so that she could reassure herself this was really the case.

"Promise you won't say anything," Gretel said. "If he finds out, everyone will know who told him."

Edith nodded, too stunned to speak. She wondered if all the salesgirls had figured out that she was Jewish and, because of that, believed she wasn't to be trusted.

That evening, Edith felt as exhausted as she had during her first months at the store, before she got used to being on her feet all day. As soon as dinner was over, she headed to bed and fell asleep.

She bolted awake shortly before one. For a long while, she lay with the pillow pressed to her ear, trying to drown out Reuben's snoring. But it was as if her mind was cluttered with jigsaw puzzle pieces that she had to assemble, or she would never be able to rest. Eventually, she went over to the chair beneath the window, unbuttoning her nightgown and exposing her shoulders to the cool night breeze.

Edith watched Reuben sleep. On his back, his mouth hanging open, he looked so old and defeated that she found it impossible to conjure up the animosity toward him that fueled much of her day. She recalled how well he used to treat his employees. How, if a worker became disabled, he would continue to pay his wages for months. How he'd kept his workers on long after it became obvious that he had no further need for them. Edith admired Reuben for this. At the same time, now that she had a better sense of the sort of things a businessman needed to do to survive, she couldn't help wondering whether his kindness had been misguided. Perhaps if he had been more cold-blooded, he'd still be in business.

Edith still was puzzled why she hadn't been asked to the picnic. Unless Sheila Lowenstein in Maternity also hadn't been invited, there had to be more to it than her being Jewish. Sheila, with her large nose and swarthy skin, really did look Jewish. Yet because of her great sense of humor, she was the most popular girl at the store, always surrounded by such a crowd in the lunchroom, it was as if she were holding court.

The following morning, Edith headed over to Gretel's department. Gretel was fitting a boxy black jacket onto a mannequin dressed in a beige crepe-wool dress from the new fall collection.

"Don't you think brown would look smarter, also something more fitted?" Edith asked. She pulled a coffee-colored jacket with embroidered lapels from the clothing rack. "Much nicer, don't you think?" she asked.

"Gorgeous," Gretel said. She had already taken the black jacket off the mannequin and tossed it across the sales counter.

Edith held out the jacket, but Gretel refused to take it.

"You do it. I'd probably end up putting it on backwards," she said.

"Gretel, really." Edith laughed, assuming this was a bit of self-deprecating fun. Then, she noticed the red patches that had formed on Gretel's cheeks. "I didn't mean to interfere. I just thought..."

"That you knew best. You always do." Gretel looked at her wristwatch. "The store opens in fifteen minutes, and I still have all these dresses to hang up." She motioned to the pile of wool crepes draped over a chair.

Edith was so flustered that she nearly forgot why she had stopped by. "Have you found out who distributed the flyers?" she asked.

"I have."

"Who?"

"Don't you think if they wanted to invite you, they would have?"

Over the next couple weeks, while Edith was tempted to warn Mr. Adler about the picnic, she never mustered the courage. But when Edith arrived at work the Tuesday following the picnic to find Mr. Adler nowhere to be seen, she suspected that he must have found out about it anyway, as she'd never known him to be even five minutes late. Then, there were the salesgirls. As they got their departments ready for the opening, there was none of the customary chatter about weekend parties and dates. The store was as quiet as a morgue.

It was afternoon before Mr. Adler showed up. He barely acknowledged Edith as he passed her department on his way to his office. She watched until he disappeared behind the gilded birdcage suspended from the ceiling that housed a pair of African Congo Parrots. It was a recent addition as was the gleaming Steinway piano atop a newly constructed platform where on Monday, Wednesday, and Friday from three to five, a man in a white tie and tails pounded out Broadway show tunes.

"I want the Emporium to be a fantasyland where customers can forget their cares," was how Mr. Adler had explained these additions at a staff meeting in July. While attendance at these meetings, held Monday mornings at eight, was mandatory, it was rare for more than half the salesgirls to show up. Face uplifted, eyelids closed, he had been too lost in his dreams to notice how the salesgirls sniggered when he revealed his plans to install a miniature carousel in the girls' department.

Mr. Adler never left his office that afternoon. Shortly after five, the bookkeeper, Mr. Lemmon, announced that Mr. Adler asked him to lock up. The salesgirls hurried toward the rear exit, from which they were required to enter and leave the store. Edith was waiting for the security guard to check her bags when she cried out, "I forgot something," causing most of the girls to turn around. She hid in a toilet stall in the Ladies' Room until she was sure everyone would have left.

When she emerged from the Ladies' Room, Edith was entranced by how the deserted store sparkled in the late afternoon sunlight. It was as if the store were indeed the fantasyland Mr. Adler dreamed of creating. Only then did Edith understand why she stayed behind. She had a bond with Mr. Adler, that being their shared love for the store. An irrational love in her case—for what, really, was the store to her, except the place where she worked?

As Edith looked around, the changes she had brought about were evident everywhere. In spite of a lack of real authority, she had managed to make the other salesgirls feel as if they were under the watch of a more critical, less forgiving eye than Mr. Adler's. As upsetting as it was to realize how much the other salesgirls resented her, she felt proud of all she had taught them. Some were things that she would have expected them to know—like how to fold a garment properly. Others were the small touches that would make their departments more appealing, like making sure all the hangers on a rack faced in the same direction and that the price tags were tucked away. The way she explained this to the other salesgirls was that, in order to make their customers fall in love with the merchandise, they had to treat it as if they loved it themselves.

Edith was on her knees, re-sorting the sales rack in the shoe department, when she was startled to find Mr. Adler standing over her, his face drawn and cheeks drained of their normally high color. She'd been examining a pair of navy and white spectator pumps with scuffed sides and worn lifts, clear signs that one of the salesgirls must have "borrowed" them for the summer. Deciding it would be cruel to point this out to Mr. Adler right now, she shoved them back onto the rack.

"Mrs. Merkal, it's after six! Your husband will be after me with a shotgun." Despite his lively words, Mr. Adler's voice was flat.

As Edith stood, she caught a glimpse of herself in a mirror. She, too, looked pale and tired. Her lipstick had worn off, and it was as if part of her face were missing. She looked at her watch. "Oh dear, I only planned on staying a few minutes. These shoes. A real mess..."

"Please, go." Mr. Adler's tone made it clear that he wanted to be alone.

Stung by his abruptness, Edith headed back to her own department. Whether due to obliviousness or indifference, Mr. Adler rarely thanked her for the extra tasks she performed around the store, and as often as she might tell herself she didn't care, she did. She retrieved her purse and cardigan from beneath the counter, watching him from the corner of her eye. He was picking up and putting down shoes in a distracted way that signaled his impatience to see her leave.

As a way of getting back at him, Edith took her time getting ready. She brushed her hair, and powdered her nose. She re-applied her lipstick, smacking her lips loudly between applications, and then finished off by bestowing a red kiss onto a tissue, which she left on top of the counter. Turning toward him, Edith asked, "Better?"

Mr. Adler said, "You looked fine before." Still holding one of the shoes, he looked down at it, perplexed, as if he wasn't sure how it got there. He then looked up with an abashed smile that made clear to Edith why he had been so abrupt. He was feeling humiliated and, of all the salesgirls, hers was the pity he least wanted.

Mr. Adler walked over to Edith's counter and picked up the discarded tissue. "Scarlet, isn't it? I think dark shades look harsh on most women, but this shade really suits you." He moved over to a display of change purses. "This one's awfully smart, isn't it?" he asked, picking up a butter-colored leather purse, the very one that Edith longed to buy for herself. As hopeless as Mr. Adler was at administration, his fashion eye could be dazzling.

"I used the afternoon to catch up on paperwork," Mr. Adler said as he played with the bag's heart-shaped clasp.

"I would imagine there's no end to that."

"At least I got the chance to take care of some things I'd been putting off."

Edith decided to use this allusion to the previous day's events as an opportunity to offer some words of sympathy. She motioned with her hand as if to take in the rest of the staff. "I can't tell you how sorry I am about all this."

Mr. Adler stiffened. "Sorry about what? They have the right to do what they want. Of course, so do I. And if it comes down to it, I might just fire the lot of them. In a funny way, I'm glad it happened. Makes things a lot clearer. Come, I'll let you out." He pulled a metal ring, laden with keys, from his pocket and started toward the entrance. For a small man with short legs, he had a remarkably fast gait, and Edith had to scurry to catch up.

As soon as they were outside, Mr. Adler thrust out his hand. Afraid this might be her last opportunity to let him know whose side she was on, Edith wrapped her hands around his. "You didn't mean that, about firing the lot of them? Of course, having not gone to the picnic, I have no idea what went on."

"I knew you weren't there. I wouldn't let Gretel leave my office until she told me everyone who was. But you're the only girl who didn't go."

"I'm perfectly happy with the way things are."

Mr. Adler studied Edith before speaking. "I hope not perfectly happy. Can ya spare the time for a cup of coffee?"

"I knew about the picnic. It's just that I didn't know what kind of picnic it was gonna be. I even gave that cow Darlene five dollars so she could buy a nice baked ham. 'Don't forget to tell the girls it's from Mr. Adler,' I said. 'Tell 'em I hope they have a swell time.' That woulda given them a laugh."

Edith sipped her coffee, so sludgy and bitter it must have been sitting on the burner for hours. "I'm sure no one was making fun of you."

Mr. Adler shrugged. "If they were, who cares?"

Edith knew he was lying. Of everything having to do with the picnic, this possibility would have been the one he would find most distressing.

"My wife, Muriel, was out, and the refrigerator was empty. All afternoon, I kept picturing those girls stuffing themselves with fried chicken, potato salad, my ham. By three, my stomach was screaming for mercy. So, I thought, why not drive over? I only planned on staying long enough to say hello and fix myself a plate of food." Mr. Adler dabbed with his napkin at the puddle of coffee that had sloshed onto his saucer. "By the time I pulled into the parking lot, the weather had gotten nasty. I was sure I'd missed 'em," Mr. Adler said. "When I saw them, I got so excited, I began running. It wasn't until I'd nearly crashed into that union broad that I realized what was going on."

"I wanted to warn you…"

Mr. Adler's eyes dropped to his spoon, which he had been running around his coffee cup. "Nah, it wasn't your place."

Edith had been sure that Mr. Adler was about to offer her a new job. Now, she began to wonder if all he really wanted to do was talk about the other salesgirls. She was so disappointed that it took enormous effort to keep her face composed.

"They're like a bunch of spoiled children." Mr. Adler grabbed the menus. "Something to eat?" It was nearly seven, and they were the only ones in the coffee shop except for the waitress. She had already lowered the blinds and switched the sign on the door from "Open" to "Closed."

"My husband's probably organized a search party." Edith slid toward the edge of the bench and reached for her purse. She would insist on paying for her own coffee, she decided.

Mr. Adler looked disappointed as he placed the menus back in the holder. As soon as he finished his coffee, the waitress slapped the check on the table. He placed his hand on top of Edith's. "Can't ya stay another minute? I never got the chance to say what I wanted. I sense you've got a real backbone, that you'd be the perfect person to whip 'em into line." So thoroughly had Edith abandoned hope of this happening that her eyes widened with disbelief. Mr. Adler added with exasperation, "I'm talking about the salesgirls!"

His proposition was simple. She'd become his manager in charge of employee relations. He'd already been thinking about some sort of promotion before the—he struggled for the right word—*incident* but had in mind something to do with fashion. For the present, this need was more critical. He gave Edith a hopeful look.

Edith smiled uncertainly. She wasn't sure what he meant by "employee relations" but was embarrassed to ask. She glanced over at the waitress, now seated on a counter stool, puffing on a cigarette. She was wearing a childishly frilled apron and had a florid, lined face. "I suppose that means I'd be in charge of the hiring and firing," Edith said.

"Oh, it's more than that. Employee relations has to do with figuring out the right staffing levels, making sure the girls show up on time and don't slack off, that they're properly trained, and that the sales floor is always covered. All the things I should be paying more attention to. See, it's not that I don't know what to do..." He exhaled heavily.

Edith pictured herself walking the floor, ordering the other salesgirls around. No, not the other salesgirls, *the* salesgirls. She would be their boss. She shook her head as she tried to make this sink in. When she looked up, Mr. Adler was smiling.

"Well, Mrs. Merkal, whaddaya say?"

"I'm flattered."

"Yes or no?"

"Yes, of course, but—"

"No buts about it. Your first job will be to quash this union nonsense." As he reached for his wallet, Mr. Adler's face changed. "Goodness me, I haven't spoken to you about the most important thing. The money! I'd imagine you'd be interested in that. There'll be a handsome raise. How much I haven't worked out yet, but handsome. You can take my word about that, Mrs. Merkal."

Money was a topic rarely far from Edith's thoughts, but for once, she hadn't been thinking about it. Mr. Adler pulled out a dollar from his wallet and placed it on the table and stood. "Shake? You can go home now, honey," he called to the waitress. "Me and my partner here are finished."

As Edith walked home that evening, she was surprised by how flat she felt. True, it had been a trying day. But she would have thought the excitement of being offered a new job would have canceled out the effects of the unpleasantness that preceded it. She wondered if the reason she felt this way was because she still didn't fully understand what she would be doing. This was not because Mr. Adler hadn't described her duties adequately, but because she would need to be actually doing the job before it became real to her.

Dusk had fallen, and there was a nip to the air. Even with a cardigan, Edith felt chilled and walked quickly. Tomorrow, school began; Jeffrey would be starting eighth grade and Harriet third. Edith supposed she was different from most mothers in that she was glad to see her children growing up. She hoped as they did, her relationship with them would improve. Of course, their getting older meant that she was, too, and that she hated. It was the sneakiness of the aging process that most terrified her, the imperceptible way it robbed a woman of her beauty, so that on a daily basis she noticed nothing. Until one day, while putting on her makeup, she discovered it was gone.

The house was in sight before Edith gave any thought to Reuben. She realized she didn't want to tell him about her new job. This surprised her, for one of the uglier things she had come to learn about herself was how much pleasure she derived from reminding him who was the family wage earner now. But this was different. Telling him about the promotion would be no mere jab; the effect would be akin to thrusting a knife into his heart. Of course, were Reuben to learn about her promotion from someone else, it would be even worse. Maybe the thing would be not to tell him all at once, but to dish it out in palatable nibbles.

She could tell him tonight that Mr. Adler had asked her to keep the scheduling roster. Then, in a few days, she could say that Mr. Adler was putting her in charge of training. Before long, she would have described the entire job to Reuben without ever having actually told him about the promotion. That was the way to do it, Edith decided. She might no longer love Reuben, but she was no monster. She still retained a shred of compassion for the man who had once loved her enough to build her a house and who used to celebrate his own birthdays by buying her jewelry.

At work, Edith felt as if she had stumbled into a sort of purgatory. Having passed the problem of his mutinous staff onto her, Mr. Adler didn't seem to care what she did with them. Whenever she asked if he could spare a few minutes, he put her off. "Can't ya see I'm busy?" he told her one morning as he slid a solo game of tic-tac-toe beneath his ink blotter. The announcement also severed whatever shreds of a relationship she had with the salesgirls. In addition to disliking her, they now feared her, and Edith discovered she was afraid of them, too.

Edith called a staff meeting for the following Friday because she figured it was the sort of thing a manager should do. She retreated to her new office, a small, windowless, and poorly ventilated space that had been a storage closet. Her intention was to work out what to say at this meeting, but she quickly realized that before she did that, she had to figure out the kind of store the Emporium should become. This was the sort of planning Mr. Adler should have been doing but wasn't. For while Mr. Adler had plenty of good ideas, he lacked the ability to transform them into a coherent vision, let alone implement the measures necessary to transform that vision into a reality.

It would be foolish to try to pattern the Emporium after the posh Fifth Avenue stores. While there were plenty of wealthy women on Long Island, there were not many who bought couture and the few who did would never dream of shopping locally. On the other hand, it would be equally foolish to model the store after Macy's given that the Emporium could never afford to carry the same breadth of merchandise, let alone sell it at such thin margins. No, the Emporium had to aim for somewhere in between. It should target the well off as opposed to the wealthy woman, one who wanted to appear fashionable but also wanted her clothing to last several seasons. The Emporium did not require the sort of elegant, knowledgeable sales staff of, say, a Saks Fifth Avenue. But it needed a sales staff with a good deal more class than you'd find at a Kresge's, girls whose advice the customers would respect, the sort they might even have to their homes.

The day of the meeting was so bright that the late afternoon sun, reflected off the sidewalk, made the cafeteria windows sparkle and scattered jewel-like orbs across the tin tables. The mood, however, was anything but cheerful as the salesgirls shuffled in. So recently united into a group, the women had already splintered into separate islands of anxiety.

Edith had rehearsed what she was going to say. Even so, as she placed her notes across the lectern, her hands began to shake. Looking over the girls' heads toward the clock on the opposite wall, she decided to allow herself a full minute to compose herself. As soon as the second hand completed its revolution, she looked back down at the salesgirls, deliberately blurring her vision so that their faces became a sea of pink. She cleared her throat and began.

She was astonished to hear her voice ring out strong and steady. Astonished, too, when after a minute or so, she found herself setting aside the speech she had labored over, a dry recitation of the performance measuring tools she'd be putting into place. Instead, Edith described her vision for the Emporium and the role she expected the salesgirls to play in making this happen.

"You girls have only yourselves to thank for my appointment. Surely you realize what a struggle it's been for Mr. Adler to keep this store going. And how do you show your appreciation?" Edith looked around as if waiting for someone to raise a hand. "Things have been too easy here. My job will be to remind you that you are not indispensable. From now on, I'll expect you to prove to me every day that you've earned your salary. If you don't, you'll be let go. That's no idle threat. I can assure you there are tons of gals out there who would love to have your jobs.

"If you arrive late or leave early more than three times in any month, you'll be fired. Ditto if you don't make your sales quotas for more than two months running. The first time a customer complains that you've been rude or inattentive, you'll be given a warning. The second time, out you'll go. There will be no gossiping, no personal phone calls, no unscheduled bathroom breaks, and no 'borrowing' of merchandise." Edith sought out the eyes of the salesgirls she suspected were guilty of this last transgression. "And no further talk about unions. Think carefully about whether you can accept these conditions. If you can't, start looking for another job."

A few days later, Edith stopped by her old department to check on the new salesgirl, Arlene. Arlene was busy with an elderly-looking woman. Nearly bald with pink patches of scalp visible beneath her short white hair, the woman was resting against her walker as with stiff fingers, she examined a red calfskin change purse.

"Hello," Edith said in her bright, professional voice.

The woman's mouth dropped open. "Edith." Her voice, though thin and weak, was familiar. With an understanding smile, she extended her hand. "Gladys Herbert."

Edith tried to mask her shock. "Gladys, how wonderful to see you! It's just that I've never seen you here before."

Gladys motioned to the slender Negro woman in a nurse's uniform, standing nearby. "I'm afraid I don't get out much these days."

Edith was debating whether to ask what was wrong with her when Gladys said, "Cancer. I was sure you would have heard."

"I'm out of touch with the old crowd. Too busy here, I guess."

"How marvelous. Which department is yours?"

"No department. I'm in charge of the entire sales staff."

"My! I heard you were working here, but I had no idea…"

"Had I known, I would have called."

Gladys placed her hand over Edith's. Her fingertips were icy. "I'm afraid it's rather hopeless. But we must make the best of things, mustn't we?" She held up the change purse. "Isn't it darling? I feel foolish buying something that's bound to last longer than I will, but mine has gotten rather ragged."

Gladys handed the purse to Arlene and then turned toward the Negro woman, who was holding her handbag. "Mavis, after you've settled up, arrange for the car to be brought around. Edith, dear, I'd be ever so grateful if you could help me to the door."

When, at the entranceway, Gladys wrapped her bony fingers around Edith's wrist and bestowed a papery kiss on her cheek, Edith became so choked up she could barely muster a good-bye. Yet later that day, Edith found herself deriving a grim satisfaction from Gladys' plight, the same sort others might have gotten from witnessing Reuben and her fall. Indeed, seeing Gladys gave Edith such a perverse lift that when she arrived home that evening to find that Reuben had failed to do the few chores she had set out on a note taped to the refrigerator, she only feigned anger. These days, she was rarely truly angry with him; it was hard to be angry with someone you'd given up on.

# Chapter Fifteen

## *September 1938*

As soon as Reuben woke on the morning of September 21, he switched on the radio. The weather forecast was unchanged from the evening before. The hurricane barreling up the East Coast was expected to veer out to sea, with Long Island experiencing no more than high tides and strong winds.

"Great," Reuben said out loud, though there was no one around to hear him. Antoinette didn't come on Wednesdays. Edith had left for work, the children for school.

With no hurricane to worry about, Reuben saw no reason to hurry out of bed. He'd grown accustomed to wiling away his morning there, listening to the radio and drifting into and out of sleep. He changed the station to CBS just in time to catch Edward R. Murrow reporting from Berlin. Hitler's army had taken control of part of Czechoslovakia. Deciding that was enough bad news for one day, he turned the radio off and went back to sleep.

It was afternoon before Reuben finally made his way downstairs. As he waited for the kettle to boil, he stuck his head out the back door. It was only sprinkling, but there was a charge to the air and a smell like burning wires that made him uneasy. He went to the living room and turned on the Motorola. It took a good deal of fiddling to find a weather report, which he took as a good sign. Even better, the forecast was unchanged.

Reuben was still at the kitchen table, thumbing through the newspaper, pausing every now and again to sip at his now cold tea, when what sounded like a gigantic moan drew his attention to the window. In an instant, it began to pour, the rain carried along by the suddenly strong winds so that it was nearly horizontal. The sky had turned a phosphorescent green.

A few minutes later, the Sea Forth fire station sounded its siren—three short blasts followed by a long one, the signal for the town's residents to evacuate. Reuben laughed. Evacuate where? The few roads connecting Long Island to the mainland were inadequate even in ordinary conditions. With everyone trying to escape, they'd quickly turn into long parking lots. He was angry with himself for believing the weather forecast instead of what his eyes, nose, and the hairs on his arms had been trying to tell him for more than an hour.

Of course, Edith's store and the children's school would close. All three were probably on their way home. Reuben decided to look for them and grabbed an umbrella. He was still on the porch when the winds turned the umbrella inside out and sent it flying. Main Street was full of pedestrians, their arms held up to protect their faces from flying debris. They spilled from the sidewalk onto the street and were weaving their way between the slowly moving cars. The noise was incredible—the ripping winds, the horns and sirens, the clatter of rolling garbage cans, doors banging open and shut, branches snapping. With so many people about, Reuben decided it would be futile to look for Edith and the children. The smarter thing would be to try and protect the house while it was still possible to move around.

It was only when Reuben caught sight of the bird feeder banging wildly against the oak tree that he thought of his mother. The bird feeder had been his housewarming present to his parents, though neither ever bothered to keep it filled. Nearly blind and infirm, his mother would be terrified in her helplessness, as well she should be given that her bungalow was just a few hundred feet from the bay.

A good son, Reuben thought, would go get her immediately. But a good husband and father would never leave until he had made the house safe for his wife and children. Reuben decided that his first duty was to them.

Reuben was crawling beneath the porch, searching for lumber, when he heard clambering above. He had already looked in the chicken shed, the attic, and the basement. He'd once been a builder; now he didn't have so much as a single spare plank of wood lying around. It was the children he'd heard, their soaked hair flat against their skulls, and buckling beneath the weight of their drenched clothing. As Reuben helped them out of their clothing, he could feel their bodies vibrating like small motors.

A few minutes later, Edith arrived, looking frantic. "Are they here?" she cried.

"Upstairs changing," Reuben said.

"I've been running up and down the street, calling their names." Edith's red cardigan had bled onto the white bodice of her dress; her mascara was running; and a filament of snot was dangling from her nose. She glanced up to the second-story landing. "I was sure something happened to them."

Reuben gave her back a few tentative pats. "I wanted to board up the windows but couldn't find any lumber." They both looked toward the living room windows, where water was pouring in from over their tops and from beneath their sills.

"What about the porch?" Edith asked. The porch floor was buckled and downward sloping, and she'd been after him to repair it for years, insisting it was an accident waiting to happen. She looked at him in a way that made clear that she was not asking his opinion but telling him what to do.

Edith had been right about the porch. The planks came up with the gentlest of tugs. Reuben was no longer used to such physical exertion, and his arm began to throb, his hand to tremble so that he could barely maintain his grip on the hammer. As he nailed the planks diagonally across the windows, he pictured his mother standing near her own window, asking Antoinette what it was like outside. Her radio would be turned up high, though barely audible for the static. By now, Reuben was sure the sandy beach along the bay would be submerged and the water seeping onto the grassy verge behind it. Before long, it would reach across to the lawns on the other side, pushing its way up to, then inside, his mother's house.

By the time Reuben finished, the winds had become so fierce that it took all his strength to open the back door. As he made his way across the kitchen, then along the moth-eaten runner that ran the length of the foyer, he left puddles in his wake. He dumped his jacket on the floor and kicked off his shoes. He was halfway up the stairs to change when he spotted Edith on the landing. She was in her bathrobe and had a towel wrapped around her head. The lights had begun to flicker, and she was holding a candlestick with a long white taper, still unlit.

"Do you have to go?" she asked, meaning to his mother's.

Reuben knew she was only asking because she was scared for him. Yet, the question irritated him. "You'd like it, wouldn't you, if something happened to her?"

A moment passed before Edith spoke. "That you could even think such a thing. By the way, I found your galoshes. They're next to the bed."

The storm drains on Main Street had backed up, and churning water was spilling over the curbs. Fierce winds rocked Reuben's car and stripped the leaves from their branches, sending them flying against the windshield, so that even with his nose pressed against the glass, Reuben could barely see.

Main Street was deserted except for the occasional car laboring through the shallow river the road had become. Elm, Maple—Reuben knew he had to be passing them, but between the rain, leaves, and his breath fogging up the windshield, he might as well have been trying to navigate the dark side of the moon. He was cold, too, his teeth chattering and body shivering, his hands so numb that he could barely feel the steering wheel.

When Reuben finally got to what he thought was Linden, he turned left, the tires spinning as they plowed through the water. He had gone less than one hundred feet when he skidded to a stop. A branch had fallen across the road, bringing the utility wires down with it. For a moment, Reuben stared, mesmerized by the crackling wires, the flying blue and orange sparks, before he began to work out other routes to his mother. He had to get there quickly. Even this far from the bay, the rains had turned the streets into canals, the lawns surrounding the houses into islands.

"Maybe the best way is on foot," Reuben said out loud. He pulled down his hat, raised his coat collar, and reached for the car door handle. The door wouldn't budge. Reuben rattled the handle, his heart thumping so hard it felt like it might break through his chest. He'd heard of people drowning in their cars, and while in his more morbid moments, he'd toyed with the idea of ending it all, he'd never been serious. He was no longer thinking about his mother, only himself. His hand trembled as he turned the key to restart the ignition. A moan, then nothing. He floored the accelerator and tried the ignition again. Now, not even a moan. He reached for the door handle again. This time, the door opened.

It was a miracle they spotted him, the cop said. Middle-aged with a ruddy Irish face, he recognized Reuben, even used his name as he hoisted him up to his feet. Reuben had made it back to Main Street, but once there, his strength gave out. His back pressed against a building, he had slid down to the pavement and was half-submerged in water, his face resting on his knees and eyes closed when this cop and his partner found him. Somehow, they managed to get him home. The three were climbing the front steps and about to step onto the porch, when one of the cops, pulling the others backwards, shouted, "What the hell!"

Reuben had forgotten about the slats.

Edith opened the back door for them. She was holding a silver candelabrum that Reuben had not seen since their days at Bliss. Both cops were careful to wipe their feet on the doormat before stepping inside. Edith put the candelabrum down and began helping Reuben out of his soaked clothing.

"I'd put him straight to bed," the Irish-looking cop said to Edith. Then he added softly so that Reuben wouldn't hear though he did, "He seem okay to you? I mean...in the head?"

The words jolted Reuben out of his daze. He looked sharply at Edith.

"He was worried about someone," Edith said. The cops, eager to leave, didn't ask whom.

The following morning, the weather was beautiful, with a sharp blue sky and a lemony sun, which made the world sparkle. Reuben watched from his bedroom window as garbage cans, lawn furniture, a chest of drawers, and an entire roof floated down Main Street. Judging from the uniform shop across the street, where the brickwork beneath the display window was no longer visible, the water had to be at least three feet deep.

People were using boats to navigate Main Street. There was even an old man in a bathtub, using a broom for a paddle. Reuben reckoned that he could probably get to his mother's, if not by foot, then by boat. But he was too afraid of what he would find there to attempt it. He paced, periodically heading over to the windows. The waters had begun to recede and, across the street, people from the apartments above the shops had ventured onto the stoop, shielding their eyes against the sun as they surveyed the damage. He was at the window when two men in mackintoshes and waders began crossing what was normally his lawn.

Reuben knew immediately why they had come. His mother was dead. He had a childish urge to hide behind the curtains. For as long as he didn't hear the words, he could pretend it wasn't so. But downstairs, Harriet answered the door and was calling out "Daddy! Yoo-hoo, Daddy..." in her bird-chirp of a voice.

Reuben heard Edith greet them and then their voices drop low.

"Reuben, some gentlemen are here to see you," Edith called up, in a voice modulated to reveal nothing.

It occurred to Reuben that these men probably had other houses to visit. He threw his clothing over his pajamas and hurried down the stairs. The men, who introduced themselves as Floyd and Al, looked like decent, working-class men, the sort the volunteer fire department was made up of, men Reuben had never had much to do with.

"All the bungalows got swept out to sea," Floyd said. He asked if Reuben knew whether Jenny had been alone. Reuben said he thought Antoinette was with her.

"I tried to get her," Reuben explained, staring down at his feet. "I had to abandon my car. On Linden, I think."

"It was just so unexpected," Al said. He laid a sympathetic hand on Reuben's shoulder. "You shouldn't blame yourself."

The words brought tears to Reuben's eyes. By the time he set out, there had been no way he could have reached his mother. But he made a choice, which was to board up his own house before going to her. Perhaps if he had loved his mother more, he would have decided differently. Then, she might still be alive.

The men persuaded Reuben to wait until the next day before heading down to inspect the damage. "We'll come by at eleven," Floyd said. "If you give us the info, we'll stop by the police station and file a missing person's report, though I wouldn't get my hopes up."

Reuben was stunned by the capriciousness of the destruction. A wall left standing here, a row of kitchen cupboards there. Amid the rubble, beneath inch-thick mud, branches, and leaves, there remained poignant remnants of lives upended—a pink eyelet bedcover, a piano, Jenny's grandfather clock. He was ashamed to discover that the more solidly built, if dilapidated, houses of the two brothers who lived across the street had survived the storm, largely intact. Al told Reuben that except for Jenny and Antoinette, all the residents had been accounted for. Several were there, digging through the debris for what was salvageable.

Reuben couldn't bear to look at them. What would they say were they were to find that it was he who built these bungalows? His motto had been "identical, quick, and cheap." He'd been proud of how, by adopting assembly line methods to a business usually regarded as more craft than science, he'd made it possible for people, who might not otherwise be able to afford it, to buy a place by the water. Except his bungalows had turned out to be as flimsy as the straw one in "The Three Little Pigs."

Neither Floyd nor Al seemed aware that Reuben had built these bungalows. What they did know was that Paul Herbert had owned them all, except for Jenny's.

"What a guy," Floyd said. He was squatting, having caught sight of something glinting beneath the leg of a chair. "Not only has he given them all places to live in his buildings, he's forgiving their first year's rent."

"Just goes to prove," Al said, "that nice guys don't always finish last." He held up a roasting pan. "Some Brillo and a bit of elbow grease, and this should be as good as new."

"Take it all," Reuben said. "Or give it to someone who needs it."

"Here's something you'll want," Al said. It was a sepia-toned portrait of Reuben's parents, taken on their wedding day. "Your ma? What a pretty thing she was."

Reuben forced his mouth into a wistful smile. "This is too hard. I'm leaving. Like I said, take whatever you want. I wish I had a better way to thank you for all you've done."

On Monday, just after Edith and the children left the house, Reuben got a call asking him to come down to the police station. The police had photographs of a body that had washed on shore and were hoping he'd be able to identify it. He could, though only from the tattered remains of her clothing. It was his mother. Antoinette's body was never found.

# Chapter Sixteen

## *October and November 1938*

More than a month had passed since Jenny's death, and there still wasn't a morning when Reuben didn't awake to find his pillow soaked. He'd feel exhausted, as if he had been laboring all night. His dreams were always about his mother. In one, she sat on his bed and held his hands. Her hands were smooth and straight, the fingertips cool, the way he remembered them from his childhood. Though she never spoke, he knew that she was trying to tell him that she didn't blame him for what happened.

During the day, Reuben could sense Jenny following him throughout the house. The air would vibrate. She had taught him that boys and men were not supposed to cry, but his tears came anyway. He would sit in his recliner, his hands clasped between his legs, and watch his tears form dark circles on his pants. He was certain that as long as he was in such a state, his mother's soul would remain tethered to this world.

At first, Edith said nothing about his crying. Nor had she complained when Adolph organized a minyan that, for five mornings and nights, gathered in their living room to say Kaddish. Reuben didn't know how to recite the prayers for his mother and had to let the other men do this for him. He would have let the funeral director talk him into a satin-lined mahogany casket had Adolph not insisted on accompanying him to the funeral home.

"You don't know that a Jew has to be buried in a plain pine casket?" Adolph roared. "And you call yourself a funeral director?"

But Edith's patience was wearing thin. One Sunday when he was in bed, the covers drawn over his eyes to block out the light, she ripped them off. "It's time you stopped feeling sorry for yourself," she said, looming over him. Later that day, she said, "It wasn't as if your mother didn't already have one foot in the grave." Reuben was unsure what shocked him more—the callousness of the thought, or the offhanded way in which she voiced it.

Reuben had known that Jews sat "shiva" and could vaguely recall from his childhood—this was before his father's anti-Semitism grew so virulent—his relatives sitting around his parents' living room on wooden crates. He remembered the mirrors being draped in black crepe, probably because he'd seen his father's sister lift up a corner of one to check her appearance. What he hadn't known was why Jews did this until Adolph explained that, according to Jewish law, from the time of the funeral until the following Sabbath, a Jew was supposed to do nothing except think about the deceased. After that, he was meant to get on with his life. But that was easier said than done. What if a person was feeling guilty because he hadn't tried hard enough to save his mother? A man was supposed to spend just a few days thinking about that?

"Not today," Reuben said when Adolph called one Monday to see if he could stop by. Since those days sitting shiva, four weeks earlier, Adolph had been calling regularly to ask if he could visit. So far, Reuben had managed to put him off.

"I'll be there in twenty minutes." Adolph hung up before Reuben could protest.

Reuben stared down at the receiver, sticky with jam, the culprit surely Harriet, who, at eight, already got more phone calls than the rest of them combined. He felt overwhelmed by all that Adolph's coming over would entail—getting dressed, shaving, brushing his teeth. As he headed upstairs, he had to pause every few steps to catch his breath.

The bedroom was a mess, his half anyway, with clothing spilling from the drawers, half-empty glasses of water on the windowsill. The sheet on his side of the bed had come undone, and for days he had been sleeping on the bare mattress. Edith no longer picked up after him. She stepped over his things or kicked them out of her way. Recently, Edith had hired a woman to come in twice a week to clean the house. Reuben had to admit that this Lenore did a better job than Antoinette had, except if he didn't put his dirty things in the hamper, they didn't get washed. He was sure that Edith had instructed Lenore not to pick up after him.

Reuben pulled one shirt after another from his dresser before finding one that wasn't too badly wrinkled. He spotted a pants leg beneath his bed and hooked its cuff with his toe. Brown gabardine, they no longer buttoned. Few of his pants did. He had just pulled them over his pajama bottoms when he heard the doorbell. By the time Reuben made it downstairs, Adolph had let himself in.

"I haven't had a chance to put on the kettle," Reuben said.

"I'm early." Adolph slung an arm across Reuben's shoulders. He looked down at Reuben's feet at they headed toward the kitchen and Reuben realized he'd forgotten to put his slippers back on.

"Sit," Reuben said as he brought the kettle to the sink.

The table was littered with the remains of the children's breakfast, flabby corn flakes swimming in bluish milk, a half-eaten slice of toast, crumpled napkins. Adolph swept the crumbs off the table into his cupped hand and dropped them into a cereal bowl. He pulled a handkerchief from his pocket and wiped down the oilcloth. While they waited for the kettle to boil, the men sat in silence. Finally, the kettle let out a shrill whistle and Reuben jumped up. As he plopped Adolph's mug down, water sloshed over the side. He was about to mop it up with his sleeve when he noticed Adolph's startled expression and grabbed a tea towel instead.

Adolph dropped his used teabag into the cereal bowl. Reuben didn't bother to remove his tea bag before taking a sip. He was more of a coffee drinker himself, but Edith kept forgetting to pick up Nescafé on her way home. Adolph had yet to take a sip, and Reuben worried that the swipe of the dishrag he had applied to Adolph's mug hadn't been enough to remove the traces of Edith's lipstick.

"Do you have any honey?" Adolph asked.

Reuben pressed his palms into the table and got up stiffly, annoyed with Adolph for being so demanding. Thank God, Adolph had asked for honey, not sugar, Reuben thought, as there was always a scattering of ants, dead and alive, among the grains. Toward the back of the cupboard, he found a crud-encrusted jar of honey. He slammed it down on the table along with a teaspoon, a can opener, and a towel, for it would surely take some doing to get the jar open.

After working the jar open, Adolph stirred two teaspoons of honey into his tea and puffed at it before taking a sip. He stretched his legs out to the side of the table. "Edith at work?"

Reuben wondered if this was Adolph's way of making him feel bad about the fact that while he was lounging around, his wife was out earning a living.

"She got a promotion. She's in charge of the salesgirls now, all of them." Reuben tried to remember her job title but couldn't.

"A very capable lady, I'm sure." Adolph took another sip of tea. "The economy's looking up, they say. It's all the war talk."

"You don't think Roosevelt is going to drag us into it?"

Adolph gave Reuben a scornful look. "As if he'll have a choice? Anyway, my point is simply that things are looking up. If you're serious about looking for a job, now's the time."

Reuben felt himself grow tense. "What makes you think I haven't started? What business is it of yours, anyway?"

Adolph pushed his cup away. "No business. Except I'm worried about you."

"I'm fine." Reuben gathered the cups and cereal bowls. Instead of leaving them in the sink, he washed them so he could keep his back to Adolph.

Adolph spoke loudly enough to be heard over the running water. "In my business, I see it all the time. You're depressed. The best cure for depression is to keep busy. And the best way to keep busy is to get a job."

Reuben turned toward Adolph as he wiped the insides of the cups. "It's not that simple. I had my own business. What am I supposed to do, now, work in a factory?"

"Why not?"

"Because it's degrading." Reuben returned the cups and saucers to the cupboard and slammed the door.

"And this isn't?" Adolph said. "I made up my mind that I was going to be blunt, even if you ended up hating me. You've got to stop feeling sorry for yourself."

"I just lost my mother."

"Everybody loses their mother sooner or later."

"Not the way I did."

"Plenty lose their mothers in worse ways. Plenty of mothers die before their time. It isn't dignified, this self-pity. Think of the example you're setting for your son."

Reuben wiped the table down and then asked Adolph to lift his feet as he swept the floor.

Adolph spoke no further about Reuben's looking for work, prattling on instead about the weather and the new sign in front of the butcher shop. It was nearly eleven before Adolph stood and, with a stretch of the arms, announced that he better be getting back to work. By then, Reuben had realized the truth in what Adolph said and was no longer annoyed with him. At the front door, he squeezed Adolph's hand. "I know you're right," he said. "You're a good friend."

All day, Reuben felt optimistic in a way he hadn't for ages. He bathed and trimmed his nails. He gathered up his dirty laundry and deposited it by the washing machine. He made the bed so tightly that it would have passed an army inspection, and went through the refrigerator, throwing out the spoiled food.

For the first time in days, Reuben left the house, whistling off-key as he visited the grocer, the shoe repair shop, and the butcher, accomplishing more that afternoon than he normally did in a week. On the way home, he spotted a chocolate cake in the bakery window and decided to buy it for the kids. When he got home, he rinsed the chicken, scrubbed the potatoes, and peeled the carrots for dinner, though he decided to leave the actual cooking of them to Edith as he didn't want to put ideas in her head.

He startled the children by greeting them at the door when they returned from school. "Is something wrong?" Jeffrey cried, fingers flying to his mouth.

Reuben laughed, though he found Jeffrey's reaction more sad than funny. Harriet was studying his face, too, but with more curiosity than concern. "I'm just happy to see you," Reuben said. "Wait till you see what I got." He steered them to the kitchen, where he had set out two glasses of milk and the chocolate cake, still resting in its cardboard box. The children stared with wide eyes as if they had never seen such a cake before.

"Sit," Reuben said, pulling out the chair for Harriet. "I thought you loved chocolate."

"I do." Harriet jabbed a finger into the frosting and then licked it. She rolled her eyes. "It's the most delicious thing ever."

"Of course it's delicious," Reuben said. "It should be—" He caught himself as he was about to say, "It cost enough." He brought Edith's pronged silver cake knife down into the cake. "Is this big enough?" he asked Harriet.

She shook her head vigorously. "Are you kidding? I'm starving."

"Are you starving, too?" Reuben asked Jeffrey.

Jeffrey shrugged. "A bit."

Reuben was about to joke that there was no such thing as being a bit starving; you either were or weren't. But Jeffrey had that closed-in look he often had when he returned from school. After he cut Jeffrey nearly as big a slice as he had cut for Harriet, Jeffrey expelled a breath as if bracing for a challenge.

"You don't have to finish it," Reuben said. He watched as Jeffrey lowered his fork and brought a small piece of cake to his mouth.

"It's good," Jeffrey said.

It pained Reuben to realize that Jeffrey was only eating the cake to please him, and although he had been eyeing the cake all afternoon, he now found his appetite leeching away. Reuben cut himself a large piece anyway and attacked it with feigned gusto. "Is this good or what?" he asked, though the cake didn't taste nearly as nice as it looked. He could tell it had been made with cheap ingredients, lard or oleo, instead of butter, and the sponge was hard, as if the cake had been sitting in the bakery for days.

Jeffrey was making a mess with his fork, pretending to eat more than he was. Harriet devoured her piece, barely pausing between forkfuls. When she finished, she raised her eyebrows at Jeffrey, and he slid his plate toward her.

"Things are going to change around here," Reuben said. "I've been sad about Grandma. Other things, too. But I'm feeling better now. It's time this family started having some fun, don't you think?"

Harriet nodded vigorously, though as far as Reuben could tell, she had never stopped having fun. He grabbed her hand and then grabbed Jeffrey's. The difference in their grips was striking: Harriet's so firm, Jeffrey's so unresponsive. It was like he wasn't there.

When Reuben woke the following morning, he still felt good. Not quite as good as the day before—but good. Again, he straightened the house, did the shopping, and started the evening meal. He did the same on Wednesday and Thursday, though he could feel his energy flagging. By Friday, his determination to remake himself had evaporated. He realized he needed to figure out what he wanted out of life. Without knowing that, how could he hope to improve himself? It would be like sailing off to the New World without the benefit of a compass or map.

That morning, Reuben saw an article in *Newsday* about the Ku Klux Klan. Kimmel had been right about the Klan; they were becoming active on Long Island, although mainly in the grim neighborhoods of red brick, two family houses that straddled Queens and Nassau. Reuben found himself pondering the nature of hate. If the Negro was inferior to the white man, then why was the white man so frightened of him? The same question could be asked about the Jews.

Although he'd been living in Sea Forth for twenty years, Reuben had never ventured inside its shantytown. Like nearly every Negro in Sea Forth, Patsy, their cook, had lived there. Now, struck by a yearning to see its tin lean-tos and plywood shacks and their inhabitants in the same way others might long to visit a foreign country, he set out. It was one of those fall days when the air is so clear, the sun so high, the golds and reds and oranges so vivid that the trees look more like paper cutouts than living things. Because he no longer got much exercise, Reuben's breath came hard, and his heart struggled to keep up with this unexpected demand for blood and oxygen. But his mind had none of its usual fuzziness. He reckoned it had to be about three miles from his house to the shantytown. That would make it six miles Patsy had to walk, six days a week, not just on beautiful days like this, but throughout the winter. He pictured her in a thin, patched coat and worn shoes, hatless and gloveless, fighting a merciless wind.

Four years since he'd lost his business. It seemed like yesterday and yet a lifetime ago. Who was he? Once, he would have answered that he was a builder, husband, and father. He now understood that those were simply the roles he had played.

"You've got too much time to brood," Adolph had told him. "Everywhere you look, there's real suffering. Be thankful for what you have."

Reuben wanted to be thankful, but it was hard when he felt as if his life was worth little more than the sum of his humiliations. A failed businessman supported by a resentful wife, a father who had his children's pity and perhaps their love, but certainly not their respect. Was that all he was now? The question tugged at him as he veered off Main Street, past the pastel-colored bungalows, some of which he had built, that eventually sputtered out into farmhouses with peeling paint and sagging porches. He continued past the fields surrounding these farmhouses, some covered with tarpaulins for the winter, others a tangle of tall grass, until, finally, beneath a blanket of hazy blue smoke, the shantytown came into view.

The narrowness of its roads surprised Reuben—roads in places hardly wider than a man's arm span, certainly not wide enough to accommodate motorcars. The roads led right up to the shacks. Plastic sheets instead of doors protected the entrances to many of these shacks. The windows were often covered with cardboard or tarpaper instead of glass. Though it was a weekday, there were children everywhere, some dressed in little more than his children would have worn on a summer's day and many barefoot. The smoke was coming from a bonfire raging perilously close by. The fumes and ash, flying through the air like confetti, made Reuben's throat burn and eyes tear.

Reuben walked slowly, strangely not afraid. He tipped his hat to a blue-lipped, toothless old woman in a faded housedress and to a girl, no more than fifteen, with a swollen stomach and a toddler straddling her hip. He paused to watch a chess game between two gray-bearded men perched on crates, an egg timer beside their board. A boy on a tire swing dug his toe into the dirt to stop himself as Reuben passed by, and housewives, half-hidden in their doorways, followed him with their eyes. He attracted attention like a bird that, while not exotic, had wandered off its migratory path.

After he had walked a block or so, Reuben came upon a smattering of shops. There was a grocer with bushels of bruised and desiccated fruits and vegetables outside his entrance and a bakery, out of which wafted the aroma of freshly baked bread. Also, a butcher shop where fat black flies feasted on the pig knuckles and chicken feet and more familiar cuts of meat in the display window. Toward the end of the road was a Baptist church, yellow brick and fairly new. A sign with gold letters announcing the times for services was staked into the grassy patch out front.

Reuben headed up the footpath leading to the church doors, which were open. He'd heard about the way colored people worshipped, how they screamed and dropped to the floor where they thrashed about like they were having fits. A primitive people, who, even after accepting Christianity, were unable to put the jungle behind them.

The honey-colored light filtering through the church's small windows provided just enough illumination to see the rows of wooden benches and the gray-tiled floor, still shiny from a recent mopping. The walls were whitewashed, unadorned except for the large wooden Christ that hung from a cross behind the altar. Off to the side sat a battered upright piano. There were no stained glass windows, no vaulted ceiling, no gilded paintings of saints. Yet, the church struck Reuben as a place of peace and refuge.

Reuben thought of his father whose insistent atheism had been a religion unto itself. As soon as Reuben was old enough to understand, his father had begun preaching. How most of what was wrong with the world was due to religion, how it was man who'd created God and not the other way around. His father's face would contort with disgust at the sight of the Chasid who attended schul in the green clapboard house around the corner from their apartment building, for no displays of piety infuriated him more than those of the Jewish people. His father had likened his own father, who had been a rabbi, to a snake oil salesman and had called his mother, the rebbetzin, a simpleminded fool.

A stringy old woman emerged from the church's shadows, carrying a rag mop and a bucket. She was light for a Negro, more yellow than brown, with a scattering of freckles across her nose and cheeks. "What you want here?" she demanded, then dunked the mop into the bucket and gave the floor a determined swipe.

"Just looking around," Reuben said with his friendliest smile. As he stepped across the church threshold, the woman took a step backward. She clutched the mop in front of her as if afraid she might have to use it as a weapon. Reuben started up the center aisle, though he knew he was frightening her and was soiling her freshly mopped floor.

"This a Baptist church, colored."

"I'll only be a minute," Reuben said as he stopped by the altar and gazed beyond it to the doleful Christ. For a short, foolish moment, he wondered whether he was finally on the verge of finding something to believe in—and in, of all places, a colored

Baptist church. Then he realized that he was mistaking the feeling of calm acceptance churches were meant to inspire for something more profound.

Reuben wanted to pray, but nothing came to mind except to ask that his children remain healthy and that he find work. But these supplications struck him as too one-sided a way for a person to acquaint himself with God. Still, he longed to believe in something. He longed for reassurance that there was some design behind all he had gone through. He understood Adolph's point, for he just had to look around this shantytown to see real suffering. But he couldn't shake the feeling that if he could only find something to believe in, he would discover the answer to who he was.

"You've got a lovely place," he said to the woman. He brought his fingers to his hat.

"This is Baptist, colored." The woman gave him one last bewildered look before closing the door.

# Chapter Seventeen

## January and March 1939

When the Rexall's first opened, Adolph hadn't been worried. "My customers trust me," he told Reuben. But gradually, his customers deserted him. Not only did the Rexall's have wide aisles and uncluttered shelves, a cheerful, confetti-speckled linoleum floor, and candy cane-striped wallpaper, there was a sparkling, stainless steel luncheon counter manned by a six-foot-tall Negro, improbably named Bitsy.

As Bitsy's reputation spread for making the juiciest hamburgers and thickest malteds in town, the luncheon counter became a gathering place for Sea Forth's mothers. There was room to park their baby carriages, and the children loved the way the stools spun and, especially, the cookies Bitsy freely dispensed. It took longer for these mothers to warm to the pharmacist, who had a port wine stain covering half his face that made him hard to look at. Word, however, began to get around about what a sympathetic listener he was and how, unlike Adolph, he never made his customers feel stupid. He also made deliveries, a lifesaver when there was a sick child at home.

When Reuben stopped by Adolph's store, Adolph blamed the drop-off in traffic in his store on anti-Semitism. "Of course they'd rather do business with their own kind."

Reuben kept his opinion to himself that this was unlikely to be the reason. Adolph's store had grown shabby. The faded blue walls hadn't been painted for ages, the floor tiles were marred and curling up at the edges, and the dust-covered merchandise looked as if it had been sitting on the shelves forever. Then, there was Adolph who could be opinionated to the point of arrogance and so stern that his customers were often afraid to ask him questions.

Reuben and Adolph had been chatting for a while before Adolph had a customer, a clownishly made-up woman with an untamed mane of gray hair, wearing a spangled red shawl.

"We shouldn't be long," Adolph told Reuben, directing him to a stool by the door. Then Adolph stunned Reuben by kissing the woman's cheek. As they talked, they kept their heads close. Reuben saw Adolph retrieve some vials from behind the counter and drop them into the woman's purse.

Finally, the cash register pinged. Adolph escorted the woman to the door.

"What was that all about?" Reuben asked.

Adolph flipped the sign on the door from "Open" to "Closed." Then, he said, "Come," as he led Reuben to a windowless room behind his stockroom. "My laboratory."

Reuben knew nothing about how medicines were compounded. Even so, he could tell this was no ordinary laboratory. The shelves above the paint-flecked workbench were crammed with roots, leaves, herbs, berries, mushrooms, seeds, barks, and twigs. Hand-printed labels identifying their contents were pasted along the shelf edges.

"My new sideline," Adolph said, "herbal medicine."

Reuben lifted a book entitled *Healing Secrets from the East* from a pile stacked against the wall and flipped through the pages.

"Any idea what that is?" Adolph asked.

"Haven't a clue." Reuben replaced the book.

"An approach to medicine that relies on the use of natural versus synthetic substances." Adolph picked up a fluid-filled vial and shook it, dispersing the sediment that had formed at its bottom. "Take this. It's just pulverized capsicum combined with a common Chinese herb called corydalis. An ancient remedy for trigeminal neuralgia, it's ten times more effective than the analgesics the drug companies push.

"Tri-what?"

"Trigeminal neuralgia? A fancy word for facial pain."

Adolph picked up another vial.

"Black cohash. It's also an herb and the best remedy there is for hot flashes. The shame of it is how many ladies suffer in silence, too shy about such matters to ask for help."

Reuben was too taken aback to respond.

"I'll let you in on a secret. Most of what the drug companies sell is garbage. You're better off flushing your money down the toilet." Adolph placed the vial in a compartmentalized tray. "Think about it! Why would a doctor want a patient to get better? If the patient doesn't get better, it means another office visit and more money in his pocket. More money for the drug companies, too, who pay off the doctors to push their crap. It's some racket they have."

"As long as you know what you're doing."

"I do. I've pushed the synthetic crap long enough to see that it causes more harm than good. Besides, what choice do I have? My regular customers have deserted me. The ones I still have, if they aren't half-dead, they're nuts."

When Adolph and Reuben returned to the apothecary, there was an elderly man leaning against two canes waiting at the door, his shopping bag slung around his neck.

"Just a minute," Adolph called. He placed a tray of his potions inside a drawer. "Can't be too careful," he told Reuben. "A fellow in Cleveland wound up in jail. Would you believe they charged him with manslaughter? Those drug companies don't just have the doctors on their payrolls, they've got the cops and judges, too."

After filling the man's order—for Milk of Magnesia, suppositories, and sanitary napkins, which Adolph informed Reuben were probably for the man himself—Adolph said, "I'm beginning to think that when people get that old, they should be shot or gassed. You have heard of euthanasia? I hear it's become quite the thing in Germany."

"Adolph, that's horrible."

"Really? Do you think that man is happy living that way? We put cats and dogs to sleep. It's considered the humane thing to do. Why should it be different for people?"

Reuben didn't know how to answer, except to say that it was different. He might have thought Adolph was putting him on were Adolph's expression not so grim. "What's really bothering you?"

Adolph shrugged. "Fifteen years I spent building this business. For what? So I can end up no better off than when I started? To tell the truth, I'm scared."

Reuben placed his arm around Adolph's shoulder. "I know how you feel. But don't make the mistake I did, and run and hide. Take your own advice. Meet whatever it is face on."

Jenny left the house not to Edith and Reuben, just Reuben. She also left him several thousand in government bonds, thankfully kept in a safe deposit box that she had opened at Marcus' bank weeks before she died, as if she'd had a premonition she was about to go. She'd placed her jewelry there, too, a meager collection that included her wedding band, which she'd worn until her knuckles became too distorted; a pair of gold earrings; a strand of pearls; and a brooch shaped like a peacock, with enameled feathers, that Reuben had admired as a child. These she left to Harriet.

The inheritance amounted to more than Reuben had expected. Between the bonds and his remaining savings, which together added up to nearly $8,000, he would be able to feed and clothe the kids for a couple of years, even without Edith's help. On top of that, he still owned the bungalow where his mother lived, and now the house. He wasn't poor, even if he felt that way and he didn't really need to get a job. Except that he did, and it no longer mattered what kind of job it was.

The bonds were bearer bonds. Anyone could cash them. A thief. Edith. Reuben supposed he could keep them locked in the desk drawer where he hid his bank statements and other private papers. He didn't think Edith knew where he hid the key—behind the bathtub hot water pipe. The drawer never looked as if it had been tampered with. But with a woman as clever as Edith, how could he be sure? She might have made a copy of the key and be biding her time until she found something worth stealing. "Things between us must really be bad for me to think her capable of such a thing," Reuben told himself as he looked out from his desk over Main Street. Edith could be self-centered and was remarkably lacking in maternal feeling, but she was not a thief. He was sure he no longer loved her, indeed, was mystified by how he could have fallen in love with her in the first place. He thought it a pity that they had to stay married. With his luck, she would probably live to be eighty, which would mean forty more years together, unless he went first, which undoubtedly he would.

The cold, bleak January day reminded him of a similarly nasty day four years earlier when he had also sat there, drawing up a list of his former friends. That had been his only real attempt to look for work, and even then, he had called it quits before reaching the end of his list. Back then, his pessimism had been warranted. Unless he was willing to dig ditches, his chances of finding a job had been slim. But Adolph was right. The looming war in Europe was affecting the economy. While he hadn't combed the "Help Wanted" pages in years, he had noticed that they'd grown thicker. There were even a few "Help Wanted" signs in the storefronts along Main Street.

Reuben sat there a long while, trying to decide what to do with the bonds. Though he'd told Edith about the house and jewelry, he said nothing about the bonds. So, if she did have a key and happened to see them in the drawer, she might well be tempted to steal them, if for no other reason than to put him in the awkward position of having to accuse her of taking something that wasn't supposed to exist in the first place.

Another option was to place them in a bank. His faith in banks had been thoroughly shaken, but he reckoned a safe deposit box would be okay. The problem was that Sea Forth only had one bank now, Marcus'. To travel all the way to Babylon or Patchogue just to open a safe deposit box seemed absurd. Besides, if anyone had something to be ashamed about, it was Marcus, not he. Of course, if Marcus hadn't been so dogged about divorcing his emotions from his actions, Sea Forth might well have been left with no banks at all. When *Newsday* reported that the president of the bank would be retiring this year, it pegged Marcus as his probable successor. But just because Marcus only did what he had to, that didn't mean Reuben would be able to forgive him.

The safe deposit room was at the rear of the bank, guarded by the humpbacked woman with a hairy mole on her cheek, who had been there forever. Reuben chose the smallest size box. As he stacked the bonds inside the rectangular slot, he noticed that they had all been bought on his birthdays. They represented fifteen years during which his mother had put aside fifty cents here, a dollar there, probably without his father's knowing. She never stopped buying them, even during those years when he was making money faster than Edith could spend it. He wondered if his mother had a premonition that his success had come too easily, and it was only a matter of time before things righted themselves.

If only he hadn't stopped to count the bonds, Reuben might have avoided bumping into Marcus and Paul Herbert.

"Reuben!" both men said, their shocked expressions quickly replaced by grins.

Paul pumped Reuben's hand. "Sport, where have you been hiding yourself?"

"I've been wondering the same thing," Marcus said.

Both men's faces were flushed and their eyes glassy. It was clear they had just been to lunch and that it had been an alcoholic one. Both were heavier than when Reuben last saw them, their fleshy necks spilling over their starched white collars, just visible beneath their stylish, double- breasted topcoats. All traces of the cadaverous haunted look had been erased from Marcus' face. Indeed, as he stepped forward to shake Reuben's hand, he radiated the sort of self-satisfied prosperity one would expect to find in a future bank president.

"Your ears must have been ringing," Paul said.

"Not twenty minutes ago, your name came up," Marcus said.

"Good seeing you both," Reuben said. He put on his cap, shabby and frayed like the rest of his clothing—his old construction uniform of dungarees, flannel shirt, and boots. As he began moving past them, Paul clasped his shoulder.

"Spare a minute?" Paul asked.

"There's something we've been meaning to talk to you about," Marcus said.

Reuben found himself being propelled toward the conference room. It had been refurbished since Reuben had last been there. The refinished walnut table gleamed, and the chair cushions had been re-upholstered in navy plush. The drapes, too, were made of navy plush and were trimmed with gold braiding. Above the door hung a stuffed and shellacked marlin affixed to a wooden placard inscribed with its weight, the date it had been caught, and by whom—Marcus.

"A tragedy about your mother," Paul said once they were seated.

Reuben recalled hearing some while back that Paul's wife was ill. He could not remember with what, only that it was serious. He supposed he should ask after Gladys, except he was afraid to, in case she had died.

"Is it true they never found the body?" Marcus asked.

"It washed on shore a few days later. It was the maid's they didn't find."

"At least you have that to be thankful for," Paul said, his tone making clear that as far as he was concerned he had done his duty in asking after Jenny. He rested his hands on the table. "A catastrophe of this magnitude comes along maybe once every hundred years. Though when I do redevelop the land, you can be damned sure I'm going to erect a sea wall."

Reuben followed Paul's eyes down to his own hands. They were rough, like a laborer's, the nails ragged and not quite clean. He recalled how when he was a builder and had an excuse for hands that looked like these, he would scrub them nightly with Lava Soap, after which he would rub away his calluses with a pumice stone and file down his nails with an emery board.

"That'll cost a fortune," Reuben said.

"Not compared to what we'd lose if we got another hurricane like that one."

"You said yourself that a catastrophe like this occurs once every hundred years." Reuben wondered why he was allowing himself to be drawn into this discussion when all he wanted was to hear what these men had to say and leave.

"What if I'm wrong?" Paul said. "Anyway, what Marcus and I want to speak with you about are the plans for your land."

"Paul's assembled a group of investors. We intend to put up a combination hotel and restaurant," Marcus said, clearly thrilled to be able to refer to Paul and himself as "we." They were, of course, referring to the land where Jenny's house had stood. Reuben had long suspected that Paul's real interest resided not in the bungalows but in the land beneath them, and that, when the time was right, he intended to raze them. How considerate of the hurricane, Reuben thought, to spare him the unpleasantness of having to evict his tenants and the expense associated with demolishing the structures.

"A place like that should be a goldmine," Reuben said. "With the economy looking up and Fire Island growing so popular, how can you lose?"

"That's how I see it." While Paul had shifted sideways and crossed his legs, there was a stiffness to his bearing that betrayed how important this discussion was to him.

"I suppose you're planning to build around my land," Reuben said.

"If we have to," Marcus said.

"What if I decide to put up another bungalow? A patch of grass is one thing, but if you have to build around a bungalow, it's going to look awfully funny."

Paul's eyes met Marcus'. "Why would you want to do that?" Paul asked.

"For the same reason you want to build down there. To make money. These days, I bet I could get four thousand for a bungalow that'd cost me, say, one thousand to build."

"Probably," Paul conceded.

"More important, it would give me a way back into the business. That's worth a great deal to me as I'm sure you, Marcus, can understand." Reuben stood, and grabbed his coat off the back of his chair. "After all these years—to have that opportunity. I'm afraid it would take a lot more than you could justify paying for such a small parcel of land to induce me to sell. Good day, gentlemen." His coat slung over his arm, Reuben let himself out.

After this meeting, Reuben felt elated. The truth was he had been too busy grieving for his mother to give much thought about what to do with the land. He was sure of one thing: he didn't have the heart to get back into the construction business. Another was that the discussion about the sale of his land was far from closed.

When more than a week passed and Reuben heard nothing from Paul and Marcus, his elation turned into despair. He was certain that if he hadn't waltzed off that way, he could have struck a deal that day. Perhaps Paul, who wouldn't be able to abide the thought of being bested, had decided the hell with him, in which case Paul would surely find a way to make his life miserable.

Reuben was trying to work up the courage to call them when Paul showed up on his doorstep.

It was a frigid day. As Paul stepped inside the foyer, he let out a long "brrrr." He unwound a plaid scarf from around his neck and handed it to Reuben as if Reuben were a servant. "How about some coffee?" he asked as he headed, uninvited, into the living room.

"It'll have to be tea," Reuben said. The only coffee they had was Postum, and he would be too embarrassed to serve that to Paul.

"Tea's fine. With lemon, please."

As Reuben waited for the kettle to boil, he thought of how Paul took it for granted that there would be lemons in the house. But there were no lemons and hadn't been for years, nor any grapefruit or oranges—fruits they had come to regard as luxuries.

When Reuben returned with the tea in two of their nicest china cups, and the milk and sugar, Paul was seated in Jenny's stiff-backed armchair. He had moved the side table so it was in front of him and covered it with papers. Paul cradled the cup, allowing the steam to warm his reddened face. "Every winter, I ask myself why I'm still living here. Then spring comes and I get my answer."

Reuben sat down on the couch, breathless with nerves. He held his teacup tightly, afraid he might spill it.

"Don't think I've been here before. It's not that bad," Paul said. "Where's Edith?"

"At work."

Paul snapped his fingers. "At that store on Corona, the Emporium, right? I'm amazed that fellow—I forget his name—is still in business."

"Adler."

"Looks a bit like W. C. Fields, except smaller, doesn't he? And Edith, don't tell me she likes being a salesgirl?"

"She's in charge of all the salesgirls."

Paul raised his eyebrows. "I always knew she was more than just a pretty face. What have you been up to?"

Paul's ploy, Reuben realized, was to erode his confidence by peppering him with questions that, on the surface, seemed innocuous but were intended as insults. "I'm sure you didn't stop by to chat."

Paul tucked his chin in as if hurt by Reuben's accusation. He donned a pair of half-moon spectacles and picked the papers up. "I hate playing games, and I do want to get going with this project. So, my partners and I have decided to make one offer and one offer only." He shook his head, as if barely able to contain his disgust at being forced to pay more for the land than it was worth. "We're prepared to offer ten thousand for your property."

Ten thousand dollars—it was more than Reuben had made in 1927, his best year.

"Take it or leave it," Paul said. "We won't be back."

Reuben walked over to Jenny's harp, tucked away in the corner for so many years that he had nearly forgotten it was there. He ran his hand along its velvet cover. Had it not been for his mother, he would have sold the land years ago for a tenth of what he would be getting now. It was another thing he had her to be grateful for.

"I suppose that's close enough to what I had in mind," Reuben said. As soon as he received the money, he'd invest it. Maybe even in the stock market, which, with war looming, had nowhere to go but up. He would not tell Edith about the sale of the land. Let her find out once the inn goes up.

One morning in March, Edith had barely settled behind her desk when Reuben called. "Something's wrong with Jeffrey." He refused to elaborate. "Come home."

Edith had lost count of the times Reuben had summoned her home, making it sound as if one of the children were dying, and the problem turned out to be no more serious than the sniffles. She probably would have remained at work had Mr. Adler not walked into her office then.

"Jeffrey's sick," she blurted, instantly regretting it.

Mr. Adler grabbed her coat off the door hook and tossed it to her. "Whaddaya waiting for! Nothing's so important here that it can't wait."

Edith stormed up Main Street. Nothing's so important! That was easy for Mr. Adler to say. He didn't have the first clue about what needed to get done. She began to run through her to-do list—interview for a new salesgirl, lay out the ad for the Easter sale. She was so preoccupied that she didn't notice Paul until she nearly crashed into him.

"Mrs. Merkal! What a surprise."

"Mr. Herbert." Edith extended her hand. Years ago, they would have called each other "Paul" and "Edith" and kissed on the cheek. His handshake, however, was warm. Then, Edith remembered. When she'd heard of Gladys' death last August, she'd gone out and bought a condolence card. She'd spent a long time composing her note. As painful as she found addressing the envelope to Mr. Paul Herbert, 20 Mowbray Street, she'd managed. What she'd been unable to do was bring herself to actually mail the card. "I never got to tell you—" she began.

Paul held up his hand. "She was very fond of you."

"And I of her." Edith felt a twinge of guilt, recalling the malicious pleasure she'd derived out of seeing Gladys that last time. "It must be hard without her."

Paul nodded solemnly. "It certainly leaves a void."

Edith was reminded of their son, who was Jeffrey's age and now motherless. "How is Lawrence?"

"As well as can be expected. I put him in boarding school. Figured he could do with a change of environment. But he does miss her."

Edith nodded. "They think they're so grown up. What they don't realize is how much they still need their mothers."

"And your son?" Paul paused. Edith could tell he was trying to recall Jeffrey's name. "They used to be such good mates." He smiled ruefully as if regretting how such a great friendship could have lapsed. As far as Edith could recall, the boys never had anything to do with each other.

Paul had aged, but Edith felt it made him even more attractive. Laugh lines fanned out from his eyes, and the furrows along his mouth had tamped down some of its arrogance. He looked more vulnerable. Perhaps, despite his philandering, he'd loved Gladys after all.

"Jeffrey's fine. Well, not at the moment. He seems to have come down with something. That's why I'm headed home."

"I hear you've become quite a big shot at that store."

"Until Gladys stopped by last year, I had no idea she was even sick."

"It wasn't Gladys who told me. It was Reuben. He must be very proud of you."

Edith smiled uncertainly. She couldn't imagine why Reuben would have been talking with Paul. With the exception of Marcus, there was no one he loathed more.

Jeffrey was asleep on the couch, his hands pressed together beneath his cheek. Edith touched her hand to his forehead. "He doesn't feel hot."

"I don't think he's sick."

"Then why did you call?"

Reuben shook his head. "He was acting strangely. When I told him we were out of juice, he started to cry."

"Because we're out of juice?"

"I don't think he knew why he was crying. Went on for nearly an hour. Eventually, he just collapsed."

Edith bent over and peered at Jeffrey's face. While he had her pale skin and wavy hair, he looked nothing like her. His face was long and narrow, his cheekbones prominent and lips full. Nor did he look like Reuben. It was odd about their children, how neither took after either of them. But while Harriet was a miniature Jenny, it was as if Jeffrey had come from another world.

"A nervous breakdown," Reuben said. "I'm not exactly sure what it means, but do you think he might be having one?"

"What in the world does Jeffrey have to be nervous about? Get up!" Edith shook Jeffrey's shoulder. "Didn't he say he had a history test today?"

"He wasn't putting it on."

Jeffrey opened his eyes. When he noticed Edith's expression, he buried his face in the sofa back.

"It's the history test, isn't it?"

Jeffrey made no response.

"Jeffrey?" Edith modulated her tone so she wouldn't sound so threatening. "Jeffrey, I'm speaking to you."

"Leave me alone." Jeffrey buried his face deeper into the cushions.

"If you won't tell us what's wrong, we'll have to assume it's nothing." Despite his height, close to six feet, Jeffrey was so delicate that it took Edith just one yank to spin him around. "Now get up, get dressed, and get yourself to school."

He stumbled up from the couch, his hands shielding his face, as if afraid Edith might smack him, though she could count on one hand the times that she had, the last being years ago.

Edith pressed her palm between Jeffrey's shoulder blades and pushed him toward the stairs. "And hurry."

"Edith," Reuben said.

She spun around. "What!"

"It wasn't the test."

"I'm warning you," Edith called after Jeffrey as he bounded up the stairs. She turned to Reuben and said, "Of course it's the test—that and hormones. You know what they say about teenagers."

"I wish Edith had been there to see it," Reuben told Adolph. He had asked Adolph to meet him at the Argosy Luncheonette.

While Reuben and Adolph discussed all sorts of subjects, one subject they had always avoided was their sons. He felt uneasy talking to Adolph about Jeffrey. As worried as he was, at least Jeffrey was healthy. Reuben still was unsure what was wrong with Ernest, except that it had to do with his heart. He wished he had thought to ask Adolph years ago. Now, it was too late.

"Sounds like Jeffrey could use a friend," Adolph said. With surgical precision, he removed the last traces of membrane from his half grapefruit.

"I think there's more to it than that," Reuben said. "Anyway, friends can't be manufactured." As he bit into his ham and cheese sandwich, he saw Adolph grimace. What was Adolph objecting to? The ham? The combination of meat and dairy? Or was his reaction involuntary, merely an unconscious manifestation of his nutritional fastidiousness?

"I'd been thinking myself that Ernest could use someone besides his old father to talk with. Why doesn't Jeffrey stop by for a game of chess?"

Reuben suppressed a sigh, annoyed at himself for not anticipating this possibility. Certainly, Jeffrey could use a friend, but the sort he needed was cheerful and upbeat, not some invalid who'd be bound to drag his spirits down further. "I don't think Jeffrey knows how to play," Reuben said. He never tried to teach Jeffrey, who'd always struck him as too fidgety for so cerebral a game.

"Ernest will show him. It's a wonderful game."

"So I hear," Reuben said. He found it less embarrassing to pretend not to know how to play than to admit that he did but had never taught his son.

"Come to dinner on Friday night. We'll light the Shabbat candles. I'll teach you the bruchas. Now that it's just Ernest and me, I tend to be a bit lax about Shabbat myself. That is, if Edith doesn't mind."

"When I explain, I'm sure she'll be okay," Reuben said. It was hardly Adolph's business that his wife couldn't care less what he did.

Adolph welcomed Reuben and Jeffrey inside with a sweep of the arm. He was dressed in an old-fashioned suit that bagged at the knees and smelled of camphor. Ernest was at a bridge table, arranging elaborately carved ivory chess pieces on a board.

"Ernest is looking forward to teaching Jeffrey to play, isn't that so?" Adolph said loudly. He waited for Ernest to respond, but when Ernest said nothing, he clapped his hands and said, "If you'll excuse me," and headed off to the kitchen.

"I hate games," Jeffrey hissed, elbowing Reuben in the ribs. It was the first time Jeffrey had spoken since back at the house when, at the last minute, Jeffrey told him he'd changed his mind about coming. To get him to go, Reuben had to chase after him, swinging his belt. He was angry enough that if Jeffrey hadn't relented, he might actually have used it.

"Something smells good," Reuben called out. In truth, the apartment was suspiciously devoid of the smells he'd been expecting: of brisket, chicken soup, the sorts of smells he recalled from his childhood, before his father put a stop to the visits to his grandparents' house. He gave Jeffrey a nudge toward Ernest, who had yet to acknowledge them.

Adolph returned, donning a frilly yellow apron. He pulled four white satin skullcaps from the china cupboard. "Yarmulkes – in English, skullcaps," he explained to Jeffrey. "Jews wear them inside as a sign of respect for God." He placed his own on his head with an exaggerated slap.

"Put it on," Reuben whispered. When Jeffrey did nothing, he snatched his yarmulke away, placing his and Jeffrey's on their heads simultaneously.

Adolph returned to the kitchen, where Reuben could hear him whistling, "I've Been Working on the Railroad." Jeffrey and Ernest still hadn't said two words to each other, although Jeffrey was inching closer to the table. When Jeffrey was alongside it, Ernest looked up. "Have you played before?"

"A long time ago," Jeffrey said. Reuben wondered whether he was lying.

Ernest motioned for Jeffrey to sit. "Each player gets sixteen pieces. These pieces are the pawns, the foot soldiers. They can only move forward one step, except on the first move. The ones in the corners are the castles. They can move horizontally and vertically any number of squares. These here are the knights. They move like this. And these tall pieces, the bishops, can move diagonally. These two in the center are the queen and the king. The object is to capture the other player's king, so it's the most important piece, but in a way, it's the queen who really is. The king can only move one square. She's the only one who can move any number of squares in every direction."

"Is that all there is to it?" Jeffrey asked.

Ernest puffed. "Is that all? Wait and see."

Adolph had opened up the drop leaf table in the hallway between the living room and the kitchen. The hallway was so narrow that the boys had to sit with their chair backs against the walls. The table was set with a white linen cloth with lace edging, bone china rimmed in gold leaf, and ruby-colored crystal goblets. In the center of the table were two well-polished silver candlesticks with long white tapers and a challah, hidden beneath a blue velvet cloth embroidered with Hebrew letters.

"It's really the woman of the house who's supposed to light the candles, but given there are no women..." Adolph said. He picked up a well-used, black leather prayer book and handed it to Jeffrey. For a moment, Reuben was afraid that he was about to ask Jeffrey to recite the prayers. "After I recite the blessings, perhaps Jeffrey will be kind enough to read us the English translations. You'll find them on page forty. Jeffrey, no not that way. A Hebrew book goes from right to left."

The meal bore no resemblance to the sort of meal Reuben had been expecting. There were roast beets, lima beans, sautéed mushrooms with onions, mashed turnips, and brussel sprouts in a mustard sauce—a multitude of dishes, all beautifully prepared and garnished, a rainbow of color against the gleaming silver bowls. But the most important part of the meal, the part without which no meal could be complete, was missing. Reuben inhaled, vainly trying to pick up the scent of broiled chicken or a roast. He shifted his eyes in an exaggerated way toward the kitchen, hoping to prod Adolph into realizing what he'd forgotten. When the bowls of vegetables were passed around, he was careful to leave space on his plate so that when Adolph did remember, there would be room for his meat.

"Oh, my," Adolph said when he spotted this hopeful expanse. "I thought you knew. Ernest and I are vegetarians. Ernest has never even tasted animal flesh."

Jeffrey's mouth dropped open.

"At first, I gave it up for health reasons," Adolph continued. "Nothing is more taxing on the cardiovascular system and clogging to the bowels than meat. Not to mention that it's so rife with bacteria, you might as well ingest strychnine. It was only later that an even more compelling reason for not eating meat came to me—the immorality of slaughtering another living creature, except in self-defense."

Reuben decided it was better not to remind Adolph of his recent endorsement of euthanasia. He also decided to keep to himself his opinion that this eccentric diet might have something to do with Ernest's enfeebled state. "I hope you don't plan on talking me into giving up meat. I have few enough pleasures as it is." Though Reuben rarely ate vegetables—and then only because a person was supposed to—he had to admit these vegetables were worlds apart from the flabby, overcooked ones he was used to.

Jeffrey stared down miserably at his food. With the back of his fork, he began squishing his lima beans against the plate.

"Eat," Reuben told him.

Jeffrey glared back.

"I said, eat!"

"Leave the boy alone," Adolph said. "Even a child should be allowed to choose what he eats."

"Like I am, right?" Ernest mumbled and began squishing his own lima beans into his plate. He caught Jeffrey's eye, and they both smirked.

"Can I have some water?" Jeffrey asked.

"In this house, we don't drink with our meals," Adolph said. "Drinking causes food to pass too quickly through your digestive tract, squandering important nutrients."

Reuben wondered what was the point, then, of the ruby goblets?

Ernest rolled his eyes and nodded to Jeffrey. "It's a proven fact."

"What did you say?" Adolph asked.

"Never mind." Ernest began pushing his vegetables around his plate. He had eaten even less than Jeffrey.

The table lapsed into silence. Without water, Reuben was unable to eat much. His mouth felt as dry as cotton and his gullet constricted, as if what food he had eaten lay plastered to its walls. Only Adolph was enjoying the meal. While the three of them watched, he cut his vegetables into tiny pieces and chewed each mouthful for what seemed an inordinate amount of time. When Adolph finally told the boys they were excused, Reuben was as relieved as they were.

"Want to see my stamp collection?" Ernest asked. He pulled a blue album off the side table and motioned for Jeffrey to sit beside him on the couch. The album was so large that when Ernest opened it, one half lay in his lap, the other in Jeffrey's. "My grandfather started it. Some of the stamps are more than one hundred years old."

Jeffrey whistled. "I've always wanted to start a stamp collection."

This was news to Reuben.

"Why haven't you?" Ernest asked.

Jeffrey shrugged. "Just lazy, I guess."

Seeing them side by side, Reuben was startled by how much they resembled each other. Like Jeffrey, Ernest was tall and skinny. His lips were thinner and his chin was strong, whereas Jeffrey's receded a bit, but like Jeffrey, he had prominent cheekbones, deep-set dark eyes, and a high forehead.

"Who's this?" Jeffrey asked.

"That was Archduke Ferdinand. From Serbia. It was issued just weeks before he was assassinated."

"Assassinated?"

"Haven't you heard the expression 'the shot heard round the world'? His assassination was what started the Great War."

Jeffrey nodded, transfixed. "I never knew what it meant."

"Of course, that didn't really cause the war; it was just the catalyst." Then Ernest asked, "What are your hobbies?" He was flipping through the pages more rapidly now. "Do you play sports? Board games?"

Jeffrey brightened. "I read a lot. Right now, I'm reading James Fenimore Cooper's *The Deerslayer*."

This, too, was news to Reuben.

"Have you gotten to the part where Natty Bumppo—"

"I thought you didn't go to school."

"That doesn't mean I'm an ignoramus!"

Reuben offered to clear the table.

"I'd order you to join the boys," Adolph said, "but I need to speak with you."

Adolph's kitchen was more like a closet than a room, with the miniature fittings typical of a residency hotel. He motioned for Reuben to sit on the stepladder. Then he filled the kettle, placing it on the two-burner stove. "You're a businessman, tell me what you think." Reuben silently thanked Adolph for not using the past tense. "As if I don't have enough problems with that Rexall's, it seems like whenever I look out my store window, I see Paul Herbert. The other day, he came in. Bought a few things, also asked a lot of questions. The way he tried to make it sound as if he were just being friendly got me so riled that I decided to call his bluff. Told him that I knew he was trying to buy the building."

"What did he say?"

"Nothing. He smiled." Adolph poured the boiling water into the sink, stepping back as the steam rose. "I swear he's scheming to buy up the whole town."

Reuben hadn't told Adolph about the sale of his land. He did this not out of secretiveness, but because he was embarrassed about having allowed greed to get in the way of his principles. "You've got a lease?"

"It's got six more months. I suppose he can do what he wants once he gets the building."

"All he'll have to do is ride out the leases."

"Do you think he might just want the building as an investment?"

"I'd be lying if I said yes," Reuben said. "That man finds it impossible to leave anything the way it is."

When they returned to the living room, Ernest and Jeffrey had put aside the stamp album and were hunched over the chess set.

"Getting on like a house on fire," Adolph said.

Reuben couldn't help laughing at Adolph's clumsy American slang. "Speak to the landlord. At least find out where you stand."

Adolph brought a finger to his lips. "I don't want the boy to start worrying."

# Chapter Eighteen

## *March through July 1939*

Edith knocked on Fred's door. "For you," she said, handing him the Emporium's spring catalog, their first catalog ever. The catalog was her idea. She hoped it might serve to lure customers to the store even when they weren't looking for something specific. She expected resistance from Fred, but without asking a thing, not even how much the catalog would cost, he said, "If you think it's a good idea, go ahead."

As Fred flipped through the catalog, Edith followed along from behind his shoulder. Not only had she overseen the logistics and chosen the photographer and printer, she had selected the merchandise and written the copy. The end result was a catalog as slick and appealing as any from the Manhattan department stores.

"I knew it was gonna be great, but it's better than great," Fred said. "Congratulations, Edie. Mind if I give you a hug?" They no longer called each other "Mr. Adler" and "Mrs. Merkal." Over the past year, they had slipped into first names, hers shortened to Edie, though Fred also called her "kiddo" and "doll." He didn't wait for permission before slipping his short arms around her. Then he stepped back and asked, "How many are we sending out?"

"Two hundred fifty." For months, Edith had been having the salesgirls ask their customers to fill out address cards, a favor the salesgirls acknowledged by placing a sachet of lavender inside their shopping bags.

"Edie, I don't know what I'd do without you."

Edith spotted a box wrapped in red foil on Fred's desk. "What's the occasion?"

"My birthday," Fred said sheepishly. "Our family doesn't make a big deal out of them, but Mr. Lemmon, being the accountant, knows when it is."

Fred's words made Edith think of her own family who, these days, also made nothing out of birthdays, not even the children's. Families, she knew, didn't just decide to stop celebrating birthdays. As love began to wither and the resentments build, celebrations became halfhearted and sporadic until they finally stopped altogether.

"At least allow me to do this." Edith gave him a peck on the cheek.

"That was lovely." Fred smiled. The lines that ran along his nose and mouth deepened, making Edith think of a ventriloquist's puppet. She wondered how old he was. With his round face and pink cheeks, it was hard to tell.

At lunchtime, Edith ducked out to a liquor store for a bottle of champagne. She kept the bottle in the cafeteria refrigerator until the end of the day, when she placed it on Fred's desk. "For you and your wife," she scribbled on the note she left beneath it, though she suspected that Fred's marriage was not much happier than her own.

A few minutes later, there was a knock on her door.

"The catalog, that really is something to celebrate," Fred said. He asked her to join him in his office. On his desk were two glasses, already filled. "I figured this way, you couldn't refuse."

Because she'd gone out to buy the champagne during her lunch break, Edith hadn't had time to eat. She was not even halfway through her first glass before she started feeling tipsy. She slid back on the couch, resting her head against the cushion and flung her arm over the side. Fred came over with the bottle.

Edith held up her hand. "I've had enough."

"It would be a crime to let such good champagne go to waste, and I can't finish it alone." Fred took Edith's glass and filled it. "As your boss, I'm ordering you to drink up."

"Aye, aye, sir," Edith said, saluting. She downed her second glass in a few gulps.

"Edie!"

"You told me to drink up!

Fred lifted the bottle. "More?"

"I shouldn't," Edith said, laughing, "which is all the more reason I will."

Fred stepped back. "I shouldn't tell you this, but I've always loved your laugh. I don't hear it often, but when I do…it makes me go all happy inside."

It was such a lovely thing to say and spoken with such sincerity. It wasn't that Edith never got compliments. She got them all the time, from Mr. Adler, the customers, the manufacturers, even the salesgirls. But these compliments were always about the job she was doing—never about her.

"Not just your laugh," Fred said. "Your smile. It lights up your face."

"My smile," Edith repeated. She tried to recall if Reuben ever told her that he loved her smile. He used to tell her how much he loved her breasts, her hair, her legs, but she could not recall him ever saying that he loved her smile.

"You must know," Fred said, pouring the last of the champagne into her glass, "what a beautiful woman you are."

"Now, you're pulling my leg," Edith said, laughing. She lifted her leg, surprised to see that she wasn't wearing her shoes. She couldn't recall taking them off.

Fred caught her ankle and kissed the top of her foot. "You better go before we end up doing something we'll regret."

As Fred grabbed her hands to help her off the couch, Edith fell against him. "God, I'm drunk," she giggled. Her legs felt so rubbery, she was afraid that if she let go, she would sink to the floor.

Fred began stroking her bare arm. "I knew your skin would be soft. I could tell just by looking at it."

"This isn't good," Edith said, pressing her face against his neck.

"But it sure is nice," Fred murmured as his hands traveled down her back and over her rump.

The next thing Edith knew, Fred's hands were inside her dress. One, in fact, was working its way into her girdle.

"You're so wet," Fred gasped. His fingers were now inside her. This seemed to Edith a shocking thing to say—also thrilling. And true. She was a puddle, a lake, an ocean. She leaned in close; the rest of her body had become as rubbery as her legs. He was pressing himself against her, pressing and releasing. She could not recall ever having been so excited. It was a new, thrilling sensation, this actually wanting to have sex.

Then they were on the couch, and he was on top of her. Her dress was up around her waist. His fingers were no longer inside her but making fast work of undoing her garters, pulling off her stockings, rolling down her girdle. As if guided by a will of its own, her hand pulled down his zipper and wrapped itself around his cock as it sprung out.

Edith used her foot to push her girdle off from around her ankles, and then she flung her legs around Fred's back, using all her strength to pull him toward her. "Put it in—now," she demanded. Her words shocked her.

The world became a carousel, spinning faster and faster, until nothing mattered except the feeling between her legs. Edith wanted Fred never to stop, to go harder, to bore down until he came through the other side. Then, she rocketed off the carousel past the clouds, now only vaguely aware of the man on top of her.

Edith had an orgasm. Her first ever.

Edith had heard women could have orgasms but never believed it. She hadn't believed Reuben when he told her women were meant to enjoy sex. She became shameless about going to Fred's office at all times of the day, closing the door behind her, unbuttoning her blouse and lifting her skirt, not caring how this made her look.

And how Fred wanted her! In ways Edith wouldn't have thought possible. Bent over his desk. Pressed up against the wall. He made her kneel on her hands and knees so he could enter her from behind. He made her straddle him on his chair, while she pretended to take dictation. He grabbed the back of her neck and pressed her mouth to his penis, and not only did she suck, she swallowed. She let him lick her as well, though the idea of allowing a man to see her "down there" would once have been inconceivable.

Edith was surprised she didn't feel guilty. She told herself that it was against the laws of nature for a man and a woman to spend so much time together and for nothing to happen. She told herself that Reuben was to blame. That if only he had gotten a job, she wouldn't have had to get one herself. Then, this never would have happened.

Fred thought they were being discreet. Edith knew better. Women being so much better than men at sniffing this sort of thing out, the salesgirls were bound to suspect. She didn't care. Nor did she care if Reuben found out. Or Fred's wife. Sex made her intrepid.

Their work didn't suffer. Quite the contrary. They attacked the store's problems with the same fervor with which they attacked each other. "We really are a great team," Fred said. He told her he was in love with her. Edith told him she felt the same way.

If sex made Edith intrepid, love made her charitable. She was more patient with her children, kinder to Reuben who, poor fool, was too pleased with the change in her to question what brought it about. Reuben began to talk about looking for work. He started scouring the want ads and going on interviews. "Any day, I'll land something," he told Edith. He was sure the war brewing in Europe would translate into more jobs at home. Edith didn't take him seriously until a few weeks later when he came home with the news that he'd be beginning his new job on Monday.

"It's not much, but it's a start," Reuben said.

It pained Edith to see what Reuben had settled for — assembly-line work with a defense contractor, Grumman Aeronautics, in Mineola. If you had a shred of dignity, she used to tell him, you'd take anything. But the thought of his punching a time clock, carrying a lunch pail, a cog in someone else's grand plans, struck her as unbearably sad. Moreover, he had been assigned to the night shift. Their car, nearly a decade old, was too unreliable to drive such a distance. He would have to take two buses, which meant that although his shift ended at four in the morning, he wouldn't arrive home before six.

Reuben stuck his head into Jeffrey's room one afternoon to remind him to be quiet, that he was trying to sleep. He found the desk gone, the dresser missing its drawers, and the only thing left of the bed was its frame.

"I'm moving to the attic," Jeffrey said. He had stripped down to his waist and was sweating. While nearly six feet, Jeffrey's body was hairless, except for some fluff beneath his armpits and a few stray hairs around his nipples. His shoulders were barely broader than his waist.

"Are you crazy?"

"I like it there," Jeffrey mumbled.

"There are no windows. It's not even heated."

"Antoinette used to live up there." Jeffrey wiped his forehead with his arm.

Reuben was about to say that Jeffrey was too old for such nonsense when he stopped himself. Instead, he said, "Let's see what you've done."

The boy's face brightened.

"That doesn't mean I'm going to allow it."

"It reminds me of a cave," Jeffrey said. The furniture was still jumbled together, and a mountain of clothing was piled atop the mattress. Reuben couldn't help marveling how skinny Jeffrey managed to get it all up the attic stairs.

The dormered ceiling was less than seven feet at its highest point and sloped down steeply to the sides. "You'll be banging your head all the time," Reuben said. Still, he liked the way the daylight pushed in between the eaves and could understand how a boy might prefer it up there.

"I'll get used to it. Remember how Antoinette always wore the key around her neck? Where did Grandma find her anyway?"

Reuben shrugged. "It's a mystery why Grandma took such good care of her."

"Not such good care. She made Antoinette live up here when there were all those empty bedrooms."

"You want to live up here."

"I have a choice." Jeffrey picked up a withered orange impaled with dozens of cloves. "Antoinette gave me this for my fourth birthday." He pushed it beneath Reuben's nose. "It still smells good, doesn't it?" Reuben had never been able to abide the smell of cloves and only pretended to sniff the orange.

When Reuben agreed to let him try out the attic, Jeffrey threw his arms around him. He was about to kiss him on the lips when Reuben pushed him away. Why was it, Reuben wondered, that Jeffrey failed to understand the most basic rules of human interaction? The sort of things most people understood instinctively.

In May, Adolph was notified that his lease was not going to be renewed. With the thirty-day grace period, this meant vacating the building by the end of July. Except that Adolph decided that he wasn't going to leave, at least not until a wrecking ball came crashing against the side of the building. Maybe not even then.

He told Reuben this on the Fourth of July. Reuben had suggested that they take a picnic down to the shore and watch the fireworks. At first, Adolph demurred, afraid such an excursion might prove too taxing for Ernest. "If he's as fragile as you say," Reuben countered, "I would think you'd want to make what time he has left as pleasant as possible." The words seemed to strike a chord with Adolph, as he agreed to come along.

The men sat on a blanket talking while the boys went looking for seashells. It was a lovely evening, the setting sun painting the sky in pinks and mauves and scattering spangles across the water. Reuben recalled how it had been the water that had drawn him to Sea Forth in the first place. The irony was that, once he moved there, he became too busy with his business to enjoy it. He had never bought the boat he'd promised himself, never once taken Jeffrey fishing. After losing his business, he finally had the time for such pursuits but had neither the interest nor the heart.

"Herbert dropped by the other day," Adolph said. His eyes were fixed on Ernest, as if, despite the low tide, the boy might be swept out to sea.

Reuben took a beer from the cooler and handed Adolph his thermos, which was filled with one of Adolph's vile-smelling concoctions. Adolph was growing so fanatical about his diet that Reuben sometimes wondered whether he was going mad. A few weeks earlier, he had invited Adolph and Ernest to the house for lunch. After lunch, Reuben had poured both boys glasses of milk and set out a plate of cookies. Adolph whisked Ernest's glass away. "I no longer allow Ernest to drink milk," he explained. "You wouldn't feed a calf human breast milk, would you? Milk is meant to nourish a species' infants, and that's all. There's no reason for anyone over the age of two to consume it."

"He pretended he'd only stopped by to pick up a few things," Adolph continued. "Mind you, he ended up buying nearly fifty dollars' worth of stuff, more than I usually sell in a day. As I was ringing up the sale, he asked if I could spare a few minutes." Adolph scanned the shoreline and pointed to two black silhouettes. "Is that them?"

"That's them," Reuben answered. "Go on."

"He asked if I had gotten the letter notifying me that my lease wasn't going to be renewed. Then asked if I'd read it."

"What did you say?"

"I told him I read all my mail. Don't you think it's time they started back?"

"Adolph, relax."

Adolph jumped to his feet. "Easy for you to say. You don't have to worry each time you say good night to your son whether it will be the last time."

Reuben got up, too. "What does the doctor say?"

"I'm Ernest's doctor now. I know more than all of them put together."

They were distracted by a teenaged boy and girl lugging an enormous picnic hamper. The pair let out exaggerated groans as they collapsed nearby. The boy lifted the girl's long hair, making himself a moustache with it, and then he kissed her. Reuben glanced over at Adolph, who was staring at them. Reuben knew he was wondering whether Ernest would ever have a girlfriend, the same thing Reuben wondered about Jeffrey.

The sky had turned dark. "Let's go find them," Reuben said. "They must be getting hungry."

As they headed toward the water, he said, "You didn't finish telling me what happened."

Adolph sighed. "I told him that I planned on staying until the walls crumbled down around me."

"That would have given him a shock. Of course, you were kidding."

Adolph turned toward Reuben. "I think it's important for people to see that while progress is inevitable, the human costs shouldn't be forgotten."

"They'll see all right. They'll see a German Jew madman being dragged away by the police. Then if you want to see your son, he'll have to visit you in prison."

A bang drew their attention over toward Fire Island. Electric pinks and greens, silver and gold starbursts, began filling the sky and lighting up the earth, transforming the figures along the shore from silhouettes back into people.

"Over there," Reuben said, pointing a hundred feet westward where two lanky figures sat, arms hugged around their knees.

"I was only making the point that just because it's convenient for him to have me out by a certain date doesn't mean it's convenient for me. Of course I know sooner or later, he'll win."

Two weeks later, Reuben decided to head over to Adolph's store during the few hours he had between when he woke up and had to leave for work. The store was dark and had a sign posted in the window: "This pharmacy has closed. Prescriptions can be filled at Rexall's, 666 Main Street, tel. 6348." Though the children and Edith passed by the store every day, they hadn't told him it had closed.

Reuben pressed his face to the glass. The shelves had been cleared of merchandise, and cartons were stacked in the aisles. He decided to go around back to see if Adolph was in the stockroom. As he made his way through the alley, he recalled that day years earlier when Adolph had pulled him in there, and how he scoffed when Adolph told him the rumor about the Nazi party starting up on Long Island. Adolph had been right.

The rear entrance was unlocked. Reuben wandered through the storeroom, also largely cleared of merchandise, calling out Adolph's name. He was about to leave when he saw light from beneath the door to Adolph's laboratory. Adolph was at his workbench, slicing a stiff brown item into slivers with a penknife. The room, which had not been packed up, was stifling, and Adolph had stripped down to his undershorts.

"Celaphonus mushroom from Northern China," Adolph said without looking up.

Reuben picked up a mushroom and sniffed it. Its odor reminded him of how the farmlands north of Sea Forth smelled in the spring after the soil had been tilled.

"Why didn't you tell me?" Reuben asked. He put the mushroom down and picked up a knobby root with beige skin and a cream-colored center. He recognized the smell – ginger – but had never seen it before in its unadulterated state.

Adolph placed the mushroom slivers inside a bamboo box. Using a small brush, he swept the powdery residue in as well. "Why didn't you call?"

Reuben resisted the impulse to make up an excuse. "I should have."

Adolph began getting back into his clothes. "The day after the picnic, something happened." Adolph pulled a blue aerogram out of the drawer beneath the worktable. "Here."

The letter was in a language Reuben assumed was German. "What does it say?"

"It's from my cousin Irma. She's living in England now. It's about my sister Gerda. She says life in Berlin has become impossible for Jews. Gerda's husband, Walter, has been fired from his position at the university, and they've been thrown out of their apartment. The children aren't even allowed to attend school." He folded the letter and put it back in the drawer.

"You didn't know?" Reuben asked.

"My parents are dead, and I've been out of touch with everyone for years. I have no idea how Irma tracked me down. My cousin hasn't been able to get them out. She was hoping I might have better luck."

Reuben found it strange to think of Adolph having a family. He had always thought of Ernest and him as islands unto themselves.

"Frankly, I never could stand my sister—and her husband I liked even less. The only time I even wrote her was when Anna died. I never got a letter back. But blood is blood, and it shouldn't have taken a letter from my cousin to shame me into doing what I can." Adolph walked over to the window, closed and locked it. "The problem is that it's bound to cost a bundle. Gabelli—he's the shoemaker next door—told me that Herbert offered him a bonus to vacate quickly. So, the next time Herbert showed up, I didn't chase him out."

With the window closed, the heat had become unbearable. "Why don't we take a walk?" Reuben asked.

Adolph sighed. "Why not?"

Though it was nearly five, heat was still rising from the sidewalks. The whole world looked vanquished—the drooping leaves, the panting dogs stretched out in doorways, the shoppers shuffling from store to store. Though he'd had seven hours of sleep, more than he got on most days, Reuben felt exhausted. And he still had ahead of him the hour-long bus ride to the factory, eight mind-numbing hours on a production line, and then the bus ride home.

Adolph picked up where he'd left off. "I told Herbert that I'd spoken to Gabelli."

"What did he say?"

"He said, 'I had a feeling it was about money. It always is with you people.'"

"You people? And it isn't with him?"

Adolph shrugged. "The last thing I wanted was to get drawn into a shouting match."

An ice cream truck was parked outside the cathedral, the megaphone on its chocolate-brown roof blasting "Pop Goes the Weasel."

"Let me treat you to an ice cream," Reuben said.

"You know I don't eat dairy. Anyway, I said the right thing. He pulled his wallet out and dropped five one-hundred-dollar bills on the counter. That's just a down payment, he said. He told me to work out how much I typically netted over three months, which is about the time it should take to find a new place."

Reuben realized that he had been so absorbed in what Adolph was saying that they had walked right past Corona, the street where the Emporium was located. They would have to head back if he were to get to work on time. "What did you tell him?"

"Four thousand dollars, figuring that he was bound to chop in half whatever figure I gave him. Instead, he told me that if I threw in my inventory and fixtures, we had a deal—assuming I was out by the end of the week."

"Four thousand," Reuben said. Adolph's store had gotten so run down, he reckoned that his inventory and fixtures couldn't possibly be worth more than a thousand. Then again, while most people would consider four thousand an enormous amount, to Paul, it was chump change.

"With that kind of money, not only should I be able to bring my sister over, I'll be able to put some aside for Ernest," Adolph said. "I should be happy, right? Well, I've never been so miserable, not since my Anna died." Adolph looked up at the sky. "If only I could believe in an afterlife. What a comfort it would be to think she was up there, looking after Ernest and me."

# Chapter Nineteen

## *September through December 1939*

On September 4, Labor Day, as soon as he woke, Reuben rushed out to buy *The New York Times*. Germany had invaded Poland on September 1, and the previous day, he'd heard on the radio that England and France had declared war on Germany.

Reuben was glad that Edith and the children were still sleeping when he arrived back home. He wanted to give the newspaper his full attention. He settled down at the kitchen table with a cup of coffee and opened the paper wide. As he read about the aerial bombardments and mass executions, he became convinced that unless Russia and the United States joined the Allied effort, there would be little chance of halting the German army machine.

Toward the back of the paper, Reuben spotted an ad, "Visas arranged, quickly and cheaply." The ad gave a Fifth Avenue address and contained an endorsement from the American Jewish Congress. He wondered whether Adolph had done anything about rescuing his sister and her family. From the way things looked, if he didn't act quickly, what little chance he had of getting them out of Germany would be lost.

He decided to walk over to Adolph's apartment. Along Main Street, small American flags had been tied to the lampposts. Though the parade would not start for an hour, spectators were already staking out places along the curbs. Outside the bank, a podium had been set up, from which the mayor, police chief, and other dignitaries would judge the quality of the floats. In the distance, Reuben could hear the high school marching band practicing in the football field.

Ernest opened the door. "Dad's in bed," he said. Though the day was warm, he had a blanket wrapped around his shoulders.

"Still asleep?" Reuben knew Adolph was an early riser.

"I said in bed, not asleep." Ernest led Reuben to the bedroom. "He's been acting strange."

Reuben had never been inside the bedroom. He was startled to discover that Adolph and Ernest shared the same bed Adolph would have once shared with his wife. Adolph's face was to the wall, his bare feet sticking out from the end of the blanket. The room was different from the rest of the apartment, all blowsy femininity, with pink floral curtains and a matching dust ruffle, a worn rose carpet, and spindly furniture painted white and trimmed in gold. It was the sort of room Reuben would have imagined for a girl, not a married woman, and Reuben wondered what type of person Adolph's wife had been—and why Adolph had left the room the way it was.

Reuben sat down on the edge of the bed. "Are you okay?"

"There's a law against sleeping late on a holiday?" Adolph reached for a bubble-filled glass of water on his night table. "Ernest, I didn't hear you offer Mr. Merkal a drink."

Ernest huffed. "So, do you want anything?"

"I'm fine." After Ernest left, Reuben said, "He's looking good. Better than you."

Adolph set the glass down. "Did you know Jeffrey stops by nearly every day? I didn't. They're funny kids, no? The things they keep secret."

Voices and laughter drifted up from outside. Reuben walked over to the window and stuck his head out. The sidewalks were filling up. Many of the spectators would have come from the surrounding towns, for the Sea Forth parade was known as the best around.

"Only two types of people love parades," Adolph said. "Americans and fascists. Myself, I can't understand the fascination. Girl Scouts, policemen, all marching in unison. Right, left, right. Tubas and drums. Not to mention the garbage they leave behind." He gave an *ugh*. "You're right. I do need to get up."

Adolph went to the closet for his robe. Looking over his shoulder, he said, "I'm fine. After all those years of getting up at six, why shouldn't I take it easy?"

"I thought you might be interested in this." Reuben pulled the ad from his pocket.

Adolph glanced at the clipping and then dropped it into the pocket of his robe.

"You heard that England and France declared war on Germany," Reuben said as he followed Adolph into the living room. "It's about time, don't you think?"

"I suppose." Adolph picked up a pair of Ernest's socks from the living room rug. "If I knew you were coming, I would have straightened up." Other than those socks, the room was in perfect order. The hiss of the shower came from behind the bathroom door. "He'd spend hours in there if I let him. I have no idea what he does." Reuben was pretty sure he knew—the same thing he did at that age.

"Have you heard of the group in this ad?" Reuben asked.

Adolph adjusted the sofa cushions. "I've decided not to do anything. Between the number of Jews trying to get out and the fact that Congress seems bent on reducing the immigration quotas, I've concluded it's a lost cause."

Reuben stared at Adolph.

"Don't look at me that way," Adolph said. "Of course, I'm worried about my sister. But I don't see the point in throwing away money. I have Ernest to think about. Even with the money from Herbert, I'll still have to watch every penny."

Reuben heard the marching band approaching. It struck him as wrong that the townspeople were celebrating while Europe was engulfed in tragedy. He wondered how it was that people who wouldn't dream of passing a beggar without tossing him a coin could be so indifferent to the plight of the millions trapped within Hitler's net.

"I have no idea whether it's too late to help your sister," Reuben said quietly. "All I know is that a year from now, you'll hate yourself if you don't try. You owe it to her—and yourself—to at least meet with one of these groups. After that, if you still think it's hopeless, so be it."

The shower tap went off. Adolph glanced toward the bathroom. "He doesn't even know I have a sister."

"What if he finds out and asks whether you tried to help her?"

Adolph began to pace. "I know you're right. I'm just scared. Who's going to hire me? A German and a Jew?"

Reuben grabbed Adolph's shoulders. "And an American citizen. Don't forget that. Let me set up the meeting. I'll go with you. That way, I can help you decide."

"You're a good friend." Adolph motioned toward Ernest, standing in the living room archway, naked except for the towel around his waist.

"The parade's started?" Ernest asked. "When Jeffrey comes, tell him I'll be outside our old store."

In late September, Adolph and Reuben took the train into Manhattan for a meeting with the agency. As they stepped out of Penn Station onto Seventh Avenue and found themselves sucked into a swarm of pedestrians, their nostrils at once assaulted by the stench of exhaust and seduced by the aroma of hot caramel-dipped apples, Reuben felt an exhilaration that he hadn't felt in years. When he was growing up in Jackson Heights beneath the shadow of the "el," there had never been a contest in his mind between country and city. A single excursion with his parents out to eastern Long Island was all it had taken to convince him that was where he wanted to live one day.

The men decided to walk to the agency, which was located across from the public library.

"Did I ever tell you that Anna and I lived in Manhattan for a few years before moving to Sea Forth?" Adolph said as they headed down West 33rd Street. It was a breezy day, and the men had to keep their hands pressed to their hats to prevent them from flying off.

There was so much that Reuben didn't know about Adolph. "What brought you to America in the first place?"

Adolph laughed. "As a boy, I loved to read. Not just German books. I especially loved Theodore Dreiser. As jaundiced as his view of America might have been, I became infatuated. It seemed like a place where the only things that could hold a man back were his own limitations. What can I say? I was naïve."

"Did you like living in the city?" Reuben asked. After crossing Broadway, the men found themselves in the tag end of the garment district. This part of 33rd Street was devoted to notions, the cluttered windows of one harshly lit store after the next, filled with dusty displays of buttons, ribbons, and trimmings. The litter-strewn street was such a tangle of pushcarts, cars, and trucks that traffic had come to a halt.

Adolph had to yell to be heard over the blaring horns. "I loved it. But Anna hated the crowds and the noise. For days, she'd refuse to step outside. After she became pregnant, I agreed to move. Fresh air, fresh food—I thought that would be best for the child, too. The irony was that within three years, she was dead. The following year, Ernest took sick as well." They turned north on Fifth. "I wanted to be a doctor," Adolph continued, "but in Germany it had become impossible for Jews to get into medical school. I thought I'd have a better chance here. Hah. They're bigots there; they're bigots here. The difference is here they're not so blatant about it. At least in Germany, a man knew where he stood."

The agency's headquarters were located in a granite-fronted office building with a marble-clad lobby. A white-gloved elevator man took the men up to the eighth floor.

"Seems respectable," Reuben said after a woman with a lantern jaw and putty-like nose led them into the reception room. The room was small and windowless with a tweed couch, a single wooden chair, and a glass-topped coffee table, on which was a book about Palestine. The sole wall decoration was a lopsided Chagall reproduction in a metal frame.

They'd been waiting about ten minutes when a middle-aged man with a round face and tiny, dark eyes poked his head through a door. "Seymour Levine," he said, shaking Adolph's, then Reuben's hand vigorously. He led them into an office where a gaunt man, who introduced himself as Myron Goldberg, sat hunched over a typewriter. There were bruise-colored pouches beneath this man's eyes, the whites of which were yellow.

"Cirrhosis," Adolph whispered to Reuben as Levine motioned for them to sit down.

"What brings you gentlemen here?" Levine asked, leaning forward.

Adolph glanced over at Reuben. Reuben nodded for him to go ahead.

"My sister, her husband, and two children live in Berlin," Adolph began.

"Berlin! Not the safest place for a Jew these days," Levine said. He broke into a coughing fit and spat into his handkerchief, examining its contents before stuffing it back inside his pocket.

Adolph looked away, his lips curled in disgust. "That's why we're here."

"You've come to the right place." Levine swiveled sideways and called out, "Myron, get me Freudenberg's file."

Goldberg had a humped back and long arms. As he scuttled over to the filing cabinet, he reminded Reuben of a cockroach. He retrieved a manila folder with a red "Approved" stamp on its cover and dropped it on Levine's desk.

Levine pulled out a sheet affixed to which was a photograph of a young woman and waved it. "Geetel Freudenberg, also from Berlin, now living in Brooklyn."

"May I see that?" Adolph asked.

"God, no," Levine said. He shoved the paper back into the file and slapped both hands down upon it. "These are confidential." He shook his head sorrowfully. "Krakow, Munich, Bialystock—we've brought them here from everywhere. From Berlin, Myron, how many? Stop that infernal clacking! I'm asking a question."

Goldberg shrugged. "I dunno. Ten?"

"Good God, man, it's gotta be at least twice that. Gentlemen, know what they call me?" He paused as if he expected Reuben and Adolph to answer. "The mitzvah man. You know the saying, perform three mitzvahs, and you're guaranteed a place in heaven. At the rate I'm going, I should be able to bring all of Manhattan with me." Levine's expression turned serious. "How long I'll be able to keep it up, God knows. What you've been reading in the papers, it's all true. But worse." His hands still pressed against the folder, Levine fastened his eyes on Adolph. Reuben turned to look at him, too. Even Goldberg stopped typing and stared at Adolph.

"How much does something like this cost?" Adolph asked.

Levine sighed as if he were disappointed in Adolph for raising so trivial a subject as money. "Myron," he said, "bring over the adding machine."

While Goldberg tapped away on the adding machine, Levine ticked off the figures on his fingers. "These are approximate, of course. Eleven dollars for visa photographs, thirty-five for application lodgment, forty for the processing fee, sixty for the departure tax, twelve dollars and fifty cents for transport to the pier, three hundred thirty-five for ship passage, one hundred fifty for gratuities, and our fee of fifty dollars per application, though I can assure you we're not in this for the money. All times four, of course."

While Reuben was not a good enough mathematician to work these sums out in his head, he knew they had to add up to at least two thousand.

"Gratuities?" Adolph asked.

Levine nodded ruefully. "A polite word for bribes. Even in times like these, especially in times like these, everyone wants their cut."

"Two thousand seven hundred thirty-four dollars and no cents," Goldberg called out triumphantly as he ripped the tape from the adding machine. "Assuming the black market rate for Reich marks stays where it is—which it won't."

As Levine explained to Adolph how 60 percent was payable up front with the balance due upon successful immigration,

Reuben looked across the alley through to the window of the building on the other side where a group of men sat huddled around a conference table. Lawyers, bankers, businessmen, Reuben reckoned, men who could toss such figures about without batting an eye, the way he once could.

"I'll have to think about it," Adolph said.

"My advice? Don't think too long. Any day that window's gonna shut." Levine slammed his hand down for emphasis. He handed Adolph a sheet of paper.

Adolph looked confused.

"Names, references, people you can talk to," Levine said. He came around to the other side of the desk and slung one arm around Adolph, the other around Reuben. "Your friend," he told Reuben, "make sure he does the right thing."

Within days of Adolph's vacating his store, demolition began. Their noses pressed against the chain-link fence installed around the construction site, Adolph and Reuben watched as a wrecking ball slammed into the remaining stubs of the building's walls, and an earthmover chomped through a tangle of concrete, steel, and brick.

"I come by every day," Adolph said. "It makes me sick, but I can't help myself."

"I hear it's going to be six stories—the tallest building in Sea Forth," Reuben said.

"What would you expect from Herbert?" Adolph said. "I called the agency today."

"Again? If you keep this up, they'll start getting annoyed."

"This time, I got through to Levine. The paperwork's finally been completed."

"I'm sure they've been inundated with applications," Reuben said.

"That's what he said. He said they can't afford to waste time going through New York anymore, so next week, he's taking the applications to Washington himself."

"I told you not to worry," Reuben said.

By the time Reuben noticed Paul approaching, it was too late to escape. Paul was sucking on a pipe and dressed like a laborer in a flannel shirt, dungarees, and a cap.

He clamped his hand on Reuben's shoulder. "Couldn't you watch forever? We're all little boys at heart." Reuben tried to disengage himself, but Paul's hand would not be budged. "Next week, we begin pouring the foundation." Paul's pipe bobbed up and down as he spoke. The woodsy tobacco scent made Reuben think of his father, who made a great ceremony of selecting his tobaccos and choosing from his large selection of pipes. "What have you two gentlemen been up to?"

Until then, Adolph had refused to acknowledge Paul. He now turned around. "Nothing. You put me out of business, remember?"

Paul chuckled as if what Adolph said was amusing. He tapped his pipe out against the fence and then checked with his forefinger to make sure it was no longer lit. "No reason to rush out looking for work. I seem to recall you made out very well."

"And I'm working at Grumman on the assembly line, night shift," Reuben said. He got a perverse kick out of trumpeting how far he had fallen.

A jackhammer started up. Adolph pointed to the side of Paul's face and said something that was drowned out by the racket.

"What?" Paul shouted.

When Adolph repeated himself, Paul shook his head, looking annoyed.

"Forget it," Adolph shouted. Reuben only knew this from reading his lips. Adolph pressed his palm against Reuben's back to signal they should leave.

"What was that about?" Reuben asked when they were able to talk again.

"He's got a melanoma," Adolph said, "a cancerous mole. If he doesn't have it taken care of, it will probably kill him."

"I should have never listened to you." The phone had woken Reuben. He was still groggy, so it took him a moment to work out this was Adolph, and he was talking about the agency.

"What happened?" he asked as he carried the phone to the living room. He hooked his foot beneath the footrest, dragged it toward him, and sat.

"Like you said, I waited two weeks before calling again. This morning, I got the operator. She told me their number has been disconnected and that she had no further information."

"That's not good," Reuben said.

"From the start, I had a bad feeling. I should have listened to my gut."

"There's got to be a logical explanation," Reuben said, though he was unable to come up with one. "Why don't we go in on Monday?"

"I'm going this afternoon."

Reuben sighed. It was Friday. He had just gotten home from work a few hours before and was exhausted. On the other hand, he knew that were it his money, he wouldn't want to wait three days. "I'm coming."

For the middle of November, the weather was unseasonably warm and, despite the increasingly grim news coming out of Europe, the city had a carefree feel. Everywhere Reuben looked he saw signs of incipient prosperity —the throngs of women streaming out of Macy's and Gimbels, shopping bags dangling from their coat sleeves, the new Packards and Cadillacs clogging the streets. Everyone who passed the Salvation Army men and women stationed outside the stores seemed to have a spare coin for their kettles. So far, the catastrophe in Europe had translated into only good things for New York.

During the walk to the agency, Reuben said, "You'll see everything's going to be fine." He found it inconceivable that anyone would be so corrupt as to exploit the disaster that had befallen the Jews. But as the building came into view, he was overwhelmed by a dreadful foreknowledge of what they were about to discover. He realized that the men had inspired the same uneasiness in him that they had in Adolph—he just refused to accept it. Inadvertently, he had persuaded his friend to do the same.

"Adolph, it isn't there." Reuben took hold of Adolph's arm to stop him from running his finger down the building directory another time. The names below where the agency's name had been had all been moved up a space. Both the doorman and elevator man professed to know nothing.

"I'm going up," Adolph said.

Reuben didn't try to talk Adolph out of this. He knew that Adolph needed to see the vacated space in the same way that a person has to peer at the corpse inside an open casket.

There was little evidence that the agency had even existed. The sign outside the door was gone. The only remaining item in the reception room was the hook where the Chagall print had hung. The furniture inside Levine and Goldberg's office had also been cleared out, except for Goldberg's typewriter, lying sideways on the floor, and a wastebasket, empty except for a length of adding machine tape.

While Adolph stood, stunned, Reuben computed his loss: roughly sixteen hundred dollars or 40 percent of what Herbert had paid him.

"Don't blame yourself," Adolph said. "It was still the right thing to do, and I'm grateful to you for making me see that."

Reuben wanted to plead with Adolph for forgiveness, but how could he when his friend was behaving as if there were nothing to forgive?

Fred's Christmas present to Edith was a ring with a square-cut sapphire, set off by diamond baguettes. It was a beautiful sapphire, the color of early evening, and Edith could just imagine the admiring gasps such a ring would have drawn from her former friends. There was only one problem. Where could she wear it?

"When you're out with me," Fred said.

"Out?"

Fred smiled sadly. It bothered him ever more than it did her that their affair, so far, had been conducted in his office. They had ventured out only once, to a motel, where they'd spent a few hours in a mildew-smelling room on a bed that sagged and squeaked.

"Put it on," Fred said. When she slipped the ring on her right ring finger, he shook his head. "Not that hand." He was staring at her gold wedding band. She'd been wearing it for so long that it had become part of her. She began to tug at it. The ring wouldn't budge past her knuckle.

He reached into his desk drawer and handed her a pot of lanolin cream.

The ring still didn't move.

He returned from the toilet behind his office with a bar of soap.

That didn't work either.

When he finally said, "The ring will have to be cut off," she must have looked startled, for he added, "Not now, eventually."

Edith's gift to Fred was less extravagant—an exquisitely carved walnut box with a green felt lining and a mirror on the inside lid. He looked perplexed as he opened and shut the lid.

"You can use it for anything," Edith said. "Cuff links, collar studs." For days, she'd wandered down Main Street during her lunch breaks, trying to come up with the right gift, until she came across the box in a store called "Jack's Junk Shop."

"I was afraid this might happen," the salesman, an effeminate man with droopy eyes, had said. "I've been saving up for it for weeks. As usual I'm a day late and a dollar short." Reminded of how brokenhearted she had been when someone bought the turquoise and silver scarf, Edith almost put the box back.

After Edith and Fred made love, Fred said, "I hate this sneaking around. I want the world to know you're my gal. We've got to find a way to be together." He was sitting at his desk, wearing nothing but his socks and garters, which was how he'd made love to her.

"Why talk like that when we both know it's impossible," Edith said. She gathered her clothes and hurried to the bathroom where she kept a douche bag and bottle of vinegar behind the toilet. She always felt so soiled after sex that she had to empty the bag into herself two or three times before she truly felt clean.

Edith's initial delight in their lovemaking had worn off. Fred never got really hard now, and even these halfhearted erections often sputtered out before Edith was fully warmed up. She no longer had orgasms, though she pretended to. She did this not to spare Fred's feelings but rather to bring what she now regarded as an ordeal to a quick conclusion. Amazingly, Fred still seemed completely satisfied, often exclaiming after he came, "That was fantastic!"

Once Edith was dressed, which she always did in the bathroom as she hated the idea of Fred ogling her, she returned to find him still seated, undressed, at his desk. He was opening and shutting the box. After they made love, he usually looked as joyous as a child on Christmas morning. This time, there was a worried crease between his brows. "Sometimes, I get the feeling," he said, "that you don't enjoy being with me as much as I do you."

"Don't be silly." Edith was grateful that he couldn't see her face as she stood in front of the mirror on the back of his door, brushing her hair. Through the mirror, Edith watched as he padded toward her, ridiculous in his nakedness with his hairless chest, skinny bowed legs, and especially his jouncing, wormlike cock. He placed his hands on her shoulders and nuzzled her neck. His breath was sour, and she averted her face to avoid breathing it in.

"You're sure you like it?" he asked, meaning the ring.

"I love it." Edith held out her hand so they could admire it. And she did—so much so that she just couldn't bring herself to remove it before returning to the sales floor. She planted a chaste kiss on his cheek. "Of course I want to be with you. I adore you!"

Fred beamed. He reached for her right hand and began covering it with kisses. "You know the expression, 'where there's a will, there's a way.' I'm gonna make it happen, Edie Rosenthal." When they were alone, he always called her by her maiden name. "You wait and see."

Edith glanced at the ring to remind herself not to lose patience. "You're such a dreamer," she said, composing her face so as to appear appropriately wistful. She was not ashamed of her behavior. She might not care for Fred as much as he did for her, but that didn't mean she wasn't fond of him. And as far as his gifts went, he clearly derived as much happiness from giving them as she did from receiving them. Besides, it wasn't as if he couldn't afford them. No, Edith decided, she had nothing to feel guilty about. At least not as far as Fred was concerned.

# Chapter Twenty

## *April 1940*

"Mrs. Merkal, aren't things looking festive?" Fred asked.

Edith smiled weakly. The previous week, she had taken ill with a stomach virus and, for the first time in three years, had been forced to miss work. This left Fred with the task of readying the store for Easter, and the stuffed bunnies and chicks with their black plastic eyes and the artificial tulips in pink foil-wrapped pots now adorning the sales counters were the sad result.

Fred picked up a raffia basket—sprayed a garish lavender—with its purple tissue-paper nest filled with chocolate eggs. "Sweets for the sweet," he said, tipping the basket toward Edith. Then, raising his voice, he said, "Mrs. Merkal, can you spare a moment to go over some figures?"

Edith cringed. Fred's efforts to mask his real intentions were as obvious as a child's.

"So, doll, what about those figures?" Fred said after he closed his office door. He lifted Edith's skirt and began the complicated task of undoing her garters.

"The store opens in ten minutes," Edith protested, though feebly, for she knew it was futile.

In the midst of disrobing her, Fred somehow managed to undress himself. With his pants and boxers bunched about his ankles, he steered Edith to his couch. Her hand clutching the top of the couch, her foot anchored against the floor, so they wouldn't topple off, Edith tried to time her thrusts to coincide with Fred's, but it was hopeless, for like Reuben, he had no rhythm. She moaned because this was what Fred would expect. He could take forever to climax, but she knew he wouldn't this morning. The only thing that excited him more than making love to her was a sale, and this was the first day of their pre-Easter sale.

As soon as she felt the shudder that signaled Fred had come, Edith pushed him off and headed to his lavatory. This morning, she wouldn't have the time to clean herself properly. Within minutes, the store would be opening, and the most serious bargain hunters would begin streaming through the doors. It had been Edith's idea to hold the sale before Easter rather than after as they had in previous years. That way, they could use markdowns on last year's hats and gloves to draw customers to the store. Once they got them inside, they could then sell them the full-priced coats, shoes, and dresses to go with these items.

By the time Edith and Fred returned to the sales floor, several women were gathered around the sales table in the millinery department, rifling through the hats. Three salesgirls stood off to the side, the girl who normally looked after the department and two others whom Edith had drafted from other departments. They were following Edith's instructions that when a department was busy, to look over the customers before honing in on any particular one. All three were wearing the black crepe sheaths and single strand of cultured pearls that were now the uniform, Edith having dispensed with the dreadful pink smocks shortly after she was promoted.

There were plenty of sales hats from which to choose—wide and narrow brimmed, felts and straws in a rainbow of pastels decorated with ribbons, artificial cherries, and flowers. All had been marked down drastically, some by as much as 70 percent. Edith believed that to draw a crowd, a store had to make its sales real ones, that women regarded the five- and ten-percent markdowns most stores took as hardly worth the effort.

Edith was sure that many of these women would end up buying hats that hadn't been marked down. For all its variety, there was really no comparison between the sale merchandise and the gorgeous confections displayed on the white trellis behind it. The point of the sale was not only to sell the coats and shoes to go with the marked-down merchandise, but to make some of the customers forget why they'd come to the store in the first place.

"Elena, straighten up," Edith whispered to the girl she'd drafted from Sleepwear. "Sylvia, smile," she said to the one from Costume Jewelry, spreading her own mouth wide to demonstrate. Though soft-spoken and waiflike, Mae, whose department was Millinery, was especially good with customers. "Show the others how it's done," Edith said, directing Mae's attention to the heavy woman puffing her way toward the department, a woman notorious for her passion for spending.

By 10:00 a.m., the store had become so crowded that the air had turned thick with the scents of perfume, powder, and perspiration—also wet wool, as the day was raw and damp. Fred, who had stationed himself in the glove department, caught Edith's eye and gave a thumbs up. It was in shared moments like these that Edith could recall how she felt during the early days of their affair, before she realized she'd been confusing her love of the store for love of the man who owned it.

So far, Edith had let the salesgirls tend to the customers. She now approached an attractive auburn-haired woman who was trying on an emerald-green toque. By the elegant cut of the woman's blue sheath, the gold bracelets lining her wrists, and her smart alligator pumps, Edith could tell she was passionate about fashion.

"Madam," Edith began, "that hat would be even more becoming tilted to the side."

"I prefer it this way," the woman said. She arranged her pageboy across her shoulders and then moving her face from side to side, studied herself in the mirror. "A hand mirror," she told Edith, holding out her arm and wiggling her fingers, so she could see how she looked from the back. "Get me that hat. Not that one, that one," the woman demanded. Uninterested in the sales merchandise, she kept Edith going back and forth until the trellis was stripped of merchandise and the hats scattered everywhere. "That can't be all there is," she said.

"I'm afraid so, Ma'am," Edith answered as she bent to pick up the hats the woman had tossed onto the floor. "I thought several were quite flattering. The apricot felt really complements your complexion."

"If I wanted your opinion, I would have asked," the woman said. She swept her coat off the counter and held it out so Edith could help her into it. After she was buttoned, gloved, and her matching alligator purse settled back on her arm, she said, "It's a mystery to me how you people remain in business." She flung her hair over her shoulders, and then clipped away in her smart shoes.

The department had gotten even more crowded, with several women now waiting impatiently for someone to ring up their purchases. But Edith was too upset to take care of them. She continued straightening up, though she could feel the salesgirls looking at her incredulously, for wasn't she the one who was always lecturing them on how they should never let anything come ahead of waiting on customers?

Had she ever been treated so rudely? Edith recalled her mother's low opinion of women who worked in the retail trade, an occupation she considered several rungs beneath the office work she eventually ended up doing. It occurred to Edith that no matter how much responsibility Fred gave her, she was still only his employee, and to the outside world, nothing more than a shopgirl. The pride she'd taken in turning the Emporium around now struck her as the worst sort of stupidity. If the time ever came when she felt she could no longer work for Fred, what would she have to show for her efforts? It would be Fred who would be left with the store and the money.

When Reuben had been at Grumman for a year, the shift manager called him over. Reuben was sure he was about to be fired, even though he could not come up with a reason why. Instead, the man told him that in recognition for his hard work, management was honoring the request he'd put in months earlier for a transfer to the day shift.

"That is, if you still want it," the manager said. He was an owlish man who, during his breaks, always had his nose inside a book. The sort who, Reuben was sure, in better times, would have ended up teaching at a university.

Reuben was tempted to say that he had changed his mind. Not only had he gotten used to doing things in reverse to the rest of the world, being on the night shift had the advantage of minimizing his time around Edith. Instead, he said, "With the wife working and all, it would certainly make things easier."

The manager squeezed Reuben's shoulder. "You'll be missed."

"I'll miss all of you, too," Reuben answered. While he hated most things about the factory work, there was one aspect he had grown to love: the camaraderie among the men and the collective sense that they were playing a vital role in something larger than themselves.

Once his body had re-adjusted to the rhythms of day and night, Reuben became eager to sample the pleasures that had been denied him by dint of his night-shift work—dinners out, the cinema, activities he had little interest in until the opportunity to partake in them had been taken away.

There was another thing that Reuben was eager to sample. On his way to and from the bus depot, he passed Sea Forth's synagogue—a modest, two-story frame house. He had been inside only twice, once for his wedding, the other time for a funeral.

Lately, Reuben had begun to question his lifelong indifference to religion. His friendship with Adolph had something to do with this. Even more so did his growing concern over the plight of Europe's Jews. He felt that, at the very least, he should be practicing their shared religion as his small contribution to ensuring its survival—also to ensure their suffering would not be in vain.

There was another, more selfish aspect to this. It had to do with the ache inside of him, which Reuben understood was only partly due to the loss of his business and his wife's love. Lately, he'd begun to wonder if the solace others derived from religion might be available to him.

So, one Friday night, without telling Edith, Reuben left the house dressed in one of his old suits that, thanks to the physical demands of his job, he was no longer too plump to wear. He timed it so he would arrive just as services were about to begin. That way, he could avoid having to explain what had brought him there.

The sanctuary was in what had once been the house's living room and side porch, the wall between them having been removed. The rabbi presided from behind a lectern on a raised plywood platform, at the back of which stood the ark made of blond wood and embellished with an abstract metal sculpture that Reuben deduced was meant to evoke the burning bush. As Reuben took a seat in the last of a dozen or so rows of metal folding chairs, he spotted Herb Pullen's block-like head and his wife's golden braids.

Enough of the service was in English so that Reuben was able to follow along in the battered prayer book an elderly man had handed him by the door. He had expected to find the prayers elegant and beautiful, to be overcome by their profundity and wisdom. Instead, all the prayers seemed to be variations on the same two themes, that of providing God with assurances of unwavering devotion and of extolling his goodness. They were so repetitive that Reuben couldn't help wondering if it was really themselves, not God, whom the Jews were trying to convince. That, at least, was something he could understand, given the unending string of catastrophes that had befallen them.

Reuben was disappointed, too, in the rabbi, a short and slight man with a wispy blond beard and a high-pitched voice. Also, the cantor, red-faced and huge bellied, who boomed rather than sang. Before long, Reuben's mind began to wander and his eyes traveled away from the pulpit to the ceiling where a pair of horseflies was dancing a minuet. Every few minutes, he checked his watch; it felt like the service was never going to end.

When the service did end, the mood in the sanctuary changed from reverence to celebration. The rabbi and cantor paraded down the aisle, the congregants spilling out behind them, everyone kissing, hugging, and wishing Shabbot Shalom to everyone else. Reuben found himself being swept into the dining room. On a table set with a white cloth and silver candlesticks were paper cups filled with a few sips of wine, a challah covered with the customary velvet cloth, and a plate of snail-shaped, raisin-studded pastries. All eyes were on the rabbi as he blessed the wine, then the challah from which he tore a chunk before passing it along.

As Reuben nibbled on the cake-like bread and sipped the too-sweet wine, it occurred to him that perhaps he came looking for the wrong thing. Maybe what the synagogue had to offer him was less the opportunity to connect with God than with other Jews, and not just with those who belonged to this congregation—with Jews throughout the world.

"This is a surprise," Herb Pullen said, slapping his back. To Reuben's relief, he didn't ask what had brought him there or where Edith was. Reuben wondered if Herb had figured out how bad things were between Edith and him. Adolph certainly had, despite the fact that his marriage was one subject they were careful to avoid.

Herb steered him over to a group of middle-aged men, all smiling congenially. As Herb introduced them as Lou, Fred, Mort, and Saul, none mentioned having met him before. Yet Reuben got the feeling he already knew them.

"Will we see you again?" Saul asked after his son appeared at his side and gave his sleeve a tug. The other men nodded in encouragement. The group was breaking up, and Reuben knew what awaited them back home. Well-scrubbed children and smiling wives, eager to join them around tables set with their best dishes. Tantalizing smells of chicken, brisket, and apple strudel wafting from their kitchens. The sort of dinners that, as a child, he had looked forward to at his grandmother's house until his father put a stop to these visits. The sort of dinners Jews had enjoyed for generations and would continue to enjoy after he was gone. At least Reuben hoped so. He once scoffed at predictions that the Jews were a doomed race. Now, he was not so sure.

It was a nasty night, with a chilling rain. As Reuben headed home, his umbrella—useless against the blustery winds—tucked beneath his arm, the thought of what awaited him brought him nearly to tears. He and Edith had no monopoly on unhappiness. But the fact that these men had wives who looked after them when he didn't struck him as a piece of bad luck he'd done little to deserve. Was this really how he was destined to spend the rest of his life?

Later, as Reuben sat over the dinner he made for himself—scrambled eggs with ketchup and a tin of Heinz molasses baked beans—he solved the puzzle of why those men seemed so familiar. It was the stamp of the tribe. He finally understood the radar so many Jews had for spotting other Jews, how the clues resided not in the their noses, which came in as many shapes and sizes as those of any other race, but in their spirits, branded with the tragedies of the past five thousand years.

A week or so later, Reuben spotted a sign in Rexall's window: "Pharmacist wanted, evenings." He became so excited that he nearly forgot what he had come for—a cough elixir for Harriet, in bed with a cold. On his way home, he decided to stop by Adolph's to tell him about the job.

By the time he reached Adolph's apartment, Reuben was having doubts. Adolph was always going on about what a second-rate operation Rexall's was, though as far as Reuben knew, Adolph had never set foot in the store. As for himself, Reuben couldn't help being impressed by the store's brightly lit six aisles and its breadth of merchandise. Whereas Adolph might have carried two or three brands of shampoo, Rexall's carried a dozen.

Adolph and Ernest were at the dining table, doing schoolwork. Since losing his business, Adolph had redoubled his efforts to educate Ernest, whom he'd begun to harbor dreams of sending to Columbia University. How Adolph intended to pull this off, given Ernest's health and the cost of tuition, Reuben could only wonder. About the only breaks Ernest got were when Jeffrey stopped by. The boys never did anything more adventurous than visit the Argosy or Kresge's. Even so, Adolph confided to Reuben about how he worried while waiting for Ernest to return.

"I was just about to put on some tea," Adolph said. "Would you prefer chamomile or rosehip? And I've just baked some flax-seed biscuits."

Ernest gave Reuben a rueful smile that said *be thankful you only have to eat and drink this stuff when you visit*. He crossed his arms and stretched out his legs. "Modern European history," he said, nodding toward a thick book. "Unfortunately, the author's idea of modern ends with the nineteenth century."

Adolph had covered the teapot with a yellow cozy that Reuben was sure his wife must have crocheted. The china cups and saucers, decorated with pink flowers, were also decidedly feminine. He waited until Adolph had poured the tea to tell him about the job, holding up his hands afterward, in case Adolph's reaction was to jump down his throat.

"Did the sign say how much they'd be paying?" Adolph asked. "Not that it matters. It's more than I'm making now."

Reuben shook his head. "I know how you feel about the place but figured you should know."

"I don't see that I have a choice. That is, if they'll have me."

"They'd be thrilled to get you," Reuben answered, though he was not at all sure. Not that they'd be able to find a more qualified candidate. It was Adolph's personality that worried him. "My advice is to be enthusiastic. Pretend there's nothing you want more than to work at Rexall's."

"I wouldn't be pretending. My finances are dangerously low."

Reuben squirmed. He still felt guilty over the role he'd played in the way Adolph had been duped. He'd offered to make up some of his loss, but Adolph wouldn't hear of it.

Adolph had taken a few steps toward the kitchen when he began to shake. Reuben just managed to rescue the tea tray from his hands before the cups went crashing to the floor. He laid the tray on the table and, while Ernest watched, drew Adolph close, the way one does an unhappy child.

"I'm so ashamed," Adolph sobbed as Reuben led him over to the couch.

Reuben ordered Ernest to his room. "Your father's just upset about what's happening in Europe."

"Ashamed about what?" Reuben asked after Ernest had gone.

Adolph pulled a handkerchief from his pocket and gave his nose a honk. "My whole life. I haven't done a single thing I'm proud of." He stuffed the handkerchief back in his pocket and buried his face in his hands. "I'm a failure."

Reuben pushed Adolph's hands away. "That's not true. You came to this country with no money. Even with your wife and son ill, you managed to put yourself through pharmacy school and then build a fine business. That a piranha like Herbert should come along and steal it from you—that's hardly your fault."

Dusk had fallen, and with only one light on, the room was filled with shadows. Adolph walked over to the windows, lowered the blinds, and switched on the floor lamp. "Herbert? With what he paid me, you can hardly accuse him of being a thief. Want to know the truth? He did me a favor. There was no way I could compete with that Rexall's."

# Chapter Twenty-One

## May 1940

Edith didn't understand how Fred could have forgotten her birthday. For weeks, she had been telling him how much she dreaded turning forty. That this was really to be her forty-second birthday was none of his business. An even bigger mystery was why this should upset her. What else could this mean except his feelings were becoming less ardent? Surely, that would make it easier to extricate herself from what was beginning to feel like a sinkhole.

Edith was packing up to go home when there was a knock on her door. "I'm busy. Go away," she called.

"Doll baby, c'mon, open up."

It was only because Edith knew Fred would stay there, knocking and pleading, that she opened the door.

He seemed surprised to see her so upset. "Of course I didn't forget. I was just having a little fun."

Edith shrugged. "So what if you did? As far as I'm concerned, birthdays are no different than every other day."

"Birthdays are special," Fred said. "You told me that on my own." He wrapped his arms around her. "Promise you're not mad?"

Edith disengaged herself. "I've got to get home. I think the kids are planning a party." The truth was she doubted her children would even give her a card.

"Of course. You can't disappoint them." Fred expressed such interest in her children that, at first, Edith had assumed he was putting it on. Later, she came to realize that Fred really did love children, though apparently more in the abstract than in real life, given that he hadn't spoken to either of his daughters, both off at college, in months. "Before you go, check my pockets."

"For God's sake," Edith said, thrusting her hand in one, then the other. "There's nothing there."

"You didn't look very carefully." Fred placed her hand back in the first pocket.

"Some loose change, some paper." She pulled out the paper.

"Read it."

As Edith unfolded it, two tickets fell out. It was a letter from the Plaza confirming a reservation for Mr. and Mrs. Fred Adler for two Saturdays from then. The tickets were for a Broadway musical.

"I hoped by pretending I'd forgotten, I'd make it an even bigger surprise."

"It's sweet of you." Edith laid the letter and tickets on her desk. "Although what do you propose I tell my husband? What do you plan on telling your wife?"

"When was the last time you spent a weekend in the city?" Fred's expression was so hopeful that Edith realized it must have been a long time for him, as well.

"Let me see those again." Edith picked up the tickets.

"Don't ya think it's time we both had some fun?" Fred said. "We'll take a carriage ride through the park and have dinner in some snooty French restaurant. We'll have some fancy maid serve us breakfast in bed."

Edith hadn't realized she was crying until Fred wiped a tear from her cheek with his thumb.

"Why so weepy? Turning forty's not that bad."

Edith squeezed his hand. It was so small. If only he were taller, better looking...less ridiculous, she thought wistfully.

Edith had every intention of telling Reuben that she'd be going away for the weekend. It was just that every time she was about to, she lost her nerve. It was one thing to carry on behind his back, another to lie to his face.

She packed while he was at work and the children at school. She hated using the buff-colored suitcase she'd bought for their honeymoon, but it was the only one that was the right size. She filled it with the sherbet-colored silk panties she'd bought months ago but hadn't worn and her prettiest nightgown, also unworn, mint-green satin bordered in lace. For Saturday night, she chose a navy jersey, utterly plain except for its lavishly embroidered bolero jacket. A gift from Fred, she'd been keeping it hidden beneath a bathrobe at the rear of her closet.

For discretion's sake, Edith and Fred had decided to travel in separately. She planned on taking the first train into the city so she'd be gone before the rest of the family got up, though she and Fred weren't meeting until noon. She slipped out of bed at six, dressed in the living room, where she had hidden her suitcase and clothes behind the sofa, and was gone before seven.

Edith's train arrived at Penn Station before nine. Because it was Saturday and still early, the terminal was nearly deserted, the thick stone walls transforming what little noise there was into a soothing hush. It had been so long since she'd been to the city that Edith had forgotten how beautiful the terminal was with its vaulted ceiling and lunette windows, through which crisscrossing shafts of sunlight poured, bathing the enormous space in an ethereal green light.

Edith took a seat on one of the varnished walnut benches in the main waiting room. Her days were filled with so much fad and fluff masquerading as more, she had forgotten the effect genuine beauty could have on a person. She thought about her life, how it, too, was like a masquerade, how she was only now beginning to appreciate the difference between the mask she presented to the world and the person she really was.

Too nervous to window shop, Edith decided to head to the Plaza and wait in the lobby until Fred arrived. There, she found a chair that was hidden behind a palm but from which she could observe the goings-on about her. With its pink and gray-veined marble pillars and walls, gold filigree-tipped ceiling, and enormous chandelier like an upturned wedding cake, the lobby was more like a parody of a rich man's living room than the real thing, but its vulgarity pleased her. She loved being enveloped in the carefree bustle of the smartly dressed guests, people who behaved as if the Depression had been nothing more than someone else's bad dream.

At noon, Edith stood beneath that chandelier—Fred and her designated meeting place. She spotted Fred before he saw her, and her spirits sank. It wasn't that he wasn't dressed smartly. If anything, his outfit, a camel-colored cashmere sports jacket, pleated brown pants, and a chocolate-colored fedora with a yellow feather was too stylish, making the effect he was after, one of urbane sophistication, so transparently obvious that it underscored what a hick he was. When Fred saw her, he began waving his hat, and Edith was transported back to that first day outside the Emporium and the ludicrous figure she had thought him to be.

Fred flung his arms around Edith and then mortified her by tilting her backward and kissing her on the mouth.

With one hand Edith pushed him away, while with the other she re-adjusted her hat. "Everyone's watching!"

"Doll baby, I'm just so glad to see you," Fred said. "When I was in the cab, all of a sudden I thought, what if she doesn't show up? My heart began pounding like a jackhammer!" Cupping her elbow, he led her to the registration desk, where a pimply young man, who looked like an organ grinder in his brass buttoned burgundy jacket, was talking on the phone, the cord wrapped tightly around his fingers. Seeing that cord made Edith think of her own fingers, rather her left ring finger. She glanced down, catching sight of the bulge of her wedding band beneath her glove, and was overcome by a sickening rush.

"Now," the clerk said breathily after he hung up, "how may I help?"

"Mr. and Mrs. Fred Adler," Fred boomed, "checking in."

"Ah, Mr. and Mrs. Adler, welcome to the Plaza," the clerk boomed back. "Give me a moment while I look up your booking. Mr. and Mrs. Adler, Mr. and Mrs. Adler," he repeated loudly as he thumbed through a sheaf of papers. "Here we are," he said, waving a sheet triumphantly. "Mr. and Mrs. Fred Adler!"

Mr. and Mrs. Adler. Each time the clerk repeated those words, Edith felt as if she were being whacked in the stomach. She had a vision of Reuben and the children huddled together, speculating on where she could be. She'd been so consumed with figuring out how to slip away that she hadn't given much thought to what sort of greeting she'd get when she returned. All three would be unforgiving, and appropriately so.

"Fred." Edith tugged at his sleeve.

Fred shook off her hand. He was scrutinizing the registration details, his index finger tracing every word while his lips formed them as if he suspected the Plaza of trying to pull one over on him.

"I need to sit down!"

"Is Madam okay?" The clerk tilted his head, his features bunched in a show of concern, his hand poised atop the desk bell. "Shall I summon the doctor?"

"No," Edith cried. She had been terrified of it somehow being discovered during check-in that she and Fred weren't really husband and wife. Now, instead of allowing the process to proceed uneventfully, here she was creating a scene. "My legs are tired," she said. "That's all."

Edith returned to the chair where she had spent the morning. She flung her legs out and threw her head back—who cared how she looked? The lobby had gotten busier, with throngs of people heading off to the hotel's restaurants and out to enjoy the afternoon. From the Palm Court came the dulcet tones of a string quartet. Interspersed with happy chatter, she could hear the ping of the elevator and, from outside, the doorman's shrill whistle and the *clip-clop* of the horses as they pulled their carriages. And she heard Fred, his voice somehow piercing through the din as he asked the registration clerk a million questions: What time was breakfast served? Afternoon tea?—oblivious to the line of people behind him.

With Fred's view of her obscured by the palm, it would be easy to slip away, Edith reckoned. By the time Fred realized that she hadn't just ducked into the powder room, she could be in a cab on her way to Penn Station. Providing she got home before nightfall, Reuben was sure to accept whatever excuse she gave.

Then it was too late; Fred was standing over her. "Doll baby, the bellman's waiting." He hoisted her out of the chair with an exaggerated groan and steered her toward the elevator.

"Get up!"

Reuben bolted awake, startled to see Harriet instead of Edith beside him in bed. "Princess?" He had a million nicknames for Harriet—Kewpie Doll, Blondie, to name two others—but Princess was the one he thought described her best.

"Mommy's run away!"

Groggy, Reuben looked around as if Edith might be found hiding in a corner.

Harriet grabbed his head and turned it sideways so that they were face to face. "I saw her, all dressed up and carrying a suitcase."

Reuben threw back the blankets. After glancing down at his pajama bottoms to make sure his private parts weren't exposed, he padded over to the window and stuck his head out.

"Silly, from my window," Harriet said. "Besides, it was hours ago."

Reuben spun around. "Why didn't you wake me?"

"I know you like to sleep late on the weekends. Besides, I didn't want you running down the street after her like a maniac."

Reuben rapped the side of his head with his knuckles. "Your old dad's sure getting absentminded. Mom told me she'd be spending the weekend with a friend." He snapped his fingers. "Sophie Silverman, that's it!"

Harriet gazed at Reuben in that unnerving way of hers that always gave him the feeling she'd been born knowing more than most people figured out in a lifetime. "Can you make pancakes?" she asked.

"Not only will I make pancakes, if something good's playing, we'll take in a matinee later." As soon as he said this, Reuben realized his mistake. If Harriet had any doubts before about whether he'd been lying, she wouldn't now.

Rueben wondered if Edith might be leaving for good, the single suitcase just to tide her over until she got the rest of her things. His heart began to thump—with relief or fear, he couldn't tell. Then, the suspicion that she had to be up to something illicit took over, and he started to feel sick.

But with whom? Edith spent all her waking hours in the store. What opportunities did she have to meet men? Surely, she hadn't gotten herself involved with that Fred Adler. As calculating as Edith could be, she would never stoop that low.

By the time Reuben made it down to the kitchen, he'd dismissed the possibility that Edith had run off with a man. He pulled down the flour, oil, and Baker's chocolate chips from the cupboard and got the milk and two eggs from the refrigerator. A cup of flour, a cup of milk, a couple eggs—his mother's pancake recipe, except that his mother would have been horrified by the addition of chocolate chips.

As Reuben mixed the batter, he began singing "Toot, Toot, Tootsie Goodbye," stopping mid-stanza to laugh at the song he had unconsciously chosen. He was beginning to get excited about the idea of a weekend free of Edith's disapproving presence. "Jeffrey, get your rear end out of bed. Daddy's making pancakes!" he heard Harriet scream. "How 'bout some bacon?" Reuben called up.

"And bacon, too," Harriet added.

Reuben just finished making the first stack of pancakes when Jeffrey appeared, his face still puffy with sleep. "Chocolate chips? Can you make mine plain?"

"This isn't a restaurant," Reuben said. He realized that had Harriet asked, he would have immediately whipped up more batter.

"I'll just have bacon." Jeffrey slumped his long body across the table and rested his cheek on his forearm. "Where's Mom?"

"Off to the city to see a friend." Reuben laid a plate containing three strips of bacon in front of Jeffrey.

"What friend?" Jeffrey began cutting away the fatty edges from the bacon, placing them on the side of the plate. "Mommy doesn't have friends."

"Of course she has friends. You're the only one who doesn't have friends." Reuben slapped down a glass of juice beside him. He wondered what it was about Jeffrey that made him say such cruel things, though Jeffrey, now nibbling at a slice of bacon, didn't look the least perturbed.

A few minutes later, Harriet appeared. She'd changed out of her nightgown into a plaid kilt and red blouse. Even on weekends, she insisted on dressing nicely. Reuben swore he detected the beginning of breasts beneath her sweater. Impossible, he told himself. Harriet wasn't even ten.

Edith and Fred's room was high up, facing the park. The walls were papered in a blue and cream stripe, and the queen-sized bed was covered with a gold-tufted satin spread, complete with matching headboard. The royal blue carpet was so thick, Edith's heels got lost in it.

The day was clear enough to see all the way to Harlem and up the Hudson, where purple-hued buildings, their top floors obscured by a low cloud, ascended to the sky. Below, Central Park was joyous with spring, all pinks, yellows, and violets.

Edith opened the window, allowing in the muted traffic sounds. "Let's go right out. I don't feel tired any longer."

Fred had been inspecting the room, opening and shutting drawers and peering beneath the bed. He joined Edith by the window. "I told that kid I wanted his best room. That if I wasn't one hundred percent happy, his boss would hear from me." He placed his hands on Edith's hips and began pressing himself against her buttocks.

Edith should have known that Fred would want to take her to bed before going out. Were he really her husband, she might have been able to put him off by saying that she didn't want to muss her hair or waste the afternoon. But he wasn't her husband, however much he spoke about wanting her as his wife.

It was after two before Edith and Fred finally left the hotel. "Wanna check out the stores?" Fred asked, meaning the elegant department stores that flanked Fifth Avenue: Bonwit Teller, Bergdorf's, Saks, Lord & Taylor.

Edith squeezed Fred's hand. Pointing to one of the horse-drawn carriages parked around the fountain in Grand Army Plaza, she said, "You know what I would love? To take a carriage ride after dinner. I can't think of anything more romantic." She kissed his cheek with an exaggerated smack. She felt whorish, pretending to care more for Fred than she did, and for what? So he would buy her a more expensive birthday present? Then these days, when wasn't she pretending? Besides, it wasn't as if Fred wasn't getting plenty out of their relationship. And didn't she deserve a reward for enduring that gruesome hour in bed?

But it was only Edith who assumed they'd be visiting the department stores as shoppers, not as retailers scouring for ideas. All afternoon, Fred led her from one store to the next, insisting they scrutinize every department, it seemed, down to its last piece of merchandise. By five, Edith was so exhausted that when the guard locked the doors of B. Altman's just as they were about to enter, she gave a silent prayer of thanks.

Had Edith's mood been better, she would have been entranced by what she saw. The main floor of Saks had been transformed into a cherry blossom orchard with artificial trees and garlands of flowers wrapped around the pillars. The theme at Lord & Taylor's was Oriental with metal gongs positioned on either side of the central aisle, over which swayed dozens of red paper lanterns. At Bonwit's, in homage to *Gone With The Wind,* models in hoop dresses strolled the aisles, handing out fragrant white gardenias. It all made Fred and her efforts to create excitement at the Emporium seem as amateurish as a high school production of a Broadway musical.

While Edith and Fred trudged back up Fifth, their efforts to hail a cab fruitless, Edith thought about Fred's frequent trips into Manhattan to check out the latest styles. Why had she never insisted on going along? As forceful as she could be when it came to matters around the store, when they involved herself, she could be as timid as the greenest salesgirl. The store would never have survived had it not been for her. Yet she still behaved as if Fred was doing her a favor by allowing her to work there. She never asked him for raises and, when he gave her one, would wear herself out thanking him.

After they had gone several blocks, Fred suggested they bus it back, which meant walking over to Madison. Peering out the bus window, Edith found Madison Avenue looking more elegant than ever, with perfumeries, milliners, couture houses, and foreign clothing boutiques lining the street. She loved the idea of the department store, of a world within a world, where the aisles represented streets, the departments, its shops. She had bought into the conventional wisdom that predicted the department store's continued ascendance and the corresponding demise of the small shopkeeper. Now, she wondered if it were that simple. While it was true that shopkeepers everywhere were being crushed beneath the weight of the retailing colossi, this was not true of all shopkeepers. All of Manhattan, not just Madison Avenue, was filled with thriving small shops. What differentiated these stores from the ones that failed?

Back at the hotel, as Edith sat along the edge of the bathtub, soaking her burning feet, her thoughts returned to Sea Forth. Reuben and her children appeared in her mind like a tableau, no longer fully part of her life. She felt detached, too, from Fred, though he was not five feet away, standing in his undershirt and shorts at the mirror, working a razor down his lather-covered face.

Though she closed her eyes to discourage conversation, Fred took no notice. "Ain't it clever the way they've mixed things up?" he asked, referring to Bonwit Tellers. "How handbags aren't next to shoes, but two departments over, so a customer has to traipse through scarves and belts? Speaking of scarves, did ya get a load of that display at Bergdorf's, the way they fanned them out so they looked like flower petals? It takes a real genius to think up something like that."

Edith opened her eyes just as Fred started to work a scissor around his nostrils.

"I'm thinking we should open a lunch counter," Fred said, "a place where our ladies can get a cup of tea and rest their legs."

"Where do you propose putting it?" Edith let the water out of the tub. She pulled a towel, incredibly soft and monogrammed with a P, off the rail and began drying her feet. "Do you have any idea of the sort of planning that goes into opening a restaurant?" She didn't either, except she was sure it had to be considerable.

"Not a restaurant, a lunch counter. A place to get sandwiches, a slice of cake. It's just an idea." And one he would drop, Edith knew. He'd come to rely so completely on her that he no longer did anything without her approval. He hoisted his foot up on the toilet seat and began cutting his toenails. "Don't wanna scratch you in bed."

In the bedroom, as Edith struggled into her girdle—for once not caring what Fred, stretched out on top of the bedspread in his undershorts, thought of her bulges—her thoughts were consumed with her future. Though it remained hazy, she was sure it wouldn't include Fred and the Emporium, or, for that matter, Reuben. Edith wondered how much the lure of financial security had to do with her initial attraction to Fred. Even during the early days of their affair, when she had been caught up in the dreams of the life they might share, she could never quite forget that Fred was wealthy. For all the pride she took in being able to support herself, she had changed very little. She was still the same girl she'd been at twenty-one, the girl who'd agreed to marry Reuben, less because she loved him—or loved him enough—but because she'd sized him up as a man "with prospects." Just that afternoon, hadn't she put on the worst sort of show, in the hopes it would lead to Fred's buying her a better present?

The joke was on her. Presents were discretionary, whereas salaries were not. Because she'd viewed Fred's presents as proof of his generosity, it never occurred to her to question whether she was being paid fairly. Not that she believed Fred was trying to pull one over on her. It was simply that he was heir to the same prejudices as every man, for that matter, every woman, too, herself included—prejudices that valued a woman's contributions more cheaply than a man's.

After returning to Sea Forth the following evening, Edith glanced up from the sidewalk at her bedroom window. She was relieved to see it was dark. During the trip home, she'd thought of little except the confrontation with Reuben that awaited her. At least if he were asleep, she might not have to face that until the morning.

Once inside, Edith slipped out of her shoes and tiptoed toward the kitchen, where she was surprised to find the sink scrubbed, the dish rack emptied, and the tea towels folded and hanging from the oven door. She was drinking a glass of milk by the sink when she heard Harriet clamber down the stairs.

"You're home!" Harriet's hand flew to her chest. She was wearing a floral-patterned nightgown with a shirred bodice. Her hair was in a loose ponytail, and she was barefoot. She, too, took a glass of milk. "Why didn't you tell Daddy where you were going?" She drank the milk with her back toward Edith.

"How's everyone?" Edith tried to sound offhanded.

"Fine." Harriet licked the milk from her upper lip as she went over to the sink. She washed her own glass but left Edith's. "I'm going back up."

"Wait!" Edith hated giving Harriet the satisfaction of seeing how worried she was, but she was desperate for a clue about what to expect.

Harriet leaned against the archway, her foot pressed into the opposite ankle.

"Are Jeffrey and Daddy okay?"

"They're asleep. We had so much fun, we didn't miss you one bit. By the way, I saw you with your suitcase. I told Daddy, too." Harriet headed back upstairs.

When Edith awoke the following morning, Reuben was already up. She had slept fitfully and was stiff from having spent the night clutching the side of the bed and trying not to move so she wouldn't wake him. Outside, the sky looked like dirty dishwater.

Her bladder full to the point of bursting, Edith made her way to the bathroom. From behind the closed door, she could hear Harriet, squeaky and off key, singing "Chattanooga Choo Choo." Harriet took more time in the bathroom than the other three combined, and ordering her out of there had become a morning ritual for Edith. But this morning, Edith decided to use the unheated toilet off the kitchen instead.

Reuben was at the stove. He looked over his shoulder, his face friendly in an impersonal way Edith found more unsettling than had he been visibly angry. "I'm making soft-boiled eggs. Like one?" He dropped several eggs into a pot of boiling water and set the kitchen timer for two minutes.

Edith shook her head as she headed toward the toilet. Jenny's one stab at whimsy in a house that was otherwise staid, it had lurid pink walls and a ruffled magenta sink skirt. Above the sink was a mirrored shelf crammed with perfume flasks, the contents of which had long ago evaporated. While Edith sat there, she could hear Reuben start whistling "Chattanooga Choo Choo," also off key. Then she heard the sounds of chairs scraping and Harriet tell Reuben that he was driving her crazy and then Reuben laugh and say, "You think you sound better?" Jeffrey asked whether Mom was back, and Harriet said, "In there."

The flush of the toilet brought silence to the other side of the door. Edith knew all three were listening for the doorknob to turn and wished she could stay in there until they left. She inspected herself in the mirror, tucking her unruly curls behind her ears and wiping the traces of yesterday's mascara from beneath her eyes.

"Good morning," Edith said, her tone falsely cheery.

Harriet raised her eyebrows. "What's so good about it?"

Jeffrey shot Harriet a glance that was a plea not to cause trouble. He had eaten little, and the sight of his yolk-encrusted spoon and soggy toast bits made Edith's already tender stomach even queasier.

Edith's eyes followed Reuben's to the clock above the window. It had been broken for so long that she had gotten out of the habit of looking at it and was surprised to see it working again. It was after seven. Reuben should have been on his way to work. She knew he stayed behind because of her, though, she could see by the set of his shoulders as he piled the dishes into the sink, not because he wanted anything to do with her.

"If no one needs me, I'll get dressed," Edith said. The absurdity of the words "needs me" made Edith cringe. Harriet had never needed her; Reuben no longer did. Jeffrey was a different matter, except what it was he needed from her, she hadn't a clue.

It was evening before Reuben referred, obliquely, to Edith's weekend away. Peering at her from over his newspaper, he asked whether she'd had a nice time.

Edith, taken aback, answered, "I did, thank you."

"Glad to hear it," Reuben said before disappearing behind the paper.

Days passed. Reuben said nothing further about the weekend. Edith found the suspense so unbearable, she might have raised the subject herself were she not so afraid.

On Sunday, Reuben asked Edith to set some time aside that evening for a talk. "Would nine be okay?" he asked. The formality of his request chilled her.

At precisely nine o'clock, Reuben nodded toward the dining room. He took his customary seat at the head of the table. Before taking hers, closest to the kitchen, Edith kicked away the door stop in case the children came down for a snack.

"I couldn't believe you would just take off without telling me where you were going," Reuben held up a hand to keep Edith from responding. "I'm not interested. I just want to talk about where we go from here."

Edith stared down at her lap.

"I think it's time we both got on with our lives," Reuben said. "You must be making enough to afford a decent place."

Edith wondered why it hadn't occurred to her that if they separated, she might be the one to leave. The house, after all, belonged to Reuben. "Are you saying you want a divorce?"

"I don't see any other way."

Edith folded her arms on the table, resting her forehead upon them. Through the top of her eyes, she watched Reuben stand.

Reuben placed his hands on the seat back. "That's all I wanted to say."

Edith lifted her face. "What about the children?"

"They'll stay here, of course."

Of course, Edith thought, lowering her face again. Even if she wanted them with her, and she wasn't sure she would, where could she take them? To a cramped apartment, where she would sleep on the living room sofa like her mother had, the children crowded into a single bedroom? It occurred to her that Reuben had not referred to what he undoubtedly suspected—that she had taken a lover.

"It's not what you think," she said. "I'm not in love with anyone else."

Reuben gave her an appraising look. "You know what I realized? That I couldn't care less. And that in itself is reason enough to end things." He pushed his chair into the table. "If you'll excuse me."

When Edith got up, she went to the kitchen for a glass of water. There'd been nothing she'd hated more about this house than this kitchen with its rusted cast iron stove, rotted wooden benches, and squat, utilitarian sink. But as she stood by the sink, caressed by a night breeze that lifted the edges of the old gauze curtains, she looked around in a kind of wonderment. Old-fashioned as it was, the kitchen was large and airy, and she found herself already missing it.

The next morning, Edith stopped Reuben as he was about to leave for work. "Who should tell the children?" She was barefoot and, she knew, slatternly-looking in her faded blue bathrobe with its frayed frog buttons.

"You, of course." Reuben grabbed his cap off the coat stand.

"Have you thought about how awful this will be for them?"

His hand poised on the doorknob, Reuben said, "What, if they learn the truth about their mother?"

Edith caught the door. "That's unkind. I do love them."

"I'm going to miss my bus." He headed down the porch steps.

"I do," Edith called as she followed after him.

Reuben looked over his shoulder. "If you say so."

Edith caught up to Reuben just as he reached the sidewalk and grabbed his arm. An elderly man walking a poodle looked at Edith curiously, reminding her that she was still in her bathrobe. "Wouldn't it be better to wait until after the school year?"

"Maybe." Reuben shook his arm free. "But the truth is I can't wait for this all to be over."

When Edith arrived home Friday evening, Reuben was at the dining table. He was building a dollhouse for Harriet, and scattered about the newspaper he'd spread over the tabletop were slats of wood, nails, screws, screwdrivers, and a hammer. He glanced up and nodded coldly.

The dinner dishes were soaking in the sink. They hadn't been properly scraped, and bits of onion, tomato, and chicken floated on the water's surface. A grease-stained recipe for "Chicken Katch-a-tore" lay next to the stove. Edith was about to leave the dishes. Then she noticed the tinfoil-wrapped plate Reuben had left for her. She added hot water to the sink and plunged her hands in, for once not bothering with rubber gloves.

"Jeffrey promised he'd do them after his homework," Reuben called out.

Edith went to the doorway. She was amazed by how much of the dollhouse he had finished in a few days. The frame was up, and he was starting to lay the floors.

"You haven't told them, have you?" Reuben asked as he eased a slat into place.

"I thought I'd wait until I rented something." This was not the reason—she had no reason.

As he hammered in a tiny nail, Reuben said, "I would think your boyfriend would be delighted to help find you an apartment. That way, he can have you anytime he wants."

Edith gasped.

Reuben looked up, stunned. Edith realized that he had tossed out the line simply to see what reaction he got. And what had she done but give herself away.

Edith tried to think of an innocent-sounding explanation but couldn't. Instead, she stood, telling him with her eyes what she was not brave enough to say—that she was sorry she hurt him.

Reuben eased another slat into place. "She's so excited. I should have made her one long ago. You'll never guess what she wants to call it. Bliss."

After insisting Edith tell the children that evening, Reuben left the house. He couldn't bear the thought of being around while she did. The night was clear, the moon full, and the sky studded with stars. Reuben decided to walk down to the pier. Because he hadn't been down there since right after Jenny died, he had never seen the Ferryside Inn, except in photos. Reuben headed to the side of the restaurant so he wouldn't be noticed, and he peered through the window. The interior had a nautical theme, the ceiling strung with fishing nets and anchors fastened to the walls. There was a backlit aquarium stocked with electric-colored fish. Every table was filled, formally dressed waiters, their trays held aloft, bustling between them.

The extravagance struck Reuben as obscene. It didn't seem right for people to be indulging themselves this way when so many were being slaughtered in Europe. When his own family was being torn apart. He no longer loved Edith but was terrified to think of his children without her, even if she had never been much of a mother. He found it impossible to imagine the bathroom windowsill stripped of its clutter of makeup tubes, the silk dresses gone from their shared closet, the dresser top without her crowd of perfume atomizers and ivory brush and comb set.

The full moon made it easy for Reuben to spot Paul Herbert as he emerged from his Cadillac and tossed his keys to the valet. "No dings, no scratches, no joy rides," Paul said. The boy saluted. As a smiling Paul made his way across the dining room, Reuben watched through the window. The diners seemed excited to see him, especially the women. Reuben recalled the way Edith would light up whenever Paul spoke to her. The admiration had been mutual. More than once, he'd caught Paul staring at Edith's chest or rump. Instead of being offended, he'd been flattered that a powerful man like Paul could find his wife attractive.

What a fool he'd been. Wives didn't just take off without telling their spouses—not unless they were up to no good. It was just that the idea of Edith and that Adler person seemed absurd. All week, he'd been racking his brains, trying to come up with who else it could be, when in the back of his mind, he must have already figured it out. Why else would he now find himself standing outside of Paul's restaurant?

Edith would regard the newly widowed Paul Herbert as quite a catch. And Paul, who regarded all women as fair game, wouldn't be above using his status as a widower to lure her to bed. Then, the most horrifying thought of all occurred to Reuben—that the likeliest spot for this coupling would be Paul's bedroom, the same bedroom he and Edith once shared. It took everything Reuben had to keep from barging into the restaurant and throttling Paul, a man who, not content with stealing his house and bungalows, just had to have his wife.

"Everyone who gets married expects to be happy forever," Edith began.

The children were staring at Edith with wary expressions. Jeffrey was perched on Jenny's needlepoint footrest, his legs folded behind him. Harriet was seated cross-legged on the floor.

Edith scanned the living room. It occurred to her that they had been living there for six years, that Harriet would have few if any memories of Bliss. Yet, there wasn't an inch of this room that didn't still have Jenny's stamp. Edith had done nothing to make the house her own.

"But it doesn't always work out that way. For a long time, Daddy and I haven't been happy." As Edith gathered her courage, even the room seemed to be holding its breath. "Because of that, we've decided it would be better if we lived apart. And so…I'll be moving out."

The children continued staring. Jeffrey's eyes filled with tears. And while Harriet's eyes remained scornful, her lower lip began to tremble. Edith longed to reassure them that she would always be their mother. But could she honestly tell them that when this might be true only in a biological sense? When, to a child, what a mother really represented was a constant presence—something her children would no longer have?

"For how long?" Harriet asked in a way that made clear that what she was really doing was daring Edith to say that terrible word—*forever*.

Edith took the coward's way out by answering, "I'm not sure." She immediately realized her mistake when relief washed over Jeffrey's face. Of course, he would latch onto the possibility that sooner or later, she would return.

Jeffrey swung his legs out in front. His pajama bottoms were too short, exposing several inches of calf. Edith was startled to see how hairy his legs had become. She grabbed his hand, already mannish in size, yet childishly smooth and plump.

"Probably forever," Edith said.

Harriet turned to Jeffrey and said matter-of-factly, "They're getting a divorce."

Jeffrey wrenched his hand away and jammed his fists into his thighs. His head lowered and shoulders shaking, he began to cry.

Harriet scuttled on her rear end to him. "There, there," she said and began patting his back.

Jeffrey buried his face in Harriet's neck. As she ran her fingers through his curls, Harriet asked Edith, "When are you leaving?"

"Soon," Edith said.

"Don't worry," Harriet said to Jeffrey. "Daddy will take care of us."

Edith stripped the closet of her suits and dresses, crammed them into her suitcases, and then scooped her shoes off the closet floor and dumped them on top of her clothes. Her shoes looked ridiculous to her with their fancy buckles and bows, their Cuban and stiletto heels. How many would she ever wear again? The years at the Emporium had taken their toll. Her feet, bad to begin with, were now so riddled with corns and bunions it was a challenge simply to find shoes that fit.

After finishing with her closet, Edith started on the dresser, cramming in her underwear and satin nightgowns, as well as the angora sweaters Reuben once said, jokingly, that she cared more about than her children. She had to sit on the suitcases to make them close. Then, she dragged them to the head of the stairs and pushed them down, not waiting for one to reach the bottom before sending down the next.

The motel room was small and boxy, the walls a swimming pool aqua, their texture rough, as if sand had been mixed in with the paint. The carpet was blue and green, so too were the polished cotton curtains and matching bedspread, which had a jarring abstract pattern. The same pattern was repeated on the shower curtain in an otherwise white bathroom, except for the rust stains in the sink and the unpainted concrete floor, in the middle of which was a drain hole that gave off a fishy odor. The rate was $5 a night, an obscene amount given that the room at the Plaza had only cost Fred $21. But this was the only motel within walking distance of the store.

As soon as Edith got to the room, she collapsed onto the bed, too tired to pull off the bedspread. She tried not to think of the people who had lain there before or the sorts of things they'd done on it. From next door, she heard the jangle of coat hangers. She wondered what kind of people stayed in a place like this when it was still too cold to swim, besides wives whose husbands had kicked them out. She had brought no books or magazines, and the room didn't have a radio. The motel's restaurant was closed until the end of the month, so her supper consisted of candy bars and chips from the vending machine, washed down with water drunk directly from the tap. Too exhausted to unpack, she slept on the bedspread in her slip.

# Chapter Twenty-Two

## *July through September 1940*

Until Edith moved out, Reuben said nothing to Adolph about the decision to end his marriage, partly from embarrassment, partly because he never quite believed it was going to happen. But now that Edith was gone, Reuben felt he had to tell Adolph immediately. He knew how hurt Adolph would be if he found out some other way.

Reuben stopped by the Rexall's, figuring the slow evening hours would offer as much privacy as they could get anywhere. Adolph was re-arranging the feminine hygiene products on the shelves beneath the pharmacy counter, just the sight of which, even after all his years of marriage, made Reuben's face grow warm. Adolph was wearing a pale green jacket with "Adolph Friestadt, pharmacist" embroidered in red script above the breast pocket.

"Edith and I have decided to separate," Reuben said.

"Really?" Adolph didn't sound at all surprised. "What about the children?"

"They're staying with me. I'm keeping the house."

A stout woman in a dark green hat with a violet plume came charging into the store. Adolph sighed as she barreled toward them. "Not a single customer all night. Why now?"

"Pharmacist," she said, snapping her fingers. She rifled through her enormous satchel and then shoved a prescription in his hand. "Make it snappy, please."

Adolph grumbled as he read the prescription, stuffed it into his jacket pocket, and disappeared into the back room.

Reuben wandered over to the magazine rack. He picked up *Life* magazine, moving past an article about this year's crop of debutantes, "the most beautiful and civic minded group to be presented in some time," to one about the German occupation of Paris. There was an aerial photo of the Champs-Élysées, its stores shuttered and sidewalks devoid of pedestrians, its roadway cleared of vehicles except for a convoy of tanks, their swastikas staring upward, making their way toward the Arc de Triomphe. The French, the article said, had put up virtually no resistance to the occupation. Though this was hardly news to Reuben, the words terrified him.

Reuben had just finished the article when Adolph emerged from the back. "Take it a half hour before meals," he heard Adolph say. "For heaven's sake, don't be a glutton. Don't eat right before bed. And lay off the fatty foods." Reuben was surprised by Adolph's bluntness, sure that this sort of language could get him fired.

But the woman, who had been tapping her foot impatiently, seemed intrigued. As she dropped the medicine into her handbag, she said, "My doctor said it might help to sleep in a semi-upright position."

"It might," Adolph said. "Though the only real solution is to lose some weight. With all that excess flesh pressing against your organs, how can you expect them to work properly?" Adolph looked her over in a detached fashion. Holding up a finger, he said, "There is something that might help and not just as a patch either."

Adolph went back to the stockroom and returned with a bottle. "Psyllium seeds. Entirely natural and completely safe."

He opened the bottle, spilling a pinch of what looked to Reuben like wood shavings into her hand.

"An unbeatable bulking agent," Adolph said. "Mix a tablespoon into eight ounces of tepid water three times a day, stir vigorously, and gulp it down. Don't let it sit or it will clump. Do as I say, and I guarantee you won't be nearly as hungry, and providing you stay away from sugars and fats, the weight should start dropping off. Just as important, it will keep you regular."

"Regular?" the woman asked.

"Your bowels. Nothing is more deleterious to one's health than a sluggish, packed colon. And promise you'll take a brisk walk every night after dinner. Thirty minutes, rain or shine."

The woman nodded.

"Do that," Adolph continued, "and not only will you lose weight, you'll sleep more soundly. In a couple of months, you should be able to toss out that stuff—the medicine, not the psyllium. That you should take for the rest of your life."

The woman looked down at the bottle and then back up at Adolph. "I believe you," she said. "I get the feeling you care about my health more than my doctor does." She dropped the bottle into her satchel and held out her gloved hand to shake Adolph's. Then, mistaking Reuben for a customer, she said, "He's very good."

As soon as the woman left, Adolph asked Reuben, "What kind of woman leaves her children to go off with another man?"

"There's no other man," Reuben said angrily.

Adolph raised his eyebrows, which over the years had grown to resemble caterpillars. "So, it's another woman! Are you going to tell me who?"

"You think sex is the only reason people separate?" Reuben asked.

"As a matter of fact, I do," Adolph said. "Not that I blame you. For a long time, it's been obvious that she hasn't been much of a wife. Besides, what business is it of mine if you're having an affair?"

"I am not having an affair. You're one to talk. The way you used to lead those old ladies on, and still do, I see."

Now it was Adolph's turn to get annoyed. "What right do you have to talk about something you know nothing about? The compounds I sell are based on sound holistic principles."

"Sell?"

"Sell! You're shocked? That a few of my customers still care enough to come to my apartment? Thank God, they do. With what I'm making here, if it weren't for them, we'd starve."

Reuben held up his hands. "I shouldn't have said that. What do I know about holistic—whatever you call it—medicine?"

Adolph laughed. "I do tend to lead them on a bit. But only because they enjoy it so, not because I don't believe in what I'm doing. I'm sorry, too. I know how hard marriage can be. As much as I adored my wife, believe me, we had our problems."

The blowzy blond cashier, who had been busy applying lacquer to her nails, began to eye them suspiciously.

"I better go," Reuben said. "For all we know, she could be a Nazi spy."

As Reuben was getting ready for bed, he had an idea. Why not ask Adolph and Ernest to move in with them? Given that he worked days and Adolph evenings, it would mean someone would always be around to look after the children. By refusing to take rent, he could ease some of his guilt over the role he played in how Adolph had been swindled. In exchange, Adolph could do the errands he was unable to do, now that he was working days. Adolph could also prepare some of the meals, though Harriet and Jeffrey would surely be unhappy about that. Not to mention how much they would each save by sharing the cost of utilities and food. Reuben also liked the idea of having Ernest around, hopeful that some of his studiousness might rub off on Jeffrey. And he had to admit that he would also enjoy the companionship.

Edith did not tell Fred she had moved out. She was afraid that he might insist on paying to set her up or worse, want to visit her at the motel. Because she could not leave the store without another job, she was desperate for the affair with Fred to continue, afraid if she ended it, he might ask her to leave.

Edith quickly fell into a routine. She would breakfast on a buttered roll and coffee in the motel's small restaurant, too worried about money to splurge on so much as an egg and bacon. Her walk to the Emporium was up a road with a wide grass divider and flanked by elms. The houses, set back on large level lawns, were mainly Victorians with turreted roofs and wraparound porches. Several had "Room for Let" signs in their windows. Edith knew that a room in somebody's house was likely to be less expensive than a motel room and also offer kitchen privileges. Undoubtedly, it would be less depressing. Yet, the impermanence of the motel appealed to her, as well as its shabbiness. She regarded living there as a form of penance.

In the month since she moved out, Edith had not spoken to Reuben or the children. She had no idea if they knew where she was living. She missed the children more than she could have imagined. She even missed Reuben. And while Fred might be too dense to figure out that something was troubling her, the salesgirls had. They were friendlier, occasionally inviting her to join them at lunch, invitations Edith seldom refused—she was that lonely. She began to let herself go. Somehow, it no longer seemed important whether her nail polish was chipped or her roots were showing. She gave in, as well, to the sweet tooth she'd spent a lifetime fighting, subsisting on candy bars and soda pop from the motel vending machine, and her hips and thighs showed it.

Reuben was asleep when the phone rang. He tried to ignore it, but when the ringing went on, he threw on his bathrobe and headed downstairs, determined to give whoever was on the other end a piece of his mind. "Who is it?" he growled.

There was no answer.

Reuben was about to hang up when he heard a rustling. "Who is it?"

The answer was barely audible. "Me."

For weeks, Reuben had been expecting Edith to call. He knew she was all right only because he'd called the store anonymously, asked if she was still working there, and was told she was. Not to have called even once, if only to ask how the children were doing, went beyond what he would have expected, even from her.

"What do you want?" Reuben asked gruffly. As relieved as he was to hear from Edith, he didn't want to give her the satisfaction of knowing. When she didn't answer, he became afraid she might hang up and said more gently, "Don't go."

"How are the children?"

"Fine." Reuben wanted to say the children missed her but couldn't, for while Jeffrey clearly did, Harriet made a point of repeatedly telling him how she didn't.

"Are they back in school?"

Was it possible she didn't know, Reuben wondered, that the first day of school was always the Wednesday after Labor Day? "Not for another week. Why didn't you let us know where you were staying?"

Another pause. "I'm at the motel at the bottom of Elm. The Tides."

If it was the motel Reuben thought, it looked shabby. "What's the phone number?"

"I don't have it on me. I'm calling from a pay phone. You can always call me at the store. Do you think the children would like to see me?" Edith asked.

"Call tomorrow evening. But earlier."

"You have to see your mother," Adolph told Harriet. He had ordered Reuben to relax and let Harriet clear the table.

"Adolph, this is none of your business," Reuben said.

"A little girl shouldn't get to decide something like this." Adolph turned toward Harriet.

"Darling, remember what I said? You need to scrape the dishes before putting them in the sink."

"I wish you'd stay out of this," Reuben said.

"Whatever you say. But if you ask me—"

"No one's asking."

"I give up." Adolph stalked out of the kitchen.

Harriet stuck her tongue out at his back. "I hate him," she said.

"Don't say that."

"Why not? It's true. Besides, his food tastes like vomit." Harriet gathered the un-scraped plates and said, "Watch," as she dropped them into the sink.

All three of them were finding the adjustment to having Adolph and Ernest there more difficult than Reuben had anticipated. First, there was the clutter. Adolph was the furthest thing from a messy person, but he had so many possessions, books especially. Reuben had watched in amazement as the moving men unloaded Adolph's cartons, 108 in all, many of which were still piled up in the living room and the foyer, making passage nearly impossible. A regular boarder, too, would have spent more time in his room. When he told Adolph, "I want you to treat this like your own home," he hadn't meant for Adolph to take it so literally.

"I hate her, too," Harriet said as she turned on the cold tap.

"Dishes have to be washed in hot water," Reuben said. "I hope you don't mean that." He was being sincere. Even so, he couldn't help feeling a bit gratified by Harriet's refusal to see her mother. He pulled a cigar from his shirt pocket and clipped off the end. These days, he rarely got the chance to enjoy one. Adolph never came right out and asked him not to smoke. He didn't have to. He made his disapproval obvious by coughing, waving the smoke away, and opening the windows.

"I do," Harriet said.

As he puffed on his cigar, Reuben studied Harriet. She had the same stubborn set to her jaw and judgmental turn to her mouth his mother had had.

"I do!" Harriet said, finally turning off the cold tap and turning on the hot. "Aren't you always telling me it's wrong to lie?"

When Reuben opened the door, he was startled by Edith's appearance. She had gained so much weight that the waistband of her skirt laid buried within a sandwich of flesh. Her inch-long roots provided a startling contrast to the rest of her hair—he hadn't realized she had become so gray, and there was a greasy sheen to her complexion.

"Are they ready?" Edith asked, looking around. Reuben could tell she was dying to know who else was living there.

"Jeffrey is. She's decided not to come." Reuben rolled his eyes.

"Oh." The word came out sounding like a gasp of pain.

"She should at least say hello. I'll get her." Reuben prayed Edith wouldn't take him up on the offer. He was sure the only way he'd get Harriet downstairs would be to forcibly carry her.

"I'll see her next time," Edith said.

Jeffrey came scrambling down the stairs and flew into Edith's arms. "I missed you!" He burrowed his face in her hair.

Reuben turned away, discomforted by Jeffrey's display of affection. He scanned the living room and upstairs landing, thankful Ernest and Adolph weren't around.

Edith pecked Jeffrey on the cheek and then gently extricated herself. "You look like a real gentleman!"

Jeffrey puffed out his chest. "I do?" He looked toward Reuben for affirmation.

Reuben nodded. He had never seen Jeffrey so carefully groomed. He was wearing a competently knotted tie—one of Reuben's—and his hair was neat, the part perfect and curls held in check with pomade. Jeffrey had even shaved the fuzz off his upper lip. Reuben was surprised to realize how handsome he was.

"I'll have him back by ten," Edith said, giving Jeffrey's perfectly lying collar a motherly tug.

Reuben felt his eyes well. He watched from the door as they headed down the path, arms linked, looking less like mother and son than lovers setting off on a date.

For Reuben, one of the few things about having Adolph and Ernest living there he found easy to get used to were Adolph's meals. He was surprised to find much of Adolph's food delicious. Adolph's lentil and spinach stew, for example, or his chickpea and escarole soup. Plus, it was economical; it was costing less to feed the five of them than it used to cost to feed himself and the children. Harriet and Jeffrey were less enthusiastic, but now that Adolph had banned snacks—save a single seed-studded homemade cookie and glass of fresh-squeezed juice after school—most nights, they finished their dinners anyway. Which was not to say all of Adolph's meals were successes. Dinner one September evening was a lima bean and mushroom stew that looked and smelled like a swamp and left them all wondering how they would get it down.

Adolph pointed his fork at the children seated along one side of the table, with Harriet squeezed between the boys. "Eat."

Harriet deposited a single lima bean on the tip of her tongue.

"None of you leave until you finish."

"I thought you said children should be allowed to decide what they eat?" Reuben said. If Adolph made the children finish their dinners, he could hardly get away without finishing his.

"Within limits. A growing child still needs to ingest the right balance of nutrients, or it will pay the price for the rest of its life."

Ernest nudged Harriet. "You didn't know you were an 'it,' did you?"

"If I'm an 'it,' what are you?" Harriet elbowed him back.

Ernest looked past Harriet toward Jeffrey. "A better question—what is he?"

Jeffrey, who had been following the exchange with a grin, lowered his face to his plate and began shoveling his food in.

Brow wrinkled, Harriet studied Jeffrey. "Maybe he's from outer space."

"One of those Martian invaders," Ernest said, nodding slowly. "He's funny enough looking. See how his ears stick out?"

"And how long and pointy his nose is?" Harriet said, laying a finger atop her own small, perfectly shaped one.

Ernest studied Jeffrey. "I've heard Martians often try to pass themselves off as humans. Maybe that's the reason..."

Reuben had been enjoying the banter. But because it was beginning to upset Jeffrey, he decided to put a stop to it. "Ernest, I'm not sure Jeffrey realizes you're kidding."

Ernest opened his mouth in mock bewilderment. "I'm not!" He turned toward Jeffrey. "C'mon, Jeffrey, tell us—are you man or Martian?"

Jeffrey threw his napkin down and charged from the room.

"We were just having fun," Ernest called out. He clambered out of his chair and bounded up the stairs—a remarkable display of energy for someone purportedly at death's door.

From upstairs, Reuben could hear Ernest banging on the attic door, pleading for Jeffrey to open up. A couple minutes later, Ernest returned, looking upset.

"He's such a baby," Harriet said. She was eating her food, bean by bean, mushroom slice by mushroom slice, wrinkling her nose after every bite.

"Shut up," Ernest said.

"Don't talk to her that way," Adolph said.

"He is," Harriet said softly.

"We shouldn't have teased him," Ernest said. Face in hand, he dug his fork into the stew and took a bite. "This is disgusting." He pushed his plate away.

Adolph gave him a warning look.

"I feel sorry for them that they've now got to eat this swill, too." Ernest carried his plate to the garbage bin. "I'm going out."

Adolph shrugged.

"Are you going to ask where?"

"Okay, where?"

"To the Argosy."

Adolph pushed his plate away. "It is awful. I admit it."

The three listened as Ernest again started banging on the attic door. "I'll treat you to a hamburger and fries." They then heard the creak of the attic door opening.

Adolph offered to make salad sandwiches for Harriet and Reuben. He was slicing a loaf of brown bread when Jeffrey and Ernest came downstairs, laughing.

"How about some shredded beets?" Adolph asked Harriet. "I know little girls don't like beets, but they're good for your liver."

Reuben winced. He had never been able to abide beets—boiled, baked, shredded, it didn't matter. He looked longingly through the kitchen doorway toward the front door, through which the boys had disappeared. He pictured them eating, meat juices dribbling down their chins, fingertips greasy from french fries.

"Reuben, some shredded beets on your sandwich, too?" Adolph asked.

In the past, Fred always took Edith to dinner on the quarterly inventory days, figuring there was nothing suspicious about a boss treating his second in charge to a meal after such a grueling day. But on the evening of the third quarter inventory, Fred left before six. He said nothing to Edith, just grabbed his hat and sprinted out of the store. He was wearing the same outfit he wore the day they met at the Plaza.

As Edith test-sampled the merchandise to make sure it had been entered into the books correctly, she wondered if Fred was meeting a woman. It had been months since he'd spoken about getting married. Or said, "I love you," except after they copulated which, Edith knew, didn't count.

One glance in the mirror told Edith why. It was the weight she'd gained. How it coarsened her facial features and transformed her figure from an hourglass into a slab. Because Fred never mentioned how stout she'd become, she fooled herself into believing he hadn't noticed. Of course he had, just as he surely noticed how unhappy she was. If he really loved her, he would have insisted she tell him what was troubling her.

It was dark when Edith left the store. Though she was exhausted, frugality had become such a habit, she didn't consider calling a cab. She had already crossed Main Street when she noticed thunderclouds drifting in from the ocean. She looked down at her calfskin pumps. The color of chocolate pudding and as soft as a baby's bottom, they were the only thing she'd treated herself to in months. But she was so tired she couldn't bear the thought of returning for an umbrella and decided to chance making it back to the motel before the rains started. Within minutes, the clouds burst. As Edith pushed her way against a suddenly ferocious wind, she began to cry. Not just her pumps, but her hat, too, would be ruined. She no longer treasured her clothing. Her distress was more pragmatic. If her hat and shoes were ruined, she would have to replace them.

Edith had gone several blocks when a horn tooted and a Cadillac pulled up. "I thought it was you," Paul Herbert said through an inch of open window. He reached across and opened the passenger-side door.

"My guardian angel," Edith said. The car had a varnished wood steering wheel and dashboard. Its burgundy leather seats still had that new leather smell. "I'm ruining your car," she cried when she realized she was dripping water everywhere.

"So I see." Paul pulled a mohair rug from the back. "Tuck this around yourself."

As Edith snuggled beneath the rug, she watched Paul's hands move between the clutch and wheel with the cocky self-assurance with which he did everything. He was wearing leather gloves with pinholes and a suit that was probably gray but looked black in the dim light. The rhythmic swish of the wipers and the heat pumping from the vents made the car feel like a cozy, self-contained world.

"Mind telling me what you were doing out there?" Paul asked.

"I'm living at the Tides Motel now," Edith said with as much dignity as she could muster. "Reuben and I have separated."

"No kidding!" Paul grinned. "The Tides? It's always struck me as a pretty grubby place."

"It's not that bad."

"And the children?"

"They're staying with Reuben." Embarrassed to leave Paul with the impression this arrangement was anything but temporary, Edith added, "for the time being."

Paul swung into the parking lot beside the motel. He patted Edith's hand. "If Gladys were here, she'd tell you how I always thought you were too good for him. What do you do for meals?"

"I make do." Edith reached for the door handle.

"My restaurant's just down the block. Let me buy you dinner."

"I'll let you in on a secret. I once had quite a thing for you. I have a hunch Gladys suspected. You still look good, a bit tired, that's all. Then again, I've always thought women got more interesting as they got older," Paul said.

Edith knew she was looking anything but attractive—her hair drenched, mascara running, her wet dress clinging to her fat thighs. Somehow, she didn't care. She took a sip of her martini and fished the olive out with the plastic toothpick. "This is some place," she said, glancing around at the starched blue linen tablecloths and napkins, the sterling silver flatware and crystal stemware, the four-person jazz band setting up on the small stage. The words were barely out of her mouth when she began to feel guilty; the restaurant stood on the exact spot where Reuben's bungalows had once been.

"I like it," Paul said. His jawline had gotten softer and his eyelids droopier since the last time Edith had seen him, making him appear sad and weary, though Edith knew it would be a mistake to read too much into what were probably just normal signs of aging. At the store, customers and salesgirls alike were always offering up tidbits about his social life and, according to the rumor mill, Paul was doing a great deal of dating, mainly of girls young enough to be his daughter.

Paul grabbed Edith's menu. "Let me order for you." He held the menu in front of his face when he ordered so that her meal would be a surprise. After the waiter left, Paul shifted sideways and crossed his legs. "Why do I get the feeling you've been a naughty girl?"

"I have no idea what you're talking about," Edith said primly. She felt her cheeks grow warm as she reached for a bread roll.

"Edith, you know as well as I do that when a marriage ends, someone's always to blame, and if I had to guess, I'd bet it was you. The way he used to moon over you – it was enough to make a person sick."

Edith dug her knife into the butter, savaging the swirls, and deposited a lump onto her bread. "Leave him out of this. What makes you such an expert on human nature, anyway?"

"Who said I'm an expert? God knows, I've made enough of a mess of my own life." Paul's expression turned somber as he tore into his roll.

The waiter brought their appetizers, two plates of clams on the half-shell on mounds of ice. Edith had a lifelong revulsion for the idea of eating raw creatures and stared at the shimmering blobs in dismay.

"You're in charge of the salesgirls, right?" Paul said after slurping several off the shell.

Edith nodded, surprised he remembered. "Only, I'm responsible for a lot more than that."

"What sort of things? But have your clams first. You won't get fresher anywhere."

Edith swallowed her first clam whole to avoid tasting it. "Very fresh."

"Like me. Although I've calmed down a lot in my old age."

"That's not what I hear around the store."

"What sort of things do they say?" Paul seemed genuinely pleased.

"What do you think they say?"

"Then you must have heard about my building."

"That's hardly what they talk about."

Paul pointed his fork at her clams. "Don't you like them?"

"They're delicious." Edith popped another in her mouth.

After finishing his clams, Paul pushed his plate to the side. "It's going to be six stories, the tallest building in Sea Forth. Very swish. Lots of marble, granite. The sort of building you'd expect to find on Fifth Avenue."

Of course, Edith knew about the building. The excavation site was like an open wound. While his building might not be the sort of thing they gossiped about at the store, the local papers talked about it plenty. A year had passed since Paul had broken ground, and the building still remained controversial, with periodic calls for an investigation into how Paul managed to get approval to put up such a tall building given the four-story height restrictions in the local ordinances.

Paul snapped his fingers. "What's the name of that guy you work for? The one who looks like W. C. Fields?" He switched plates with her. "Why didn't you tell me you don't like clams?"

"Fred Adler."

"Right. Besides looking after the sales gals, what else does W. C. have you doing?"

Edith was pleased to have this opportunity to brag. "That's a big part of it. A retail store is nothing without the right employees. I figure out the staffing levels and set the wages. I also design the sales promotions, which includes deciding when to mark down items and lay out the advertisements. Then, I— "

"Whoa, what don't you do?"

"I don't handle the books, although I do keep dibs on our inventory levels."

"It sounds like you run the place."

"Hardly. It's just that after you've been around a place for a while, you begin to see the whole picture, and if you've got the sort of big mouth I do..."

"Forgive my being nosy, but how much is W. C. paying you?"

"Enough to get by," Edith said.

"Really?"

"Enough."

"One thing's for sure. It isn't enough. Want my opinion? You've probably learned all you're going to learn from W. C.

From here on in, all you'll be doing is making him rich. You should think about going into business for yourself."

By then, their main course had arrived, which, to Edith's relief, was Sole Veronique.

"I mean it," Paul said.

Edith thought Paul was being ridiculous. "What do I know about starting a business? Besides, there's the little problem of money."

"Don't let anyone tell you it's love that makes the world go around. Money can buy you love, but the opposite sure isn't true."

"That's one lesson I learned long ago."

"I'll tell you something else. Even if he paid you five times as much, and for the next five years you saved every penny, you still wouldn't have enough to start your own business. The number one reason businesses fail is due to a lack of capital. Whatever you figure it'll take to get a business up and running, multiply that number by three."

"Then, why encourage me? So, I can end up selling apples on some street corner?"

"All I'm saying is that if you do go into business, make sure you go about it the right way."

The band began to play "Slaughter on Tenth Avenue," making further conversation impossible. It was not until they'd finished their desserts—chocolate cake topped with whipped cream, so delicious that Edith could barely resist running her finger around the plate—that the band took a break. By then, Paul had lost interest in discussing whether Edith should start her own business. "This boyfriend, does he want to marry you?"

The alcohol had loosened Edith's tongue. "Who cares? There's no way I would marry him."

"I still think it was rotten of Reuben to make you move out."

"It's his house."

"That's hardly the point. You must miss the kids. I know how much I miss Lawrence when he's away at school, and I'm only his father."

"Can we talk about something else?" These days, the mere mention of her children could reduce Edith to tears. She felt Paul's eyes upon her as she scanned the room. Even on a rainy Tuesday night, the restaurant was busy. She caught sight of George and Marianne Rule across the room. From the intensity with which they were talking, shoulders hunched, heads leaning in, it was clear they had spotted Edith and Paul and were trying not to be noticed.

"How about an after-dinner drink?" Paul raised a finger to get the waiter's attention.

"Are you trying to get me drunk?" Edith joked. She thought this entirely possible. Paul knew where she was living, probably sensed how lonely she was. She decided she rather liked the idea of spending the night with Paul.

When Paul didn't laugh, Edith realized she had been wrong about his intentions. He ran his finger around the rim of his glass, and Edith knew he was thinking about Gladys. "I shouldn't have said those things about Reuben. I always liked the guy. I can only imagine how awful it was for him when he lost his business."

"Only him? Anyway, that was a long time ago. I'm over it now, and so is he."

"Except for what it did to your marriage."

"Except for that," Edith said.

# Chapter Twenty-Three

## *November 1940*

---

In early November, Edith began planning the Christmas work roster. Forecasts were for the strongest Christmas in years and, based upon how robust sales already were, Edith saw no reason to question these predictions. Her challenge was to translate these forecasts into a series of practical decisions, such as determining the appropriate level of sales coverage in the weeks leading up to Christmas and figuring out the extent to which she should rely upon temporary help versus having the permanent staff work overtime.

Nothing made Edith forget her problems the way work did. It was Wednesday, one of the two nights each week when Edith took her children out to dinner, the other being Sunday. Edith found these dinners a strain, especially now that Harriet had agreed to come along. She planned on leaving work by seven, which was early for her. She was spending more time at the store than ever, not out of loyalty to the Emporium but because she dreaded returning to the motel. To Edith, the saddest thing about the waning of her and Fred's relationship was how her love for the store had wilted along with it. Fred never did muster the courage to break things off. He avoided her, which she made easier by spending most of her time inside her office. When Fred needed something, he would slip a note beneath her door or ring her on the telephone.

The children weren't ready when Edith arrived at Main Street. She waited for them in the living room, surrounded by Adolph's boxes. She'd been astonished to learn that it was Adolph who had moved in, a man whom Reuben once crossed the street to avoid.

"Where are we going?" Harriet asked while she rubbed at the spot on her cheek where Edith had kissed her. She was scarf-less and gloveless, and the backs of her anklets were trapped inside her shoes.

"The Argosy. Button your coat; it's cold."

Harriet undid several more buttons. She whipped off her hat and stuffed it into her pocket. "That place makes me puke. Why do we have to stay in Sea Forth?"

"Because we do," Edith said.

Edith hated the Argosy, too, but it was the only restaurant in Sea Forth that was reasonably priced. The food was awful, and the décor—if it could be called that—even more so with scarred wooden tables and torn plastic benches that snagged her stockings. Plus, it was dirty. The windows were smudged with grease, and the linoleum floor was so sticky their shoes made sucking noises as they headed to their booth.

"I'll have a grilled cheese and cocoa," Harriet told the waitress with a sigh. She folded her arms across the table and rested her head upon them.

Jeffrey methodically read out loud from the menu, pausing after each item as if to consider it, oblivious to the waitress who was tapping her pencil against the order pad. At last, he looked up and said, "I'll have a hamburger, well done. Without the bun." It was the same thing he always ordered.

"Fries or coleslaw?"

"Neither."

"Something to drink?"

"Water. No ice. I hate ice."

As soon as the waitress left, Edith tilted her head, and assuming an artificially bright expression, asked, "What's happening in school?"

Her face still on her arms, Harriet answered, "Why do you care?"

"Jeffrey?" Edith asked.

Jeffrey played with his fork. "We had a chemistry test. On esters. I did okay." He spoke haltingly as if he had been called on in class and was afraid of giving the wrong answer.

At a loss for what else to ask, Edith blathered on about the store. "Harriet, you should see the alpaca scarves we got in. They're so soft, and the colors are just beautiful. Would you like one?"

Harriet didn't respond.

"How about a red one? Though there's a lovely royal blue."

"Fine, blue." After taking a few bites of her sandwich, Harriet folded her arms again and laid her head back down. "Can we leave now?"

"Not until Jeffrey finishes. Besides, don't you want dessert?"

Jeffrey was taking rabbit-sized nibbles of his hamburger while he stared off into space.

At the mention of dessert, Harriet perked up. About the only thing good about the Argosy was the ice cream, made by a local dairy, and ice cream was Harriet's favorite food.

"I'll have two scoops. Chocolate and vanilla," she told the waitress. "And he'll have the same," she added, foreclosing the possibility that Jeffrey might decide to skip dessert.

The waitress had just pulled two parfait glasses down from the shelf above the freezer when Harriet jumped up. "You never got my mom's order," she cried. "She wants strawberry. Two scoops." Turning toward Edith and smiling for the first time that evening, Harriet said, "Don't worry, I'll eat whatever you don't finish."

Edith had just let herself into her room when the phone rang. She looked at it in disbelief. The only person who ever called her was Reuben, and he called her at the store.

"Is this Edith Merkal?" The line was so crackly that Edith could barely make out the voice at the other end.

"Who's this?" she screamed.

The caller had to shout his name twice before Edith understood. Paul Herbert.

Edith yelled back what a pleasant surprise this was as she slipped out of her shoes. Between the ringing of the phone and the fact that it was Paul, her heart had begun to pound.

The crackling intensified, and Edith was afraid they'd been disconnected when, finally, she heard, "How about dinner Sunday night?"

Dinner, Sunday night? Edith thanked God that Paul was unable to see the state he'd reduced her to. "I'd love to!" she gushed.

It was only after she hung up that she remembered. Sunday was her night with her children. She considered calling Paul back, but only for a moment. What harm would there be if she missed one night, so long as she didn't make a habit of it?

What Paul hadn't mentioned, or Edith missed because of the bad line, was that they'd be dining at Paul's house. Her old house. "I hope you don't mind," he said as they drove past Jenny's house toward Mowbray. "This way, we'll have more privacy."

Did she mind? Edith wasn't sure. She longed to see the house. At the same time, she was afraid of how she'd react to seeing it changed. She felt conflicted, too, about Paul's reason for bringing her there. While she found the idea of being alone with him thrilling, she felt vaguely insulted. Did he think that because she was older and about to become a divorcée, he could dispense with the customary wooing?

As Paul unlocked the door, he said, "We never had you here, did we? I think you'll get a kick out of the changes we made."

For years after losing Bliss, Edith would dream they were back living there, but as squatters. The house would be changed in awful ways. In one dream, it had a funhouse feel, all mirrored hallways and rolling floors. In another, the rooms were much as they had been, except for the ropy vines that had pushed through the windows and snaked along the walls and across the ceiling.

The real house had been stripped of its romantic embellishments. The sweetheart staircase that once dominated the foyer had been replaced by a more practical wall hugging one. In the living room, the whipped cream swirls had been sanded down, the walls now covered with bamboo-textured wallpaper. Gone, too, were the pressed metal ceiling and the ornately carved pink marble fireplace—a large gray stone one stood in its place. Moss-green, wall-to-wall carpet had been laid over the walnut parquet floors.

"Very modern," Edith said.

"Gladys preferred a contemporary look. Let me show you the kitchen."

The kitchen, with laminated countertops that Paul referred to as "Formica," was the most modern Edith had ever seen. There was an electric stove and a Kelvinator refrigerator with a separate freezer compartment. Beside the sink was an appliance Paul told her was an automatic dishwasher. "You stack the dishes, attach the hose, and forty minutes later, voilà—clean dishes."

"Did you keep anything the way it was?"

Paul thought about this. "I don't think we changed the sun room. Poor Gladys ended up sleeping there once she could no longer handle the stairs."

"What about upstairs?"

"We didn't do much. Come to think of it, didn't one of the bathrooms have purple tiles? Of course, Gladys got rid of them."

Paul offered to make a pitcher of martinis while they waited for dinner. He slid back a pair of louvered doors, revealing a mirror-backed cupboard stocked with glasses and liquors, and a stainless steel sink. "Saves a lot of back and forth to the kitchen when we entertain," he said, oblivious to his use of the word "we."

He sat down on the couch and directed Edith to the love seat diagonally across from it. "To old times." As he leaned forward to clink glasses, he said, "Dammit, I should have made champagne cocktails!"

"The last time I had one was at your party."

"That was some night! Gladys didn't speak to me for days. Of course, I was right, though even I never imagined things would get so bleak."

"Not for you, they didn't."

"I took my share of beatings. But comparatively speaking, we were lucky." Paul took off his jacket and laid it across the sofa back.

"At least it finally looks like things are on the mend."

"With war around the corner, not even Roosevelt will be able to muck things up now." Paul checked his watch. "I better go see about dinner."

After several minutes passed, Edith walked out into the foyer to see what was keeping Paul. She could hear him on the phone, so she decided to use the time to look around. Because the house was so altered, she didn't find being there nearly as upsetting as she'd expected. She especially wanted to see the sunroom, given it was the one downstairs room Paul said was unchanged. But the French doors leading to it were locked, and the curtains on the inside windows drawn. Edith had a hunch Paul no longer used it, maintaining it as a sort of shrine to Gladys.

For all of Paul and Gladys' infatuation with the contemporary, the living room had a cluttered feel. The fireplace mantle was filled with a hodgepodge of items: a porcelain shepherdess with a broken staff, an ashtray from Paul's restaurant, a pair of tarnished silver candlesticks encrusted with wax drippings. There was also a photo, askew in its frame, of a youthful Gladys stretched out on a picnic blanket. Dusty rubber plants flanked the windows, which were covered with equally dusty wooden venetian blinds.

Edith was looking through the blinds at the front lawn, lit by floodlights, when Paul returned.

"Reuben did a nice job out there," Paul said.

Edith couldn't make out much except the silhouettes of the rhododendron bushes. Runt-like when Reuben planted them, they were now at least six feet tall.

"He loved this house." It surprised Edith how much saying this hurt. "It was his wedding present to me."

"It's a beautiful house. As Gladys used to say, it has good bones."

"He wanted Harriet to get married in the backyard."

"I looked for champagne," Paul said. "I used to always keep some on hand, but since Gladys died..."

They returned to the couches. "I might as well begin telling you what I have in mind." Paul crossed his leg over his thigh, resting his hand upon his ankle. "You know how much I love this town. It has so much going for it. Good public transportation, the beaches. But what excites me most is its location. The island's ninety miles long and Sea Forth's right in the middle, which makes no place on the island more than an hour away."

Edith tried to hide her confusion. If Paul was trying to seduce her, he had an odd way of going about it.

"I don't need to tell you," Paul continued, "what a chore it is to commute to the city from here. But I think we can turn that into an advantage. Long Island's population is about to explode. It'll happen first in Nassau, but eventually this growth will have to spread eastward."

The cook poked her head through the doorway. "Dinner's ready."

"A few minutes, Ellie." Paul raised his index finger. "My prediction? Within the decade, the population on Long Island will be large enough to support another urban center. Not another New York, but big enough to be a commercial hub. It doesn't have to be Sea Forth. Any number of towns, Mineola or Glen Cove, for example, could fill the bill. And will, if we don't start positioning ourselves."

Edith wondered if Paul had gone mad. She'd heard that could happen after the death of a spouse, especially when a person had something to feel guilty about. Sea Forth—a mini New York! "That sounds exciting," she said.

"It is. My office building—"

"Mr. Herbert, dinner's getting cold!"

Paul stood. "Can't get Ellie off side. I barely know how to boil water."

Though the dining room walls were covered with the same bamboo wallpaper, and a smoked glass and chrome configuration hung in place of Edith's crystal chandelier, the room bore enough resemblance to how it once looked that Edith couldn't help thinking back to the dinner parties she had thrown there, how she'd insisted on only the best: pure Irish linen tablecloths, Spode china, Stuart crystal, prime cuts of meat, French wine. For a girl who had grown up eating dinner off chipped plates at a kitchen table covered in oilcloth, she'd learned awfully fast.

It was not until they were on their main course, roast lamb and creamed spinach, that Paul picked up where he had left off. "I'm only accepting first-class tenants. An insurance company has taken the third floor, and my old law firm's signed up for part of the fourth. What I want to talk to you about is the retail space."

Edith sipped her wine. Surely, Paul wasn't going to try and talk her into opening her own store, not after having lectured her about why most businesses failed—for lack of capital!

"The shop that ends up there will set the tone for the building. What I'm thinking about is a high-end women's clothing store," Paul said.

"I didn't know you were interested in women's clothing," Edith said, confused.

Paul laughed. "Only the removing of them. That's where you come in."

So, he wants me to run his dress shop, Edith thought. She laid her knife and fork across her plate, scarcely able to hide her disappointment. How could Paul think she'd be happy managing a small shop after having run the Emporium?

"You don't seem excited. I thought you'd jump at the opportunity to start your own business."

I was right the first time, Edith thought; he's trying to pitch his retail space. "I'm afraid I'll have to pass. As you can imagine, I'm finding money a bit tight these days."

Paul patted Edith's hand. "I don't think I'm getting through. What I have in mind is more than a frock shop. We're talking two floors! Secondly, why would I try and talk you into something you can't afford? So I can end up saddled with a vacant storefront, while I sue you for the rent? I want us to become partners. You provide the talent, brains, and fashion know-how, and I'll provide the money."

Edith was stunned. Paul's faith in her—what could it be based upon?

As if he read her mind, Paul went on to say, "Believe me, I'm not proposing this out of the goodness of my heart. My sources all tell me what a fabulous job you're doing at that store. Besides, a businessman has to trust his instincts. Mine tell me I couldn't find a better partner."

Only later did it dawn on Edith who Paul's sources were—her own salesgirls. She wondered how many of them he had bedded. He really was a lecher!

On a bone-chilling day that same week, Reuben woke with a scratchy throat. As he stood waiting for the bus, his collar drawn up and hat pulled down against the wind and sleet, he regretted having set off for work. Everyone else took sick days. Why not him?

As the morning wore on, Reuben realized he had more than a cold. One minute, he'd be hot and sweaty, the next he'd be shivering. His mind felt dull, and his reflexes were slow. He became concerned about his physical safety and the quality of his work, for his job, which involved riveting the forward section of the fuselage, required vigilance and precision.

Shortly before noon, he asked the foreman for permission to leave.

By the time he arrived in Sea Forth, Reuben felt so debilitated, he did the unthinkable and taxied it home from the depot. He was startled to find Adolph entertaining a woman in the living room, as Adolph never expressed the least interest in dating. Not wishing to disturb them, Reuben headed upstairs without saying hello. It was not until he was in bed, where even with the covers pulled up to his chin he continued to shiver, that he realized he recognized the red-spangled shawl draped over the back of her chair. It belonged to the madwoman he'd seen in Adolph's store. Adolph was conducting his snake-oil business inside his own living room.

"I made some tea..." Adolph said. Reuben was puzzled why Adolph would be bringing him tea in the middle of the night. Adolph set the tray down on Reuben's night table and switched on the light. "You've got a high fever. I also made some sorrel soup. I'll bring some up before I leave for work."

Reuben shifted up against the headboard. His mouth was as dry as sandpaper, and he accepted tea gratefully.

Adolph pressed his hand to Reuben's forehead. "You're hot. A bit of a fever's a good thing. Too much—that's another story. I've run an oatmeal bath. That should cool you down. When you're finished, I'll help you up."

It was then that Reuben remembered. He placed his cup down with such force, its contents went splashing over its sides. "What was that woman doing here?"

Adolph assumed an innocent expression. "Leonie Cochrane? I would have introduced you, but I could tell you were sick." He pushed a sweat-drenched lock of hair off Reuben's forehead. "It's early for flu, but I can't think what else it could be."

Reuben threw the bedcovers back and stood. "Who gave you permission?" he asked, the severity of his tone undermined by the fact that his pajamas, which he'd forgotten to tie, had begun sliding down his thighs. The world began to spin, and he collapsed back down.

Adolph placed his fingertips against Reuben's pulse and began counting. "It's so fast, I'm having second thoughts about that bath."

The rest of the night was a blur. Later, Reuben would recall his children at the door, Jeffrey looking terrified, Harriet appearing more curious than worried. Adolph came in regularly to offer him liquids and wipe his brow.

Nearly a week went by before Reuben was able to return to work. He recuperated to the constant sound of the doorbell, followed by women's voices. It was quite a business Adolph was running down there. But Reuben was too grateful to Adolph, who brought him his meals, sponged him down regularly, and changed his linens twice a day, to say anything. No one, not his mother and certainly not Edith, had ever looked after him so well.

# Chapter Twenty-Four

## December 1940

---

It would be a year before Edith's store would be ready. Even so, she no longer felt as if her life was in limbo. She began looking for an apartment and found one that had been carved out of the side of a house. It had a parlor, a kitchen, and two bedrooms that faced a rear garden. Edith loved that no one had lived there before. Plus, it was only blocks from Reuben's house and not much farther from where her store was to be.

On the Sunday after she moved in, when Edith went to pick up the children, Adolph let her in. He was wearing her yellow apron and holding a spatula. "Mr. Merkal is in the living room," he said coldly, though Edith could see that for herself. He then disappeared into the kitchen. The house was suffused with the smells of garlic and rosemary.

Reuben adjusted his recliner to a more upright position and dropped his newspaper. Edith was surprised by how good he looked. He'd lost so much weight, he was even thinner than when they met.

The day was unseasonably warm. Still, there was a fire roaring. Edith recalled Jeffrey telling her, "If Ernest catches a chill, he could die." Though the house was stifling, Edith kept her coat on, embarrassed about the weight she'd gained.

"You're early," Reuben said.

"I need to talk with you." The kitchen was quiet, and Edith wondered whether Adolph was eavesdropping.

Reuben picked up a half-smoked cigar from the ashtray and relit it.

"I've rented an apartment," Edith said.

"It's about time."

"I was wondering if I could take some of the furniture in the barn."

"Take what you want. I'm never going to use it again." Reuben waved his cigar around. "Also, anything you'd like from here. You'd be doing me a favor."

The room was as crowded as a warehouse. Edith's art deco wrought-iron lamp, its base like intertwined vines, was crammed between Jenny's harp and a hat stand. The black lacquered box with an inlaid mother of pearl dragon on its lid, where she used to store coasters, toothpicks—the accoutrement of entertaining—was resting on a stack of cartons.

"Maybe a few things," Edith said. At least, then, they'd be looked after. From upstairs, she heard footsteps. "I was also hoping..." Edith felt her throat constrict. It was incredible, being scared of the man she'd been married to for so long. "That the children could stay over on the evenings I see them."

Reuben kept his gaze fixed on the cigar smoke curling toward the ceiling. "School nights are out. Maybe if you took them on Saturdays instead of Sundays. I'll have to think about it."

Edith had anticipated that Reuben might react this way, but to hear him say these words was another story. It had been six months since she'd moved out, and she still hadn't gotten used to not living with the children. It wasn't them she missed so much as being around them. Not only the pleasures, such as peeking into their bedrooms while they slept, but the annoyances, too. The schoolbooks scattered about, the half-empty glasses of milk left to curdle on windowsills, Harriet's phonograph playing too loud.

"They're my children, too," Edith said.

Reuben flicked his ash into the ashtray. "When are you going to hire a lawyer? I want to get on with my life. While we're on the subject of the children, I might as well tell you, I'm determined to get custody."

Edith fell back against the couch. She noticed that their wedding portrait had been removed from the fireplace mantle and replaced by one of a young woman, presumably Adolph's wife. "You don't get to decide that," she said.

"I'm not saying you won't get to see them. But let's face it, you've never been much of a mother."

Edith wondered how she could defend herself when this was what she also believed, when she wasn't even sure she wanted the children to live with her. But she was not prepared to hand Reuben such an easy victory. "Children are happier with their mothers. It's what nature intended."

Reuben slapped his thighs and stood. "We can argue about this after you've hired a lawyer. Until then, I call the shots."

That she was to be the first tenant in the apartment had delighted Edith. She loved how everything gleamed, from the varnished floors to the brass switch plates and doorknobs. She loved that the refrigerator, with its separate freezer compartment, was brand new, as was the electric stove, the only one besides Paul's she had ever seen.

But when Edith returned later that evening, all this pristine brightness seemed a mockery. As she walked from the living room toward the kitchen, she hated the way her footsteps reverberated through the largely unfurnished space. She put the teakettle on to boil. While she sat staring at the stove elements as they made their leisurely progression from black to red, she had to laugh at all the fuss being made in the women's magazines over electric stoves.

Finally, the kettle let out an incongruously cheerful whistle. Edith brought her tea to the table. She longed for something sweet, a cookie or slice of cake, except there was nothing in the pantry. Upon moving in, one of her first resolutions had been to banish sweets from the apartment. All she had were several packets of sugar she'd swiped from the Argosy. She ripped them open, watching the contents of each dissolve before dropping in the next. As she sipped her unpleasantly sweet tea, Edith thought of how there was a steeliness to Reuben she'd never noticed before. Had it been there all along, simply hidden beneath his love for her and the children? She had never thought to question Reuben's mother's contention that he was too soft on his workers, an accusation she had parroted, though there was no way she could have known whether this was true.

As Edith washed her cup—cheap pink plastic from Woolworth's—she reflected on how she'd come to enjoy her solitude, even if there were moments such as this, when it pressed down upon her like a pair of heavy hands. In looking for an apartment, she'd decided that it had to have two bedrooms. But it was also true that in the weeks between signing the lease and moving in, whenever she pictured herself inside the apartment, she was always alone.

Edith returned to the table. While she knew little about the intricacies of divorce, she was sure there had been a fair bit of bluffing in what Reuben said and that if she fought him for custody, she was likely to win. There were reasons to do this that had nothing to do with the children. It was bad enough that as a divorcée, she would be branded as morally suspect; there were few people society looked down upon more than women who gave up their children willingly. If she decided to give them up, it would be a colossal act of bravery, one Edith wasn't sure she was capable of performing. But it would also be an act of pure love, one of the few truly unselfish things she had ever done.

Reuben, Jeffrey, Adolph, and Ernest pulled the dining room chairs around the new Philco, in its walnut console, which Reuben had bought to replace the ailing Motorola. Harriet was leaning against the archway. Outside, rain was coming down in sheets, causing the windows to rattle and the porch door to bang against its frame.

Despite the weather, the Philco's reception was so good it was as if Edward R. Murrow was reporting not from Warsaw but from the next room. His deep, soothing voice couldn't mitigate the horror of his words: how every day, truckloads of Jews could be seen passing through the gates leading to the ghetto; how every evening, wagons loaded with corpses could be seen headed in the opposite direction; how the inhabitants regularly tried to escape over the twenty-foot walls, despite the fact that they were topped with crushed glass and patrolled by guards with orders to shoot. He closed by saying, "It's estimated that twenty percent of Polish Jewry has already perished due to disease or starvation." The broadcast went back to New York where, after several seconds of sympathetic murmuring by the local commentator, a jingle for Fels-Naptha, the laundry whitener, cut in.

Adolph turned off the radio. "Who wants tea?" It was the same question he asked every evening, though the children didn't drink tea and Reuben preferred Sanka.

Ernest stood and stretched. "I think I'll turn in. School tomorrow."

Adolph removed his glasses. He breathed on the lenses and wiped them with a felt cloth. As he spoke, he held them to the light, examining them for smudges. "So, you'd rather go to school than have me teach you? Don't let me stop you. That way, you can grow up ignorant, like every other American boy." With a flick of his glasses, he motioned toward Jeffrey and then walked over to Ernest, not stopping until their noses were practically touching. The smirk gone from his face, Ernest clutched the edge of the china cabinet for support.

"You were expecting me to forbid it?" Adolph asked. "Go. Have a heart attack and die. See if I care." He pushed his palm into Ernest's chest and stormed from the room.

Ernest followed his father upstairs. He pounded on their bedroom door for at least a minute before Adolph let him in.

"We shouldn't listen," Reuben told Harriet and Jeffrey despite the impossibility of this. Even with the bedroom door closed, they could hear Adolph's and Ernest's voices, and while the content of their accusations was muffled, the names they hurled at each other rang out clear: "Ingrate." "Hypocrite." "Tyrant."

"All families fight," Reuben told Harriet as she snuggled against him in his recliner. "It's because they care about one another so much."

Harriet looked puzzled. Reuben wasn't surprised. His explanation didn't make sense to him either. He ran his hand down her back. Beneath her blouse, her vertebrae felt like a necklace of tiny pearls.

"Tell me a story," Harriet said.

"Would you like to hear one, too?" Reuben called out to Jeffrey, who was making a circuit of the downstairs, ramming one fist against the other. Reuben had never been one for telling stories, but a story seemed the sort of distraction they needed.

Jeffrey turned around, his face contorted with grief. "Tell them to keep it down!"

"I can't."

"Then I'm going out." Jeffrey grabbed his coat off the stand.

"It's pouring!"

Jeffrey slammed the door behind him.

"He's upset," Reuben said to Harriet.

"I don't know why Jeffrey likes him so much. He's so mean to him," Harriet said as she twirled one of Reuben's shirt buttons around.

"Adolph?" Reuben gently pried her fingers away.

Harriet let out an exasperated breath. "Ernest. It's like he's in love with him."

"They're best friends. I bet Ernest spends more time in Jeffrey's room than in his own."

"Hhhm." Harriet began playing with the button again. Reuben wanted to ask her what she meant by that "hhhm" but was afraid. "The story," she said, giving the button a tug.

"Okay." Reuben searched his mind for something to tell her. "Have I ever told you what it was like growing up in Flushing?" He already knew the answer, which was no.

"The three of us, grandma, grandpa, and me..." Reuben was about to tell Harriet about what it had been like to grow up in Queens so close to the "el" that, from his bedroom window, he could see the passengers inside the carriages, when he was struck by a memory of gazing through the slats of a crib at his baby brother, Harold, who died as a toddler when Reuben was six.

Reuben began again. "I bet you didn't know I had a younger brother." As he spoke, it came back to him so clearly it was as if he were turning the pages of a picture book. He realized why, in his memory, the room was dark except for a stripe of sunlight that had seeped in from around the drawn shade. "He died of the measles. He caught it from me. Grandma warned me to stay away from him, but I didn't."

"Daddy, you were just a little boy. You didn't know any better."

"I did know better. But you're right, I was only little." Reuben recalled how jealous he was of Harold, which was the reason why, while no one was looking, he bent over the crib and kissed Harold on the lips. Although his parents never found out, they still blamed him for Harold's death—never to his face, but he could tell they did. It was after Harold died that his father put an end to the Shabbat dinners at his grandparents' house. Reuben had never made the connection before.

# Chapter Twenty-Five

## September 1941

Edith ducked out of the Emporium to meet Paul in front of his building. While there was still work to be done on the inside, the façade was complete. With the European war-related ramp-up in defense production, material and labor were in short supply on Long Island, and most of the local construction projects were facing delays. Paul's project, however, was proceeding according to schedule, with the first tenants slated to move in the following month.

"What do you think?" Paul asked. Instead of his customary gray suit, Paul was wearing dungarees and a blue and white checkered shirt, the sleeves rolled up to his elbows.

"It's wonderful." In truth, Edith wasn't sure what she thought, not because the building— peach-speckled granite through the third story and limestone for the three floors above—wasn't handsome. Rather, it was because of how out of place it looked surrounded by two- and three-story red brick buildings, across from the brown stone cathedral, formerly the pride of Sea Forth, but which now looked like a dowdy old maid by comparison.

"Let me show you your store." Paul led Edith through the revolving doors into the marble-clad lobby.

Her space was still unfinished, all struts and beams. But as she and Paul ducked beneath the tangles of wires, she could envision how it would look. From the beginning, she'd known that the walls, curtains, and carpets should be beige and the woodwork varnished blond oak; that the fittings, while elegant, should be forgettable, merely a backdrop for the merchandise displayed in series of U-shaped bays accessible from a single long aisle.

"Have you decided on a name?" Paul asked as they took the plywood stairs to the second floor. "We need to order the sign next week."

Edith hesitated. Paul might not be self-conscious about the name he'd chosen—"Herbert Towers," proclaimed by a brass plaque that ran the length of the building's entranceway—but she certainly was about the name she'd chosen. "Edith's," she murmured.

"Edith's," Paul roared. "I like it. After all, that's what you're really selling, your style and taste. Though what I really love is how it's bound to stick in Adler's craw."

Edith started. "You don't even know him. Why should you care?"

"I just do," Paul said. He had sworn Edith to secrecy about the store, telling her he wanted to "create a buzz." "Also, the longer we keep Adler in the dark," he had explained, "the less time he'll have to prepare for the assault."

Edith thought she understood. The store's first few months would be tough enough without giving Fred the chance to buy up the advertising space in the local papers. What Edith hadn't grasped was the significance of Paul's choice of the word "assault." More than mere civic-mindedness lay behind Paul's plans for Sea Forth. He wanted to own Sea Forth even if it meant destroying whoever stood in his way.

Back on the street, as Paul shook Edith's hand, a breeze caught the white collar of her dress, causing it to fly up against her mouth. Edith patted the collar back into place. She glanced down, distressed to see a lipstick smudge along the collar's edge. Paul was staring at the collar, too, but in a distracted way that told her he had already moved on to the next item on his to-do list. As Edith hurried back to the Emporium, she wondered what place she occupied in Paul's schemes. When he called her "his partner," did he mean forever or for only as long as it served his purposes?

For the first few months after their affair ended, Fred had treated Edith with exaggerated courtesy, as if he wanted her to know that just because he no longer loved her, that didn't mean he didn't value her as an employee. As time went on, however, he began to take her for granted until she felt like she'd become as invisible to him as one of the store fixtures.

So, when the time came to give Fred her notice, Edith couldn't help feeling an anticipatory thrill at the shock this would give him. She knocked on his door and, ignoring the annoyance that flickered across his face, took a seat on the couch that had been the scene of so many of their trysts.

By then, word had gotten around that the butcher paper shrouded space in Paul's building was to be a dress shop. Fred, himself, had mentioned it several times, sounding more amused than worried. "I betcha it's some out-of-towners who don't know the first thing about the local market," he said. "I can just imagine the kinda lease Herbert's hoodwinked 'em into signing!"

"I'm leaving," Edith said.

Fred blinked stupidly.

"I'm giving you a month's notice."

Fred laced his fingers, leaned forward and gave her a knowing smile. "What do you want? Five? Why don't we make it ten?"

It took Edith a moment to comprehend that he was offering her a raise. "I'm leaving."

"That's five hundred twenty a year. I'd say that's pretty generous."

"I'm opening my own store."

As her words sank in, Fred's face drained of color. "It's Herbert's building, ain't it? I must be an idiot not to have figured it out."

"Why should you have?" Edith said, though, had their roles been reversed, this possibility would have occurred to her weeks ago.

Fred walked over to the couch, looming over Edith. "It's taken me a long time and a king's ransom to get where I am, and I'll defend my store any way I need to." His eyes bulging, his complexion scarlet, Fred looked so comical that Edith had to suppress the urge to laugh. She found herself feeling sorry for him for failing to perceive that the true threat to the Emporium wouldn't be her store, which was unlikely to do more than nibble at the edges of his, but rather the loss of her.

"Do what you have to," she said. "I didn't go looking for this, but when I was offered the opportunity, felt I had to take it."

"I understand," Fred said, sounding defeated now. "No need to stay a month. Two weeks should be plenty. I'm sure you've got lots to do. When's your store opening?"

Was Fred unaware of how much she did around the store? Barely able to keep the scorn from her voice, Edith said, "Around Thanksgiving. Truly, I'm happy to stay."

"That day I saw you on the street, who woulda dreamed?" There was a far-off look to Fred's eyes, and Edith realized he was speaking not to her but himself.

A few mornings later, Edith found a memo on her desk from Fred to the staff, announcing her departure. She was stunned to read whom he'd chosen as her replacement: a bleached blond named Faye with a beauty spot that migrated around the right side of her face, someone who looked as cheap as the costume jewelry Fred hired her to sell. She and Fred had to be having an affair, which, when Edith thought about it, wasn't that surprising. Hadn't Clara, the salesgirl he'd had an affair with before her, been just as trashy? Perhaps she had been the aberration, and Fred was just reverting to type.

"I want ya to show her the ropes," Fred said as he pushed the giggling girl into Edith's office. He waggled his finger at Faye, "There's gonna be a test this afternoon, so take lots of notes."

Faye was chewing gum, in breach of the Emporium's rules. She fingered the large cross around her neck, the wearing of which was yet another rules violation, as were all displays of religiosity, as she said, "Who knows, if I'm lucky, maybe I'll end up owning a dress shop, too."

"Let's get started. There's a lot to get through," Edith said. She pulled out the work roster she maintained on ledger paper, its many columns each devoted to a different department. More time consuming than intellectually taxing, it was a task she believed even the limited Faye could master.

Before long, Faye began picking the pilling off her tight, red mohair sweater and allowing her eyes to wander around the office.

"Any questions?" Edith asked.

Faye yawned, exposing the pink wad of gum. "Nah."

"It's a lot to take in. It might not be a bad idea to take notes." Edith slid a writing tablet and pen across to her.

Edith began talking faster, aware that with each word, she was leaving Faye further behind. Every few minutes, she would pointedly glance down at the writing tablet, which remained blank.

"That's probably enough for now," Edith finally said, closing the ledger book. She stood, in case Faye failed to get the message that she was free to leave. "We'll pick up where we left off this afternoon. How's one?"

"One?" Faye sounded shocked by the outrageousness of this suggestion.

After Faye left, Edith rested her forehead in her hands. Faye's too-strong perfume, still lingering in the air, had given her a headache. Within minutes, there was a knock on the door.

"How'd she do?" Fred asked.

Edith was too angry to lie. "How'd she do? The girl's an imbecile. Though I'm sure she has other talents."

"What a thing to say!"

"Well, she is. So are you, for that matter."

Fred sniffed in Faye's perfume with a dreamy expression. "Admit it. You're jealous." Fred dropped his voice. "I've been a heel. The way I ended things, or rather didn't end 'em. Don't think I don't feel rotten about it."

Edith held up her hand. "This is a discussion I don't want to have."

"Edie, I hate to see you angry." Fred placed a hand on Edith's shoulder. "I'm sorry I hurt you."

"Hurt me!" Edith shook off his hand. "Every time you touched me, my skin would crawl. Your rotten breath, your corny jokes. Whenever you summoned me to your office, my heart would sink. But I was afraid to break things off. Because I needed the job!"

Fred turned pale. "You're lying."

"I'm finally telling the truth. Do you think that floozy's screwing you because she loves you? Because she thinks you're sexy?"

"Keep her out of this," Fred shouted.

"Okay. But as long as I'm being honest, I might as well let you in on how the others laugh at you behind your back. You know how you've got nicknames for them? Toots, Sweetie Pie? They've got them for you, too. Addle-brain, Cornball, W. C. for W. C. Fields, who, come to think of it, you do resemble." That it was Paul who called Fred W. C. seemed beside the point. "The way you slobber over the customers, it's a miracle you haven't driven them away. You may think you're charming. They think you're a buffoon."

Fred lifted a chair off the ground—Edith was afraid he was going to throw it. Then he slammed it down. "Why don't you leave now? I managed fine before I hired you, and I'll manage again. My manufacturers—all I have to do is tell them that if they want to sell to me, they'd better not sell to you."

Edith slapped her cheek. "Goodness, you're scaring me! Then again, maybe they'll decide they'd rather sell to me than to you." She extended her hand. When he refused to take it, she looked at it with mock hurt. "I hate that things have to end this way. But I'm sure Faye will do a marvelous job."

Upon arriving home from work one evening, Reuben was surprised to be greeted not by the usual clattering of pots and pans and exotic aromas wafting from the kitchen. He found Adolph seated at the kitchen table, Edith's yellow apron tied around the argyle sweater vest he wore from the first day of autumn through the last day of winter, his hands wrapped around a cup of tea. Chopped onions, peppers, and garlic lay in piles on wooden cutting boards. The only thing on the stove was a simmering pot of water.

Adolph motioned toward the front door. "He's not home yet."

"It's only half past five."

"He knows he's supposed to come straight home from school." Adolph shuffled over to the stove and turned the flame up beneath the pot. "Sorry, I'll start dinner."

"He probably stayed after to get help with his lessons." Reuben went to the refrigerator and poured a glass of milk. Adolph might insist that cow's milk was meant only for calves and that drinking it made humans vulnerable to all sorts of allergies and infections. But this was one of the few food battles Reuben had won; the children, Ernest included, regularly drank milk now—and with their meals.

"What they're covering, I taught him years ago." Adolph pulled a frying pan from the drawer beneath the oven. "Something's happened."

"He probably went home with a friend," Reuben said. "Besides, if something was wrong, Jeffrey would have called."

"Jeffrey's upstairs."

As he rinsed his glass, Reuben noticed that Adolph seemed to be applying a good deal more concentration to the task of browning the garlic than it required. "I thought Jeffrey and Ernest did everything together."

"Not anymore," Adolph said, dropping in the onions.

The aroma of the onions and garlic filled the room. Reuben's stomach growled. "Did they have a fight?"

Adolph dropped a handful of chopped peppers into the pan, along with another splash of oil. He stepped back as they began to sizzle. "Can we talk about this another time?" Adolph pointed to the cupboard. "Get me the rice. And a measuring cup."

"Adolph, he's almost sixteen. If he's not home by ten, then worry," Reuben said.

Adolph pulled a packet of crushed Pall Malls from his pocket and tossed them onto the counter. "I found these in the chicken coop. I'd been wondering why Ernest was spending so much time back there."

"How do you know they're not Jeffrey's?" Even to Reuben, his words sounded lame. Jeffrey sneaking out to the chicken coop for a smoke—it was unfathomable. "What boy doesn't experiment with cigarettes?"

"Boys with damaged hearts, that's who." Adolph motioned to a cream-colored block sitting in a bowl of water. "Cut that into quarter-inch cubes."

Reuben had no idea what he was cutting into.

"Coca-Cola, milk, cigarettes. I can't help wondering if moving here was such a good idea."

Reuben whacked the knife down so hard that the shimmering cubes went skittering off the board. "You know perfectly well that whatever Ernest's been up to, it has nothing to do with Jeffrey."

"Tofu." Adolph scooped up the cubes and dropped them into the frying pan. "Compressed soybeans, a staple of the Asian diet. All I know is I never had a moment's trouble with him before."

"That's because you kept him locked up like a prisoner. Ernest is just behaving like a normal adolescent." It was something Reuben would have given a great deal to be able to say about Jeffrey.

"But he *isn't* normal. You should listen to his heart. He hardly lets me listen to it anymore."

The High Holy Days came early that year. Early or late, Reuben wouldn't have known had he not bumped into Herb Pullen.

"Haven't seen you in schul lately," Herb said, "lately" an odd word choice given that Reuben hadn't been back since his one visit more than a year before. "We'll be seeing you next week?"

His tone made clear that this wasn't a question so much as a command, one Jew to another.

Reuben lied that he was planning on going.

"Let's hope it cools off. You'd think the ladies would learn. But every year, they insist on wearing their new wool suits. And when they suffer, we men end up suffering more." Herb winked. "Come to dinner after. I won't take no for an answer."

Maybe he could pretend to be sick, Reuben thought, as he watched Herb lumber down the street. He knew nothing about the High Holy Day services, except what he recalled from his childhood when he'd sit on the stoop of his apartment building and watch the other Jewish families on his street head off to schul in the morning, where they'd remain until dusk.

There had been all sorts of Jews in that neighborhood. There were the ones he used to think of as "normal," who didn't look that different from the Irish and Italians with whom they lived side by side. Then there were the ones who looked very different, foreign in a way that even the greenest greenhorns did not. The men, their beards untrimmed, wore ringlets like girls, and their skin was pasty in a way that made Reuben think of subterranean creatures. They dressed in oversized black wool suits that never looked clean, beneath the jackets of which hung fringes that flapped in the breeze as they walked. The women, always trailing behind, with a swarm of children tugging at their hands and skirts, looked cleaner than the men, but sexless in their obvious wigs, long sleeves and skirts, bulky shoes, and black woolen stockings. He'd felt a repulsion for these people that extended beyond their strange appearances to their clannishness and smug sense of superiority—not just to the neighborhood Gentiles but to all other Jews.

It was one thing to ignore the High Holy Days. Another to promise you'd attend services and then not show up. Reuben was not especially superstitious. Even so, he couldn't help worrying that if there were a God, he was bound to hold such duplicity against a person when choosing what sort of year to give him. On his way home, he decided to detour to the synagogue for a schedule of the services.

"You didn't know you need a ticket?" the woman who ran the temple's business office asked. She lifted a metal cash box from beneath her desk. "Three dollars for one ticket, four dollars for two, children come free."

"What do they think this is, Broadway?" Reuben asked.

"Of course if you were a member…"

"Just give me two tickets." Reuben pulled three wrinkled bills from his wallet and began fishing around his pants pockets for loose change. Twenty, thirty-five, sixty, seventy, seventy-one, seventy-six.

"Here," the woman said impatiently, dropping one of her own quarters into the box. "Row R, seats eighteen and nineteen."

Reuben wasn't sure why he bought two tickets, except with one ticket costing three dollars, two for four dollars seemed like a bargain. He arrived home to find Adolph by the stove, stirring a cauldron full of leaves that smelled of peppermint.

"For you," he said, placing one of the tickets on the counter.

"For congestion." Adolph bent over the pot and sniffed. "Needs more oil of eucalyptus."

"For the High Holy Days."

Adolph tapped a few drops from a brown bottle into the cauldron. "Not interested."

"Rosh Hashanah, Yom Kippur." Reuben hoped he was pronouncing them correctly.

"Take your son."

Reuben didn't want to take Jeffrey, who was bound to get restless, nudging him every ten minutes to ask if it was time to leave. Wasn't Adolph the one who used to lecture him about how a Jew should never forget who he was? "What about that Shabbat dinner?"

"That was then, this is now. I'm not interested."

Just as Herb feared, the first day of Rosh Hashanah was miserably hot. So many folding chairs had been jammed into the sanctuary that when the rabbi and cantor paraded down the aisle with the Torahs, their thighs banged against the aisle chairs, and their tallis fringes tickled the congregants' noses. As the morning wore on, the air became pungent with sweat. The women fanned themselves with their programs; the men loosened their ties and undid their top shirt buttons.

As if the Jews don't already suffer enough, Reuben thought, as the service dragged on through late afternoon. By then, most of the women had left, their buttocks spilling into their neighbors' laps as they made their way to the aisle. Reuben remained for the duration. Even though Yom Kippur, not Rosh Hashanah, was the Day of Atonement, he looked upon this as his way of atoning for all those years when he had not only not attended services but hadn't known enough to feel guilty about it.

The Pullens lived above the tailor shop in a five-room apartment that was similar to the one Edith once shared with her mother. It was the sort of apartment Reuben feared his family would end up living in before his mother offered them her house.

Though cluttered, the apartment was cheerful, the living room walls painted a lemon yellow. Everything appeared shiny and smudge-free, which Reuben found miraculous given that the Pullens had two teenaged sons. Despite her long days in the tailor shop, Trudy Pullen apparently found the time for needlework. On the walls hung her handiwork, scenes of hearth and home emblazoned with sayings like "God Bless This Happy House" and "The man may earn the gold, but the woman rules the roost."

The meal was thankfully light given the weather. There was a broiled chicken, beautifully browned and fragrant with herbs, a tossed salad, green beans, and roast potatoes. At the end of the meal, Trudy brought out something she called tagelach, a mountain of honey-soaked pastry balls, as well as apple slices and a pot of honey. The apple, Herb explained, was meant to signify the world and was dipped in the honey to express the wish that the upcoming year would be sweet.

"More than our brothers and sisters in Europe can hope for," Trudy said.

There was a guilty moment of silence broken by the slap of Herb's palm against the table. "And what is our government doing? Nothing!"

Trudy laid a hand over his. "Dear, how can one reason with a madman?"

Herb kissed her hand and then placed it down on the table. "The person who witnesses a murder but does nothing is as guilty as the murderer himself. Our president is a coward."

"I'm sure it's more complicated than that," Reuben said. Despite the many ways in which Roosevelt had let him down, he felt the old, reflexive urge to defend him.

Herb slapped his palm down again, this time so hard, the plates rattled. "We should be fighting alongside the Brits."

"They probably wouldn't be fighting themselves if Hitler hadn't invaded their country. If this were only about the Jews, the rest of the world would be celebrating," Reuben said.

"You're right." Herb looked across the table at his boys, both blond and good-looking like their mother. Excellent students, too, according to Herb. They had sat through the entire services on either side of their father, all three heads bobbing in unison as they recited the prayers. "What do you think?" he asked them.

The boys looked at each other, and then the older one said, "We should join the Allied effort."

"It's immoral to stand by and do nothing," the younger one chimed in.

Herb nodded approvingly. "You may be excused."

The boys began clearing the table. When they got to their mother, they thanked her and bent to kiss her. They did the same to their father.

"Happy New Year," they wished Reuben before disappearing into the kitchen.

A moment later, Reuben heard the taps running and the clatter of dishes as the boys began cleaning up.

Though the factory allowed three days off a year for religious observances, Reuben had been too embarrassed to tell his supervisor why he was staying out and called in sick on both days of Rosh Hashanah. Later, he worried whether the fact that he had been too embarrassed to tell the truth would negate whatever good will he might have chalked up with God. Then, what about Yom Kippur? Would his supervisor get suspicious if he called in sick again? But if he took a religious holiday, even a vacation day, would his supervisor figure out that he'd lied about Rosh Hashanah?

That was the problem with lies, the way one led to another until it was only a matter of time before a person got caught in his own tangled web. So, Reuben told his supervisor the truth about Yom Kippur, right on the factory floor and in such a loud voice he was sure to be overheard down the line.

The supervisor nodded, made a note on his clipboard, and walked away. Reuben stood waiting for the penny to drop, for the supervisor to return and ask about the previous week. He didn't, nor did anyone on the assembly line so much as glance at Reuben.

Adolph had gone to work on both days of Rosh Hashanah. Reuben was sure Adolph used to shut his store not just for the High Holy Days, but on most of the lesser Jewish holidays.

Reuben stopped Adolph as he headed upstairs to change for work. "Rosh Hashanah's one thing. You can't go to work on Kol Nidre." Until the week before, Reuben had never heard of Kol Nidre, let alone known it referred to the evening prayer service that ushered in the Day of Atonement. "Call in sick."

"What if someone needs to fill a prescription?"

Reuben followed him upstairs. "They can do the same thing they did before Rexall's opened."

Adolph glared at Reuben. "When did you become such a Jew? Besides, if anybody should be atoning, it's God, not us."

"Weren't you the one who was always reminding me of how the Jews needed to stick together?" Reuben decided to try to appeal to Adolph's sense of thrift. "You already let the Rosh Hashanah ticket go to waste."

"No one told you to buy it."

"I wanted to do something nice for you. Do the same for me. Say you'll come."

Adolph sighed. "If it's that important to you."

While dressing for synagogue, Reuben kept thinking about what he'd said about the Jews needing to stick together. That really was the crux of this going to temple for him. Even if there were a God, which he doubted, he surely didn't deserve any accolades. Reuben doubted, too, that he would ever be able to find solace in the prayers and rituals. But it was not what these rituals meant to God that mattered. They were the glue that bound his people together, ensuring their survival. Only now did he see the things about the Jews that had repulsed his father—their refusal to blend in, their strange practices, their dress and dietary customs—for what they were: a form of defiance, daily acts of bravery, and the only true weapons the Jews had against the likes of a Hitler.

"I'm glad I came," Adolph said after the service. "Not that I'll ever get used to American synagogues. They're so different from the ones I grew up with. Ancient stone, as beautiful as churches, everything much more formal."

It was a balmy evening. As they walked home, Reuben slung his jacket over his shoulder. He found it odd to see Main Street taken over by so many Jews. Back when he moved to Sea Forth, there were only a handful.

"Are you going to fast?" Adolph asked.

"No." Reuben toyed with the idea but decided enough was enough.

"Neither am I. Though nothing beats an occasional fast for ridding the body of toxins."

They stopped outside of Herbert Towers. The fountain was going, the revolving floodlights turning the water green, red, and blue. Another set of floodlights sent arcs of colored light up the building walls. The lobby was lit, as were many of the floors, providing glimpses of sumptuous wood paneled offices. Only the retail space remained unoccupied.

"Impressive." Adolph whistled.

"Too grand for Sea Forth, I'd say."

"Maybe now," Adolph countered. "But who's to say what this place will be like in ten years. I'll give Herbert credit for one thing. He's not afraid to take chances."

"An herbal drugstore—isn't that what you called it?" Reuben asked Adolph later that evening while they were relaxing over garlic tea, which, according to Adolph, was unequaled in its ability to stave off everything from colds to cancer.

"Herbal drugstore, health store, the name doesn't matter. My dream is to open a store dedicated to helping people ward off illness instead of waiting until they get sick. A store based upon the philosophy of treating the body as an interrelated system, instead of a collection of symptoms. I'll be right back." Adolph left the room. Reuben groaned, realizing he was about to learn more about herbal medicine than he could ever care to. When Adolph returned, he was carrying a pile of books bearing titles such as *Holistic Harmony, Doctor Herb,* and *The Pharmacy in the Forest.* He placed them on the coffee table. "I think you'll find these fascinating."

Adolph cradled his teacup as he spoke. "Take constipation. Don't wince. That's the problem with you Americans, you're so childish. What does the pharmacist recommend? Ex-lax. Do you know how Ex-lax works? By irritating the bowel so that it's forced to evacuate its contents. Use it often enough, and the bowel forgets how to work. We holistic practitioners try to figure out what's causing the constipation. Maybe the patient isn't consuming enough whole grains, fruits, and vegetables. Or drinking enough fluids. We try to get the bowel working again, maybe by prescribing a bulking agent like the seeds of the psyllium plant and an early morning walk."

Reuben stood up and stretched. "That's interesting. I think I'll head up to bed."

"As long as you asked, let me finish." Adolph began to pace. "Here's something I bet you didn't know. Thirty percent of manufactured drugs are nothing more than adulterated versions of the seeds, herbs, and roots people have been treating themselves with for centuries. Take digitalis, which is used to treat congestive heart failure. You know where it comes from? The flower foxglove. Even aspirin was originally derived from extracts of white willow bark and meadow sweet."

Reuben feigned a yawn. "Adolph, I've got to be up by six."

Adolph sighed. "Go. Sorry I got carried away. It's just that to open a drugstore like that—it's my dream."

It was nearly midnight. As tired as Reuben was, he was unable to sleep. He kept thinking about Adolph's concept for an herbal drugstore and decided it wasn't as crazy as he first assumed. He kept thinking, too, about what Adolph said about Paul, how he was not afraid to take chances, something that once might have been said about him.

As a young man, he'd been willing to risk everything in pursuit of his dream of building summer getaways for city folks. When he went into business for himself, he thought he knew what he was doing. But all he really knew was how to build houses. With time, he learned about the importance of cash flow and an even more important lesson about human nature—that there were people who could shake your hand and, later, stab you in the back. It never occurred to him to wonder about the extent to which his success had been due to the exuberant times rather than his business acumen. Because of that, he hadn't realized how essential it was to protect himself from the forces outside of his control, like the state of the economy, which could destroy a business as thoroughly as a tornado.

Wisdom made him timid. The only courageous thing he had done in years was to ask Edith to move out. As Reuben stared at the bedroom ceiling, his life, once so full of possibilities, unfurled as a straight, predictable road. He would continue working in the factory for the duration of the war, perhaps into his old age. With luck, he might be promoted to line supervisor. He would spend the rest of his life in this house, probably die in it.

An herbal drugstore wasn't an office building. But it was a way to start. The way his first bungalow had been. If the concept did catch on, perhaps another store would follow, and another after that. If the business did fail, at least he couldn't blame himself for not trying. As the night wore on, Reuben grew excited. Given that this part of Main Street was mixed use, they could operate right out of the house! If he closed in the front porch and the sunroom to its side, there would be enough room for a small store. The warehouse would have to be in the old chicken coop, a minor inconvenience but hardly insurmountable. Or, he could finish the basement.

As soon as the first licks of light appeared over the horizon, Reuben knocked on Adolph's door. When there was no answer, he let himself in. He stood over Adolph's bed until Adolph woke. "Adolph," he said, "I have an idea that just might work."

# Chapter Twenty-Six

## November 1941 through March 1942

Paul insisted on assembling the guest list himself for the opening day party. "After all, you've been off the social circuit for a while," he told Edith, oblivious to how hurtful she might find this comment. He invited fifty women, many of whom she, indeed, did not know. The rest, former friends, she knew too well.

On the morning of the party, Paul surprised Edith by showing up at the store for, as he put it, a last-minute inspection. He made his way methodically from the front to the rear, fiddling with the flowers, straightening the picture frames, running his fingertip across the counters like a housewife checking up on her maid.

Not everything was the way Edith wanted it. The curtains, delivered the day before, were more of a mustard shade than the beige she ordered and would have to be returned. The embroidered gowns she planned on showcasing in the evening wear department had not arrived. But these weren't things Paul would notice, and Edith was proud of having achieved what once seemed impossible: which was to put the store together in less than two months.

"How does it look?" she asked.

"It doesn't matter what I think," Paul said. "It's what they think that counts." He pulled a wool sheath from the rack and examined it with a disapproving eye. "A bit matronly, no? If Gladys brought home something like this, I would have sent her back to the store."

Edith found Paul's comment ironic, given the sacks Gladys wore. "Not at all. But like you said, it's not what I think that matters." Edith returned the sheath to the rack.

After he'd completed his inspection, Paul said, "I think I'll skip the party. The idea of being the lone man in a crowd of fifty women is a bit daunting, even for me."

The first guests to arrive were Marianne Rule and Bunny Fleming. Marianne had grown plumper, and her makeup and jewelry were more garish than ever. But the change in Bunny was shocking. Bunny's hair had gone entirely gray, and she had grown so thin that her dress, hanging off her shoulders, gave no hint of breasts or hips.

Marianne inclined her head toward Bunny as a signal for Edith to be careful what she said. "Isn't Edith looking splendid?" she asked Bunny loudly.

"Splendid," Bunny parroted.

"And the store..." Marianne made a sweeping gesture. "Isn't it something?"

Bunny nodded like an obedient schoolchild.

Marianne led Bunny to one of the upholstered "husband" chairs by the dressing rooms. "Is that the saddest thing you've ever seen?" she asked Edith when she returned. "After Art's dealership went under, she fell to pieces." Both women glanced over at Bunny, who, her purse clutched against her, was looking around like a cornered animal. Edith recalled that she meant to call Bunny when she heard about Art's dealership, but she had been so preoccupied with her own problems that it slipped her mind.

Marianne's attention was caught by a chartreuse silk evening gown. "Is that gorgeous," she exclaimed. "Edith, be a dear. See if you have it in my size."

Edith had just returned from the stockroom when five women burst through the door, Rosemary Groschal among them. She was wearing a Chanel-style black knit suit, which she had accessorized with opera-length pearls, an outfit that made clear her husband, who had given up his local real estate law practice to go work for Paul, was being handsomely rewarded.

"Edith, darling," Rosemary said, extending her hand palm down as if she expected Edith to kiss it. "It's about time someone opened a quality dress shop in this town." She shook her head as if she could hardly believe how she'd survived without one. From time to time, Edith would spot Rosemary at the Emporium, where she would run the salesgirls ragged, looking for different styles or colors, and then leave without buying anything. Rosemary breezed past Bunny without even a hello and, like Marianne, began tearing through the racks.

The guests now arrived in a swarm, most dressed in the two-piece suits with exaggerated shoulders and cinched waists, the hemlines shorter than they'd been since the '20s, which were in fashion. Edith had arranged for a light lunch—dainty sandwiches of watercress and chopped egg and smoked salmon and capers, arranged in pyramids upon tiered silver platters. But the food was hardly touched. It was as if the women were in a fever, pulling this dress, then that one off the racks, jockeying in the most unladylike fashion for places in front of the mirror. By two o'clock, there were lines outside the dressing rooms and discarded items everywhere. Edith's five salesgirls looked shell-shocked as they scurried from customer to customer.

Edith felt a tap on her shoulder and was startled to see Paul. "Changed my mind and glad I did," he said, looking gleeful. He had on a different outfit from the morning and looked elegant in his chalk-striped, gray flannel suit and burgundy silk tie, his shoes as shiny as licorice mirrors.

Paul's entrance had not gone unnoticed. The ransacking through the racks slowed as a ripple of excitement spread through the crowd.

"Ladies," Paul shouted, holding his arms aloft and flashing a movie star smile, "welcome to our store! I hope by now you've all met my partner, Edith Merkal!" Paul turned toward Edith and began clapping. The women, dutifully, did the same. Unbeknownst to Edith, Paul had called in a photographer. The man, squatting amid the crowd, began snapping away, the flashbulbs blinding her. In a tone of voice more suitable for a political campaign, Paul called out, "If you'll bear with me, I'd like to spend a minute telling you about the building."

Paul spoke for closer to ten minutes, not just about the building—about his restaurant, his garden apartments, even the old-fashioned street lamps he procured for the town years earlier. Had it been anyone else, the crowd would have grown bored, but Paul had such a hypnotic effect on women that he could have gone on for hours.

After he finished, Paul said to Edith, "I don't want to steal the show, so I'll slip out now," though he had already "stolen" the show. And he hardly "slipped out," stopping to hug nearly every woman on his way to the door, feigning boyish embarrassment when a few took the liberty of kissing him.

Once Paul left, it was as if the air had been sucked out of the room. The women gathered up their purses and parcels and repositioned the dolls' hats so popular that year on their heads. By three o'clock, the last of the guests had gone.

"It was like a stampede," the cashier said as she began counting up the sales receipts. "I hope there are no mistakes."

Edith collapsed into an armchair while the salesgirls, flushed and disheveled, their arms weighed down with the discarded items, began putting their departments back in order. She poured herself a tumbler of warm orange juice, pulled a couple of sandwiches from a collapsed pile, and removed her shoes.

Nearly everyone had shown up for the party, and the merchandise was clearly a hit. Yet, as Edith headed home that afternoon, she felt deflated. The way Paul hogged the spotlight had a lot to do with this, but the fact that she had no one to complain about this to, even more. No husband or lover, no relatives, and though she had spent the past few years immersed in a world of women, not a single friend.

As soon as she was back at the apartment, Edith took her housedress from the closet. But the thought of all that was involved in changing out of her clothes, the undoing of all those buttons, zippers, snaps, and garters, defeated her. For a long while, she sat on the side of her bed, staring at the floorboards. After nine months, the apartment still did not feel like home. Indeed, she felt even lonelier here than she had back at the motel. The motel, at least, had seemed like an intermission. This was her life.

Though she kept the door to the second bedroom closed, she was always aware of the two single beds behind it, of her hopeful attempt at decorating the room. The poster of Betty Grable she'd hung beside Harriet's bed, the poster of Babe Ruth she'd hung by Jeffrey's—as if he'd ever shown a lick of interest in baseball. The desk tucked into the corner with its cup filled with sharpened pencils and stack of writing tablets. The wardrobe she'd bought, which she kept empty for several months, until finally she began hanging her own clothes inside.

Sometimes on Wednesdays, Edith would pray for Reuben to call to say that the children couldn't go out that evening. This wasn't because she didn't miss them. It was because having to drop them back at Main Street after dinner, as if she were their aunt instead of their mother, made her miss them too much.

She probably talked with the children more during the two evenings a week when she saw them than she used to during an entire week when she was living at Main Street. But there were things that a mother couldn't learn through words. In order to truly understand her children, she needed to see them stumble to the breakfast table, and sprawled out on the carpet, listening to the radio. She needed to peek through their bedroom doorways and watch their innocence return as they slept.

As January 2, the opening day for the health food store grew near, Reuben became despondent. He'd sunk fifteen hundred dollars into the store, Adolph one thousand. Yet, in fitting out the space, they still had to cut corners, and it showed. The store was a depressing place with fluorescent lighting, hospital white walls, and a speckled linoleum floor. Bins filled with loose tea, seeds, grains, and beans lined one wall. The unvarnished pine shelves along the opposite wall held several brands of soy milk, a section devoted to yeasts—brewer's yeast, cakes of yeast, powdered yeast—all giving off a nauseating smell, as well as cod liver oil and other digestives in ugly brown bottles. There was also a refrigerator containing blocks of tofu in buckets of cloudy water, some tubs of yogurt, and a variety of strangely colored vegetable juices. Reuben understood this was not meant to be the sort of store where a customer went to browse. Still, he couldn't help wishing the merchandise was a bit more appealing.

The men announced the opening by placing an ad in the *Sea Forth Beacon* and by sending Jeffrey and Harriet around, passing out flyers, an exercise in which Ernest refused to participate. Then it was up to Adolph to sit by the cash register and wait for the customers. On a good day, there might be two or three, invariably the same women who used to buy Adolph's potions at Friestadt's. As the weeks passed, both men tried to remain upbeat. "These things take time," Adolph told Reuben, the same thing Reuben told him.

"I can't believe you let my crazy father talk you into this," Ernest said. It was a Saturday, the one day when Reuben watched the store. Ernest was leaning against the doorway that separated the store from what had once been the living room and was now the warehouse. He had a date with a girl for the matinee and was jingling the change Adolph had given him around in his pocket.

"Your crazy father didn't talk me into anything," Reuben said. He'd begun to dislike Ernest. He hated the way Ernest spoke to his father, alternately dismissive and defiant. He was rude to Reuben, too, which put Reuben in the awkward position of having to decide whether to reprimand another man's son. But what irritated Reuben the most was how Ernest had begun to treat Jeffrey.

Were Ernest rude to Jeffrey, at least there would have been something tangible to chastise him about. Instead, Ernest patronized him. He would hear Jeffrey out with a smirk and then respond in a slow, simple manner as if Jeffrey were feeble-minded. The thing Reuben found most painful, however, was Jeffrey's dog-like gratitude for every morsel of attention Ernest threw him. Pale, thinner than ever, Jeffrey wore his hurt like a cloak. Whenever Reuben tried to talk with him about Ernest, Jeffrey's face filled with such mistrust that he would back off. All those years during which he'd tried to remake Jeffrey into someone he wasn't meant to be had had their impact. His son was afraid of him.

"Thank God we weren't stupid enough to quit our jobs," Reuben said as Adolph was about to leave for work one evening. Half an hour later, Reuben heard the front door open. Though late March, the weather was wintry, and a gust of cold air accompanied Adolph into the foyer.

"I've been fired." Adolph stared at Reuben in disbelief.

"Give me your things," Reuben said. Then, thinking better of it, he unwound Adolph's scarf, removed his hat, and helped him out of his coat. He steered Adolph into the dining room. Because the living room was now used as a warehouse, they'd moved the couch and recliner in there, pushing the dining table off to the side.

"What can I get you?" Reuben asked.

"A cup of tea would be nice."

Reuben was on his way to the kitchen when he spotted the dusty huddle of liquor bottles on the sideboard. He held up a fifth of bourbon. "This will warm you up a lot faster than tea."

"You know I don't drink." Adolph leaned back against the couch and closed his eyes.

Reuben poured them both shots of bourbon anyway. By now, Adolph's news had sunk in, and he was beginning to realize the impact it would have on his own situation. Because Adolph's savings were nearly depleted, Adolph would now be able to contribute little to the household and business expenses.

"What happened?" Reuben asked.

Adolph took a sip of bourbon. He put the glass down, sputtering and coughing. "The manager found out about our store. I hadn't even taken off my coat when he dragged me into the stockroom. He said people like me belonged in jail. It was only when he called me a traitor that I realized why. It was the loyalty oath Rexall's makes its employees sign. I thought it was just a bit of red tape."

Reuben took a cigar from his breast pocket. Cigars had become part of his evening routine, though out of consideration for Adolph, he normally refrained until Adolph left for work. He slipped off the White Owl band, placing it off to the side for Harriet, who had begun to collect them. "What do we do now?"

"I go find another job," Adolph said.

"The next nearest pharmacy is two towns away. On top of that, he's not going to give you a good reference."

"Something's bound to turn up." Adolph ran his finger around the rim of the glass. "I had to throw the tofu out. It was starting to smell." He drained his glass and set it down on the floor. "It was also a mistake to buy so much bulgur. I suppose we can still get away with selling it, but it's starting to go stale."

Reuben walked over to the living room archway. The glass-paneled door between the living room and the store was closed, but the streetlights coming through the store windows provided enough illumination to make out the silhouettes of the barrels. The challenge, Reuben knew, would be figuring out when to cut his losses and walk away. He'd already held on to one business for too long and didn't want to make the same mistake twice.

"Maybe people can't see the sign from the street," Adolph said.

"It's pretty big."

"Maybe we should advertise more."

"People know we're here. They're just not interested in coming."

The men listened as Harriet clomped down the stairs. Slight as she was, she made more noise than all of the males of the house combined. The refrigerator door slammed, and a moment later, Harriet appeared in the kitchen entranceway, holding a glass of milk, her pink quilted bathrobe knotted loosely around her. She sniffed in. "I just love the smell of a cigar." She brought two fingers to her mouth and pretended to puff, and then she plopped down in Reuben's recliner, causing the milk to slosh over the sides. "Aren't I a clumsy goose?" She laughed as she rubbed at the wet armrest with her sleeve.

"Mr. Friestadt and I are talking," Reuben said.

"Adolph doesn't care if I stay, do you Adolph?" Though Reuben reprimanded her repeatedly for not calling him Mr. Friestadt, Harriet always "forgot." Harriet rested her head against one armrest and slung her legs over the other. "Don't mind me," she said.

"Your poppa and I were talking about the store," Adolph said. "We're trying to figure out what we're doing wrong."

Harriet nodded. "Do you have any customers at all?"

"Not a lot," Adolph admitted.

Harriet sucked on a strand of hair. "Maybe people don't like what you're selling."

"If you can't keep quiet, you'll have to go upstairs," Reuben said.

"Let her stay." Adolph shifted over to the end of the couch nearest her. "Tell me, darling, what kind of things should we be selling?"

Harriet gave Reuben one of her "so there" looks. After a moment's pause, she said, "I know! Malteds, candy bars, stuff people like. You don't have to stop selling the disgusting stuff, but you should sell delicious things, too."

"It isn't that kind of store." Reuben shot Adolph an apologetic glance.

But Adolph looked thoughtful. "She's right," he said. "Given the mess I've made of my life, the last thing I should be doing is trying to tell other people how to live theirs."

# Chapter Twenty-Seven

## April 1942

---

Before heading to bed each evening, Adolph would set the kitchen table for breakfast. He would use a freshly ironed cloth and his wife's china so that the table was a pretty clutter of bowls, plates, cups, and saucers. At the center of the table, he would line up boxes of Raisin Bran, Shredded Wheat, wheat germ, and unprocessed bran—the only cereals he approved of.

One morning, when Reuben came downstairs, only Harriet and Ernest were at the table. Both were eating Kix, Harriet's favorite cereal. The Hershey's Syrup was out, and the milk in their bowls was brown.

"Where's Jeffrey?" Reuben asked.

Harriet shrugged and continued shoveling cereal into her mouth.

"Have you seen him?"

"This morning or ever?" Ernest asked.

Harriet giggled. Reuben looked at her sternly; Ernest was insolent enough without giving him encouragement. He was about to pour himself a bowl of cereal when it occurred to him that he hadn't heard Jeffrey's footsteps from above his bedroom. He decided to make sure Jeffrey hadn't slept through his alarm.

On the stairs, Reuben passed Adolph, who never came down to breakfast until he'd completed a half-hour of calisthenics.

"You know teenagers," Adolph said when Reuben explained where he was headed. Reuben gave a rueful shake of the head, meant to signal agreement, though both their sons were about as far from being typical teenagers as two boys could be.

It had been months since Reuben had been up to the attic. He hated what it symbolized—Jeffrey's retreat from the world. His friendship with Ernest had made such a difference. For the first time, Jeffrey had seemed genuinely happy. Except now, Jeffrey seemed unhappier than ever.

The attic door was locked. Reuben knocked and shouted. When there was no answer, he panicked, convinced that Jeffrey had killed himself. He pictured him swinging from a rope hanging from the rafters, his neck broken and tongue hanging out.

Reuben felt a tap on his shoulder. He turned around to find Ernest holding out a screwdriver.

"Pop asked me to give you this," Ernest said.

Reuben felt a murderous urge to drive the screwdriver through Ernest's eye until he noticed that Ernest was white-faced, his expression stricken.

There was no body hanging from the rafters. No sign of Jeffrey anywhere. Other than the unmade bed, everything was in order. On the pipe rack where Jeffrey hung his clothing, all the hangers were facing in the same direction, the shirts to the left, the pants to the right. On Jeffrey's desk, the pencils, their sharpened points facing up, were in the holder, his school books stacked neatly to the side. At the center of the desk, there was a black and white copybook, "Jeffrey's journal" printed in the space for a name.

Reuben flipped through the journal. When Jeffrey was young, whenever he picked up a pencil, fork, or spoon with his left hand, Mrs. Goldsmith would slap his hand. Jeffrey eventually learned how to eat and write with his right hand but with an awkwardness that even now was painful to witness. Jeffrey's handwriting was large and childish, the letters slanting in all directions and meandering across the lines.

Reuben was just a few lines into the first page when he heard rustling. It took him a moment to realize that it was coming from the bed. He pulled down the covers, exposing the back of Jeffrey's head and neck.

"Are you all right?" Reuben asked.

There was no response.

"Did you forget to set your alarm?" Reuben asked.

Jeffrey tugged the covers back up. Reuben pushed his hand away and pulled the covers completely off. He was shocked by Jeffrey's nakedness, not the fact of it, but by the line of dark hair ascending from his buttocks. He had a flash of himself at Jeffrey's age, how, in bed, his hand would travel down between his legs. He recalled the sense of release, his remorse afterward, his vows of never again, the "never" rarely lasting more than a few days.

Jeffrey rolled over, the ragged imprint of the bedding on the side of his face. "I'm dropping out of school."

"You are not!"

"The law says I'm old enough to decide for myself."

Reuben realized there was nothing he could do to stop him, short of threatening to throw him out on the street. "Why?"

"Because I hate school, that's why." Jeffrey swung his legs over the side of the bed. Reuben couldn't help staring at his penis, longer than his own, and the thatch of pubic hair above it. "Toss me some underpants," Jeffrey said, nodding toward the dresser, "then get out. I want everyone just to leave me alone."

At the factory that day, time and again, Reuben was jarred to attention by the clank of one piece of fuselage colliding into another. He'd realize that instead of watching the assembly line, he'd been thinking about Jeffrey. He wondered whether his journal might provide answers to why Jeffrey hated school and to other questions he didn't know enough to ask. He recoiled at the idea of sneaking up to the attic to read it. But he decided he had no choice. What if Jeffrey ended up doing something stupid—Reuben wouldn't allow himself to be more concrete than that—which, had he read the journal, he could have prevented?

As Reuben stepped off the bus that evening, the garden that Sea Forth's beautification committee had planted outside the depot provided him with his first bit of pleasure that day. The daffodils and hyacinths had come up, so, too, had an early variety of tulips. On the walk over to Main Street, he spotted signs of nascent prosperity. This area, north of Main Street, had long been regarded as the poor side of town, but that demarcation had begun to blur. A cluster of houses had been constructed on land that had once been part of a potato farm. The houses, built around a cul-de-sac, were well-designed, with all sorts of amenities including attached garages. On Main Street, there was virtually no space to let. Indeed, rents had become so high that the shoemaker and laundry had been forced to relocate to side streets.

Then, there was Herbert Towers, which, in spite of its Manhattan-style rents, was fully occupied. The sight of this building never failed to upset Reuben, less because of its owner and ostentation than because of what it signified: a momentous step closer to the obliteration of the small town hominess that had drawn him to Sea Forth in the first place. Reuben's feelings about "Edith's" were even more complicated, vacillating between pride in her accomplishments and a fervent hope she would fail.

Reuben planned on telling Edith about Jeffrey, only not that evening when he wanted nothing more than to collapse into his recliner. All the same, he paused, as he often did, by her display window, hoping to catch a glimpse of her inside. Most nights, he was disappointed. Tonight, just as he was peering in, Edith happened to pass by the window and glance out. Before Reuben had a chance to escape, their eyes met.

Edith opened the door. "Reuben?"

Reuben was sure she was wondering if he'd been spying on her, which, in an innocent way, he supposed he was.

Over the years, Edith's taste in clothing had grown more conservative. Today, she was wearing a high-necked lilac blouse and a straight gray skirt, the only bit of flair provided by the paisley scarf tied around her shoulders. Even so, Reuben thought she was looking better than she had in years. She'd lost the weight she had gained. And while she mostly wore her hair up these days, today it was loose. He was surprised how long it had grown, nearly to her shoulders, and found the contrast between her girlish waves and her no-nonsense outfit alluring.

Edith was looking over his outfit as well—his jeans, worn through at the knees, his dusty work boots, his shirt, soiled and reeking of sweat. Reuben dug his hands into his pockets. At the end of his shift, he always washed his hands with Lava Soap, but no matter how hard he scrubbed, he could never remove the last traces of grime from his knuckle creases and from beneath his nails.

"This is a surprise," Edith said in what Reuben used to call her party voice. She led him toward a pair of armchairs at the rear of the store. "Everything okay?"

Reuben was almost glad that everything wasn't okay. It made it less embarrassing to have been caught peering through her window. "Yes and no."

"They're not sick?"

"No, they're fine."

"Thank God for that."

They were sitting so close, their knees were nearly touching—so close that Reuben could smell Edith's perfume, not Arpege, the one she wore while they were married, something stronger. He found it bizarre how she could be so familiar that he could picture her naked body perfectly yet seem like a stranger.

"It's Jeffrey," Reuben said.

"Is he in trouble?" Edith glanced around to make sure no one was eavesdropping.

"He's decided to drop out of high school," Reuben said.

"What brought that about?"

Reuben shrugged. "I only know what he told me—that he hates it there."

"What kid doesn't hate school? Of course, we can't let him."

"We can't stop him. He's nearly sixteen."

Edith bit the side of her thumb. "He's still a baby."

"Not according to the law."

"You didn't try to talk him out of it?"

Reuben felt a familiar anger rise up. Did Edith think he told Jeffrey he thought it was a great idea? He took a long sip of the lemonade one of the salesgirls had brought him and looked around. Outside, it was April. Here in the store, it was already summer, the mannequins dressed in sundresses or two-piece bathing suits that exposed a lot more flesh than he'd ever seen at the beach. Their colors were defiantly cheerful, a thumbing of the nose to the wars raging in Europe and the Pacific.

Reuben's anger dissipated as quickly as it had flared up. He realized it had less to do with Edith than himself, for allowing the gulf between his son and him to grow so wide. He could try to reason with Jeffrey until he was blue in the face and it wouldn't make a difference.

"I was hoping you might talk to him. Maybe you could take him to dinner—without Harriet." Reuben pulled a wad of cash from his wallet, but Edith waved it away.

"What makes you think I'll have better luck?"

An image came to Reuben of Jeffrey and Edith walking down his front path, their shoulders touching and footsteps in sync. "Because he loves you."

Edith looked uncertain. "I can't believe he's serious. I bet he had some sort of test, and this was the only way he could come up with to get out of it."

Now that Jeffrey had stopped going to school, he no longer came down for breakfast. For dinner, he would fix himself a plate of whatever concoction Adolph had cooked up, and take it up to the attic. Other than that and to use the bathroom, he rarely left the attic. Reuben had no idea what he did up there. He had no radio, nothing to amuse himself with besides his dozen or so well-read books, his chess set, and, of course, his journal. When Reuben pictured him up there, he imagined him hunched over his desk, scribbling away in that copybook.

Now that the dining room had been turned into the living room, the household ate all their meals crammed around the kitchen table. "It isn't fair," Harriet grumbled, scraping her fork tines across her plate so that they made a screeching noise. "He doesn't have to get up early. He doesn't have to go to school. He doesn't have to finish Adolph's glop. He gets to do whatever he wants."

"Your brother has a name," Reuben said.

She glared at Reuben. "Everyone knows who I'm talking about."

"Don't talk back to your poppa," Adolph said.

Harriet turned her glare on Adolph. "He's my father, not my poppa. Besides, it's true."

"Your brother's unhappy," Adolph said. "Why he's so unhappy I have no idea." He turned to Ernest. "Maybe you can shed some light on that?"

Harriet and Reuben looked toward Ernest. Reuben found it hard to connect the young man before him with the emaciated boy he'd been when Reuben met him. Whatever resemblance Ernest once had to Jeffrey had been obliterated. Ernest was husky now with muscled arms that he helped along by lifting weights despite Adolph's objections. His beard had become as heavy as a man's, and black hairs covered the back of his hands.

"Did either of you know he was planning to drop out?" Adolph asked.

Harriet had stuffed an entire slice of bread in her mouth. She sprayed crumbs as she spoke. "I knew nothing, Adolph, I swear. Jeffrey never even talks to me except to complain how loud I'm playing my music. Not that I play it loud." She nodded toward Ernest. "I bet he knows something."

Ernest grabbed the table's edge. "If I knew he was planning to drop out, don't you think I would have tried to talk him out of it? The way he never leaves the attic—it's like he's gone crazy. I like Jeffrey, but I want other friends, too. Jeffrey—all he wants...Aw, forget it." He stood up, knocking his chair backward. "Can I be excused?" He dashed from the room without waiting for permission.

As soon as Edith and Jeffrey left for dinner, Reuben ran upstairs. He eased the screwdriver into the attic door keyhole, afraid that Ernest or Harriet would catch him trying to jimmy the lock. But the lock opened easily and, in seconds, he was on the other side.

The copybook was still on the desk along with one of Reuben's fountain pens, an expensive one he had given up for lost. A minute or so passed before Reuben could bring himself to open the journal. He reached into his breast pocket for his reading glasses, but they weren't there. To decipher Jeffrey's handwriting, he had to hold the journal at arm's length.

The first entry, dated October 2, 1941, was mainly a recitation of what Jeffrey was studying in school:

> In algebra, we're learning quadratic equations. Problem is, Mr. Swinburne's getting senile and keeps losing his place on the blackboard.
> In biology, we have to dissect a frog tomorrow. The idea makes me sick. Why do I need to know what the insides of a frog look like?

As Reuben read on, he calmed down. The entries, nearly all about school or Adolph's meals, were what he'd expect from a fifteen-year-old:

> Dinner tonight looked and smelled like dog crap and tasted even worse. I don't know why Dad lets him get away with cooking stuff like that.

The journal contained so little of a personal nature that Reuben soon became bored and began to skim. Then he got to December 3: "Today is Ernest's sixteenth birthday," it began. Until then, Jeffrey had made no more than passing references to Ernest:

> He should really be in eleventh grade, not tenth. I bought him a display box for his stamps. It cost $3.00. I cleaned out my piggy bank—that made $2.50. Don't ask me where I got the rest. He barely looked at it. He told me he had better things to do than collect stamps.

After that, the references to Ernest became frequent. Jeffrey's handwriting became even unrulier, straying so far beyond the lines that the words collided with the ones above and below.

> Ernest got a haircut. It's so short, you can see his scalp.
> Ernest was so upset with the B+ on his history exam, he went to see Mr. Cox after school.

It was not the content of these references to Ernest so much as their frequency that made Reuben uneasy. By late January, the entries themselves had become disturbing:

> I waited until four o'clock for Him in the freezing cold after school. Finally I gave up. That's the third time this month. When I was walking home, I saw Him in the Argosy, with some kids from school. I got so upset I ran into the alley to hide.

In February, Jeffrey wrote:

> Sometimes I feel like I don't want to live. Sometimes? Most of the time. I keep begging Him to tell me what I've done. He tells me I haven't done anything but I must have or why would He be treating me this way?

Reuben couldn't bring himself to read more. Though it was chilly in the attic, he was sweating, and when he stood, his legs almost gave way. He glanced at the clock by Jeffrey's bed. He'd been up there nearly an hour. Edith hadn't said where she was taking Jeffrey, but he had a hunch it was to the Ferryside Inn. He thought back to that evening when he'd stood off to the side, looking through the window. He could picture Edith and Jeffrey inside. All week, he could hardly wait for Edith to report back on what Jeffrey told her. Now, he decided he would rather not know. He was sorry he read the journal. There were things it was better for a father not to discover about his son.

**

On the cab ride over to the Ferryside Inn, Jeffrey kept playing with the door handle, his legs jouncing like they had motors inside. Edith was already regretting her choice of restaurant. As the maitre d' led them to their table, she glanced around, afraid lest they bump into one of her customers, or worse, Paul.

The maitre d' sat them at a table overlooking the bay. It was a clear night, lit by a brilliant quarter moon. Edith touched Jeffrey's forearm, directing his attention to the window, where, beyond their ghostly reflections, the lights on the pier sparkled and turned the swooping seagulls into silver flashes. After dutifully shifting his eyes sideways, Jeffrey turned his gaze to the few square inches of tablecloth beyond his plate.

It was going to be a long evening, Edith thought, rising out of her chair and trying, unsuccessfully, to catch the waiter's eye. Now that she was sitting across from her son, she realized she and Reuben had been fretting about the wrong thing. Jeffrey's decision to drop out was the least of their worries, a mere symptom of the torment within.

The redhead at the next table shifted sideways and crossed her legs, causing her unfashionably short dress to slide up to her knees. She pulled a cigarette from her purse, placed it in a long black holder, and waited for her much older companion to light it. The woman's makeup was garish, her hair obviously dyed, but it was this very cheapness, Edith knew, that many men would find attractive. Edith guessed this woman was the man's mistress, though she undoubtedly harbored hopes of becoming his wife. Edith saw nothing shocking about this. Since the dawn of time, women and men had been trading sex for security and calling it love. She, herself, had done it twice.

The woman took a drag of her cigarette, releasing smoke in Jeffrey's direction.

Jeffrey made a show of waving the smoke away. "Can't you tell her to stop?" It was the first full sentence he'd spoken all evening.

"She has a right to enjoy a cigarette."

When the redhead released another plume of smoke, Jeffrey began coughing in an exaggerated way, eliciting dirty looks from the redhead and her companion.

It was always such a balancing act with Jeffrey. Edith was afraid that if she were too sharp with him, he'd withdraw, ruining any chance of discussing his decision to drop out. On the other hand, she could hardly allow him to make a scene. She scanned the room for something to distract him with and caught sight of the fish tank at the opposite end of the room. It was backlit and the tropical fish glowed.

"They're finishing up," Edith said, referring to the couple. "Go check out the fish. I'll get you after they leave." She wasn't hopeful that Jeffrey would follow her suggestion. To her surprise, he did.

A minute later, their waiter, a hawk-faced man with a small, tight mouth appeared. "I can come back," he said when he noticed Jeffrey's empty chair.

"No!" Desperate for the meal to proceed quickly, Edith ordered without looking at the menu, two Manhattan-style clam chowders and two filets of flounder.

"Anything to drink?"

Edith rarely drank and reflexively shook her head. The waiter was on his way to the kitchen when it occurred to her that some wine might be what they needed to get through the evening. "On second thought," she called out, "I'll see the wine list." She scanned the list until she found an inexpensive white and then pointed to it, afraid to say its name lest she mispronounce it. "And two glasses."

The waiter raised his eyebrows. While Jeffrey was tall, he had a boy's face.

Edith raised her own eyebrows. "Right away, please."

By the time the waiter brought their soups, Edith had finished her first glass. Already she was finding it hard to recall why she had been feeling so anxious. She rose to get Jeffrey, who was squatting by the fish tank, his hands and nose pressed against the glass. She tapped his shoulder and he looked up, smiling for the first time that evening.

"Aren't they beautiful!" Jeffrey said. "See the speckled yellow one with the long tail? And that striped one with the silly whiskers?"

"Your soup's getting cold."

"That blue one—you can see its skeleton right through its skin."

For a moment, Edith, too, stared, transfixed by the fishes' vibrant colors, their rhythmic swishing motions, their round dark eyes. She was struck by the extraordinariness of how such simple creatures could be born knowing everything they needed to survive, something it took most humans a lifetime to figure out.

Jeffrey's mouth fell open as the waiter poured him a glass of wine.

"It's okay," Edith told him. "Drink."

Jeffrey scooped the soft middle out from his roll, nibbled at it with a dreamy expression, and then took a sip of wine. Edith was about to ask whether he'd tasted wine before, but she forgot. Just two glasses and her mind was already sludge.

"My date," Edith giggled when the waiter came to clear the soup. The restaurant had gotten busier, and they were surrounded by the sounds of clinking glasses and laughter. The waiter topped up Edith's glass and then placed the bottle back in the ice bucket. "Haven't you forgotten something?" She pointed to Jeffrey's glass.

"Do you think he believes I'm your date?" Jeffrey asked. His eyes were shining, if not quite with happiness, at least with more animation than she had seen for a long time. He gazed past her toward the fish tank. "I bet you didn't know that all land animals, even humans, evolved from fish. Whales and dolphins were just smart enough to realize how much nicer the ocean is."

Edith laughed, assuming Jeffrey was joking.

"I learned it in biology. That's why even though they look like fish, whales have lungs. Their blow holes are just nostrils that have migrated to the top of their bodies."

Jeffrey's words reminded Edith of the reason she had brought him there—to try and talk him out of dropping out. "See, school's not all bad. If you hadn't taken biology, you would never know that, would you?"

Jeffrey began tracing circles on the tablecloth with the dull side of his knife. "I don't want to talk about school."

Edith decided to wait until their main courses arrived before raising the subject again. She poured herself another glass of wine and topped up Jeffrey's glass. She'd certainly done the right thing in ordering the wine; she felt calmer than she had in weeks. And if Jeffrey didn't yet want to talk about school, at least he was talking.

"What's this?" Jeffrey asked after the waiter brought their main courses. He lifted the corner of his fish with his fork.

"Filet of flounder," Edith said.

Jeffrey's eyes flitted toward the fish tank.

The waiter lifted the bottle from the ice bucket. It was empty.

"Another bottle, please," Edith said, careful to enunciate her words.

The waiter glanced pointedly at Jeffrey, making clear his poor opinion of Edith as a mother.

"You have to eat," Edith told Jeffrey after the waiter left. "Or you'll get sick."

Jeffrey impaled a tiny piece of fish on his fork, brought it to his mouth, and wiped his lips with his napkin.

"You spat it out," Edith said.

"No, I didn't!" Jeffrey cried. It was such an obvious lie—spitting his food into his napkin had long been a trick to avoid eating—that they both began to laugh.

As the waiter cut the foil from the bottle, he stared at Jeffrey's plate. "Is something wrong with the fish?"

Edith's and Jeffrey's eyes met. The air between them appeared wobbly to Edith, as if they were underwater. She knew why he couldn't eat the fish, that while it would never occur to most people to connect the beautiful creatures in the tank with what was on their plates, Jeffrey was not like most people. His sensitivity, exasperating as it was, was also one of the things about him she loved most. While Harriet was the sort of child who squashed houseflies with her thumb, Jeffrey captured them beneath a cup and set them free outside.

"Maybe Adolph has a point," Jeffrey said.

Edith rolled her eyes. "Adolph."

"I know what you mean." Jeffrey shuddered. He ate around the fish, picking at his carrots and potatoes.

They helped themselves to the second bottle of wine, as the waiter now seemed to be avoiding their table. Edith tried to calculate how many glasses she had drunk. Whatever it was, it was more wine than she had ever had before. As for Jeffrey, now that he had gotten used to its taste, he was downing the wine like it was water.

His fork still impaled in a carrot slice, Jeffrey suddenly pushed his plate away and laid his face on the table. "I don't feel so great."

"You're not going to be sick?" Edith asked, though the greenish cast his face had taken on made the question unnecessary. She motioned for the waiter and was mortified when, instead of the waiter, Paul appeared, informing her as he helped Jeffrey out of his chair, that their meal was "on the house."

He drove them to her apartment in his Cadillac and helped her put Jeffrey to bed. Smiling and whistling all the while, Paul claimed to be amused, and Edith was sure this was true. Drunk as she was, she recognized how it was possible for a person to be amused and disapproving at the same time.

The following morning, Edith could hardly believe her ears when Jeffrey told her he was starving. Her hands were shaky as she cracked the eggs into the mixing bowl. She put on the percolator thinking coffee might revive her, but her stomach heaved at the smell of it brewing. All she could manage was a few sips of orange juice. Jeffrey finished the eggs and two slices of buttered toast, washed down with several glasses of milk.

"I want to stay," he said.

"You'll be alone," Edith said. "I leave for work in an hour."

"I mean forever."

Her glass poised mid-air, Edith said, "It's fine with me. Though it may not be with your father."

"Dad will be happy to see me go," Jeffrey said.

"What a thing to say." It occurred to Edith that Jeffrey might be right. The irony was, after all those months when she missed her children so much it was practically a physical ache, she was beginning to enjoy living alone. As she scraped the last bits of egg from Jeffrey's plate into the bin, she looked at him over her shoulder. "I'll ask. Just don't get your hopes up."

The warmth and openness Jeffrey displayed that morning proved ephemeral. Within days, he had retreated back into himself, hardly speaking and skulking around the apartment like an unwelcome guest. Edith found herself treating him like a guest as well, bombarding him with questions, mostly having to do with his physical needs and all asked with painfully false cheeriness: "What foods should I buy?" "Do your clothes need washing?" "Anything need ironing?"

This last question was laughable, given that Jeffrey hardly ever changed out of his pajamas. Then, why should he when he never left the house? Edith found the sight of Jeffrey in his pajamas especially disturbing not only for what it implied about his mental state, but because it brought up unpleasant memories of Reuben. Also, when Jeffrey was in his pajamas, she could see how emaciated he had become. His body, visible through the thin cotton, appeared no wider from the side than a plank of wood. Believing that, at least, was something she might be able to do something about, Edith embarked upon a campaign to fatten him up.

Every morning, Edith would make Jeffrey a hearty breakfast such as pancakes with maple syrup or oatmeal with brown sugar and cream. She would sit across from him, nibbling at her toast, not leaving for work until he finished every bite, though this cut into the most productive part of her day—that window of time between her arrival and that of her staff. She made a point, too, of leaving the store early enough to prepare Jeffrey a proper dinner.

Edith stuck to this routine for weeks. Had Jeffrey shown an ounce of gratitude, she might have kept it up longer. But as he methodically chewed his way through her decently prepared meals, he showed so little awareness that he might as well have been eating cardboard. Plus, as far as Edith could tell, he hadn't gained so much as an ounce of weight. Before long, she started skipping a breakfast here, a dinner there. She rationalized this by telling herself that the store also needed her, which, while true, was hardly the whole story. She hated being around Jeffrey.

# Chapter Twenty-Eight

## May and June 1942

Since Jeffrey moved in, Edith had been having the salesgirls close up without her on Thursday nights when the store stayed open late. As pleased as she generally was with the salesgirls, on Fridays, she would invariably arrive to find the lights left on or a door unlocked. Then, in May, the girls forgot to close the windows in the shipping bay. That night it rained heavily. Water poured in through the windows, ruining a trio of silk dresses that were about to be sent out.

"I simply have to stay until the store closes," she explained to Jeffrey at breakfast the following Thursday.

"Okay," Jeffrey said. Cheek resting in his palm, he was stirring his oatmeal but had yet to eat a single bite. There were purple smudges beneath his eyes. His hair, which lay plastered to his scalp, exuded an odor like stale cooking oil. It occurred to Edith that it had been a while since she had seen any evidence in the bathroom of his having bathed.

"For dinner, there's leftover pork in the refrigerator. Heat it in the oven at 350 for ten minutes. Also, some baked beans. Put them in a saucepan over a low flame." Edith wasn't sure why she was telling Jeffrey this. She knew she would arrive home to find the food untouched.

It was after ten when Edith got home. From beneath Jeffrey's door, she could see that his lights were off. Exhausted, she went to bed. After a great deal of tossing about, Edith realized she was too wound up for sleep. She clicked on the lamp and grabbed the pen and pad she kept on her night table, in case she thought of something about the store that needed attending to. She made a few notes, but nothing that would explain her growing agitation. She became hot and breathless. Wondering if this could be the start of menopause, she threw the covers off.

But it was not the store or menopause. It was Jeffrey. For a minute, dread kept her pinned to the bed, listening to the *tick-tock* of her alarm clock and the purr of the refrigerator. When she did get up, Edith had to grab the bedpost to steady herself.

"Jeffrey, Jeffrey," Edith called out as she crossed the short distance between their rooms. She expected no answer; yet, when she didn't get one, her panic grew. She paused before trying his door, half-hoping it would be locked.

Jeffrey was sprawled out on his stomach, the blankets twisted about his middle so that his legs and arms were bare. Just asleep, Edith told herself, laughing at her foolishness. She was about to close the door when it occurred to her that Jeffrey never slept on his stomach. He had a peculiar way of sleeping—on his back with his knees bent. Her breath caught and, as it did, she got a whiff of an odor like spoiled milk. She went to his bed and rolled him over. His eyelids fluttered. His mouth was slack, something white and granular dribbling from the corner.

Edith slapped his cheek. A single moan was the only sign his body registered the slaps.

"He tried to kill himself," Edith said out loud. She had to grab her wrist to steady her hand before delivering one last stinging slap. The slap sent Jeffrey's head crashing against the wall. He still didn't wake.

A lucid calm descended on Edith. She was sure Jeffrey had taken pills and that she needed to get him to the hospital. While waiting for the ambulance, she checked the medicine cabinet and his room. She found two empty vials—one for aspirin, the other for sleeping pills—beneath his bed.

*He tried to kill himself.* The words kept playing in Edith's head as the attendants loaded Jeffrey onto a stretcher and into the rear of the ambulance. Back when she was living next to the hospital, she'd grown so used to the ambulance siren that it would barely register. Now, it regained its former ability to terrify. As the ambulance swung into the entrance bay, Edith wondered whether the siren had drawn Reuben to the window.

"He tried to kill himself," Edith said softly as they wheeled Jeffrey into the harshly lit emergency room. The words no longer shocked her; they had already taken on a ring of inevitability.

"Do you know how many pills he took?" the doctor asked. He had driven over from his home, his blue pajama bottoms visible beneath his doctor's coat.

"No more than four or five aspirin. The bottle was nearly empty."

"How about the sleeping pills?"

Edith shook her head.

"Anything else?" the doctor asked, finishing off with a yawn.

Edith did a mental scan of the medicine cabinet. "I don't think so."

The waiting room was empty except for them and the receptionist, who was following their conversation, her face cupped in her hands.

"He's already starting to wake, so it couldn't have been many," the doctor said.

"He's going to be okay?"

A flicker of impatience crossed the doctor's face. He glanced at the clock. It was nearly midnight. "I told you; he's started to wake."

"Why would he do such a thing?"

The doctor shrugged. "You know teenagers. They take everything too seriously."

"When can I see him?"

"In the morning. I suggest you go home to bed, which is what I'm going to do."

Edith put on her cardigan and hooked her purse over her arm, but as soon as the doctor had gone, she sat back down. The doctor might be used to teenagers trying to kill themselves, but she wasn't.

At midnight, the receptionist left, her presence replaced by a bell and sign that said "Please Ring." With no one in sight, Edith headed down the hallway to the patient rooms. The floor, speckled green tiles, still shone from a recent mopping, and the air had a reassuring disinfectant smell. Edith was relieved to find Jeffrey behind the first door she tried for by then, she could hear the slap of rubber-soled shoes against the corridor floor.

Jeffrey was on his back, an IV line attached to his arm. He had fallen back asleep. Edith sat by his side and stared at his forehead. She wished she could bore into his brain so she could comprehend how he saw the world. His genius for saying and doing the wrong things, the way he jerked and twitched as if his body were an ill-fitting suit—all were lifelong traits that had alternately shamed, exasperated, and pained her. Like any parent, she wished for his life to be filled with successes, the path to his future smooth. But she had never tried to understand him, nor had she given him the unconditional love that was every child's birthright. Reuben was right; she hadn't been much of a mother. But nor had Reuben been much of a father.

While Jeffrey was in the hospital, Edith went through every drawer and shelf in the apartment. She collected the knives, scissors, bleach, and other caustics, packed them in a box, and brought them to the store. The only things she left behind were a set of steak knives and sewing scissors. She hid these in her closet, behind her shoes. She didn't kid herself. She knew if Jeffrey were determined to kill himself, he'd find a way.

When Edith picked Jeffrey up on Saturday morning, he looked none the worse for his ordeal, which was not to say that he looked good. She'd taken a cab to the hospital and paid the driver to wait but, after glancing up at the cloudless sky, Jeffrey said he'd rather walk. "I don't get out much these days," he explained as if there was something beside himself to blame for this.

The streets were busy. A gaggle of girls around Harriet's age careened by on roller skates, forcing the two of them off the pavement. They passed a trio of boys lugging mitts, bats, and balls. Edith's heart tugged as she thought about all the childish pleasures Jeffrey had missed out on and how diminished his childhood was because of this. She didn't have a clue whether Jeffrey also felt this way, and that by itself said a lot about the sort of parents she and Reuben had been.

They hardly spoke during the walk but, unlike most of their silences, this one felt companionable. Edith could tell Jeffrey was enjoying the pleasant weather. He even stopped to glance at a few shop windows. Maybe he's finally realizing how precious life is, Edith thought. Maybe, he's ready to start really living. But what if she were wrong? What if the reason he seemed so at peace was because he had finally made up his mind and, because of that, his next suicide attempt wouldn't be so halfhearted.

"You can tell me anything," Edith told Jeffrey at dinner that evening. "By this stage in my life, I've heard it all." She heaped a mound of scrambled eggs on his plate—he'd told her he was starving—and a smaller one on her own.

Jeffrey studied her.

"Well, you can," Edith said, though she was beginning to have her doubts. She began to get teary.

"Are you okay?" Jeffrey asked through a mouthful of egg.

"It's been a long two days."

"Here," he said, grabbing some paper napkins and holding them out.

She blew her nose. "Please eat. I'm sorry."

He took a few more forkfuls, but Edith knew she had ruined the meal and that he wouldn't finish. It was that more than anything else, which caused her to break down completely.

Soon, Jeffrey was standing behind her. "Don't cry," he said, stroking her hair. "Would you like a glass of water?" He held the glass as she sipped. "Do you want to lie down?"

"It's me who should be asking you that," Edith said, in her mind, adding, *I'm not the one who tried to kill myself.*

The following Monday morning, Edith was startled to find Jeffrey staring down at her from the side of the bed. "Is everything okay?" she asked.

"I came by to look at the birds," Jeffrey said.

There was a sparrow's nest in the tree outside Edith's window. The week before, the eggs had hatched and, even with the window shut, she could hear the tiny things' plaintive cheeps. She wondered why, if Jeffrey had come to look at the birds, he was standing over her bed. The room was not yet fully bright, its beige walls tinged with gray. Edith glanced at her alarm clock. "It's not even six."

Jeffrey widened his eyes in an unconvincing show of surprise.

"I have to get up soon anyway." Edith patted the bed. "Sit."

Jeffrey remained standing, his glance flickering between her face and the window, and Edith could tell that whatever surge of courage had propelled him into her bedroom was seeping away. She grabbed his forearm, pulling him down. "You're not leaving until you tell me what's on your mind."

For a while they sat in silence, listening to the birds and the garbage trucks rolling down the streets.

"Remember what you told me?" Jeffrey finally said. "How I could tell you anything."

"You can." Edith suddenly felt frightened. It occurred to her that what she meant by "anything" and how Jeffrey chose to interpret it could be very different.

Jeffrey traced the rose petals stitched into Edith's quilt with his finger. "It's hard."

"You'll feel better if you talk about it," Edith said.

"I'm different than other people."

Edith laughed, an involuntary response, brought on by nerves. But when Jeffrey looked offended, Edith realized that he took it as affirmation of what he'd said. "I'm sorry." Edith reached for his hand. He refused to give it to her.

"Maybe I should just forget it," Jeffrey said.

"No! Besides, you've already woken me."

Jeffrey walked to the foot of the bed and wrapped his arms around the post. He looked out the window as he spoke. "What I meant is that I'm different than most men. Different than Dad."

An ambiguous statement, by which Jeffrey could have meant any number of things. Yet Edith knew, even though she didn't yet fully comprehend that she knew, that there was only one way to take it. And that what he was about to say would come as no surprise.

"I like boys in a way that's supposed to be wrong."

Even so, to actually hear these words had the impact of a blow to the stomach. A long moment passed before Edith was able to speak.

"You don't know what you're talking about," she said.

Jeffrey stared at a golden patch of sunlight on the hardwood floor. "I've known since I was a little boy. The way most men feel about women, that's how..."

Edith leaped from the bed. "Men, women...Do you have any idea how ridiculous you sound?" She pushed Jeffrey away from the bedpost and grabbed her robe off of it. She belted it tightly and began to pace. "Boys your age, they're like animals. They have such strong urges, they can't think straight. The key is not to give in to them."

"Even when I dream, it's about boys."

Edith waved her hand. "Jeffrey, enough. This isn't the sort of thing you should talk about to anyone, even your mother. You'll end up talking yourself into believing something that isn't so."

"But it's true."

"I said—enough." Edith swirled around. "I don't want to hear another word. I might as well go make coffee. No point trying to get back to sleep."

As the days passed, the shock of what Jeffrey told Edith began to wear off. This was not because she found it easier to accept. She was angry with herself for encouraging him to confide in her and angry with him for taking her up on the offer. She could hardly bear to look at him and wasn't a good enough actress to pretend otherwise. She threw herself into the store, leaving before he was up and not returning until well into the evening.

But no matter how much time Edith spent at the store, it was never enough. As devoted as she had been to the Emporium, she had been able to view it as a thing apart, maybe because it was Fred's store, not hers. Here, it was her name out front, the embodiment of her vision inside. If the store failed, it would be her reputation, and hers alone, that would suffer.

The irony was that the store was not really hers. To the outside world, it might appear that way, but that was not how Paul saw it. He visited the store every day, sometimes more than once. The salesgirls adored him. Paul remembered their names, even the names of their mothers and beaus. He noticed if they were wearing something new or had done their hair differently. They loved how Paul joked with them, how he would pretend not to know which way a frock was supposed to be worn, scrunching up his face with mock perplexity as he held it back to front before a mirror.

All harmless fun, Edith supposed, especially given that as far as she could tell, Paul had not propositioned any of the salesgirls. The customers adored him, too, invariably seeking his opinion about their selections. That Paul's visits were good for morale and boosted sales was unarguable. But they did something else, something Edith suspected Paul was aware of, which was to diminish her authority in the eyes of both staff and customers.

Edith was the only person Paul didn't try to charm. With her, he was all business, so formal that she found it hard to remember they had once been friends. While bantering with the salesgirls, he would mentally be taking notes, forming the questions to grill her with back in her office. Questions that required her to know everything there was to know about the store in excruciating detail.

"How many pairs of calfskin gloves sold yesterday? In black? Taupe? When's that shipment of plaid shawls due? What's the inventory of size ten pink mohair sweaters? Size twelve?"

No matter how thoroughly Edith prepped, Paul always came up with at least one question she couldn't answer. When she fumbled, or worse, gave the wrong answers—answers he often seemed to know already—all traces of pleasantness would vanish from his face. "If you can't stay on top of the numbers," he warned her, "I'll find someone who can."

Not "we'll"—"I'll." Paul might refer to her as his partner, but she was not and never would be. Paul was incapable of regarding anyone as his equal.

Jeffrey's sixteenth birthday was the first Monday in June. Edith felt obliged to make him a birthday dinner, not that there hadn't been plenty of years when she'd done nothing to mark the day, and he hadn't seemed to care. Before leaving for work, she set the table with a linen cloth and napkins. She had to use everyday cutlery and dishes. She'd never asked Reuben for any of the flatware, china, or crystal, now undoubtedly gathering dust, and it was too late now.

Jeffrey asked what she was doing.

"It's your birthday," she said. He looked so surprised that she believed him when he told her he'd forgotten.

Because she didn't have a clue what he'd like, she'd put off buying a present, hoping that by the time his birthday rolled around, she would think of something. But she hadn't, and for much of that morning, she wandered in and out of the Main Street stores. She was about to resort to handing Jeffrey a cash-filled envelope when she remembered Culver's Hobby Shop, a dingy place a few doors from her own store, so long a fixture on Main Street that she had nearly forgotten it was there.

"What are his hobbies?" the elderly owner shouted.

"He doesn't have any," Edith shouted back.

The old man shook his head. "Not a boy alive that don't have hobbies." He studied the dusty shelves as he fiddled with the volume first on one, then on the other of his hearing aids. "How's about a model building kit?" He handed Edith a cardboard box.

Edith examined the B-59 on its cover and skimmed the instructions on its side. At least a model would keep Jeffrey busy.

How many nights had she returned home to find him lying on top of his blankets, staring at the ceiling?

"I'm thinking," he told her once. "Something wrong with that?"

She'd answered, "Of course not." But later, she couldn't help wondering if there was, if what Jeffrey needed was something to distract him from his problems.

Then Edith recalled how clumsy Jeffrey was with his hands. How bad his handwriting was. How he never even learned to use a fork and knife properly. A model, with those tiny pieces, would only frustrate him, make him feel worse about himself than he already did. "I don't think so," she said.

"Wha? I'm tellin' ya, all boys love models." The man looked offended. Using a pole with a claw hand, he pulled a box from the top shelf. "Lionel train set," he said. "This here's the deluxe model. Tracks, trains, signals, you name it. Trains is somethin' he'll never outgrow. Even old codgers like me love trains."

Edith, too, loved trains and had ever since she was a young girl and would lie on her bed, listening to their whistles as they pulled into or sped away from the Sea Forth station. She stared at the artist's rendition of the miniature world she and Jeffrey could create, complete with stores, trees, overpasses and mountains, and thought of how wonderful they would find it to escape, if only for a couple hours, to such a perfect, predictable place. She was about to fish out her wallet when it occurred to her that there was no space in her tiny apartment for a train set—not unless she gave up her front parlor. The room was hardly used. She never invited anyone over and neither did Jeffrey. But to give up her parlor would mean that she had no intention of ever doing so, and she was not prepared to reconcile herself to that.

"Thanks anyway," Edith shouted. She was nearly to the door when she spotted a revolving display of colorful stamps in cellophane packets, many from countries she had never heard of.

"Lotsa boys like stamp collections, specially the quiet ones," the man hollered as he fished out a large blue album.

Jeffrey threw his arms around Edith and kissed her on the lips. She laughed nervously and pushed him away. "Only sweethearts kiss on the lips," she told him.

"How did you know?" Jeffrey removed the stamps from their packets and, after laying them out on the floor, sprawled out on his stomach to study them. Then, turning his attention to the album, he began turning the pages. "I'm not pasting them in until I'm certain where they should go." He shut the album and ran his hand across its smooth leather surface. "I've wanted to start a stamp collection forever."

"Why didn't you tell me?" Edith asked.

Jeffrey shrugged.

Edith tried to recall the last time Jeffrey had asked for anything. It was his tenth birthday, and he had wanted a bicycle. Not that he had gotten one, their finances being what they were at the time. He probably hadn't even gotten an apology.

At dinner, Jeffrey asked for seconds of chicken and potatoes. Then he mopped up the gravy with his bread. "This is the best meal I've had in ages," he said. "You should see the stuff Adolph fed us. Turnips, beets, cauliflower. You can't imagine how disgusting."

Later, between mouthfuls of a store-bought iced sponge cake, Jeffrey said, "I'm so much happier living here."

Edith could hardly believe her ears. Jeffrey had to sense how difficult she found having him around. Though maybe the way he was feeling didn't have a lot to do with her. Or even with this place itself so much as with being away from Main Street. Also, with the relief that came from getting his secret off his chest.

Edith pushed away her plate and laced her hands. As his mother, she had an obligation to make him understand that this relief was illusory. She hated doing this on his birthday, but if not now, when? They talked so infrequently.

As if he could read her thoughts, Jeffrey became somber. He began pressing the cake crumbs against his plate with the back of his fork.

"What we were talking about a couple weeks ago," Edith began. "I won't pretend it didn't upset me. But I meant it when I said nothing could change how I feel about you."

Jeffrey's eyes, the right one twitching, searched hers. Edith had the uncanny sense of being able to look past them to his essence, utterly good, kind and trusting, qualities which he had in such abundance as to transform what were normally virtues into curses. This guilelessness made it all the more imperative that she be blunt with him.

She began to talk, stumbling at first, later with more conviction. She spoke without pauses so Jeffrey couldn't interrupt. She kept her voice even, in an attempt to keep it free of emotion and judgment, while she explained how the urges he spoke about were against the laws of both man and God, and that the reason for this was because they were perverse and unnatural. How if he didn't want to end up an outcast, perhaps land himself in jail, he must never give in to them, not even once.

"Promise me that you'll make yourself date girls and that you'll eventually marry. If you do as I say, I guarantee that those unnatural urges will keep getting weaker until, with time, they disappear completely."

Jeffrey placed his hand over his face to hide the twitching, which had taken over the entire right side. "Sometimes, I wish that I had killed myself."

Edith took his chin between her thumb and forefinger so that he had to look at her. But it was as if a shutter had come down across his eyes. "Such a silly thing to say," she said. "You don't really mean it." A lie—insipid and unforgivable. Words she knew would only push him deeper into himself. But, as his mother, what was she supposed to say?

# Chapter Twenty-Nine

## *July and August 1942*

Reuben arrived home from work one Friday to find Harriet and Adolph seated cross-legged on the living room floor. In front of them were two metal canisters and a dasher. Adolph was reading out loud from an instruction manual. Through the doorway to the store, Reuben spotted another acquisition, a white enamel-coated chest.

"What's this all about?" Reuben could hardly believe that Adolph had bought more equipment when it was obvious that the store would have to close. When he was working all the overtime he could get to make up for the loss of Adolph's salary.

"It's an—"

Harriet clamped her hand over Adolph's mouth. "Make him guess!"

Adolph mumbled something behind her hand, and Harriet squealed, "No!"

Reuben was in no mood for games. He was tired from the long week and hot from the walk home. He took the booklet from Adolph.

"An ice cream maker. Did she talk you into this?"

"As a matter of fact, she did," Adolph said, standing. "She's not just a pretty face. She's got a real head on her shoulders."

Reuben lifted the lid of the chest. It was a freezer.

"No point in making ice cream if it's going to melt," Adolph said.

"I'm going to be his assistant," Harriet said. "We're going to make two flavors every day. One with fruit. The other with nuts. I get to choose."

"Since when did ice cream become a health food?" Reuben asked.

"Since I became desperate enough to try anything."

"How much did this stuff cost?" Reuben asked.

"I sold my grandfather's pocket watch to pay for it," Adolph said. "And I've still got enough left over to buy the ingredients for months. You won't be out a penny."

The store had been his own idea, Reuben reminded himself. And five months was probably too soon to throw in the towel. After all, few businesses made money the first year, though, by now, he would have expected the business to have begun to show a bit of promise. On the other hand – no, there was no other hand. "Just keep me out of it," Reuben said.

According to Adolph, at ten o'clock each morning, Harriet would drag a table, chair, and blackboard out to the sidewalk. She would print the ice cream flavors for the day on the blackboard using a different color chalk for each letter. Regardless of how hot it got, she would remain all day, periodically looking up from her stack of movie magazines, Nancy Drew and Cherry Ames books, to ring her bell and call out "Fresh ice cream!"

On a given day, a fair number of people would pass by on their way to the hospital or to the shops, which had continued to creep eastward so that they now extended past the hospital on both sides of Main Street, leaving the house looking stranded upon its lawn and quaintly incongruous. Few passersby could resist Harriet, who, after taking their orders, would ask with her most fetching smile, "Have you seen our store?" Before they had a chance to refuse, she would have them by the hand and be leading them there.

"She's something, that daughter of yours," Adolph told Reuben at dinner one night while Harriet listened proudly. The sun had turned her hair nearly white and her face pink. The skin on her nose and arms was peeling off in strips. "You should hear her with the customers, telling them everything they never wanted to know about tofu and linseed oil. What she doesn't know, she makes up. The other day, she told a lady with a wen on her chin that if she rubbed goat's milk yogurt on it, the wen would disappear! The woman bought up my entire stock."

Ernest wasn't home. These days, he often ate dinner at his girlfriend Ruth's house. Reuben suspected he wasn't the only one who preferred it when Ernest wasn't around. The Saturday before, Reuben had heard Ernest and Ruth upstairs in the bedroom. She was crying out "Stop, stop," though hardly sounding like she meant it. Stop what? Both sixteen years old and up to God knows what. It was a miserably hot day, and Adolph had taken Harriet to the movies so they could cool off. Reuben knew he should go upstairs to investigate. Instead, he locked up the store and went for a walk.

In August, Reuben arrived home to find Adolph and Harriet arguing in the store. Arms crossed, Harriet was looking around. "I hate to break this to you, Adolph, but it's going to take a lot more than ice cream."

Adolph's forehead, back, and underarms were drenched with sweat. "Go watch your stand."

"Brownies, chocolate chip cookies, that sort of thing," Harriet said.

"I don't even get a hello?" Reuben asked. He kissed her on the cheek.

"Can't you see we're in the middle of a discussion?" Harriet asked, the same thing Edith used to tell the children when she and Reuben argued.

Harriet walked over to the bushel of licorice tea and sniffed it. "If this stuff is so good for you, the real stuff's got to be even better."

"Get your daughter out of here," Adolph said. "I'm busy." He removed his penknife from his pocket and slit open a burlap sack that had been sitting by the register for days.

"I'm not leaving until we discuss this," Harriet said.

"Do you want a slap?" Reuben asked. In truth, he agreed with her. Plus, if anyone could persuade Adolph that the store had to change if it were going to survive, it was Harriet.

Harriet walked over to the burlap bag. "What is this stuff, anyway?"

"Wheatberries."

"Who's going to buy them?"

Adolph gave Harriet a shove. "You're being a pest. Go."

"I just don't see the point of wasting money on stuff no one wants. But I'm just a kid. What do I know?" Flinging her hair over her shoulders, she pranced from the room.

Adolph pulled down the window shades and turned off the lights. "I shouldn't have snapped at her," he said. "The way she sits out there day after day, when I can't even get my son to pass out a few flyers."

Earlier that week, Reuben had dropped in to see Jeffrey for the first time in weeks. He did so mainly out of guilt, but also because of the journal, which was always on his mind. He was finding it difficult to recall exactly what he read and was beginning to wonder whether the conclusions he'd drawn had merely been the product of his own dirty mind.

Jeffrey looked better than he had in a long time. He had gained weight and was tan. He told Reuben that he'd been going to the beach nearly every day, having taught himself how to swim.

Just as Reuben was about to leave, Jeffrey said offhandedly, "By the way, I've decided to go back to school in September."

Sensing it might be a mistake to make too big a deal of this, Reuben kept his words mild. "I'm glad to hear that." He clasped Jeffrey's shoulders.

Jeffrey squirmed in a halfhearted attempt to free himself. "Not Sea Forth, Brentwood High. Mom's arranged it."

Why hadn't Edith told him? Reuben wondered. Did she think he didn't care? At best, this was a barely excusable oversight, the obligation to keep each other informed about their children, having not yet become a habit for either of them.

At the door, Jeffrey asked, "How's the store doing?"

Reuben's instinctive reaction was to tell Jeffrey, "fine." He then realized by doing so, he'd be implying that Jeffrey lacked the maturity to handle the truth. "To be honest, lousy. It's time we started thinking about shutting down."

Jeffrey grabbed Reuben's hand. "Can I do anything to help?"

As Reuben squeezed Jeffrey's hand, he was struck by the concern in Jeffrey's eyes. Their relationship, damaged though it was, was not irredeemable.

Back in the store, Adolph had been flushed from the heat. But as the two men relaxed in the comparative cool of the dining room, his face appeared drained of color. Reuben made gin and tonics, ignoring Adolph's protests as he slipped an already sweating glass into his hands. "What an idiot I've been," Adolph said between sips, "to think I could make people see the connections between the poisons they stuff themselves with and their rotting teeth and expanding waistlines."

Reuben nodded, thinking of how he'd been an even bigger idiot, given where he'd come from, an initial position of total skepticism. Despite that, he found himself unable to blame either of them; their need to believe in something was too fresh in his mind. He glanced through the archway into the living room. For months, they'd been buying next to nothing, and there were still stacks of unopened inventory, enough to keep the store going for at least six months. Reuben reminded himself what a mistake it would be to allow this fact, or sentiment, to influence the decision whether to close the store. A decision like that had to be based upon a cold-hearted assessment of the store's prospects, and those couldn't be clearer.

For a couple of hours, Adolph and he sat weighing the pros and cons of remaining open through Labor Day, bandying about how to get rid of the inventory and fixtures. Reuben thought the matter was settled. So, when he arrived home the following evening, he was startled to find Adolph busy, not with dinner, but with flour, sugar, shortening, things Adolph once described as being as lethal as arsenic.

"I'm not giving up," Adolph said, raising a batter-encrusted finger. "There's got to be a way to satisfy people's craving for sweets—yet make them nutritious. The key is to figure out a way so they can't tell that what they're eating is actually good for them!"

"I thought we agreed..." Reuben never finished the thought, for just then, Harriet emerged from the toilet off the kitchen, her braids wrapped around her head and covered with a hair net, her plaid jumper protected by a nearly identical yellow apron to Adolph's. He would wait until later to talk to Adolph, Reuben decided, and excused himself to go clean up. By the time he was upstairs, he had changed his mind. Why not humor Adolph in this last-ditch attempt, given that whatever money he spent on this crazy scheme wouldn't amount to peanuts compared with the money they had already thrown away?

That was to be the first of many nights Reuben would arrive home to find not dinner, but whatever new concoctions Adolph and Harriet had come up with. Every surface in the kitchen became cluttered with canisters of oatmeal, whole wheat flour, pumpkin and sesame seeds, carob, and dried fruits—especially prunes because of their laxative properties. There were also pureed bananas and applesauce, which Adolph added to his cookies and cakes as a way of reducing the amount of refined sugar. While Adolph made a point of asking Reuben's opinion about the results, the only opinion that really mattered to him was Harriet's.

Eventually Harriet gave her blessing to two of Adolph's experiments, a fig and walnut-studded oatmeal bar and his coconut-covered, almond-filled dates. It was her idea to toss together the leftover nuts, dried fruits, seeds, and rolled oats, and divide them into snack-sized packets, which they called "Energy Mix." It was also her idea to offer samples at her stand. Not all of their experiments were hits—their applesauce and carob cake was a dud. But many were. And because people were willing to pay more for prepared foods than for the same ingredients in their unadulterated states, by the time Harriet went back to school, the business was no longer bleeding cash.

This was not to say that the store was providing the men with anything close to a living. Moreover, with the ice cream stand tucked away for the winter, the drop-in business had dwindled. But at least Reuben and Adolph knew they'd finally come up with products people were willing to buy. In fact, the real surprise was how much people liked the idea of snacks that were actually good for them.

It was Reuben who came up with the next idea. "Why don't we try selling to the local restaurants and stores?"

Adolph looked skeptical. Who was supposed to do this selling? Reuben worked during the days, and he knew himself well enough to realize that people didn't warm to him, at least not at first, and first was the only thing that mattered when it came to being a salesman. They both thought of Harriet at once, who, even at twelve, could turn on the charm like no one else, and who yearned to be part of the business.

Every day, Adolph would pick Harriet up after school. Over the course of a week, they would make a circuit, one day visiting the stores and restaurants in Sea Forth, the next day in Babylon, the third day in Islip. The following week, they'd begin again. By December, Adolph and Reuben were so overwhelmed by the press of pre-Christmas orders that they were forced to shutter the store. By spring, they had outgrown the Main Street kitchen and relocated to a commercial one. Reuben quit his job to concentrate on the administrative side of the business. Adolph did the baking and Harriet oversaw sales. The wholesale business was on its way.

Edith lacked the courage to visit the Emporium. Whatever she knew, she knew secondhand. "It's like a morgue," Marianne Rule told her. Marianne visited Edith's store several times a week to see what had come in. She was spending so much money that Edith was becoming alarmed and couldn't help wondering what George Rule, who by all accounts was barely hanging on to their two remaining jewelry stores, thought about this.

According to Rosemary Groschal, however, the Emporium was as busy as ever. "If you want my opinion, it's looking fabulous," she told Edith. "Please don't tell me this is all you have?" she said with a shake of her cocker spaniel curls, as she rustled through the size twelve dresses. She laced her skinny, cold fingers through Edith's, her garishly large rings pressing into Edith's flesh. "Darling, you'll never survive if you can't do better than this." Given that Rosemary never found anything she liked, it was a mystery to Edith why she kept coming back.

Edith suspected that Adele Fellowes' assessment of how the Emporium was doing was the one closest to the truth. She stopped by Edith's store before Christmas for "something festive." Finding something that would fit her, let alone that was festive, was going to be challenge enough, for Adele, who had always been plump, had grown alarmingly fat. She had surrendered completely to middle age, letting her hair go gray, no longer bothering to tweeze her eyebrows, which now met above her nose, or to depilate her moustache.

"Admit it," she said, laughing, as Edith struggled to work the zipper up her fleshy back. "I've grown as big as a house. Bigger than some."

After Edith found her a dark red silk with a dropped waist and long sleeves, which, if not wildly festive was about as chic and slenderizing as any dress its size could be, Adele turned serious. "Have you been there?" she asked. There was no need to explain what she meant by "there." "Every now and again, I stop by," Adele continued. "Mainly out of curiosity. The place doesn't look that different. A bit less orderly, that's all. But it doesn't feel the same. The spark is gone. The magic. And that poor little man. He always looks so sad."

Edith hadn't seen Bunny Fleming since her opening party. According to Marianne, these days, Bunny rarely left the house. "Why don't we girls have a reunion," Marianne suggested. "If that doesn't cheer the poor thing up, nothing will."

As the date of the reunion drew near, Edith was surprised to find herself growing excited. She was under no illusions; the women couldn't recapture the past. The years had left their mark on them all, and the alchemy—of youth, prosperity, and innocence—that had drawn them together could never be recreated. It occurred to her that this was precisely why she was looking forward to the party. Not only did she no longer pine for the past, she wouldn't have been able to dredge up the hurt, resentment, and betrayal she once felt—even if she tried. She could enjoy the party for what it was: a gathering of middle-aged women out to have some fun.

As to how her life would unfold, Edith could only guess. It was clear that this store was not to be the destination she had hoped it would be. Once she had amassed enough capital, she would start up another store, one that would truly be her own. Perhaps on the North Shore, in one of those beautiful towns like Cold Spring Harbor or Locust Valley along the Sound. She would move up there, returning to Sea Forth only when she had to.

She would probably not remarry. A dress shop provided few opportunities to meet men. Besides, as stylish as she was, she was no longer beautiful, at least not in the way that mattered to men. She was surprised at how little this troubled her. The Depression had robbed her of so much, but by forcing her to realize that, in the end, the only person she could really rely upon was herself, it had given her much more. She was proud of what she had accomplished, prouder than she had ever been of Bliss or of her youthful good looks.

Of course, there was still Jeffrey to worry about. When she told him that if a person behaved the way society expected him to behave, he'd eventually grow into that person, she'd known she was being dishonest, but it had been a dishonesty that had sprung from the noblest of motives, the desire to protect him. Still, she couldn't help wondering whom she was really trying to protect—him or her? For what sort of life would Jeffrey lead if he did as she said? It wouldn't be a happy one. A life grounded in hypocrisy, spent in constant terror of being found out, couldn't be. Not that if he rejected her advice, his life would be easy. Either way, his life was destined to be arduous and lonely, the way it had always been. Nothing would change that. The best she could do, would be to be there for him in a way that, for too long, she hadn't been—cheering him on, helping him to muster the courage he would need to reach out for and then hold onto whatever happiness he could find.

# Acknowledgments

To Jenna Blum, Lisa Borders, Rebecca Brown and Darcey Steinke for their help in bringing this story to life

To the staff of the Newton Public Library for creating such a wonderfully tranquil and well-resourced working space

To my late father, Samuel Ringler, my mother, Rita Ringler, and my sons Eric, Andrew and Jack, all of whom I cherish, for their support and love.

And especially to my wonderful husband Anthony for—well, for everything.

# ABOUT THE AUTHOR

Rhonda Ringler Cutler's 26 year banking career was challenging and often fun, plus took her to every continent, except Antarctica. Between that and raising her three sons, it left little time for her true passion—fiction writing. So one day, after much agonizing, she announced to her incredulous staff and boss that she was quitting to pursue a Masters of Fine Arts in Creative Writing. After obtaining her degree, she spent years wandering through a creative wilderness filled with false starts and dead ends. But tempted as she was to return to the safety of banking (not to mention the paychecks), she persevered and THE END OF BLISS, her debut novel, is the result.

In addition to her MFA from Goddard College, Rhonda has an MBA from Columbia University Graduate School of Business and BA from Barnard College. Rhonda and her husband, Anthony, divide their time between Newton, MA and Sydney Australia. When Rhonda is not writing, consulting on a pro bono basis to small businesses, or visiting her sons—currently living on three continents, she enjoys working out, knitting, cooking, and reading.

To learn more about Rhonda's work, visit www.rhondaringlercutler.com

www.ingramcontent.com/pod-product-compliance
Lightning Source LLC
LaVergne TN
LVHW050923080826
845145LV00001B/192

* 9 7 8 0 6 1 5 6 9 7 6 4 2 *